LIN FINITY

AND THE

WORDS UNSPOKEN

Other Books By Edward Allen Karr

* * * * *

SERIES: Fringes Of Infinity

Lin Finity And Her Mayhem Rising – Book One

Lin Finity In Holding On
(A Fringes Of Infinity Novella)

Lin Finity And The Islands Of Time – Book Three

Lin Finity And The Flights To Forever – Book Four

* * * * *

SERIES: Thrills N Kills In The Hills

Dayzee Dazzle And The Kildare Killers – Book One

Dayzee Dazzle And Her Manic Mansion – Book Two

* * * * *

LIN FINITY
AND THE
WORDS UNSPOKEN

Fringes Of Infinity
Book Two

Edward Allen Karr

LAKESIDE
LETTERS, LLC

Lakeside Letters, LLC
30628 Detroit Road, #247
Westlake, OH 44145

This is a work of fiction. Names, characters, businesses, events, and incidents are the products of the author's imagination. Any resemblance to actual persons, living or dead, or actual events is purely coincidental. Certain long-standing institutions are mentioned, but the characters are imaginary. The opinions expressed are those of the characters and should not be confused with those of the author.

Lin Finity And The Words Unspoken
Fringes Of Infinity Book Two

First Edition, 2020
www.lakesideletters.com

Cover design by JD Smith Design
Front Cover Model: Kim Hendrickson as Lin Finity
Back Cover Model: Lea Goldsmith as Lee Ternity
Scroll & Tower Sketches by Eric Brock, Somerville, MA
Editing by Preferred Proofreading, LLC

ISBN-13: 978-1-950886-04-3

"Gabby," Lin said, her voice shaking, "what good is all that endless magic if we can't understand it? If we can't even remember it?"

"There's a challenge for you, Lin. Just know that the magic is real. And understand, too, that when you're in this world,"—Gabriel pointed to the floor—"you're experiencing only a small part of all the wonder,"—Gabriel pointed to the empty black beyond the window—"out there."

Lin stared into the darkness before looking back at Gabriel. One tear escaped.

"Gabby," Lin whispered, "I don't . . . I mean, what should I—"

"Rest, Lin. You need to rest."

From Chapter 4 – Light & Night

Dedication

This work is dedicated to all who seek the unknowable magic swirling just beyond the borders of our world. To journey there, find the stillness within you, where your intent lies waiting.

Table of Contents

Chapter 1 – Long Ago

"Your bones and your flesh. Your heart and its streams. All will be reshaped to bear the Words across time."

"Yes, Queen Gloriana."

"Of all the volunteers, you, Renato, have shown the required resilience and desire. And most importantly, the patience."

"I am thankful to be selected, my Queen."

Tiago could barely believe he witnessed such a scene. He'd only recently come of age and been allowed to advance in the ranks as a helper to one of Gloriana's attendants. The ceremony would be brief, he knew that much, and he listened closely to every word. He and the attendants, along with select members of the military, were present to display their support to Renato. And to keep him from losing his resolve. What followed the event required Renato's complete and unconditional submission.

Gloriana sat on the edge of her plain, polished coral chair at the far side of the room, with Renato kneeling before her. In the center of the floor stood a simple table holding an open box fashioned of undersea oak. Her cinnamon gown had few adornments but showed enough of her form for all to know she remained a warrior. Despite the curious faces studying her from every direction, her caramel eyes remained focused on the man cowering before her.

Renato wore a common cloak and sandals. His sun-streaked dark hair fell to his shoulders, braided and ending in a variety of teeth. His eyes never looked up.

"There will be no path back to what you are today. You must accept that."

"Yes, my Queen."

"You will span many lifetimes yet live only one. You will speak the Words for brief moments, and centuries may pass before you are called upon again. Ask now if you have questions."

"Yes, my Queen. What of those centuries? What of my life during those times?"

"Ah, Renato, you will know what every living thing knows except for humankind. You will feel what every human heart longs to feel but cannot. It is a comfort that you, right now, are unable to comprehend."

The purpose of the ceremony, Tiago had been told by the attendant he served, was to focus the volunteer, to prepare him for the change. Tiago had asked what that meant, but the man could explain no more. It involved magic, he'd said, and Tiago should remain cautious, doing only as instructed. Fear kept the man from speaking of it again.

"Look into my eyes, Renato, and repeat after me. 'I carry the Words so that others may know truth. I will never forget the Words, and my patience has no end.'"

Renato fearfully looked up and repeated it. Then again. And again.

Tiago grew weary of hearing Renato repeat it so many times. But as it continued, he felt a change within himself. He became calm and felt a sense of purpose. He began to understand the need for the repetition. He knew the importance of Renato carrying the Words.

The round room covered almost all of the tower's top level. A single door led to the walkway circling all around. The domed ceiling defied gravity five warriors above the floor at its center, and many large openings at the top of the circular wall allowed in light and air. An opening at the roof's top let in sunlight and rain when it fell. Forty paces would be needed to cross the room and five more to view over the parapet. The low wall rose half a warrior high, except for a section near the door, five paces long, where nothing would prevent a careless fall. Rainwater could flow out from there and drop to the canal far below.

Tiago wondered why the ceremony needed to be held so high up in the tower since most of the palace below remained above water.

Gloriana rose and guided Renato to the middle of the room. A sign from a general prompted all spectators and attendants to file through the door and take places along the parapet, facing away from the room and out toward the islands. Tiago quaked at seeing the ground so far below. But when he looked farther, he could see the Great Ocean at the end of the canal, and it calmed him. The general closed the door from the outside and took her place with the others. No one spoke a word.

It seemed forever to Tiago as he fought to look out over the islands and not back at the room. But it had been only moments before he heard the first screams. Chills clawed up his spine as he listened. The screams didn't sound human. Renato wasn't wailing from pain or even fear. His were cries of madness.

Tiago looked to his left and then to his right. Everyone he could see had closed their eyes, as if they hoped that would block their hearing as well. Tiago quietly turned and crept back toward the wall. With only one pace remaining, he froze, stunned from the sight. The wall appeared liquid, with countless waves and swirling ripples, though it had been formed from mountain stone. He took another step, and his curiosity overcame his fear as he listened to Renato's howling laughter.

He reached out to touch the wall and gasped as his finger disappeared beneath the surface.

The sounds of insanity inside stopped abruptly, and the wall's shimmering had gone—it was again solid mountain stone. And Tiago's finger had merged with the wall. He dared not call for help and pulled frantically to free himself.

All at once, everyone opened their eyes and turned toward the room. Tiago's master scoffed at his predicament and said, "There is always one of you, there is."

Without another word, he unsheathed his knife and slid it smoothly down the hard wall surface, freeing Tiago from the wall's finger. Tiago wanted to scream, but his fear and embarrassment denied him his voice. He'd been told. He'd been warned. And still, he'd been a fool anyway.

He felt important, though. Whatever the fate of the tower, he'd forever be a part of it.

* * *

Gloriana had summoned Marco, her most trusted general, and he stood with her near the far wall, away from the center of the tower room. He'd brought a scribe as the queen had commanded. All others had been dismissed and had filed down the series of stairways to the palace below.

With his helmet cradled beneath his left arm, his black hair could be seen, trimmed flat across the top, according to his rank. His ceremonial uniform left his thick arms uncovered, and out of habit, his right hand remained close to his dagger.

He made a quick study of the room. It contained only Gloriana's chair, a small table supporting a closed box, and a folded cloak beneath sandals and some teeth. It was obvious to him that the transformation had been completed.

Marco had high enough rank that he could look at Gloriana directly. He did, and he was taken aback, as always, by her beauty and strength. Wild brown hair coiled down far past the dark skin of her bare shoulders. And her features were graceful, in contrast to her athlete's body. Her thin garments couldn't conceal legs that were at least as strong as his own. As she looked down on him, for she was taller, he trembled inside. He knew he had no reason—they'd been friends, even lovers for many seasons. But still, he struggled to meet her gaze.

"Marco, our lives here are nearing their end. The fortitude inside that had once seemed boundless will be gone soon. And all of this with it." She extended her arms to each side.

"I do not want to tell you goodbye, and I ask that you grant me this request. And it is a request, not a command, because it requires your steadfast resolve long after I have gone. For that reason, I am speaking to your heart. You must be a willing general, a friend like no other, until your very last breath."

"I will do anything you ask of me, Gloriana. You have had my heart for many seasons, and you will always have it. Just tell me what you desire."

Marco willed his breaths to stay calm as he reflected on all the golden seasons they'd passed together. Be thankful for those times, he told himself. None of it had been given easily. He knew that only Gloriana's intent had made it all possible.

"That box is crafted from undersea oak. As you know, when that wood is dried properly, it has the toughness of iron. But it is light. A child can lift it. Inside, I have saved the Words of God.

"The Words cannot be revealed to anyone who does not possess great power. I have made it this way because it takes uncommon ability to accept the message of the Words. The Words must be protected and preserved until the day one who can know them will come.

"Take the largest boat in our navy. Secure the box at the far end in the hold. Do not allow any of your crew to remain within twenty paces of it for more than one tenth of a sea tide. The box itself offers some protection but not enough. If you were to open the box, within a dozen breaths, you would forget your own name. If you were foolish enough to open the clasp and let your eyes hold the Scroll, within several waves of your heart, your mind would be forever lost. This protects the Scroll from all too weak to learn its contents.

"Set sail toward the rising sun and pass through the Pillars. Travel the water until the old sea can take you no closer to the next day's sun. The Words must wait there.

"Your life must become a shield for the Scroll. When your seasons are reaching their end, pass it to one you can trust. Instruct them to do the same. It must continue this way as centuries are counted. Do you understand, Marco?"

"I do. But I beg of you, Gloriana, set sail with me."

She shook her head but continued to look into his eyes.

"I can go nowhere, Marco. Soon . . . I will be lost between the Islands, and these islands will be no more."

"I . . . I do not understand, my Queen."

"I speak of my life here ending, Marco. All I have built will end."

Marco began to speak, but his head tipped forward, and he stayed silent.

"Scribe, are you ready?"

"Yes, my Queen."

"Marco, carry my telling with the Scroll. It might help guide others that follow.

"Go with my love, Marco."

He looked up and stared without fear into her eyes one last time, letting their warmth burn into his soul. His heart begged that their bond might somehow defy fate. But after several long seconds, she looked past him, through the doorway at the rising ocean.

Marco studied the lines of the stone floor as he left his queen to stand near the parapet, with his jaw clenched tight to keep trapped all he would never say.

* * *

The mid-day sun glared into the tower, and reflections off of the long canal cast Marco's shadow on the far wall. His shade twisted in silent anguish while he, too, appeared built of mountain stone. Military ships shared the waterways with merchant vessels. Only Marco's ship would remain.

The work of transforming Renato had weakened Gloriana, but she knew that at least one more task needed to be completed. She leaned back in her chair and looked to the scribe, who still awaited her direction.

She nodded her head, and her voice broke at first as she narrated the story of the Words.

"After . . . a long, precious life, full of countless wonders and triumphs, I felt my days approaching their end. I stood on the tower before dawn and looked out at all that I had built. All that I had supported and nourished and loved. And I saw the sadness, fear, and cruelty that had woven itself into the joy, peace, and kindness I had intended.

"I looked to the Heavens and asked God, 'Why? For what reason are we subject to every imaginable nightmare until the day when all our efforts are swept away, lost in oblivion? Why are we, for all our days, separate from your peace and truth?'

"God's Words came unspoken. A few shone with the rising sun. More fell with the morning's light rain. Yet more were carried on a warm afternoon wind. And others descended with the sounds of flocks, fleeing toward tomorrow's new sun. Still more Words were entwined with the weak light of sunset as I looked down at the islands of my intent, once teeming with life. Islands that I could no longer hold. Lives I had become too weak to hold."

She paused and closed her eyes.

"God's final Words rode the pale rays of an uncaring moon as my strength faltered, and the waters began to rise."

She opened her eyes and continued.

"I gave the Words to the Scroll so that others may know. The Messenger will tell why evil is forever present in our world, even these islands. God's Words tell us why we are forever stumbling through chaos and sin, while we are made to strive for order and good. Know these Words, and have the answer your heart seeks. Learn what God says about the nature of our lives.

"Perhaps it will be you that finds comfort."

Chapter 2 – Sunday

<u>J O E L</u>

Night had fallen quickly in Savannah, and Joel welcomed the darkness with another round of manhattans for his friends and himself. The party had been out of control for quite some time, and he'd had so much liquor that he could no longer speak. But still, he drank and danced. Over the sounds of drunken karaoke and screaming and an occasional glass breaking on the patio's concrete, sirens could be heard approaching from the north. That only prompted more laughter, but they had just enough judgment left to realize they'd best disappear into the night. And Joel couldn't deny that his shabby clothes and long, greasy hair had always made him a target for the authorities.

Joel had staggered off, led away by someone, and before the sun had risen, he awoke and knew it was time to get back to the Island. For a moment, he considered rolling back the sheets to see whose bed he'd shared. But the drumming in his head drowned out any curiosity. He needed to focus on the drive home and his job at the keyboard. In the house of God.

He knew that playing for Mass would be a struggle since he was hungover and lacked any real enthusiasm. But he knew he could fake it well enough to pull it off anyway. He also knew that not a single parishioner would have any idea what he'd been doing so recently and with whom. He smiled, thinking he didn't know either, and pulled his knit cap down to his eyebrows for the drive home.

His amusement faded when he recalled the true reason he would always make it to Mass, no matter what fun led him astray. Playing for the service provided some satisfaction, and it paid the bills. But the real reason, the one that he wished he could forget, was the simple task he'd been asked to continue fifteen years earlier by his dying father.

Joel's father had played for Mass, too, until his declining health prevented it. In one of their final conversations, he'd told Joel about strange events that had occurred on the Island when Joel was but three. A man mutilated himself in a grotesque way, and he hanged himself shortly after. No one could prove foul play. Only a teenage girl had been in the house, a pretty blond girl named Lin, and there was no evidence she was involved. But people that had known the man were baffled, saying he'd never do that to himself, not in a thousand years.

A few days later, he'd been contacted by a man claiming to be a paranormal investigator. Someone looking for proof of the evil in the world. His mission was God's work, he'd said. He'd made a case that there could have been supernatural forces at work. And he had a simple request for Joel's father: to listen, to watch, to pay attention to everyone in the church. If he were to hear any talk about strange powers, about magic even, he should call the number provided. He'd promised great financial rewards for any leads he could report and told him again that he'd be doing God's work.

Joel's father had scant belief in his public faith. But out of fear, he believed much more in Hell than in Heaven. And he didn't want a ticket to Hell. So, he'd committed himself to doing as he'd been asked, and he did just that for the last fifteen years of his life. On his deathbed, he'd confided in Joel, and his request had been so impassioned that Joel had kept the number for his own fifteen years as the organist. Joel doubted he'd ever witness anything noteworthy, but still, he listened and watched everything.

As he sat at the console in the empty church, resting his eyes one last time behind his stringy brown hair, Joel remembered that grim conversation with his father. He wanted to laugh about it because it seemed ridiculous. But no, the man had been serious. And since that had been his father's dying request, he'd been honoring it ever since.

So, for fifteen years, he'd been watching and listening, and he'd never heard a single thing.

Until that Sunday morning in early November.

Joel expected it would be a routine Mass, and like usual, God would no doubt be pleased with the attendance and fervor. After he'd rubbed his face and began preparing the music, he heard Father Steve ambling his way to the front door to prop it open. Seconds later, he heard a low conversation at the door between the pastor and a female voice. A quick, quiet walk down the stairs led him to a perfect vantage point, just around a corner and out of sight, but well within hearing distance.

He couldn't see the woman speaking with Steve, but he could hear every word clearly. It felt like another routine waste of his time until he heard her say, "Maybe it's a power of some kind."

Joel's eyes opened wide, and he froze on the spot. Could something really be happening? After fifteen years of hearing nothing, did he finally have something to report? Maybe, but he figured he needed more than that.

". . . I can see that the world is magic."

Joel struggled to accept that he'd really heard that. Someone in his church had actually spoken of magic. The conversation ended shortly after, and he heard the woman's heels clicking on the pavement as she walked away. He waited, unnoticed, as the pastor shuffled back toward the altar. Joel walked quickly to the open doors and peeked around the corner to watch a blond woman climb into a car and drive away.

* * *

After Mass, Joel called the number he'd kept for fifteen years. It took only one ring before someone answered, but no one spoke.

"Hello?" said Joel. "This is Joel Squires, and I have something to report. I was—"

A female voice answered. "Yes, Joel, tell me what you witnessed."

"Okay, um, I'm an organist at—"

"Tell me what you saw."

"Okay, there was this woman at the church talking to the pastor. He called her Lin. She seemed to be bothered by something. She talked about having some kind of power. And she said maybe it was magic. She really used the word magic, and—"

"I need her last name."

"Her last name? I don't know. She never said. And she's gone now. She drove—"

"You need to find her last name. The pastor should know."

"He might, but why would he tell me? Why would I need to know that? I'm just—"

"Find her last name. Quickly. You must do whatever it takes."

"Me? I'm just an organist here. How would I convince him to tell me—"

"Listen, Joel. This is important. Get that name. You are doing God's work. Would you rather I send a team down there to visit you?"

"A team? What? No, no, don't do that. Okay, um, I'll get the name. Just give me a few minutes, and I'll call you back, alright?"

"Good." The call ended.

*　*　*

Joel mumbled and brushed his hair back as he knocked on Father Steve's door. A soft "come in" prompted him to open the door and step inside the modest room.

"Joel, what brings you here? I thought you'd be gone by now. Beautiful music this morning, as always."

"Hi, Steve. Thanks, those were some of my favorite hymns. Um, I saw you talking to that blond woman before Mass, and I think she looked familiar. What's her name? I think I might know her."

Steve's badly cut gray hair framed a confused expression.

"Oh, I doubt you know her, Joel. She's only visiting from Pennsylvania, and she's leaving today. I knew her as a child many years ago."

"But, Steve, I need to know her last name. It's Lin, right? But what's her last name?"

"Joel, where do you think you know her from?"

Joel felt a new rage and determination spring up inside.

In a deeper voice, he said, "I just need her last name, Steve. Lin who?"

Joel had approached the pastor's desk and stood looking down on him. Both of his fists rested on the tidy surface as he stared into Steve's eyes. He began to twitch.

"Joel, I don't feel I can share that with you. You probably don't know her. Perhaps we should call it a day, hmm?"

Joel watched his own hands reach over the desk and grab Steve by his robes, pulling him forward and knocking papers to the floor. His eyes had become mere slits.

"Joel, what are you doing? Let me go!"

"Tell me her name, Steve. It's not much to ask. The name. Now, Steve," Joel said with more authority than he'd ever said anything before.

When the pastor reached for his coffee mug to his right, Joel let go with one hand and landed a solid punch to his jaw. The old man went limp in Joel's hands, with blood running down his chin and his eyes wide.

"The name, Steve," Joel said and punched him again.

The man faded quickly, but he managed to say, "Finnerty, you don't know her, it's Finnerty, why are you—" before Joel punched him again, and his head slumped to one side.

Joel released him and stood straight up, looking down at his own hands. His chest swelled as he studied through squinting eyes Steve's blood on his knuckles.

A second later, his hands dropped to his sides, and his eyes stretched open.

"Steve. Steve! I'm sorry, I don't know what . . ."

With his hands shaking, Joel dug out his phone and dialed the number.

"Yes, Joel."

"Finnerty. Her name's Finnerty, and she's from Pennsylvania. Steve said she's going back today."

"Very good. You have done well, Joel. Tell me, what did you have to do?"

"Oh, I'm in so much trouble now. I punched Steve a couple of times. I don't know what got into me. He's unconscious in his study. What do I do now? What will happen to me? I should call the police—"

"You will not call anyone. We will take care of the priest. We will get help there as soon as possible. It might be several hours, though. Stay with him all afternoon if you need to. They will have a generous payment for you. Wait for our help, Joel." The call ended.

Joel sank into the guest chair and hid his face behind his trembling hands. He hoped that Steve wouldn't wake up before they arrived, but what then? What will they do with the priest? What will they do with him?

And he wondered who he'd just become.

ANNA

The call from Joel had reached Anna Kelgina just before she'd convened a meeting of her team. Reports had already arrived on her laptop about strange events in Pennsylvania, and at the meeting, she would assign agents to investigate.

As she walked through the spotless hallway deep beneath a vacant warehouse in Baltimore, she stopped outside the heavy concrete block covering the tunnel entrance. The small dog she carried whined and burrowed deeper into her arms. In all her years with The Shield, she'd never seen the barrier moved. She glanced down at the large motor that could be used to drag it to one side. Could the item housed at the very end of the tunnel be that dangerous? she wondered.

"Benson, you have been with us many years. I have never been in the tunnel. I have only heard stories of the last time it was opened. It was more than twenty years ago, I think. Tell me what you have heard," she said with a Russian accent.

Derek Benson gave every impression of being ex-military, with the rarely blinking eyes of a fanatic. Always in combat boots, always a short, neat haircut, and rarely a smile. That day was no different.

"Ms. Kelgina, I doubt I know any more than you. That thing in there is a nightmare. The box is supposed to have something special, something sacred inside. But all it does is destroy people. And whatever's inside the box, if that's opened, too, they go insane almost instantly. Hell, even if you stood just inside the doorway for long enough, you'd be finished."

"That is what I have heard, too, Benson. Sometimes, it seems too crazy to me. It helps to hear it said out loud by someone. And we still need to know what is in there. All we have is that 'Telling'—a confusing story handed down through the ages. But the story does say there is an answer there. The Words of God. That is why we do what we do. What we have been doing for many centuries now."

She quickly smoothed out her blue suit and picked off a few pieces of dog hair as she and Benson resumed walking to the meeting. The black dog she cradled in her left arm remained silent. Anna's shoulder length brown hair seemed molded into a shape that prevented any disarray. Her white shirt was buttoned to the top, and her eyeglasses resembled oversize windows pieced together with thin wires.

Her work in Moscow had ended more than twenty years earlier, the day the Director of The Shield had approached her at the United Nations. He'd made a compelling case. If she valued helping humanity, he'd said, she'd join their cause.

Anna had often hoped to alleviate the sadness and despair so many people felt as they struggled through difficult lives. She'd been ready to play her part.

And she'd found it impossible to tell him no.

* * *

"Please open the folders in front of you," Anna said. "They describe first reports of unusual events in two locations in Pennsylvania. One in Erie, in a motel room. And one out on a road between Erie and Pittsburgh.

"In Erie, a fugitive was delivered to police by an unknown person. We have been unable to secure information on who delivered him. The man displayed remarkable psychological damage, according to our contact at the jail. The fugitive had been there before, and he was known to be an outgoing, lively person. Something changed that. He is now unresponsive, but there is no sign of injury.

"Daria, you will investigate in Erie."

"But I'm still new. I'm not sure if—"

"You will go, Daria. This is how you learn. Go and find out all you can."

Daria nodded and tilted her head back, shaking her thick black hair over her shoulders.

"The other location is along a road closer to Pittsburgh and near a pond. In that case, there is clear evidence of violence. But the violence is of such an unusual nature that it warrants our attention. Look at the photos. He had been a sane man before that. No sane man would do what he did to himself. He is in a local hospital, and though he is physically able to communicate, even if just by writing, he will not.

"Ms. Kelgina, are we sure he did that to himself?"

"Yes, Benson, it is quite conclusive. Look at the photo of his hands. That is his blood. And gravel dust.

"We have other evidence related to this case. It is a recording of a call to 911 from a man who identified himself as 'John.' He can be heard talking to another named 'Tommy.' Listen to this short recording:"

"Hi, John. Where are you?"

"She's amazing, Tommy, isn't she? We'll find her. Hi, I don't know—Pennsylvania, I think. But man, Davey's really messed up. She seemed to care about him, so that's why I'm calling. In case you were curious."

"Who cared about him, sir?"

"The blond lady. The *most* amazing lady ever. Her eyes . . . if you could see her eyes. *I* saw her eyes! If you saw her eyes, you'd know. She's all I care—Tommy, wait, you'll never find her walking. Wait . . ."

Anna clicked off the playback.

"My God, he sounds insane. What's wrong with him?"

"We do not know, Benson, but we believe he and Tommy are eyewitnesses to whatever happened.

"There is no useful dialog beyond what you heard. It seems this John forgot he was on the phone and also forgot to end the call. It went on long enough that they were able to track his signal. By the time the first responders got there, the two were gone. Possibly they hitchhiked. No further information on them is known.

"Benson, go there and learn all you can, including the whereabouts of John and Tommy.

"One more item. A call just came in from a man in South Georgia. He reported hearing an unusual conversation between a woman named Lin Finnerty and a local priest. She lives in Pennsylvania now. Her address is in the report, and we believe it has not changed. We opened a file on her and her parents over thirty years ago in St. Simons Island. But after several years of surveillance, with no unusual activity, the work there ended.

"Tayo, we need your talents for her. Go alone and learn what you can. She might be there by the time you arrive."

Tayo pushed his thick glasses higher up his nose and said, "Yes, Anna. You can count on me."

"That will be all. Good luck."

T A Y O

Tayo Tersoo had gathered Anna's report and a few items for traveling and promptly left for Pennsylvania. Likely another dead end, he thought, as the miles played out under a cloudy sky.

But his sense of purpose never lessened. Diligence. Discipline. The words continually echoed in his mind. The task was noble. The fate of the world depended on his dedication.

He'd left his car one block and four houses away from Lin's home, and under cover of night, he'd crept into a hidden place behind thick shrubbery in front of her house. His tall, thin frame couldn't be completely hidden behind the bushes, but his dark clothing and darker skin helped conceal him in the unlit space. His long black curls spilled out below a thick wool cap. The air chilled him, and the ground even more so. He hoped it wouldn't be a long wait.

His photographic memory went over the report again and again. The picture of an attractive blond woman in her late forties. The reported conversation she'd had with a priest. Talk of a power. Talk of magic. Maybe it wouldn't be a dead end, he told himself.

The strong rumble of a car approaching prompted him to put away his mental notes. The garage door opened, the car pulled in, and the door closed after it. Five and a half minutes of silence followed, finally broken by a single, loud bark. Tayo noted that the deep bark indicated a large dog. And likely only one dog. More silence followed. On a chilly Sunday night, Kingsbury Court remained quiet and devoid of traffic.

Thirty-seven more minutes of silence passed, and Tayo felt the temptation to raise his head to look into the living room window above him. But he didn't look. Discipline. Above all else. God's work. He would continue to wait in the cold, all night if necessary.

A loud shriek broke the still of the night, piercing the wall at Tayo's back. Then, silence. He wanted badly to look, but stealth was crucial.

The shriek was valuable information to report, and it was recorded in his mental notes. The exact time, its duration, even the estimated decibel level through typical construction for homes of that type. But it was not enough on which to draw a conclusion.

So, he waited in the cold. He slept, with his ears tuned to hear mostly sounds from inside, and just enough focus left to hear of any approaching danger.

L E E

Just the sight of him had become a heavy chain pulling her to the ground. She struggled to remember why she'd ever let him into her life. Lee Turner avoided second guessing her life decisions, but Alex had become enough of a burden that it needed a clear reminder.

She'd met him at the community college ten years earlier, at a time when she hadn't yet figured out how things work. She'd needed him for financial reasons, and, she hated to admit to herself, for emotional support too. Her congenital health problems had been overwhelming then, making even supporting herself almost impossible.

Lee knew she should have ended it with Alex after she'd learned the proper arrangement. Instead, she'd allowed him to stay, and before long, they'd welcomed a daughter into the world.

"We might as well get some lunch, Lee. We should have time."

"Sure, let's eat," she said as she brushed back her straight black hair.

His drinking had gotten excessive following the birth of Alessa, a year after she'd found the key. Maybe he couldn't deal with her not needing him anymore. Either that, or he was afraid of her.

Lee sat across from him at the mostly vacant airport restaurant, grateful that he'd agreed to go to the treatment center in Austin. She'd convinced him that the family he had in the area would help. She knew he'd get the same help right there in Jacksonville, but she'd wanted him gone. At least for a while.

"It used to be you'd look for something healthy, but not anymore, right? Doesn't matter what you eat, does it?"

Without thinking, Lee flexed her leg muscles against the faded denim stretched over them. "I feel pretty healthy, if that's what you mean."

Her answer seemed to enrage him, but beneath his anger, she saw mostly the panic of a control freak whose life had gone off the rails in an instant. Still, his attitude seemed like it would never stop. He started an argument, and like usual, her calmness only made it worse, driving him dangerously close to violence. She had even prepared herself to use the knife at the side of her plate.

And then, the most amazing thing happened.

Lee felt an odd sensation all over, a pressure of some kind, and instantly, Alex was on the floor. She instinctively looked away, focusing on what she believed was the source of the strange feeling. She could only see the back of a woman's head, her long blond hair hanging down over the chair back.

The blond woman turned and looked at Alex, then at Lee. Lee sensed something, a reality that she couldn't describe. But it seemed familiar. And powerful. She gazed into the woman's green eyes, knowing that answers waited there.

The woman looked away quickly and rose from her seat, grabbed her bag, and headed for the exit. As she paused at the door for a final look, Lee saw a patch on her luggage, and she memorized it.

Chapter 3 – Monday

Just before the sun would begin battling the thick clouds, Tayo heard sounds of life again inside the house. He surmised that Lin would likely leave her home soon, so before the sky lightened any more, he stretched his legs and hurried to his car. The motor fired right up, and he wanted to curse the cold air blowing from the heater. But he didn't. Focus only on Lin, he reminded himself. A short drive left him within viewing distance of her driveway, and warmer air rewarded his patience.

Forty-nine minutes later, he watched the garage door open, and Lin's car backed out. He followed the car as it took as direct of a route as possible to a parking lot across the street from a row of storefronts in downtown Allentown. She'd driven at such high speeds, as high as sixty-seven percent above legal limits, according to his calculations, that he could barely keep up.

He found a convenient place to park to keep watch, and he was grateful for the warmth of his car. Three more people parked and went inside after Lin, at roughly three-minute intervals. Likely other employees, noted Tayo.

After twelve minutes of no activity around the shop's entrance, he stepped back out into the cold. A short, shivering hike brought him almost within reach of Lin's car. But the rate of passersby in that area, all with the opportunity to observe his actions, drove him back into his own car.

Tayo watched as, one after another, shoppers, workers, vagrants . . . all continued to walk near Lin's car. To his dismay, a street vendor opened a mobile hot dog stand close by as well. His assignment would have to wait.

But could he at least purchase lunch from the vendor? No, he concluded—he might have been seen already walking in that area. A second appearance might arouse suspicion. Hunger was acceptable. Failure was not.

Six hungry hours later, Lin appeared, and he followed her back to her home, where he remained in his car, slightly over three houses away. Hunger was his only companion. Along with his dedication.

Two hours and ten minutes later, he again tailed her car back to Allentown, risking a speeding ticket to keep her in sight.

After she'd parked and gone into a restaurant, he walked past her car, slowing just enough as he passed it, and he placed a magnetic tracking device in the driver's side rear wheel well. He continued into the restaurant, grateful for the opportunity to eat while continuing the surveillance. He took a seat at a small table on a balcony, where he had a view of Lin looking through the patio doors before walking to her seat at the bar.

He found he needed to correct a specific entry in his mental notes. The small photo of Lin's face got replaced with his vision of her standing near the glass. The image of her short skirt, shapely legs in high heels, and flowing blond hair burned into his mind. The blue of her beret became his favorite color. From a distance, outside her work, he hadn't noticed. But up close, he struggled to remember his purpose. The mission could easily have been forgotten.

But Tayo refocused himself. She was just a woman. A woman who talked of magic, he reminded himself as many times as he needed. Discipline.

* * *

Lee's detective work, along with an unplanned flight and a drive in a rental car, took her straight to Allentown. The patch on the woman's bag read, "Vets Without Regrets." A quick search for the group's website led her to photographs of various animal health care teams that had traveled all over the world. One photo showed the blond woman, identified as Lin Finnerty, with a team that had traveled to Kashmir. She worked at a place called Sweet Pets.

Lee looked at the photo of Lin closely, and nothing out of the ordinary was obvious. Not like what she'd seen in Lin's eyes in Jacksonville. And what she'd felt. She looked at her own eyes in the rearview mirror for several seconds, shrugged, and looked for the nearest fast food drive-through.

"And cookies. Do you have cookies?"

She parked her rental car near the Sweet Pets entrance and watched intently. She'd picked up a bag of burgers and fries and a dozen cookies for dessert, and she settled in for what might be a long wait. To her surprise, she'd only just finished the burgers and all the fries before an employee turned off the "Open" sign, stepped out to the sidewalk, and locked the door.

Lee calculated that she had enough time before the woman would reach her car, so she brushed her hair back over her black leather jacket and closed her eyes. She remained motionless, doing what she needed to do, setting things right, and opened her eyes just in time to see the woman climbing into her car.

She began devouring the cookies as she pulled into traffic to follow.

* * *

Tayo watched as a crowd gathered around Lin. Diligence, he reminded himself as he fought to observe the rest of the room, not just Lin. The bar area had become shoulder to shoulder, and he congratulated himself for finding a seat with a good view. The balcony was mostly empty, with only a few guests at neighboring tables. It all looked routine, and he anticipated his mental report might not have any more entries.

Until he saw a large, unkempt man elbowing his way through the crowd toward Lin. He stopped six feet from her, and she rose from her seat. Tayo studied them closely, but he also noticed that a man two tables from him had gotten up to watch as well.

Without any deliberations, Tayo stood, spilling coffee on his sleeve. An unnecessary thought raced through his mind—a hope that the drink would stain the black stripes, not the white—and then it was gone, and he focused only on the confrontation unfolding below. His mind struggled, but his self-discipline carried him through, allowing him to witness and remember every detail. And he fought to record those details, to treat them as reality, when he doubted they possibly could be.

The woman stood without speaking a word, and her eyes closed slightly less than halfway. He saw a wave emanate outward from her to a distance of about twenty-five feet in every direction. He'd quickly counted four-foot-wide wall panels to arrive at an accurate estimate. Tayo's black eyes stared, and he muttered under his breath after he'd seen every single person touched by the wave go out of focus, then quickly return to normal.

A voice inside contended that yes, her eyes had been glowing . . . a soft green. No, they couldn't have been. Yes, he saw it. That fact went into his mental notes too.

As quickly as the wave rushed out and dissipated, the man confronting her began dropping to the floor. Tayo heard a glass crash on the concrete below, and he saw Lin look down on the man, who was out of his view behind the bar. She soon looked up, tried to pull her skirt down, gathered her things, and ignored the clamoring crowd as they parted for her to pass through.

To Tayo's surprise, the man seated two tables over bolted down the stairs and met her at the door. They exchanged a few words and exited the building together.

Always do what's right, Tayo reminded himself, as he threw cash onto the table before jumping down the stairs four at a time. He snaked his way through the crowd, which for some reason unknown to him had clogged the exit area, trying to get outside.

He finally made it out into the chilly air, looked for Lin, and saw only the crowd milling around, chattering and snickering.

* * *

Several quick miles and half a dozen cookies later, Lee followed the car from Sweet Pets into a restaurant parking lot just as a swarm of giggling people poured out into the windy air. At the other turnoff into the lot, she saw a gleaming black car waiting to turn onto Broadway. She parked her rental car and began walking toward it, with the brisk wind lifting her black hair forward and over her shoulders. She stopped when she saw a man get out on the passenger side and swing the door shut. The car turned right onto the road and traveled a short distance before it jerked to a stop. The man walked out to the sidewalk and stood gazing at the car, which rumbled with its brake lights lit.

Lee walked over and stood next to him, staring at the car through her mirrored sunglasses. Neither spoke a word. Within seconds, the engine roared, tires screamed, and the car rocketed toward the sunset.

Chapter 4 – Light & Night

"Yesterday, I killed a man, Gabby. Crippled a couple more before that. Drove Jack insane with pleasure too. And now, you're telling me we've only begun?"

Gabriel's jeans, sweater, and hiking boots were a stark contrast to Lin's tight black sweater and short black skirt. She shifted her long legs, careful to not snag her black stockings under the steering wheel.

Gabriel glanced at her and laughed, saying, "You've learned a lot in the last week, Lin. It took over thirty years for you to get control of what you became, what you *made* yourself, when you were fifteen. We're not going to wait thirty more years for the next step."

"There's more? More than my mayhem?" she said with a smile.

"Yes. When you've used your mayhem, and you saw the endless depths of magic below the calm world of reality, you must have suspected that there's more. Much more."

"Oh, I don't doubt it. There's so much I don't understand. I guess I'm surprised it took me only thirty years to get this far."

"Well, it might have taken longer, except I pushed you. You do know that, don't you?"

Lin paused and looked back on their peculiar relationship. It had all become clear just minutes before, after she'd pulled off the highway. Several hours earlier, she'd sped away from everyone in her day-to-day life in Allentown. She'd used her mayhem to heal Ben, and that had turned friends and coworkers into infatuated fans. But not Jack, who only stood on the sidewalk and watched her leave.

Several hours of ignoring the posted speed limits had passed, and she sat with Gabriel in the quiet of midnight. She'd felt a strange confusion deep inside, growing with every mile her Temt8tion traveled, and she'd had to pull over.

Gabriel had somehow found her—miles from home, in her car, on a deserted Pennsylvania highway—and did something to her, something that had cleared her mind.

She'd met Gabriel a moment after her mayhem had first erupted and destroyed the uncle that had abused her for three years. She remembered how she'd felt after that: too weak and overwhelmed to do anything but retreat and maybe never return. Then, Gabriel appeared, held her and comforted her, and became an internal friend. Her best friend. She'd been living some impossible mind trick, not knowing if Gabriel were real, but not really asking either.

And of *course,* Gabriel had pushed her lately. She could see it clearly. Gabriel had criticized her frumpy clothing, which encouraged her to change her style. Wearing the sexier clothes had helped her reclaim her sexual identity, which she'd locked away when she was fifteen from feelings of guilt. For over thirty years, she'd kept her sexuality, and her mayhem, and knowing the real Gabriel buried deep inside. But with Gabriel's coaxing, walls had begun to crumble, and what had been hidden away inside began fighting its way to the surface.

Only a week earlier, her mayhem had erupted in Erie, saving her from a violent attack. After that, Gabriel had gently pushed her into dangerous situations. That very same day, in a risky confrontation with a stranger near a pond, Gabriel talked her into getting out of her own car and dealing with whatever unknown danger might be waiting. Gabriel knew that she could no longer be hurt. Her mayhem would always protect her. And it did protect her on its own until she finally got complete control of it on a lonely road in Georgia.

Through all of it, Gabriel had always encouraged her to choose good while prodding her to take control of her power. Her mayhem. And only minutes before, Gabriel had caused Lin to remember all of it. Every memory for her last thirty-plus years had to be rebuilt with the truth of Gabriel.

"I see it now, Gabby. You knew it was time. But still, your patience astounds me. I truly would not have survived without you. I can't thank you enough."

"You're welcome, but I want you to remember something. You're very important. We'll talk more about that someday soon. But now, what are your plans? Will you try to find the end of this road number 76?"

Lin released the steering wheel of her Temt8tion and placed her hands on her lap. She still felt the magic just below her surface, and she knew it would never be lost again—her hold on her intent was unbreakable. But after using her mayhem in Allentown, that odd side effect that she'd seen before had changed everyone close to her. Life with them would be impossible, and she had no reason to believe that would ever stop.

"I don't want to leave my life. I really don't. But you know what John and Tommy were like, after what I did by that pond. How could I possibly live with so many people acting that way?"

Gabriel stretched then lowered the window, hanging an arm out for air.

"Now, Lin, please don't think for a minute that I've been anything but happy to be with you for the last three decades. But I have to tell you, it's good to be real again."

Lin laughed. "I'm probably happier about it. It's been so unnerving having you with me but not knowing if you were even real. I've known something wasn't right, but I couldn't look directly at it. Couldn't even question it. How is that possible?"

"It's actually pretty easy, Lin. Someday, you'll see for yourself. But for now, we need to discuss your converts."

"Converts?"

"Yes, what your mayhem does to anyone close enough. The most important thing for you to know right now is that it's not permanent."

"What!"

"John and Tommy are likely back to normal by now. Or whatever normal is for them. The people in the restaurant will take longer. The stronger you get, the longer that effect lasts."

"Oh my God, Gabby, that's great news. I can certainly start a new life—I can still feel that fever inside. It was burning so hot when I left it all behind. But that's a good life, back there. I'd always miss Jack. And Nomad."

"Leaving the way you did, committing yourself to an entirely new life—that's what was required. That changed you in an important way.

"It's the leaving that mattered, Lin. What ground you actually stand on means nothing."

* * *

A short drive brought them to a crumbling motel shrouded in shadows and tucked into the forested hills near Somerset. The chilly air carried aromas of burning wood and pine, and they hurried to check in under the silent moonlight. Gabriel volunteered for the sagging couch so Lin could claim the bed.

"What you've been through has tired you, Lin, and you probably don't know just how much. Using the magic, as you call it, takes a kind of strength that few ever acquire. When you healed Ben, you pushed beyond your limits."

"I feel good, Gabby. But you're right—I am pretty tired. I'm still so amazed by it all. The magic and what it can do. And I'm amazed by you too."

Lin had changed into sweats and slippers, but her hair remained impeccable. She sat cross-legged on the bed, and Gabriel leaned against the plain wood dresser.

"Do you feel you understand things better?"

"Yeah, I really do. Once I got control of my mayhem, my life began to make some kind of sense again. I need things to make *some* kind of sense."

"I understand."

Gabriel studied Lin closely, then spoke.

"Before you sleep, there's someplace I'd like to take you."

"Oh, maybe I shouldn't have changed?"

"We're not leaving this room."

Lin still felt beyond needing explanations after everything that had happened in the previous week. She'd used her mayhem many times, injuring some, killing one, and healing another. And she'd almost wrecked Jack with the pleasure she'd forced on him. The world seemed boundless. She'd go wherever Gabriel wanted. She rose from the bed and stood near Gabriel.

"Take my hand, Lin. Try to not let go. There are no signposts where we're going."

"Oh, um . . . sure. Okay," she said and took Gabriel's outstretched hand.

Immediately, she saw Gabriel's eyes begin to close, only partially blocking a deep green glow. The wave from Gabriel hit her like a hurricane. Her eyes said that she hadn't moved, but she felt the wave whip her impossibly high and snap her back down. The feeling of falling was like a brick in her gut, and she felt she'd traveled miles in an instant. As she neared the bottom, the room began to blur, and she felt the odd confusion that she used to feel before she'd gotten control of her mayhem.

Every sense overlapped with all the rest. The alarm clock's ticking tasted like honey. The white of the walls felt like hot sunshine. And the sound of her own heart beating was a soft shade of blue, then waves of wet and dry. Then, each beat was a puff of wind through lilacs, a scent that she could see bouncing around and that felt rough like sandpaper. Then, the room was gone, and she was alone with Gabriel in the magic.

And everything hit like an explosion.

Every sense she had staggered under the onslaught of chaotic sights and sounds and scents. Her mind collapsed as thoughts and memories and ideas and dreams swept through and were gone, making room for more. Feelings raced to every extreme in countless directions, and she sought anything solid, anything that would just hold still long enough for her to know it, to understand it. But there was nothing that made sense. It was a screaming storm, its only purpose to devour her.

And still, she felt her hand in Gabriel's being squeezed tight. Gabriel's grasp became a sound, then a scent . . . then again, only a touch. They'd found a calm corner of the swirling insanity, but she still clutched Gabriel's hand in fear for her life.

She wanted to look at Gabriel, but something else had captured her attention—something that seemed near and far, gigantic and tiny at the same time. Lin gazed at a stillness being born amid the spinning hysteria. Something was being created there for her alone.

She continued to hold Gabriel's hand, and she felt like laughing and crying. It was a jewel resting on a cloud, beating like a heart, and shining with a color that she could not recognize. A color that didn't exist in the world she knew. She could tell it wasn't a blend of other colors. It was an entirely new color!

How could that even be possible? She knew she had to remember it and somehow bring the memory of it back into the world. What an incredible find, she thought—something that couldn't possibly exist. A new color, there in the magic, a brilliant color with no name, a color that—

Abruptly, she felt a pull from Gabriel, followed by a sense of breaking a barrier. She felt the whipping force drag her dangerously high and snap her back down. With her free hand, she held her stomach and opened her eyes in the motel room.

An undefined turmoil seeped into her mind as she turned to look at Gabriel, whose eyes were slowly returning to their normal brown.

She felt something move deep inside. Something that had been rooted loosened.

"Gabby, I . . . I don't know what to say . . ."

"There are no words for it, Lin. We can try to talk about where we were, but our words will fail us. Try to tell me what you saw."

"I don't know what it was. A jewel, I think. A magic jewel? But maybe it doesn't really matter. What matters is that its color...I've never seen that color before. It doesn't exist. But I saw it. I remember seeing it and knowing that it doesn't exist. But I can't remember what it looked like now. I really did see it, didn't I, Gabby?"

"Yes, you really did see it."

"But why can't I remember it?"

"Your eyes, your mind, even your memory, are made for this world. They will never know that color."

"That's crazy . . . I should be able to remember it."

"You never will."

Lin felt hot tears lined up and ready to go. She could only bite her lip and stare at Gabriel before again finding her voice.

"But you . . . you remember it, right?"

"No."

Lin turned away and grabbed the dresser with both hands. She shook her head slowly, her long hair hanging down past her shoulders, and wondered how any of that could have just happened. The world's a place where everything is possible, she reminded herself, and everything is accounted for. But that color—it had no place in the world. And while she lived in the world, she knew she'd never see that color. No one would.

A feeling of excitement surged then vanished, replaced by an unfamiliar fear. She'd never known that she lived only a heartbeat from insanity.

Something inside her felt like it was shaking itself loose, breaking apart. Suddenly, her world, the entire world she'd known all her life, seemed no larger than the motel room, surrounded by a vastness stretching to infinity. A realm that literally could not be described. Or even remembered.

She'd seen the endless magic below the calm surface of reality every time she'd used her mayhem. But it had seemed separate, something that existed as a secret part of the world. Almost like a game.

But no, she could see now that the world she inhabited was just a small, easily managed portion of all that existed. What wonders, what mysteries—and what terrors—lay waiting in all that magic? She knew that she'd never be able to bring any part of it back into her life. She couldn't even remember a simple color.

"Gabby," Lin said, her voice shaking, "what good is all that endless magic if we can't understand it? If we can't even remember it?"

"There's a challenge for you, Lin. Just know that the magic is real. And understand, too, that when you're in this world,"—Gabriel pointed to the floor—"you're experiencing only a small part of all the wonder,"—Gabriel pointed to the empty black beyond the window— "out there."

Lin stared into the darkness before looking back at Gabriel. One tear escaped.

"Gabby," Lin whispered, "I don't . . . I mean, what should I—"

"Rest, Lin. You need to rest."

She had a thought of their room being but a single speck of light, surviving only because of those thin walls. A light lost in infinite night.

Lin ended her gaze into Gabriel's kind eyes and lay down across the bed. She struggled to raise an arm of lead to switch off the lamp on the nightstand. She heard only silence, and she wondered if Gabriel even needed to sleep.

Her thoughts raced until they hit their own wall and could go no further.

Lin fell into the deepest sleep she'd ever known. Her dreams courted delirium and flirted with lunacy. But even with all the madness her mind could concoct, it could not conjure up that color.

Chapter 5 – Fans & Allies

"You're building this house? Are you a carpenter?" said Lee.

"Yeah, I'm working on this house too. But I'm not a carpenter, alright?"

"I guess I'd agree with that," she said, looking around the unfinished room.

"Funny."

Jack Madison took pride in being handy with a hammer, and he could usually tolerate Lin calling him a carpenter. He could perform just about any work that a house needed to make it livable. Any house except his own. Half-painted walls crowded in on unfinished floors, most ceiling lights answered to no switch, and many doors remained unhinged, waiting to be installed. They'd been waiting a long time.

He sat deep into a worn vinyl couch, and Lee stood near the front door, her stuffed backpack still hanging from her hand. Both stared at Ben Barlow, waiting for him to recover from his experience at the restaurant in Allentown. They'd left him slumped against an old upholstered chair framed by towers of paint cans and rolls of vinyl flooring and carpet.

"Thanks for helping me drag him here," said Jack. "I didn't know what else to do. I couldn't take the chance Lin would get into some kind of trouble for . . . for what she—"

"No problem, Jack. I want to talk to him too. I want to know what Lin did to him."

Jack rubbed his chin, remembering the hard punches Ben had dealt him in St. Simons Island just two days earlier. And he wondered if more were headed his way.

"Maybe we should try to get him up onto that chair. What do you think?"

"Leave him. He's fine," Lee said as she pulled back her long black hair. "He probably wouldn't fit in that chair anyway."

As Lin had sped away from the chaos she'd caused in the bar, Jack could only stare at the love of his life leaving him forever. He'd felt empty, demoralized. The engagement ring in his pocket kept reminding him of how high his expectations had been and how far they'd crashed. He let go of the ring and ran his fingers through his wavy brown hair.

"What are we going to do? I don't know what Lin did to him, and maybe he'll be even more pissed when he wakes up. More pissed than when he beat me down at Lin's reunion."

"We'll handle it."

"You didn't see it, Lee. My mind can't accept what I saw. She did something incredible. Ben was about to attack her, and then, something, I don't know what, some kind of wave shot out from her, and Ben fell to the ground. I ran down the stairs, and Lin and I walked out to her car. It was really weird, but all her friends came outside, laughing and trying to find her."

"No, I didn't see that. But I did see something back in Jacksonville."

"Is that why you're here?"

"She knows something. Something I need to learn."

"Yeah, she knows something alright. I can't describe something else she did once. All I know is that I loved it, and it scared the crap out of me at the same time."

Jack smiled, reliving that magical night in a cool hotel room on the Island. He took a deep breath, expanding his strong chest, remembering the ecstasy. He blew the breath out sharply and shook his head as he remembered the terror that came with it.

"So, we should stick together like we agreed, and maybe we can find her again. But I have no idea where she went. She seemed determined to leave everything behind. Even me. Hell, even her dog."

Ben groaned softly and dragged a hand across his face and over his bald head, rubbing his eyes until they could crack open. His eyes grew wide, looking around at Jack's living room and Jack and Lee staring at him.

"Where am I? What day is it?"

"It's still Monday, and don't start anything again, Ben. We're not looking for any trouble," Jack said quickly. Ben's greasy jeans and the skull and crossbones on his black t-shirt gave him more memories of being knocked to the ground.

"I don't want to start anything. Hey, I remember you from the reunion in St. Simons."

"Yeah, I remember you too. Thanks for not killing me, I guess. I'm Jack, and this is Lee."

"Jack, Lee," he said, looking each of them in the eye.

"Jack, I apologize for what I did. I'd blame it on some kind of temporary insanity, except it lasted most of my life. I feel different now. I don't want to hit anyone again."

Jack stared and didn't know what to say. The man who'd punched him without a second thought, who seemed to have no respect for life, no decency at all, sat there apologizing. Could it be a ploy, he wondered? Did he really deserve any trust?

"Sounds good to me, Ben. But you should know, you sure can hit."

"I do know," Ben said with a laugh. "I've had a lot of practice."

"What did Lin do to you?" Lee said.

"First of all, who are you? I don't know you, do I? What are you doing here?"

"I met Lin, sort of, at the airport in Jacksonville. I need to talk to her."

"So, you two are partners now?"

Jack and Lee looked at each other, then back at Ben, nodding their agreement.

"I'd like to talk to her too. Where is she?"

"I'm not sure you should be anywhere near her. All you've done is try to kill her. I'm not sure you won't try to kill us too."

"I don't blame you for feeling that way. But I'm telling you that I've changed. Lin changed me."

"What do you mean?" said Lee.

"In the restaurant. I walked up to her, and you might not believe it, but I only wanted to talk to her. And then, something so crazy happened. I got hit with something, and I was paralyzed. I wanted to speak, but I couldn't. I could feel that Lin had taken control of me. How is that even possible?"

"Oh, it's possible," said Jack.

"And then, all the anger inside me, all the rage and craziness that had become part of me, started to fade away. I could feel it being replaced, piece by piece, with something, I don't know what, something that felt good. Felt right. And that's the last I remember until waking up here. And where exactly is 'here' anyway?"

"This is my house, just north of Allentown. We couldn't just leave you there. And believe me, it wasn't easy getting you into my pickup."

"You're living . . . here?" Ben said as he looked around the room.

"Yeah. Yeah, I am. Look, it's a project. I still need to do a few things . . ."

"We want to find Lin," said Lee.

"I do too," said Ben. "Not to hurt her. To thank her."

Jack said, "Between the three of us, maybe we have a chance. If you're serious about not trying to hurt her, you're welcome to stick around."

"I feel like I owe Lin my life. I'd give it up for her in a heartbeat."

Chapter 6 – Madness & Reality

"It will take time to build your strength. Even that short journey into the magic has weakened you."

Lin heard the words from Gabriel shortly after she'd crawled out of the motel bed. She'd never known such a deep sleep, and finding her footing in the real world took longer than she expected. The shy morning sunlight creeping in didn't help.

"I feel fine, Gabby. Just a sort of confusion in the background, that's all. I keep thinking about how there's a color that exists out there, in the magic, but my mind can't even conceive of it. It's unsettling."

"Yes, that unsettled feeling is the weakness. It will be replaced with acceptance. But until it does, you're going to feel a little wobbly."

"There's more, isn't there? I mean, more than just one color."

"Yes, that's very true. Just as the magic is boundless, so are all the things that can be witnessed there. You could spend a lifetime, many lifetimes, trying to unravel all of it."

Lin wiped the sleep from her eyes and headed for the bathroom, where she showered and dried off. She smiled at the clothes she was about to put on. She felt lucky that she'd left her travel bags in the trunk of her Temt8tion when she'd made it home late Sunday. At the time, she didn't want the distraction of carrying luggage when she played the game with Nomad at the door. She'd won the game—Nomad broke down first and barked—and being home was such a relief that she'd left the bags where they were.

She put back on her black skirt, stockings, and heels. But since the Pennsylvania air in mid-November carried a chill, she donned a thicker gray sweater instead of the thin black one she'd worn the night before.

The jacket she'd taken to the restaurant hung from the chair, ready to help with the cold.

"Do you plan to keep dressing that way, Lin?"

"Yeah, I like it. I don't need to anymore, I know that. But it feels right. This is my style."

As she walked out into the motel's main room, she stopped abruptly and leaned against the wall with a hand on the dresser. She stared at Gabriel and felt faint convulsions deep inside. They were barely noticeable, like weak thunder from over the horizon.

"I know I shouldn't focus on unimportant details, with all the magic and mayhem. But you only became real hours ago. And right then, you already had clothes. It doesn't make sense. None of it makes sense. How is any of that possible?"

"You've already answered your own question, Lin. Sense. It doesn't make sense. Does sense have any place in the magic?"

"Not from what I've seen of it, that's for sure. Without your hand to hold, I would have been lost there. It's the exact opposite of sense."

"You would have found your way."

"Can we not test that?" Lin managed a smile. "I can't imagine how I'd ever survive there."

"You only need more strength. It will come in time. Then, you won't need the magic to make sense."

"But, Gabby, in this world, where we are, things *do* need to make sense."

"That's true, but I'm mostly magic. I only make as much sense as I want to. Soon enough, you'll see that even in this world, there's only as much sense as *you* expect there to be."

Lin grabbed tightly the edge of the dresser as she felt a foundation inside start to weaken. Gabriel's answer seemed true, but something in her core continued to break loose.

She saw that the idea of the world making sense, that was the basic canvas on which her life had been painted. Everything that happened had an explanation. It all fit on that neat, limited surface. And even those things that couldn't be explained, they were assumed to have explanations that made sense, though the answers might still be out of reach.

"I'm going to take a shower, too, Lin. And before you ask, no, I don't need to. But it's a joy of being alive."

Gabriel retreated to the bathroom and Lin heard the shower start up. She'd thought she had the world figured out when she'd gained complete control of her mayhem. It had taken nearly being strangled to death on a road in Georgia for her to claim that ability. After that, her power over the magic—her mayhem—would never again be unreachable. But that feeling of being on solid ground had started to slip away. Starting with seeing a color that doesn't exist. And then, Gabriel's calm assertion that the world doesn't *have* to make sense.

She found her blue beret and set it on the dresser. Her brush was already out, off to the right, and she reached for it as she looked into the mirror. Her hand fumbled while she continued to look into her eyes, green and sleepy beneath her cascading blond hair.

She realized that she'd miscalculated the brush's location, though, and her hand found only the dresser top. She looked down and saw that the brush was actually to her left. She shrugged, thinking it must be like Gabriel had said—that she was still weak from their journey into the magic.

She reached for the brush with her left hand, keeping her eyes on it to be sure, and she let out a short scream as she saw the brush vanish. Her first thought was that she must still be asleep and dreaming. But everything seemed so real. Every detail of the room was visible, and even the sound of the shower could be plainly heard. She looked at herself in the mirror, wondering how to wake up . . . how to get back to the real world.

Then, she felt her attitude flare up, demanding that she charge forward, whether it was real or a dream. She had to pick up that brush and finish her hair. She looked down and saw the brush off to her right. She reached for it and missed as it vanished and reappeared to her left.

Perhaps a different approach, she thought. She crept her left hand toward the brush, not wanting to startle it, and knowing that that thought was crazy. Her hand inched closer and closer until her little finger almost touched it.

The brush remained in its place. Lin cautiously moved her hand in circles around it, keeping her fingertips in contact with the dresser. The brush stayed.

Her manicured finger was a fraction of an inch away from the brush and slowly closing in. Soon, she'd touch it and know that it was real. Soon, she'd feel the smooth, hard surface of the handle, and from there, it would be easy to grasp it and pick it up.

She watched as the tip of her finger closed the distance, and she let out another sharp scream as her finger disappeared into the handle. No, she thought, that's impossible. But she knew it wasn't a dream. She'd actually pushed her finger into the plastic.

Lin drew her hand back and stared at the troublesome brush, and it seemed to be waiting patiently. With tears rising to the surface, she grabbed the brush and jerked it up to her hair. Her hand shook as she finished her hair while studying the uncertainty she now saw in her eyes.

After dropping it onto the dresser and hearing the solid rattling, Lin backed away until she hit the bed, and she sat. She looked inside and felt her mayhem still there, still ready to rise up if needed. But what good would her mayhem do with a brush that couldn't be real when she needed it to be?

She fell back into the soft blankets and stared at the ceiling. Several minutes later, the shower stopped, and several more minutes passed before Gabriel came out and leaned against the dresser.

"Are you alright, Lin?"

Lin laughed out loud, almost hysterically. "No, I don't think so. I don't know where I am. Is this real? Is this a dream?"

"Yes. And yes."

"Gabby . . . I . . . I—"

"Did something happen while I was in the shower?"

"Oh, God. Yeah, something happened. I think I'm losing my mind."

"Yes, you did for a while when we were in the magic. Is that what you mean?"

"No. I mean here. Now. I need the world to be real, Gabby. It has to be. And for a while there, it wasn't."

"I think what you're saying, Lin, is that the world is more comfortable when you believe everything makes perfect sense. But there's a more complete comfort from living in the truth of the world. It takes strength, though."

"Who could live in a world where things don't behave like they're supposed to? That's madness. No one could live like that."

"Madness is a relative term, Lin. Sanity, things making sense—that's the world of your mind, the world you're most comfortable with. But you know that there's so much more. You've seen it. You've been there. And you've used it. The limitless magic that supports everything in this world. That's reality."

Lin lay on the bed, staring at the ceiling and shaking her head slowly back and forth. She felt her mayhem inside, still waiting, but useless in a world she couldn't control.

Gabriel stood in front of the wall sconce, looking down on her. The light fanned out around long brown hair like an aura.

"What am I supposed to do? This all seems impossible."

"Your mayhem seemed impossible to you as well. Now, you accept it, and you control it. Keep moving forward, Lin. Your strength will not disappoint you."

Chapter 7 – Rings & Revelations

"I guess I believe you—that I can somehow learn what the world's really about. I mean, you're right, I thought my mayhem would destroy me. But my mayhem always seemed like something apart from me, apart from the world. And the world was constant. I could depend on it. I don't know how to adapt to a world that doesn't have to be real."

"Yet here you are, and you will adapt."

They'd packed their things, checked out, and climbed back into the Temt8tion. In contrast to the unnerving behavior of a simple brush, Lin's car gave her a welcome sanctuary. The black leather seats adjusted to her every curve, keeping her posture just right and amplifying the benefits of her low-cut sweater. The big engine started with a deep roar, and she held the steering wheel, contemplating the day ahead.

"I can't tell you how relieved I am that that weird side effect of using my mayhem—making converts—is only temporary. But what of the fear? You know I caused a lot of fear in Jack, and I also used my mayhem to turn him into a convert. I'd hoped to balance the two, so he'd just be the same old Jack again. What of the fear? Does that wear off too?"

"It will for Jack, but that's because he loves you, and you had no desire to hurt him. For anyone else, like that fugitive you tangled with in Erie, or that Davey guy that you dealt with near the pond, they'll always be terrified of you. No amount of magic will fix that."

"You said that the stronger I get, the longer that effect, the convert effect, lasts? But for everyone back home, they'll get back to normal eventually?"

"Yes."

"I need to call Jack. I have to tell him I'm alright, and we'll see each other again. I know how he feels about me, even with all my mayhem mixed in. That must have broken his heart for me to say goodbye and drive away like that."

"Jack's strong, too, but not like you. Just in a normal human way. He'll be fine, especially if he hears your voice again."

Gabriel switched on the radio and tuned it until an agreeable station was found.

"Classic rock, Gabby?"

"Sure, why not?"

Lin could only smile.

"I know it's too soon for me to go back. Things back home need to cool down a little. I feel I've left some kind of trail behind me with all that's happened. Let's just drive, and when we come across someplace to eat, let's stop and get some breakfast. You *can* eat, can't you?" Lin said with a laugh.

"I'm as human as I want to be. And right now, I have a human hunger for the biggest breakfast we can find."

* * *

After Ben had declared his devotion to Lin, which Jack still found unlikely, he'd slipped back into a sleep that rivaled that of a dead man. Jack and Lee had continued to watch him for a while after midnight, unsure of his real feelings about them and about Lin. Lee had wanted to restrain him using the twisted mess of electrical cords piled in the corner, but Jack had talked her out of it. Eventually, they both slept too.

Jack awoke to find Lee had sat next to him after he'd fallen asleep and leaned her head on his shoulder. Her leather jacket felt warm where it pressed against his arm. He looked across the room to see Ben snoring exactly where they'd dumped him. He found it hard to believe that Ben had ever spoken to them.

Lee shook herself awake and sat straight up, extended her arms in front of her, then dropped them back down and closed her eyes. Jack watched as she sat there motionless, eyes closed, and not moving a muscle. After several seconds, she let out a deep breath, got up, and walked toward the kitchen.

"We need to eat. Do you have food?"

"Uh . . . yeah, I should have something. I couldn't help but notice, but you're some kind of bodybuilder, right?"

"Some kind, yeah."

"I work out sometimes, too, but I don't think I have anything healthy in that kitchen. I'll—"

"Anything, Jack. It doesn't matter."

Jack looked up and down her lean, muscular frame.

"Well, I know there's a box of cookies and some leftover pizza, and there's probably . . ."

Lee turned and walked into the kitchen. She returned with all of it and stood by the door, eating one thing after another.

"Well, alright then. Um . . . what should we do with him? I don't have any idea when we might see Lin again. It might be soon, and it might not. But we can't just sit around this house forever, waiting."

"We have no idea where she went, Jack. Where would we even look? All we can do is wait. Maybe she'll call you. Or why don't you call her?"

"I can't call her, Lee. You didn't see her, how she had to leave. I have to give her whatever space she needs. Maybe she will call, though. God, I'd love to see her again, just to know for sure that she's not gone forever."

Jack's right hand held the engagement ring in his pants pocket.

"We both need to see her. The three of us need to see her," said Lee.

"So, let's just hang out, then. Ben's not waking up anytime soon anyway."

* * *

Before Lin's Temt8tion had eaten up too many miles of Interstate 76, she and Gabriel found a diner near Bedford, wedged into a thick stand of evergreens. She pulled in and parked, hoping that Gabriel's hunger could wait a few minutes.

"I'd rather not wait. I think I'll call Jack right now."

"That's a great idea. I'll be fine."

She heard his cell phone ringing and waited nervously, not knowing what she'd say. She heard Jack's voice.

"Lin, oh my God, it's so good to hear from you. Are you alright?"

"I'm fine, Jack, and it's good to hear your voice too. I apologize for leaving like I did. The last week has been incredibly difficult for me to get my head around. And after the scene in the restaurant last night, all I could think of was leaving. I felt I had no choice. I'll explain that better when I see you."

"You're coming back? When? I can't wait to see you, I—"

"Yes, but not right away. I'm only calling to let you know that I'm fine, and I wanted to know you were okay too."

"God, Lin, just knowing that you're coming back, whenever that might be, is the best news I've ever heard."

"It's good news for me too. I didn't want to leave like that, but it felt right, like I had to. It was like a fever, Jack."

"I saw it. It seemed like something was pulling you away, like you couldn't fight it anymore."

"Did you make it home okay?"

"Yeah, and you won't believe what's been going on. Ben's here too."

"Ben? Why is he with you? Are you at your house?"

"You won't believe it, Lin. He's changed. He's polite now. And he hasn't punched me again, thank God. Yes, we're at my house."

"But why is he with you?"

"We went back into the restaurant after you left, and Ben was still crumpled on the floor where you'd left him. We helped him into my truck, and I didn't know where else to take him. We didn't think we should leave him for the police or whoever else might show up."

"What do you mean, 'we?'"

"Lee. Her name's Lee. You must have seen her. She was on the sidewalk with me."

"Yeah, I did see her. And I remember her from Jacksonville. What's she doing here, Jack?"

"She's not very talkative, but she said she needs to speak with you. Who is she?"

"I'll have to leave that explanation for when I see you too. It won't be long. Maybe even later today. I just want to get some things straight in my mind first. It's always something with me, isn't it, Jack?"

"I wouldn't want you any other way. Come back soon, alright?"

"I will, Jack. I'll call soon. Goodbye."

*   *   *

"If you can wait a little longer, I'd like to call my boss too. Can you hold off a bit more for a big stack of hotcakes?"

"Sure, Lin, take care of things. I'll be fine. The longer we wait, the more I'll want, though," Gabriel said with a laugh.

Lin smiled and shook her head at the sight.

"Gabby, I still can't get past you being real after being with me for so long. You're my best friend, but I can't even begin to understand who, or what, you are."

Lin dialed the number and listened to the ring.

"In time, Lin, you'll understand. For now, though, your life is waiting. I'll stay with you a while longer."

Lin felt a sharp stab somewhere inside. She'd never considered, never imagined, a life without Gabriel. She fought back tears as Dr. Grayson picked up.

*   *   *

"Dr. Grayson, this is Lin. Do you have a few minutes?"

46

"Oh my God, Lin, it's so good to hear from you! Where are you? How are you? We need you back. We—"

"Doctor, I'm fine. I just had to take care of some unexpected business. Sorry for not giving notice sooner. I plan to return as soon as I can."

"That's fine, Lin. Do whatever you need to do. But come back soon, okay? We really do need you. I need you. I've never told you how unbelievable you are. I guess I always knew it, but I never felt it so much as last night at the bar. God, that was incredible. I felt it. I really felt it. I—"

"Dr. Grayson, it's okay. Take a breath! Will you keep my job for me? I don't think this will take too long, but it's going to be hard to put an exact time on it."

"Well, of course, Lin. Of course, I'll keep your job for you. I'd do anything for you. Anything at all. Just ask. Just *tell* me. You're the most stupendous person ever, and you can take as much time as you want. But please, don't take too long because we—"

"Okay, okay, Dr. Grayson. Look, I've got to get going. I'll check back with you soon, okay?"

"Yes, yes, of course. Check back soon. Come back soon. We all miss you, and all the critters miss you, and—"

"Okay, Doctor, I've got to go. Talk to you soon."

Lin ended the call, feeling like she'd gone another round with John and Tommy. Could it be true about those two, what Gabriel had said? Perhaps they'd recovered and were no longer her converts. Being around them had been a huge challenge. Working alongside Dr. Grayson if he were acting the same way . . . that would be impossible.

* * *

"Gabby, you weren't serious, were you? About leaving?"

"I can't stay here forever, Lin. But I'm not leaving anytime soon. Don't let it bother you, okay?"

"Okay, I'll try. I can't even think about you being gone. Dr. Grayson is definitely one of my converts now. Are you sure that effect wears off after a while?"

"Yes, I'm sure, Lin. At least for now. But there will come a time when it's permanent. Luckily, by then, you'll have enough control that you won't ever accidentally convert anyone. When you're strong enough, you won't send out a wave blindly. You'll be able to focus it. If you choose to convert someone, you will. If you choose to use your mayhem on them, it will be only on them."

Lin stared in disbelief at Gabriel revealing details about her mayhem that she hadn't even considered possible. Could she really someday have that kind of control? She felt a new exhilaration rising inside, a new optimism for the future. She saw that her life could truly be infinite. It made even more sense that she'd changed her name to Lin Finity.

"Will you ever stop surprising me? I can't even imagine how much more there is to learn."

"No, and no. There are many more surprises for you. And no, you can't possibly imagine how much there is to learn. Neither can I."

Chapter 8 – Free Will & Hotcakes

"Of all the ways you amaze me, your appetite takes the top prize. That's your third stack of hotcakes, and you're not even slowing down."

"Ah, Lin, food is such a great joy of being alive. Everyone knows that. But what few know is that almost every joy in life brings with it great responsibility. A simple pleasure like eating can also hasten your death. You must walk a fine line, not taking more joy than you're able. Or that joy will lead to your end."

Lin had expected to have an uneventful breakfast, with good food, good company, and pleasant conversation. Gabriel had wrecked that in a masterful way. But she knew Gabriel spoke the truth.

"But you're eating like there's no tomorrow. How is that okay, then?"

"A better question would be about how you, a mostly complete human, could do that too."

"I'm a 'mostly complete human,' huh?"

"Yes."

Lin laughed nervously.

"Okay, you're right, I'd love to know that because I miss eating chocolate. I used to eat it every day. When I changed my style, and I liked the way it looked, I figured I'd better cut it out."

"Lin, you must have noticed. You were eating a lot of chocolate, and it didn't change you in any way. Didn't you ever wonder why?"

"You're right—I never did gain any weight from all that, but I figured it was just my metabolism. I can't keep taking that chance."

"You've had magic working inside you, helping you in small ways since you were fifteen, when your mayhem first showed itself. You really have no idea how much the magic can do, do you?"

"No, Gabby, I really don't. I've used my mayhem many times now, and I can summon it whenever I want. But I don't have a clue what it is."

With cheeks stretched around blueberry hotcakes, Gabriel continued.

"Your mayhem, as you call it, is only possible because of that narrow space you've found that exists between a person's body and their spirit. Most people aren't even aware that it exists. That leaves it open for you to take it."

"So, if they were aware of it, I wouldn't be able to squeeze in there?"

"That's one thing that could stop you."

"But what is that space? Why is it there? When I tried it on Nomad, there was no space at all. His spirit was completely connected to his body. The harder I tried to squeeze in there, the crazier it made him. And it eventually knocked him out, the poor dog."

Gabriel paused to load the fork with more hotcakes, ready for the next chance to pile it in.

"Lin, there are many things I can't tell you. It's not that I'm not allowed, it's just that most knowledge you need to claim for yourself. Like you did with your mayhem. I coaxed you and encouraged you, but you had to find it yourself.

"That gap, that narrow space, is one of the things I can tell you about. You might be surprised. It relates to a fundamental human condition. When it's explained to you, you'll understand your life, and everyone's life, so much more."

Lin sat on the edge of the bench in the diner's corner booth. Her breakfast had been forgotten as she became mesmerized by the words from her best friend, a being she could barely believe was real.

"Humans have been given that narrow space between their bodies and their spirits. Through that narrow space, their spirits have limited control over their bodies, and not just to move around. Remember that the world of reality is magic too. You've seen that—it's just very slow compared to all the magic swirling beneath it. Humans are given enough control over that slow magic to make themselves into almost anything they want to be, within reason, by the choices they make. They're using magic, and they don't even know it.

"It's called free will, Lin."

Lin could only sit and stare at Gabriel as more hotcakes continued to disappear.

Free will. Of course. She'd never really thought about it. It had always been an abstract concept, something people mentioned but never took any time to examine. To her, it had become synonymous with being able to make choices.

Gabriel's explanation hit her in a place deep inside. Free will wasn't just a concept. It was a real condition related to humans having a small amount of control over magic. The world all around was magic, she'd seen that. But no one else seemed to know it. Yet everyone, every day, used magic in very small ways.

"I've seen that the world we live in, it's magic too. It's just very, very slow magic. That gap allows us to use that slow magic? And that's free will? We've been given the ability to use magic in a very small and slow way to change the world?"

"Usually not the world. To change yourself, Lin. All your life, you've witnessed people changing themselves for better or worse. Mostly worse, though, because time spent in the world inevitably degrades everyone. That's the natural direction. But with free will, with the focused use of the magic we all can control in small amounts, that natural decline can be held back. People can even reverse the trend, improve themselves. But it takes focus. It takes intent.

"And of course, free will also gives humans the ability to make choices. Actually, they have no choice but to make choices about everything they do, whether they realize it or not."

Lin sat back in the booth and brushed her hair back over her shoulders. She knew she was overdressed for a diner, with her short black skirt, black stockings and heels, and a low-cut gray sweater. Her blue beret crowned her flowing blond hair, and her green eyes opened wider with every word from Gabriel.

"Why doesn't anyone know this, Gabby? All we have to do is tell them, right?"

"It's not that easy, Lin. Your words would mean nothing to them. Most would have to see it for themselves, and they never will. But there are some that have developed a feeling for how things work. They've learned to focus, to hold their intent, without knowing exactly what's going on. You could say they have faith."

Gabriel stuffed in more hotcakes and chewed them quietly, gazing at Lin, letting it all sink in.

"Faith? Faith in what . . . God?"

"That's one way of seeing it. Maybe we should say faith in their intent."

"How does anyone get the faith to begin with?"

"It takes intent."

"You're saying you need faith to use intent, but it takes intent to get faith?"

"Yes. Is it little wonder so few learn?"

Lin sat in silence.

"Remember that free will works on the slow magic of the world. Very, very slow magic. It's not easy for anyone to believe that their intent, the use of their free will, could ever work. Nothing changes quickly. The natural tendency is to give up because any change takes a long time.

"Unless the change you're aiming for hastens your decline. That goes much more quickly. And it seduces many because they can sense that they're using magic. They get a misplaced satisfaction from using magic as they destroy themselves.

"If you're trying for any significant *positive* change, your thoughts tend to tell you to stop. And that's just being rational. Only faith in your intent lets you continue. Lets you shape the slow magic of the world."

Gabriel broke Lin's stare and turned to call the server. Another order of hotcakes was soon on the way.

"But, Gabby, how could . . . if—"

"Lin, save yourself the trouble. You can't even form a question about it. Your mind will never solve this riddle.

"Remember when you were being strangled by the criminal Ivan on that Georgia road? You looked inside yourself, maybe because there was nothing else left for you to do. But you looked inside, and at first, it appeared to be a switch, a switch that you could flip to summon your mayhem. But you knew it wasn't really a switch. And it was so simple: it required only that you be what your mayhem demanded you to be.

"You were close to your death, and it required faith to stop fighting and find your intent. Your faith was a stillness inside you, and you searched for your intent despite your circumstances.

"What you found wasn't a thought, it wasn't a memory, it wasn't even a feeling. That *thing* that you can't name, I'm calling it your intent.

"The word means nothing, Lin. We must give things names so that we may speak. And using names convinces us that we know what we attach names to. But many times, we don't. That part of you will never have a real name.

"It will never be known by your mind."

* * *

Many silent minutes had passed as Lin sipped her coffee and watched Gabriel continue to eat. She knew that everything she'd just heard was true. She felt it. But why, she wondered, was it so unsettling? She'd just heard profound truths, explained in a way that she could understand on some level. Why did it shake her inside?

Finally, she began to see. Free will put her, and everyone else, on a razor's edge. They all had responsibility for their lives. They had to make choices about everything and live or die by their decisions. She felt the weight of it, the impossibility of trying to figure it out. No wonder, she thought, that most people struggle to find any comfort in life. Why they turn to habits that dull their senses and wreck their bodies. And why they so easily give up control of their lives.

"It all seems so much clearer now. But why are we like this? Why do we have free will?"

"I've seen a lot in my many years, Lin, but I have no answer to that."

"Nomad didn't have that narrow space. So, that means he doesn't have free will?"

"That's mostly true. No other creature has free will like humans. They still make choices as they go about their lives. But the ability to change themselves, to control the slow magic of the world like humans can . . . no, they don't have that."

"That seems kind of sad."

Gabriel finished chewing and swallowed, and Lin smiled as she watched the large mass spreading Gabriel's throat as it made its way down.

"Don't pity them, Lin. Not for a minute. They all have something we can't even dream of."

"What, Gabby?"

"It's like that color, the one you can't even imagine right now. When you're stronger, I can show you. But not now. You'll need much more strength, or you'll never come back."

Chapter 9 – Impossible & Deadly

Anna shivered. She'd just turned seven, and white traces of the Moscow winter whistled in through cracks around the door. Their apartment building should have been leveled years before, but since it hadn't, many desperate families had continued to live there. She and her mother and two younger brothers huddled inside, waiting for the storm to break before they could venture out in hopes the grocer had anything on his shelves. If her father had still been with them, Anna knew, he'd find a way to feed them. And keep them warm. But he was gone, taken by masked men years earlier while playing a piano recital . . .

The rattle of the door opening woke Anna from her reverie, and she stared in silence as she watched Lancaster Wolfe, Director of The Shield, stride into the conference room. It had been over twenty years since she'd seen him in the flesh. His charisma and ageless good looks defied explanation—he hadn't changed at all since she'd first met him many years earlier. His hair was still completely black, short and neat, and a closely cropped beard ended in a sharp point. Blindingly white teeth flashed as he smiled at her, matching the crisp white of his shirt beneath his black jacket.

"Anna Andreyevna Kelgina, my darling, don't get up. I'm here to observe your meeting. It's more significant than you know. Pretend I'm not here."

"Mr. Wolfe, I did not know—"

"Shh . . . it's okay. Carry on as usual," he said while giving her another excited smile.

Anna felt a desperate laugh inside, knowing that no one would be able to forget he was there. Somehow, she knew, she'd have to continue the meeting and hope it met his expectations. She'd been mostly running the entire organization, with only an occasional call from Wolfe. Seeing him was unexpected until she remembered the topic of their meeting that morning. It made perfect sense that the Director would be present.

Benson entered the room and froze when he saw Wolfe. But he said nothing and took his seat to Anna's right. Daria followed shortly after and took a seat to Anna's left. Several other associates entered the room and found seats, struggling to pretend it was a normal meeting.

"Please open the folders in front of you," Anna said, after shifting Ozzy to the side and flicking several dog hairs to the floor. "We have new information about recent events that we need to review. Once that is covered, we will discuss the next phase and your assignments."

She looked to Wolfe, who sat motionless with his eyes closed in the room's corner in an extra chair. He rested his martini on one leg.

She continued. "Daria found no new information in Erie. The victim is still unable, or unwilling, to communicate, and she was not able to identify whoever it was that brought him in. For now, at least, that appears to be a dead end.

"Benson has filed an interesting report on his findings near the pond between Erie and Pittsburgh. Please brief the group on what you found," she said as she looked to Benson.

"As you can see in your folders, a victim was picked up at the site and taken to a local hospital. He was injured in a bizarre way. He'd shoved as much gravel as possible into his mouth while lying on the ground. His injuries are extensive. But there's been no damage that would prevent him from communicating, by writing for instance. Still, he won't.

"I've interviewed people that know him, and they claim he'd never harm himself in any way, especially not like he did. He had no history of being self-destructive or mentally ill.

"We'll continue to monitor him, and hopefully, he'll speak again and tell us what happened."

"And what of the man, John, who phoned in the 911 call?" Anna said.

"John and another man mentioned in the call haven't been located. They'd left before the first responders arrived, and no one knows where they might have gone. We don't have any leads on them at this time."

"Do you have any theories about John and why he sounded so strange in the call?" said Anna.

"No, Ms. Kelgina, I've never seen anything like that. Most likely, he's just an odd person. I can't imagine it being related to what happened to the victim."

"Very good, Benson. We also have a report from Tayo. He has been following Lin Finnerty, who recently changed her name to Lin Finity. This is the biggest story we have right now. Lin is the main focus of our work going forward. Tayo says he witnessed Lin using a power in a restaurant in Allentown Monday evening.

"Tayo is not here today because he is en route to South Georgia. That is where Lin spent most of her childhood and where something strange happened when she was fifteen. We opened a file on her, but nothing more surfaced, and we let the investigation lapse. However, we do know that she spent last week there, and more curious victims have appeared during the time of her visit. Tayo will investigate that.

"He also told me some things in a phone call that are too outlandish for me to repeat here today. I do not want to believe that Tayo has somehow been corrupted or is the victim of some form of mental trickery. I will discuss all of it with him when he returns and files his full reports.

"I do believe that he had a good vantage point, as he told me, from which he looked down at Lin and an unidentified assailant. But the rest of it . . ." She shook her head slowly. "I will speak with him. He did manage to plant a locating device on Lin's car. We are tracking her as we speak, and at this time, she just left Bedford, Pennsylvania.

"Benson, take a small team and intercept her. We would like her to come back here willingly, so please, try being diplomatic. But if she refuses, you are authorized to use force if necessary. Do not harm her, though. We need her.

"That is all from me. Good luck."

* * *

"Sit tight, everyone," said Wolfe, taking a sip from his glass before rising from his seat.

"You've all worked diligently for years, and The Shield has been at this for many centuries. We're getting close now. You've probably guessed that from Anna's report. Interesting things are happening. Finally, we're catching a break.

"It's time for a pep talk. A reminder of who we are and why we watch everywhere we can for signs of magic. Yes, magic. Let's just call it what it is.

"I applaud all of you here today for your steadfast pursuit of our goal: to read what's written on the Messenger Scroll. Our numbers are dwindling around the world. It's becoming more difficult to sign on new team members. Perhaps our goal seems pointless to newer generations. Thankfully, we always have large donations that keep our work alive.

"I mentioned the Messenger Scroll. You all know that it's stored at the end of the tunnel. There's a reason no one goes in there. In a word, it's 'madness.' If you stay just inside the tunnel entrance for more than two to three hours, you'll lose your mind. Really, that's all it takes. If you were to open the box, within a minute or two, you'd be a howling lunatic. The Scroll is bound with some sort of clasp. If you were to open that and view the Scroll directly, in a heartbeat, your brain would be fried. Like a crispy ball of bacon," he said with a laugh.

"We know all this because I've tried, over the centuries. *The Shield* has tried, over the centuries," Wolfe said with a grin. "Many volunteers have attempted to learn the Scroll's contents. Brave men and women, every one. All have failed. We haven't been able to read the Scroll's message, but still, we have learned a lot.

58

"The box holding the Scroll is made of an unknown material, which has been called ironwood over the years. But it's not wood, and it's not iron. It seems to be strong like iron because we haven't been able to get a sample of it. But it's very light. Undoubtedly, it was selected to help preserve and protect the Scroll.

"Let me try to describe the Scroll: Imagine two cylinders on which a parchment is wound. View both cylinders from their ends on the left-hand side. The parchment rolls over the top of the left cylinder down to the bottom of the right cylinder. So, from the left side, you can see that you'd need to rotate both cylinders clockwise to unroll the parchment.

"Viewed from the right side, you'd see the same thing. From that side, you'd also need to rotate both cylinders clockwise to unroll the parchment.

"Do you understand the problem yet? There's only one parchment wrapped over one pair of cylinders. But to unroll the blasted thing and view the message, you'd need to rotate both cylinders in opposite directions at the same time. It doesn't make sense. It's an impossible configuration.

"Anna, you wish to ask something?"

"Yes, Mr. Wolfe. I have never heard such a detailed description before. It does sound impossible. How can something like that exist?"

Wolfe had walked to stand behind Anna, and he reached past her to place his drink on the table. His hands found her shoulders, and he rubbed them vigorously while looking around the room.

"It can't exist. Not without magic! That thing was made with magic, and that's why it's so deadly.

"Now, if I may continue?

"The clasp in the middle region of the parchment covers the transition from one side to another. The mystery of how the Scroll connects from one end to the other is hidden by the clasp. The clasp has no distinguishing features—it's a boring, flat thing that looks to be the same material as the rollers."

"Mr. Wolfe?"

"Daria Kelgina, isn't it? Yes, Daria, what's on your mind?"

Wolfe took a step to the left and had a hand on each of their shoulders.

"Maybe it's not one paper rolled around them, or maybe each side opens on its own. Maybe there are really two Scrolls!" She looked up at him with a smile.

He took another step and had both hands on Daria's back. He wrapped his hands around her neck and laughed as he shook her forward and back.

"Good thinking, Daria! No one has ever considered *that* before!" His laughter almost drowned out Daria's gagging until he released her.

"Good people of The Shield, there's only one Scroll. It doesn't make sense because it was created with magic. We know this. We've checked.

"Several volunteers over the centuries have been bold enough and quick enough to open the clasp. Each one, without exception, has been able to speak for a few seconds before sliding into uncontrollable madness. Each one has said that the Scroll makes perfect sense. Of course, it can be unrolled, they said. It's as simple as anything else. And each time, we needed to lose at least one more volunteer to rush in and replace the clasp.

"We thought to leave the clasp open and photograph it that way. We captured a very clear, detailed view of it. The man who focused the camera lost his mind right after he snapped a beautiful shot. And anyone that viewed the image lost their mind immediately too. There was no alternative but to send more good people to their undoing to cover the Scroll. And the photo had to be destroyed.

"I see some skeptical faces here, questioning my knowledge of this diabolical Scroll. You are all welcome to traipse down the tunnel and look for yourselves."

There was nothing but silence in the room.

"That's what I thought. Trust me, people, when I say even the sight of an image of the Scroll will destroy you. And here's why: The way that thing is made, it cannot exist in our world. It simply can't. But anyone that looks at it will somehow see that it *can* exist. Why, now it makes perfect sense! And once *that* thing makes sense, the rest of the world—our world—will be a nightmare that does *not* make sense.

"That thing captures you. Your imagination, your focus, whatever you want to call it. Seeing it is the worst. Seeing an image of it is almost as bad. Even being near it for long enough, just its existence close to you, will finish you off quite nicely.

"We need someone that can use magic to read it. There's no other way. But here's the thing, people: anyone that can use magic is a curse to mankind. They're evil and will bring nothing but disaster to anyone that crosses them. It happens to be *our* curse that we need someone like that, someone evil, to read God's Words. But once they've read it, once I know the Words, well . . . we don't need to suffer their existence another minute.

"And that's why we watch religiously," he said with a quick laugh, "for signs of magic. Any questions?"

He walked back to the head of the table.

"Mr. Wolfe?"

"Yes, Daria. What is it this time?"

"How did all these people ever get back out of the tunnel?"

"Ropes. Tied around their waists. They were dragged, and they screamed the entire way. Any other questions?"

Daria crossed her arms and shook her head.

"The Shield is an old group. Our first records of it are from a little over two-thousand years ago, but it was around long before that. How long we don't know. But we do know the age of the Messenger Scroll. This is where it gets even more strange.

"Years ago, one brave volunteer removed a small shred of the parchment. He immediately lost his mind and couldn't continue. A second volunteer retrieved the piece of parchment and brought it to the tunnel entrance. She was also lost. A third volunteer—"

"What is it this time, Daria?"

"Why would so many people volunteer for something so dangerous? What were they thinking?"

"My dear girl, when I need a volunteer, I *get* one. I can be very, *very* persuasive."

He held her gaze as his smile faded, and Daria looked down at her hands in her lap.

"As I was trying to say, the third volunteer was able to bring the piece out for analysis. Being so small, the piece's effects were much reduced. All involved still paid a price, though, including everyone that had any contact with it in the laboratory. And even transporting it.

"What we learned is that the Scroll is about eleven-thousand years old. Here is the big surprise, though: its chemical analysis is exactly the same as a human body. It has the exact same proportions of chemicals and compounds.

"Ladies and gentlemen, the Scroll was made from a human body. An *entire* human body. Plus the fish he had for breakfast."

Chapter 10 – Salt & Sanity

Several hours of peaceful driving eastward on I76 had passed, with Lin savoring every moment of controlling her powerful car over hills and through forests in Pennsylvania. She felt her tight skirt hugging her curves, and the leather seat cradled her just right. Gabriel seemed to be recovering from all the hotcakes that had been consumed, and she was left with the pavement racing under her Temt8tion and her thoughts.

The events at the restaurant in Allentown had seemed monumental after they'd happened. She remembered the fever she felt, the need to leave it all behind. But that whole affair paled when compared to the simple conversations she'd had with Gabriel since then. And the disappearing hair brush. She still felt a trembling inside just thinking about it, but she hoped it was only a natural aftermath of Gabriel taking her into the magic. Where she'd seen the color. The color that doesn't exist.

"I'm tired and would like nothing more than to sit with you and have a cup of hot coffee. Are you up for another stop? Maybe when we get to Reading?"

"Sure, Lin, the next diner you find. Count me in."

"I will always count you in, Gabby. You . . . you've been a part of me for so long. I can't imagine life without you."

"I'll miss you too, Lin. Even I don't know how magic could help with that. But I'm curious about how fast this car of yours can go."

"Nice try, changing the subject like that. I'm supposed to believe you have a real interest in cars?"

"I've driven a few, you know. A chariot or two as well, back in the day."

"Oh, Gabby," Lin said. "That's pretty good, actually. Now, I'm imagining you holding a sword."

She continued to smile as the road rushed up to meet her.

"This one looks good. Mostly deserted too. Perfect for some peace and quiet."

She pulled the car into the lot and looked once more at the small lights lined up straight down the Oblivion Black hood. There would be no need to see them all lit up again, she thought. Unless she floored the accelerator for fun.

After settling into a booth with a window view, Lin ordered coffee and Gabriel requested a menu.

"Oh, you've got to be kidding me!"

"Lin, think of how many items on that menu I haven't had in over three decades."

"Oh, okay. I see your point," she said with a smile.

Before long, Gabriel had a huge omelet and a stack of toast, and Lin sipped her coffee and stared in astonishment at how quickly it all disappeared.

In between large bites, Gabriel said, "Lin, something upset you in the motel room while I was taking a shower. I could tell you didn't want to talk about it then. How about now?"

Another large bite stuffed Gabriel's cheeks.

"You're right. It was too weird and scary. I hoped it might be something from having traveled with you into the magic, and maybe it would never happen again."

"What was it?"

"My hair brush. My stupid hair brush. Gabby, it disappeared! It was there, I reached for it, then it was gone. And it reappeared on the other side of the dresser. I thought I was losing my mind. Finally, I was able to grab it, and it was just a normal brush again. Magic is exhilarating but pretty damn scary too."

"It's probably nothing, Lin. Could you pass the salt?"

Lin looked down to find the shaker, which was off to her left, near the window. As soon as she laid eyes on it, it disappeared. Instantly, it reappeared less than an inch from her left hand.

She stared in disbelief, feeling the insanity bubbling up inside her. Not again, she thought. Not again.

Before she could move her hand, the salt shaker was gone again, this time materializing off to her right, next to her coffee cup.

Lin stared at the salt, feeling a tear of frustration and fear crawling down one cheek. She tried to not think about the salt, and it remained in its place. Without a thought, she reached out and grabbed it. It was solid and didn't move.

She looked down at it with a feeling of triumph. Maybe the secret is to not think about it, she reasoned. The shaker felt solid in her hand, just like it should.

She was about to look up when the coffee mug vanished, and for the shortest possible instant, she saw the coffee there by itself in the shape of the cup before it collapsed and spilled out in every direction.

Lin froze and stared at where the cup should have been, hearing the coffee drip onto the tile floor and feeling it dribble onto her lap. The tear continued its march down her cheek.

Still staring at the coffee puddle, she heard Gabriel's voice.

"Lin, look into my eyes."

She looked up, and the sight rocked her. Gabriel's eyes were half-closed and glowing with a deep, cool green. As if she were hypnotized, she could not look away.

"Don't be afraid or even concerned, Lin. I moved your hair brush. I moved the salt. I took away the coffee cup. It no longer exists. But we can ask the server to bring another. We'll need a lot of napkins too."

Lin couldn't speak. She could only gaze into the deep green of Gabriel's eyes. She watched as their light began to fade, and they opened all the way. They were again a normal shade of brown.

"Say something, Lin. It's just me."

Silence.

"Tell me your name."

"I'm Lin. But what . . . how—"

"I told you there was much more. Did you think that invading the narrow gap all people have is the only way to use the magic?"

"I don't even know what to say, Gabby. So, I'm not crazy?"

"Well, no, but you're getting there."

"What do you mean—"

"It only feels crazy, Lin, but you'll understand when I explain it to you, although you'll still feel crazy for a while. Remember that your mind, your sanity, has no place in the vast magic out there. But here, in the real world as we call it, your mind is in control. It *needs* to be in control. When you break that control, when the magic spills into the real world, you feel like you're losing your mind. Because you are."

"Why would I want to lose my mind, Gabby? How could anyone live like that?"

"Not just anyone can. But *you* can. You're building the strength, the power, to control the magic within you. To let it be part of you. Without that strength, you'd be like any ordinary person that had gone insane."

* * *

"Benson, are you getting close yet?"

"We're about two miles out of Reading, Ms. Kelgina. Do you really believe Lin's the one that can do it?"

"No one else has been able to, not for centuries. And he would not share the message with The Shield. Instead, he took it upon himself to go out and convince people of something, something he believed was right. A message of having faith."

"What do you think the Scroll says? Do you think it's really the Words of God?"

"I believe it is, but I have no idea what to expect. I know what The Shield thinks it says. Or rather, what Mr. Wolfe thinks it says. He believes it is a message of hope for humanity. That somehow, it will promise peace and forgiveness to the world and to everyone. And he meant everyone. He told me it is the most important thing anyone can do—learn those Words of God. He said they came close twenty centuries ago, but he would not tell anyone what was written on the Scroll.

"Now, it seems like Lin Finity is another one that can somehow read it. Wolfe thinks she is the one. He is betting on it."

"And don't forget the staggering bonus I'd get for bringing her in. Right?"

"Yes, of course . . . a very large bonus. You have to bring her back, Benson. Ask her nicely, okay? But bring her back. This is bigger than all of us."

*   *   *

"Things must be going well because I do feel I'm losing my mind. It's not fun."

"Maybe we shouldn't take any of this too seriously, Lin. You wouldn't know this, but I was once just like you. I didn't call it 'mayhem,' and I wasn't abused like you were. But my life was hard, and I took it head on. Every moment, with every breath. I called it my secret storm. And it erupted many times before I got control of it. I, too, had help, but they're gone now.

"I had the same doubts and fears, all the questions, the feeling that I was losing my mind. But look at me now. I turned out okay, don't you think?"

Lin shook her head, and a smile spread across her face as she gazed at the friend she couldn't explain.

"Gabby, you amaze me. Thank you for everything. I feel like you and I are at the center of a storm, a small calm place. Oh, I was going to say it was a place where things make sense, but that's not correct, is it?"

They shared a laugh as only friends for more than three decades can.

"Okay, it doesn't make sense. But it's peaceful here with you. And despite all the doubts and fears and questions that I'll have to answer myself, right now, this feels right. I wouldn't trade my mayhem or the wonder of all the mysteries out there for anything.

"I just want to sit and enjoy my coffee. And your company."

The bells on the diner's entrance door danced wildly as it was yanked open, and two men were shoved inside.

Chapter 11 – Mayhem & Creation

Gabriel glanced over Lin's shoulder just long enough to size up the two men who stood inside the diner. Lin continued to sip her coffee and keep a wary eye on the salt.

*   *   *

"Steve, I'm really sorry I got you into this. And sorry I hit you too. God, I don't know what got into me."

"It's a little late for that, Joel. You wanted to know about Lin? Well, there she is, sitting in that booth. This is nuts. Who are these people?"

"Maybe if we do what he said, just get Lin to go back with him, then they might let us go. They should, right? I mean, I'm just an organist. Who would want anything—"

"You have more faith than I do. There must be a back door in this place. Maybe we could—"

A rapping on the restaurant's glass door caused them both to turn, and they saw Benson's angry face and his gestures for them to get moving.

"I hope you learned a few prayers from all your years in the church. Let's get this over with."

Father Steve and Joel the organist began the walk toward Lin and Gabriel.

*   *   *

"Hi, you're Lin, right?" said Joel. "Uh . . . you don't know me, but I work at the church you went to Sunday morning. I play the organ and do a lot of other stuff. My name's Joel. I've been there—"

"Lin, you're probably wondering what we're doing here."

Lin turned farther in her seat to see Father Steve, and a smile lit up her face.

"Father, I'm surprised to see you here in Pennsylvania! How are you? What brings you here?"

"Lin, we're in a bit of trouble, Joel and I. I'm hoping you can help us out."

"Sure, Father. What's going on?"

"There are some people that we're, um, working with. They wanted us to help them find you, and we thought that would be enough. But they want us to convince you to go with them. They say it's extremely important."

Lin had turned in her seat, and her right leg was bent at the knee, resting on the cushion. Her short skirt didn't cover much. Joel couldn't help but stare, and Steve struggled to look her in the eye. Gabriel sat quietly.

"What people, Father?"

"They're part of a group that call themselves The Shield. I don't know who they are, Lin."

At the mention of the group's name, Gabriel wrapped both hands around the mug and stared into the hot coffee.

"The Shield? What the heck is that? And why would they want me?"

Joel's eyes had narrowed, and his chest puffed out. "Too many questions. You need to get up and come with us. There's a car outside."

"Joel, I'm not going anywhere with you or anyone else."

"You have no choice." A twitch animated his cheek. "We tried to convince you. Fine. We'll just take you. We'll—"

"Easy, Joel," said Steve. "Give her some time to think it over."

"There's nothing to think over. I'm here with my best friend, and I'm in no mood to be pushed around."

Lin flicked her long blond hair back over her shoulders, and a look of calm power filled her green eyes.

Father Steve's voice cracked as he spoke.

"Joel, I think we've given it a good try, but she's not—"

"Listen, Lin. Get up out of that booth, and walk to the front door. Don't make me force you."

Joel's eyes had closed down to thin slits, and his voice had gotten much deeper. Clenched fists poked out of the sleeves of his jacket. The twitching increased.

In a slow, controlled voice, Lin said, "Joel, you really don't want to take that tone with me."

Lin felt her mayhem swirling just beneath her surface.

Gabriel spoke without looking up. "Lin . . ."

She snapped her head around to face Gabriel.

"What, Gabby?"

"I know of The Shield. You must not let them take you, but Lin . . . be kind"

She turned back to look at Joel just as he reached into an inside pocket and took out a hypodermic needle. His face had taken on a determined sneer. He pointed the needle straight up and squeezed, sending a few drops flying into the air. Like he must have seen in the movies, thought Lin.

Without any hesitation, all of Lin's life focused sharply on her intent, and time stopped. She viewed the calm surface of reality, with the drops from the needle lined up like tiny pearls waiting to fall. Below the world of reality, she saw the churning depths of magic writhing and cavorting in a timeless dance.

Lin Finity saw infinity in every direction, with her eyes half-closed and glowing with a green light of their own.

There was no danger. And there was no hurry.

She slowly drew in a deep breath and held it. Doing so was no longer necessary, but the pleasure she felt was incalculable. With that captured breath, she felt all the magic from below funneling up into her, rushing ecstasy to every tiniest part of her until she felt she might burst.

She looked outward to the two men who believed they could threaten her in any way. She almost felt sorry for them as she exhaled the trapped breath and felt she was falling from the sky. Instantly, a massive boulder crashed into the calm surface of the world as Lin's life broke her fleshly bounds and rushed outward. The massive wave of magic washed through the two men as she had intended. The wave continued outward for a short distance, but she rested in the narrow spaces of each man, those thin gaps where their spirits connected to their bodies. Lin's intent had positioned her between their realities and their magic.

Lin's *mayhem* had taken complete control.

Each man let out a silent shriek as they felt their souls ripped from their bodies. There was no sound, but Lin could still hear their heartfelt screams. Then, their terror settled in, just as she knew it would.

She felt some affection and respect for Father Steve, despite the questionable task he'd taken on. There would be time to deal with him later. For now, she left him standing in place.

But Joel, the cocky organist, he needed stronger treatment. How he'd gotten involved, Lin had no idea, but his attitude would be his end. She was about to silence him, not having any need for his excuses and apologies. But at the last moment, she thought to leave him, to let him speak in the haunting, silent way of a life snared by her mayhem.

As she focused on Joel, a shocking realization hit her. Something about his spirit was damaged. No, not damaged, but blurred somehow. There were overlapping pieces. The dark regions weren't from any kind of injury like she'd seen in Ben before she'd healed him.

She finally recognized that another spirit had hitched a ride on Joel's. A spirit that seemed to shift around and hide behind his. She heard his silent shrieking for help and another voice, more subtle, speaking only to Joel.

The moment Lin understood, the other spirit fled somewhere back into the swirling magic. Joel's spirit again had a normal appearance, like it should have had all along.

Lin didn't want to take the time to contemplate what had just happened. She still had work to do.

She considered Joel's spirit and determined that he'd been an unwilling participant. He still presented a risk, though. She quickly surmised that the injection wasn't lethal since they'd wanted to take her with them. That knowledge led to the most reasonable solution.

She caused him to raise the needle up, and she heard him begin to shriek more urgently. As the needle moved closer to his neck, the shrieking got more intense. But he couldn't resist. She forced the needle into a soft, fleshy spot and pierced the skin. An unwilling Joel squeezed the liquid into his own neck, and Lin felt his consciousness rapidly fade. She allowed him to collapse without harm to the floor.

Ah, but what to do with the priest, she wondered. She sensed no dark presence clinging to his spirit, and she knew that he'd been dragged into the misguided operation against his will. She thought it best to smother his consciousness until he had just enough sense left to curl up in the next booth.

Both men had been rendered unconscious, and she hadn't harmed either of them.

Lin returned to her own body. As her eyes opened completely, the glow in them faded until their normal green color had returned. Her mayhem stayed a fraction of a second away, ready for her intent to summon it again.

The airborne drops from the needle splatted without a sound on the chipped tile floor.

"I was kind, Gabby. No broken bones. Not even a broken heart."

"Yes, you were kind. I'm glad you saw that there was no need to kill them."

The bells on the door jangled once more, and Lin turned to see another man looking in on the scene. He hesitated, looking from Lin to the two sleeping men and back to Lin. He approached their booth slowly with his hands raised.

"Lin, my name is Benson. I represent a group called The Shield. Maybe I shouldn't have sent these two clowns to talk with you. I thought since you knew the priest that might convince you to help us."

Even without a green glow, Lin's eyes were fierce, but she hadn't yet engaged her intent. Her mayhem remained just below her surface. Benson bit his lip and trembled as he looked into her eyes from the short distance.

"Are you with the military?"

"What? No, not at all. We're a private group that has one, and only one purpose. To find someone with the ability to read the Messenger Scroll."

"Some kind of scroll? That's what this is about?"

"Not just some kind of scroll. *The* Scroll. We believe it's the Words of God."

Lin gazed at Benson as if he were a madman.

"An old priest, a sloppy organist, and *you* have the Words of God?" She laughed at him.

"Good luck with that, Benson. We're enjoying our coffee, and I have no interest in whatever weird mission you think you're on. Frankly, your group seems pretty lame."

"I understand, Lin. But tell me, please, what the hell did you do to these two?"

"Who says I did anything? You were watching from the door, weren't you? You must have seen them both collapse. Next time, Benson, choose some better minions."

"Okay, you're right. They weren't any good—"

"That's for sure."

"—but I still need you to come back with me."

"To read your scroll. The Words of God, you say. Why don't you read them yourself?"

Lin watched Benson closely, her mayhem swirling just beneath her surface.

"We can't. People have tried for centuries. All have failed. They've gone mad, every last one of them. But we believe you can do it. We believe you have the power to do it."

She reached up quickly to sweep her long hair back over her shoulder, and Benson flinched.

"Even if I did have whatever power you think I have, why would I want to go read it?"

"Aren't you curious?"

That caused Lin to pause and consider his question. Yes, she was curious. But she didn't trust him. Not even a little.

"You need to leave, Benson. My friend and I have had enough of you. And take these two out of here, or maybe you'll join them. Or worse . . ."

Benson looked at Gabriel, who only shrugged while never looking up from the coffee cup.

He began reaching inside his jacket, and Lin said, "Careful, Benson. Are you sure you want to do that?"

Her eyes glowed just enough that Benson couldn't be sure what he saw. His hand froze, then he pulled it back out.

"This isn't over."

"Go."

Lin turned to face Gabriel and picked up her coffee.

Father Steve had begun to stir, and though he struggled to stand himself, he helped Benson drag Joel out of the diner.

* * *

"You know about those people?"

"Yes, and they won't stop, Lin. Now that they know about you, they'll continue to hunt you down. Today went easy because they hoped you'd come along willingly. It will only get worse."

"And there really is some kind of scroll?"

"Yes, I've heard of the Scroll. It's real, Lin. I know of this group, The Shield. They've been around, in some form, for many centuries."

"And no one can read it?"

"Not for a long time. I believe it was created out of magic. A great power over the magic."

"You don't know what it says either?"

"No, but I've heard about the creator of the Scroll. She was powerful beyond belief. Her name is lost in history, but her words about the Scroll are preserved. The Shield probably has that too."

"Her words? What did she say?"

"I only know that she asked God for an answer, and an answer was given. I'd like to know God's answer too."

"What kind of power did she have?"

"She took the power like you've begun to use and went way beyond what even I can do. It was at a time when people were more open to magic. She didn't have as many roadblocks as exist today. But those who witnessed her were terrified, and she was persecuted. She could have wiped them all out, every single one. But she chose to leave on her own.

"She created her own world far out in the ocean. I mean that literally, Lin. She took the magic that swirls beneath us all, and by her own intent, she shaped it into islands. And she arranged to have people come there to live. She created it all with her intent.

"Eventually, even she began to lose her strength. And when her strength faltered, the islands were no more. There's no trace of them because they didn't exist the same way everything else in the world exists. It all went back to the magic."

"That doesn't sound possible. How could anyone have that much power? Was she God?"

"Oh, Lin, what that woman could do was nothing compared to God. It was astounding that she could channel so much magic, use it to create islands, and she could sustain it using only her intent. But remember, God is doing that every moment with every tiniest thing you and anyone else considers real."

Lin leaned back in her seat and poked at her plate without any real interest. She needed time to absorb what Gabriel had just said. That

God is creating the world, every little part of it, at every moment. That flew against everything she'd been taught, the whole idea of matter and energy existing, not able to be created or destroyed.

"Gabby, everybody believes that matter can't be created or destroyed, only changed. Things were created, and now they exist. They don't need continuous help. Are you sure about God creating it all constantly at every moment?"

"Science is quite clever, Lin. That explanation is very close to fact. But the truth is, it's only *magic* that can't be created or destroyed. That coffee cup earlier—it has returned to the magic.

"Nothing . . . *nothing*, Lin, has the ability, or even a reason, to exist another moment longer. Not a single thing should take its continued existence for granted."

"People too? I mean—"

Lin froze in her seat.

"Let's talk about this later. We need to get going. Maybe everyone I care about is in danger too."

Chapter 12 – Hunted & Healed

A quick exit brought them to her car, but before they got in, Lin stopped and looked at Gabriel.

"How did The Shield find me? Even I didn't know where we were going."

She walked around her car, and after a short search, she'd found the tracker in the wheel well and threw it into the woods.

"Okay, how did that get there?"

"They're resourceful, Lin. They obviously know who you are."

"Oh no, Gabby, they might know a whole lot about me. Where I live, where I work, even Jack. And Taylor! How ruthless are these people?"

"They won't let up now that they know about you."

"Let's get in, but I need to make a call, okay?"

Safely inside the luxurious car, she dialed Jack.

"Hi, Lin. Damn, it's so good to hear your voice. How are you?"

"I'm okay, Jack, but life is getting a lot more complicated. Are the other two still there with you?"

"Yep, we're all just hanging out, hoping to hear from you. We knew we couldn't go looking because—"

"Listen, don't get alarmed, Jack, but I'm kind of in some trouble. I'm being hunted."

"What? Hunted?"

"Yeah, sort of. These people want me to go with them and help them with something."

"What people? You're not going, are you?"

"No, no way. But they're not going to stop trying, that's for sure. Here's what I need from you right now. Please, don't offer any information. Just listen to what I ask you to do, okay? I don't know, but they might be picking up your calls too."

"This is sounding pretty scary, Lin, but alright."

"I want to meet with all three of you. Before you get in the car, though, look it over carefully. It might be bugged. I found a tracking device in the wheel well of my Temt8tion. If you find one, don't destroy it, just leave it somewhere a few miles from your house.

"Next, listen closely. I'd like you to bring me three pieces of chocolate, just exactly like you did before. Exactly like before. Do you know what I mean, Jack?"

She hoped he would remember their first date at a cute little restaurant west of Allentown. After they'd finished dinner, Jack had placed four pieces of chocolate on the table. Lin had assumed they'd split them. But no, he pushed three in front of her, and he told her she'd always get three to his one. She'd loved him from the start.

"I understand, Lin. How long before you can get there?"

"Give us an hour, Jack. And make sure you're not followed."

"Us? Who's us?"

"Oh yeah, you've never met Gabby. Oh my, Jack, we have some catching up to do. See you in an hour."

Lin brushed her hair back and started the Temt8tion's powerful engine. Her sharp heel caught in the floor mat carpet, and she had to pull it back before pressing down on the gas. The car quickly reached Lin's cruising speed, and her many glances in the rearview mirror convinced her that no one followed them.

*　*　*

After a long morning packed with mundane tasks, Anna sat alone, trying to digest what Wolfe had disclosed at the meeting. The Scroll was made from a human body? An *entire* human body? How was that even possible? Especially eleven-thousand years ago. It made no sense. Nothing about The Shield or its mission made sense anymore.

She hugged Ozzy tight and considered fleeing back to Russia, a familiar haven with family and old friends. Perhaps it was time to forget about the Words of God and resume a normal life.

The feeling passed. Her conscience, that voice inside, told her to stay, and Anna refocused herself on the goal. It didn't matter what the Scroll was made of, only what was written on it. They needed to learn the Words of God.

She'd gotten word from Benson that his mission had failed. He'd taken the two reluctant accomplices to a safe location and was awaiting further instructions. She called him.

"Benson, what happened? Is everyone alright?"

"We're all fine, but I don't know what to tell you about what happened. I sent those two stooges from Georgia into a diner to get Lin. She was sitting with a friend in a corner booth. I thought since she knew them, or at least the priest, that maybe she'd at least consider helping us. But that organist, he turned into a maniac and pulled out the needle right away.

"And here's the crazy thing—I watched through the window as he injected himself right in the neck. He was out cold. And then, the priest, he just crawled into the next booth and went to sleep. What the hell, Ms. Kelgina. What are we dealing with here?"

"I do not know, Benson, but obviously, she has some kind of power that will require better planning from us. Maybe she can hypnotize people. Do you know where Lin is now?"

"She found the bug and tossed it. No, I don't know."

"We had a bug on her boyfriend, Jack, but he removed his too. That was only a short while ago, so he is probably near his last known location. I will send you the directions. Take those two 'stooges' of yours and go there to see what you can find. I am sending Daria to help out too.

"And Benson, next time use the tranquilizer gun from a safe distance. She will be out and will not be able to use any kind of power. Bring her back here where we can contain her. You got that?"

"Yes, got it. We're on our way to find Jack."

* * *

Lin pulled her car into a spot next to Jack's pickup and killed the engine. She and Gabriel got out and began the short walk to the restaurant entrance.

"Lin, I'm curious about the food here."

"I bet you are, Gabby. It's all good. Really good," she said with a laugh.

As soon as Lin laid eyes on Jack, she felt that everything would work out. She walked toward his table, and when he rose to greet her, she reached around his waist and rested her head on his shoulder. After giving him a smile and a kiss, she looked around him to see Ben and Lee sitting at the table. Ben looked happy to see her, but Lee's face couldn't be read. She only stared directly at Lin.

"Jack, it feels like it's been so long, but it really hasn't been. It's so good to see you again!"

"Lin, if I had a choice, I'd never let you go again. I know that's not possible, but hey, that's how I feel."

She ran her fingers through his long brown hair, smiling and looking into his eyes. She saw no fear and no senseless adoration either. There was no trace of her mayhem's effects on him. It was just Jack, with normal Jack feelings.

Without letting go of him, she again looked over at Ben and smiled, not sure what to expect. When Ben stood and smiled back, she guessed that what she'd done to him in the restaurant the evening before had worked. She'd felt he was about to attack her, her mayhem rose up instantly, and she invaded him, taking over that narrow space between his body and his spirit. But from there, she'd seen the damage to his spirit, a wounding that he'd been carrying with him most of his life.

Damage she'd given to him when they were fifteen, back in St. Simons Island.

After seeing the ruin she'd caused to his life, she knew she had only one good option: to heal him. And that's what she did, carefully replacing all the darkness with light. With fresh magic.

"Hi, Ben."

She let go of Jack and stepped closer to Ben. As usual, she knew she was a sight, with her short skirt showing a lot of her legs. But Ben didn't look her up and down. He looked her in the eye.

"Hi, Lin. It's wonderful to see you again. I want to tell you now that I'm sorry for any problems I've caused you. I don't feel that way anymore. I don't understand anything that's happened or anything that you've done. But I believe you fixed me last night at the bar."

"I'm sorry it took so long, Ben. I never meant to hurt you all those years ago. I was out of control, and I didn't even know what had happened to you. I'm so relieved that I could help. How do you feel?"

"This might sound stupid, but I feel like a new man. Even better than I would have been if you'd never, um, done what you—"

"I'm happy for you, Ben. I hope you can forgive me."

"Forgive you? God, I owe you. Whatever you need, I'm your guy."

"What about Luanne?"

"I'm sure she's fine, but she has no idea what I'm up to. I'll call her to tell her I'll be a little while and that she shouldn't worry."

"That's great, Ben, because I do need you. I have a big favor to ask."

"Whatever you want. What do you need?"

"There are people after me, and maybe they'll go after other people in my life. Would you take the next few days until this is all worked out and go guard my daughter?"

"I didn't know you had a daughter," said Ben.

"Neither did I," said Jack. "Since when?"

"Hardly anyone knows about her. I'm sorry I never told you, Jack, but she's not really a part of my life lately. We've had a falling out. We still talk, but I haven't seen her in years."

"I'm sorry to hear that," said Jack. "What's her name?"

"Taylor. And she's not well. I'm not sure she ever will be completely well. Lately, she's been in a hospital in Philadelphia, getting some treatments that aren't exactly mainstream. But there's not much else left to try. Ben, if you could, please just go introduce yourself. You'll need a letter from me to get in. Just stay close, and keep an eye on her until things back here get straightened out."

"Of course, I'll do that, Lin. I feel I owe you my life."

She hugged him close, and even in her heels, she couldn't lay her head on his shoulder. He embraced her politely and patted her back. She felt like a lion tamer at first, risking her life getting that close, but she could tell that he'd changed. She'd changed him.

Lin let him go and sat at the table, looking at Jack and delaying her introduction to Lee.

"Jack, this is Gabriel. Gabby, Jack."

"Hello, Jack. I feel I know you already."

"Has Lin talked about me? Because she hasn't said a word about you."

"Lin and I have been friends for many years, but I haven't been keen on socializing for quite a while. I've been sort of withdrawn from the world."

"Well, any friend of Lin's is a friend of mine. It's a pleasure to meet you."

"Likewise, Jack."

Lin finished writing up a letter for Ben to take to Philadelphia, including the hospital's address. She stood and handed it to him.

"And Ben, please take this. You're doing me such an incredible favor. This should help."

His eyes opened wide at the sight of a fat wad of bills.

"Thanks, Lin, and don't worry. I've got it covered. If anyone tries anything, I can still be the old Ben."

"Thanks, I know Taylor will be safe with you."

Ben nodded, turned to leave, and bumped solidly into Jack. Jack flinched and looked up at him, and Ben looked down with the beginning of a scowl. But he burst into a huge laugh and hugged Jack tight, saying, "Jack, the past is gone. You're my friend now too. Please remember that I'm your friend as well."

He slapped Jack's back, let him go, and walked out of the restaurant.

The relief on Jack's face was plain to see, and Lin just shook her head and smiled.

"Jack, why don't you and Gabby go and get a few menus, okay?"

Jack seemed to understand and so did Gabriel. They took a walk toward the bar.

"Hi, I'm Lin."

"I'm Lee. You're probably wondering why I'm here."

"Yeah, of course. I remember you from Jacksonville in the airport. You followed me back to Pennsylvania?"

"I'm not a stalker. But I saw what happened, I mean what you did, back in that restaurant. I had to meet you."

"What do you think I did?"

"Please, Lin, let's skip all that. I know it was you, what happened to Alex. He deserved it, so don't think I'm mad or anything. But I want to know how you did that. I need to know."

Lin sized her up while remembering the encounter. She'd been eating lunch and waiting for her flight to board. Lee and a man took seats a couple tables behind her. He was obnoxious, even threatening, and Lin had reached her limit. So, she used her mayhem and invaded him. She raced his heart until he passed out twitching on the floor.

She also remembered what she'd seen in Lee's eyes as she walked past her table. Her eyes showed a cold determination. She'd seen Lee as someone of uncommon internal strength. Looking at her across the table only confirmed it.

But what had surprised Lin was that Lee hadn't fallen victim to the convert effect from her mayhem. She'd only looked calmly at her. Yes, Lin concluded, they should skip all the nonsense. For some reason, Lee had an understanding of her mayhem, and she'd seemed immune to it.

"I'm not sure I can explain anything to you, Lee. I'm not sure I understand it well enough."

"Try. Please."

"I can try. But first, tell me why you want to know."

Lee hesitated but continued to stare into Lin's eyes.

"Lin, I've had to fight some impossible odds in my life. I was born with some serious health problems, but I never gave up. I always believed I could beat it. And I did. About nine years ago, I figured it out. Nothing will ever harm me again."

Lin sensed her mayhem wanting to rise at her being confronted with an unknown force, but she kept it in check. She'd expected some sort of morbid curiosity or some quest for power. But not a simple, confident declaration that "nothing will ever harm" her again.

"Okay, Lee, but one more thing. Did you feel anything when Alex had that . . . um . . . experience?"

"It was like I got hit by something. Something ran into me, and it felt like it tried to go through me. But it couldn't. I wouldn't let it. I knew it came from you."

Lin felt the intrigue building, learning that her mayhem couldn't get into Lee, into the narrow space between her body and her spirit. Why? Obviously, Lee had incredible strength, but why couldn't her mayhem wash through her like it had so many times with everyone else?

It hit Lin in a flash—a memory of what Gabriel had said earlier. That she could take that narrow space from people because they weren't even aware that it existed. Lee knew it existed. And from her mention of having conquered her health issues, she must also know how to use it. She knew how to use the slow magic of the real world. She'd healed herself.

"Lee, we can learn from each other, I believe. This might not make sense to you, but I believe it will someday. You've learned to control something inside yourself, and you used it to correct the problems you were born with. I've learned to control something outside myself, and I know how to use it to control other people.

"We need to talk more, but not here. Not now."

Lee only stared at Lin for a few seconds, nodded her head once, and looked to the bar. Jack and Gabriel were on their way back.

Chapter 13 – Candies & Histories

Jack and Gabriel walked the short distance back from the bar and joined Lin and Lee at the table. A few other diners enjoyed the quiet restaurant, but none were near enough to hear their conversation.

"Okay, well, this is an interesting group we have here, huh? Jack, I was sure surprised to see you at the restaurant in Allentown last night. Where were you?"

"I was up on the balcony."

"Why didn't you come down and join me?"

"I . . . um . . . I just got there, and it was so crowded I thought I'd go up there and see if I could spot you. And I did—you looked absolutely magnificent. Still do."

Lin saw the normal adoration in his eyes along with a playful twinkle. Jack loved her; she had no doubt. She knew he had to have noticed her low-cut sweater with her hair spilling down far past her shoulders. But still, he appeared happy with only what he saw in her eyes.

She took a long look into his eyes, always feeling a heat inside from his rugged good looks. His wavy brown hair and solid chest made her squirm a little in her seat as his big brown eyes smiled at her. She felt a need to take him, much like when she woke up in that cold hotel room on the Island when her mayhem was rising.

"So, you must have seen . . . everything?"

"I saw something, but really, I wouldn't know how to describe it. Then, I saw Ben drop to the floor."

"Yeah, that sure was a crazy night. I had to leave. With how I felt, there was no choice."

"I didn't even know what to say, watching you leave. I thought I'd never see you again. But hey, it's been less than twenty-four hours, and here you are. Damn, this might be a perfect time."

Jack found the ring in his pocket.

"I was—"

"Lin, I don't believe I've met your other friend," Gabriel said.

Jack looked at Gabriel, then back at Lin, but he said no more.

"Oh, sorry, Gabby. Lee, this is Gabriel. Gabby, Lee. Lee came up from Florida to visit a while."

"It's a pleasure to meet you, Lee. You have business in Pennsylvania?"

Lee hesitated and only stared at Gabriel.

"It's nice to meet you too. I wouldn't call it business. There are some things I want to discuss with Lin."

"Like what?" said Gabriel, looking calmly into Lee's eyes.

Lee paused even longer, staring directly at Gabriel.

"It's not something I want to discuss with a stranger."

"Yet, you're a stranger to Lin yourself, aren't you?"

"Okay, Gabby, maybe we should all just look at our menus, okay?" Lin said.

Gabriel and Lee continued to stare at each other, but neither spoke. Gabriel was the first to look down at the menu.

"Lin," said Jack, "I knew what you meant when you mentioned the chocolate. So, of course I brought some. Not enough for everyone, though. Sorry."

He pushed three pieces in front of her, keeping one for himself.

"Oh, Jack, you're so sweet. I think I'll risk ruining my appetite and have one now."

She grabbed one piece of candy and wrapped her hand around it.

"Thank you, Jack," she said and gave him a bright smile.

Her smile faded quickly when she felt it disappear from inside her grasp.

Oh no, she thought. Not again. What kind of crazy world is it where things can disappear at any given time? She saw Jack waiting to watch her eat the chocolate, and she had no clue what to do.

She looked at Gabriel, who could barely contain a grin and never looked up from the menu.

"Gabby, you don't like chocolate, do you?"

That caused Jack to look over at Gabriel, and Lin started to drag her hand to the edge of the table.

I'll pretend to drop it, she thought, and I'll never pick it up.

She continued to stare at Gabriel, who finally looked over at her.

With a big grin, Gabriel said, "Lin, be careful. You might lose that chocolate."

Her hand froze near the table's edge.

"Of course, even if you lost it, it wouldn't be too difficult to find another, would it?"

She felt the candy reappear in her hand.

Jack looked a bit confused, but Lee looked on without any change in her expression.

Lin turned her hand over to see the candy, which she unwrapped and ate. Before it disappeared again, she thought. She felt a gentle tremor inside, something working itself loose. She also felt a little crazy. For a few seconds, she held Gabriel's gaze, which had become more serious, then she composed herself and looked to Jack.

"Jack, now that Taylor's safe, I can think about some other possible complications. You probably know I'm talking about Nomad. Jack, I'd die of sadness if anything happened to that big fluffy boy. We have time to eat, but after that, could you go and get him?"

"Sure, Lin. Of course. Get him and do what?"

"I'm going to find a place to rent for a while. Maybe a suite. We need a place to hide until I can straighten this all out. I'll feel much better if I know Nomad is safe."

"Great idea. I'll bring his food too. Good thing I have a truck," Jack said with a big smile.

"Okay, he needs to eat a lot, you know that. But don't bother with the scale. I don't care how much he's eating anymore."

* * *

Their orders were placed, the plates and a bottle of wine arrived, and the food vanished quickly. Gabriel was the first to raise an interest in dessert, and Lin smiled as she took a large sip and wondered when it would end. And her amusement left just as quickly when she remembered that her time with Gabriel could end at any time.

After everyone had finished, except for Gabriel, who gave complete attention to a large piece of chocolate cake, Lin attempted to get the operation moving.

"Jack, maybe you and Gabby could drive over and get Nomad. Lee and I can go rent that suite. Remember, I don't know if they're snooping on your phone, so when you get him, meet us back here in the back parking lot. No one ever goes back there. And then, we can head over together."

"Lin, I think it's best if I stay with you. Perhaps Lee would like to help Jack with that?" Gabriel looked directly at Lee and waited for her response.

"Sure, why not?" said Lee.

"Sounds good to me," said Jack. "We'll round up that big boy and meet you back here."

After Jack and Lee had exited the building, Lin turned to Gabriel.

"There's a reason I wanted to be alone with Lee. There are things we should discuss. She's different. I can tell."

"I think she's more different than you know, Lin."

"What does that mean?"

"Just be careful, okay? Anyone that knows, or even suspects, that you have some kind of power, you can't be sure of their intentions."

Lin realized the truth of what Gabriel just said, having to admit to herself that the world had become a much different place for her.

"Gabby, I'm pretty sure she has some kind of power herself. I think she came here only to learn what she could from me. And who knows, maybe I'll learn something from her too."

"That's all very good, Lin. But remember, you've had someone whispering in your ear,"—Gabriel paused to smile—"reminding you, encouraging you to choose good. Has she?"

"Oh, right. I have no idea. But I know what you mean. That Joel guy back in the diner—he had something tagging along with him. I heard it talking to him. And as soon as I saw it, it disappeared."

"It's good that you didn't have to kill him, then. Those things have an easy time with the weak."

"I don't believe Lee has anything like that. Can you tell, Gabby? Can't you figure her out somehow?"

"We've never talked about this before, Lin, but no, I can't interfere in human lives. I'm here only for you."

"That's some kind of law that you have to live by? Who said?"

"No one said, Lin. I just know. The same way you know that you shouldn't capture cute little animals and torture them. Did anyone ever tell you that exactly?"

Lin shuddered and looked at the table.

"No. No one had to tell me. I get it. Why *are* you here with me?"

"You remember I told you that you were important, don't you?"

"Yes, but—"

"Your power, your mayhem as you call it, is truly rare. The last time it happened was twenty centuries ago. He struggled, much like you, and he learned, much like you. But those were difficult times. The converts he made were more serious. People lived much harder lives back then."

"That can't be right. I'm the first in two-thousand years?"

"Yes, Lin, that's exactly right."

She felt another tremor deep within her. Whatever had begun to loosen, loosened a bit more.

"Why me? How is any of this possible?"

"Lin, I once told you that when you confronted your uncle Ray, during those years of evil abuse, that you had the strength to not become a victim. You did more than just tolerate it, though. A lot of people can do that. But you never stopped seeking the power to correct the injustice of your life. And more than that, you had the *intent* to get stronger. It's all about your intent, Lin.

"Everyone uses a small amount of intent to shape the slow magic of themselves, but they're not aware of it. You've learned to focus on that intent, and it grew with every hardship that you experienced. Your intent grew stronger every time.

"That very strong woman, many centuries ago, had such strong intent that she created a complete world from the endless depths of magic that supports the world of reality."

"Okay, but how is that possible? What happened when she slept?"

"She could sleep whenever she wanted. It made no difference. Her intent never changed."

"I can't even imagine that."

"Maybe not today. But two weeks ago, could you have imagined what you now do with your intent?"

Lin had to stop talking and slow her racing thoughts. It all fit, even though it didn't make sense. No, she had to clear up her observation of the whole situation. It didn't make sense to her mind, but it made perfect sense to her *intent*. That nameless part of her inside, that part of her that shaped the slow magic of the world. That part of her that she could use to focus and raise her mayhem in less than a heartbeat.

"I accept all that, Gabby. But why am I important? Why are you here? Why does it make any difference what I do with my life or with my mayhem?"

"There's a reason why it's possible for you, or that man two-thousand years ago, or anyone else, to be able to control their intent, to learn about the magic that supports the world. But I don't know what that reason is. I only know that there are battles raging, even now, in dark places within the endless fields of magic. Battles of good versus evil.

"It's important that the power of your intent is used for good. I don't trust The Shield. But the answer might indeed be contained in the Messenger Scroll."

Chapter 14 – Fires & Missions

Ben gasped after leaving the restaurant when he unrolled the pile of bills Lin had just handed him. He laughed out loud at having his hands on more cash than he'd ever before had at one time.

But the laughter trailed off when he remembered the importance of the mission she'd trusted with him. He knew he needed to focus and not let her down. Anyone but her. She'd saved him in a way he couldn't explain. He could never thank her enough.

He fired up his old truck, trying not to notice the empty beer cans and other trash scattered everywhere inside. He vowed he'd clean it up when he had a chance. He reached beneath the seat and found his pistol, and he remembered the rage and lust for violence he'd felt when he purchased it in Brunswick. Well, he laughed to himself, it would be there if he needed it.

The truck rattled out into traffic without the benefit of a working radio to keep him company. Oh well, he thought . . . that was his own fault. There had never been a good enough reason to punch the radio.

As he sat listening to the truck shaking itself apart all around him, he reached into his jacket pocket and found his cigarettes. He got as far as hanging one on his lip and reaching for his lighter before he stopped. He held the cigarette up and studied it before tossing it out the window. The entire pack followed it, and he rolled up the window as he continued his drive.

Ben found he could ignore the garbage the truck carried with it, but his clothing . . . that he could not see past. At the next department store, he pulled in, parked, and walked inside.

* * *

It took him only a minute to find the extra-large section, and when he did, he quickly located new jeans, a t-shirt, and a couple of button-down shirts too. For now, he thought, his big boots would have to do.

After paying the bill, he exited, stuffing the bills in his pocket before aiming for his truck. As if he were a magnet for trouble, two young men fell in behind him and tailed him into the deserted parking lot.

Ben turned and stopped, staring from one to the other. That startled them, but they likely had reasons for needing the wad of cash that Ben had flashed in the store.

"Let's have that money, baldie."

"Yeah, and make it quick. Maybe we'll let you walk away."

Ben felt an explosive fire light deep inside, but he held it back. He shook his head and laughed. Not at the two would-be thieves but at his new ability to control his violent nature.

"Boys, you should probably just crawl back into your sewer."

"Don't make me cut you up, man," said the larger one as he pulled out a long knife that glared briefly in the weak light.

Ben didn't hesitate. They'd been warned.

Rather than backing away from the knife, he stepped toward it. The thug lunged it forward, aiming for Ben's belly. The knife found only the bags of new clothes, which Ben immediately dropped and got a solid grip on the man's wrist. He pulled the knife arm out straight, grabbed the shoulder with his other hand, and brought the arm down and his knee up. He laughed out loud at the cracking sound when the arm bent backwards and the blade clattered on the pavement.

He yanked the punk close and ratcheted down a snug headlock, tight enough to silence him. His cohort danced a short distance away, throwing weak punches, until Ben leaned forward at the right time and leveled him with one blinding jab. Blood and chips of white littered the lot.

Ben uncurled his arm and held the crying thief by the scruff of his neck. He gave him a brief, up-close look at his other knee. The crying stopped, and his body collapsed across his partner.

"I did warn you guys. Sorry."

He picked up his bags and looked through his purchases.

"You put a hole in my new t-shirt."

He gave each downed man a sharp kick to their ribs. Only one of them groaned.

After a quick change in his truck, Ben resumed his journey to Philadelphia.

*   *   *

The young girl at the front desk asked Ben if he needed any help. He looked respectable in his new clothes and his calm demeanor instantly put her at ease.

"Yes, I do, thank you. I'm looking for Taylor Finnerty. I'm a friend of her mother's, and she asked if I'd stop to visit and keep her company."

"Just a minute . . . let me look and see . . . yes, she's here, but she's flagged to not get any visitors other than her mother."

"Yes, Lin knew that, and that's why she wrote this letter. Please, take a look. You can even call her if you'd like. You probably have her number on file."

Ben laughed inside, thinking how he would have handled the situation just a few days earlier. Things would have been broken. People would have been broken. He knew that was a bad strategy, and it wouldn't have worked. But he saw that the Ben he used to be wouldn't have thought that far ahead. He would have charged up to see Taylor.

The girl called a supervisor over to help. Ben watched the woman read Lin's letter and call her phone, and he listened to her side of the conversation.

"Hello, Ms. Finnerty? This is Lisa calling about your daughter, Taylor. There's a gentleman here that says he's a friend of yours, and you'd like him to visit Taylor."

"Yes, he's tall.

"Yes, that's correct, that's how he looks.

"Okay, I appreciate your patience. You know that we have to check.

"Yes, I'll let him up. She'll probably be happy to have a visitor.

"Yes, she's holding steady. We'll be starting the next round soon.

"Okay, take care, Ms. Finnerty. We'll contact you if we need any more information. Thanks."

She looked back up at Ben.

"Okay, you're in. Here's her room number. And please, remember that she's probably not as energetic as she'd like to be, so don't disturb her. And if she needs to rest, please let her rest."

"I will," said Ben. "I wouldn't dream of disturbing her in any way. Thank you."

He set off for Taylor's room, grinning all the way.

* * *

"Hello? Taylor?"

"I'm Taylor. Who are you?" said a weak voice.

Ben stepped in and saw a bed surrounded by equipment and smelling of antiseptic. The cute but gaunt blond girl in the bed looking up at him was clearly Lin's daughter. Even though her hair was shorter, she flicked it back much like Lin would have.

"Hi, I'm Ben. I'm a friend of your mom's. She asked me to stop in and visit."

"Really. Why?"

Ben did some quick thinking.

"No real reason. She just knew I'd be in the area, and I was happy for the chance to meet you."

"My mom never mentioned you. How long have you known her?"

"A long time. We were in high school together, back in St. Simons. We hadn't seen each other in quite a while, but we sort of ran into each other at the reunion last week."

"You knew my mom in high school? What was she like? Did she have a lot of friends?"

The conversation fell into a comfortable zone, and Ben was relieved that he'd gained some of Taylor's trust. He tried to answer her questions, but he didn't know enough about Lin to even fake answers.

"Taylor, do you mind if I sit a while? It's been an exhausting couple of days, and it'd be great to take a load off."

"Of course, Ben. Have a seat."

He pushed aside some curtains and saw a comfortable chair, which he grabbed and started dragging over.

"Hey, that's for my nephew when he visits. He'll be here soon."

Ben looked at the elderly man who shared Taylor's room. A spark lit inside but quickly got under control. The fire never took off.

"Sorry, sir. I should have seen you there. I'll ask the nurse for another."

"Why, thank you, young man. I wish more young men were as considerate as you."

Ben smiled as he retreated back to Taylor's space, but he kept the spark alive. He thought it might be needed.

After another chair had been brought in for him, Ben sat and talked with Taylor, which was mostly him listening to her talk. She had so much to say and not just about Lin. He recognized how lonely she'd become, spending so much time by herself in a cold hospital room with grim medical problems.

The longer he listened, the more he liked the role Lin had asked of him.

"Do you have kids, Ben?"

"No. No, I don't. But maybe I should have . . ."

He dragged a hand over his bald head and rubbed his moistening eyes.

He'd walked into the hospital on a mission for Lin, and after only a short while with Taylor, he knew it had become a mission for Taylor. She became his purpose. Protecting her mattered more than anything he'd ever known before.

He looked for that fire deep inside, that spark that could erupt into extreme violence in an instant. If it were needed, it would be ready. He'd die to protect Taylor, and he'd take to the other side anyone foolish enough to try to hurt her.

Chapter 15 – Horns & Halos

"Joel, what the hell have you gotten us into? I just want to go home."

Father Steve picked at the wound on his upper lip and rubbed his chin as he slumped further into the back seat of Benson's car.

Benson had stepped outside to take a call, and Steve found himself alone with his attacker, his friend for the last fifteen years. He looked over at Joel, who had recovered from the injection he'd given himself in the diner.

Joel could only turn his head slowly to look at Steve before exhaling loudly and looking down. He shrugged his shoulders.

"Steve, I'm sorry I hit you. I never meant to. I only wanted to know her last name, and then something came over me. That wasn't me. It felt like I was watching it happen."

"Right. Sure, Joel. I just bet it wasn't your fault. Why did you need to know her name anyway?"

It was the first time they'd been left alone since Steve woke up in the car barreling north to Baltimore. And for the last hour, since leaving the diner, they'd only looked at each other, too afraid to speak.

"It's a long story. It has to do with my dad and his deathbed wish. He said he'd been watching for years, waiting for someone to talk about power or magic. He had a contact, some investigator or something, that had asked him to report anything, and he'd get a big reward. Sounded crazy to me, but he was dying, and he asked me to keep doing it for him. It seemed like mostly a game, Steve, until I called the number after I heard Lin talking to you Sunday. Something came over me when I was asking you about it. I swear, Steve, I didn't mean to hit you."

"Who are these people? Why do they want Lin?"

"I don't know, but I'm scared. We have to do what they say, don't you think? And back there at the diner—what the hell, Steve, I didn't want to inject her with anything. I couldn't stop. And I injected myself! I don't understand—"

The car door opened, and Benson climbed back in. He turned to look over the seat at the two scared men behind him.

"Alright, you two, we're off to continue our work. Just sit quietly, and don't cause any problems. With any luck, you'll be successful next time. And honestly, after that, you can return to your lives. You will never mention any of this to anyone. You got that?"

"Yes, of course, we just want to get back home," said Steve.

"After we let you go, we'll have you monitored for quite a while. You'll never see us, but we'll be there. And if you do anything that causes us concern, well . . ."

"No, don't worry, we won't," said Steve quickly.

"Good. For now, just sit quietly. We need to locate Lin, and this time, we won't take any chances."

Steve worked his jaw to each side several times and stared at the floor. Joel rolled his head back and closed his eyes. They sat quietly.

* * *

Several hours later, Benson slowed the car and pulled into a gas station.

"If you boys need to take care of business, now's your chance."

Joel looked over at Steve, and with a shaky hand, he opened his car door and got out. It felt good to move his legs again, and he considered dashing into the woods. But he knew that wouldn't work. Even if he could elude Benson, which he doubted, he'd die out there. He could mix a manhattan with his eyes closed, but that was the extent of his survival skills.

As Joel walked back to the car with Steve, he saw another car pull in next to Benson's. An attractive young woman with thick black hair, and wearing a short camouflage dress and black boots, got out and stood talking with Benson.

Joel stopped, and he stopped Steve with him. Should he interrupt them? Would that get them in more trouble? Or should they stay back and wait? No obvious answer presented itself, so Joel kept walking very slowly.

"Get over here already. What's with you clowns?"

"Daria, these are the two I told you about. They've volunteered to help."

Joel looked at Steve but said nothing.

"Great, they should be a big help, Derek. You know, I'm still kind of a rookie at this."

"In a lot of ways, we're all rookies. This woman, Lin, definitely has some kind of power. Hypnosis or something. I guarantee you, no one with The Shield has ever dealt with this before. When we bring her in, you'll have shown your worth and so will I. That's good for a fat pay raise. Trust me."

"I'd love a pay raise! And a bonus too."

"Clothes are expensive, huh?"

"You have no idea, Benson. No reason I can't look good while kicking ass."

"Just don't forget this is serious business."

Daria nodded but continued to smile.

Benson directed the two men to their places in the backseat, and Daria joined him in the front. Benson followed Anna's directions to the last known location of Jack's truck.

"Hey, Mr. Benson, why do you want this woman so bad?" said Steve.

"That's not your problem. Your only concern is following our instructions, and maybe you'll survive. You got that?"

"Steve, quit bugging him," said Joel. "Let's just do this, and we'll be fine. Like he said."

"Your friend's got the right attitude, padre. Just keep quiet back there until we need you."

* * *

"I'd like a two-bedroom suite for a week."

Lin unrolled a stack of bills, signed the papers and grabbed the key.

After walking into the room and locking the door, she dropped her bags and turned to Gabriel.

"I don't know how to deal with things disappearing and then somehow coming back again. You did that with the chocolate, didn't you?"

"Yes, I did, Lin. But it wasn't for fun, although it happened to be fun too."

"First of all, why weren't your eyes glowing? Back at the diner, that weird deal with the salt shaker and the coffee cup—your eyes were glowing then."

"Eyes don't have to glow. Nothing has to change if that's your intent. But if you let things run their course, your eyes will glow. It's a magic thing."

"What? All those times I've used my mayhem, I knew my eyes were glowing. I could have stopped that?"

"Sure, but would you want to?"

"Probably not. It *is* pretty cool. So, if I want, nothing will change?"

"Or something else can change. It's up to you."

"Oh no, you can't be serious. Like what? What else can change instead?"

"We're talking about magic, Lin. You know I ended that coffee cup's existence. Should it surprise you to learn you can sprout a halo if you wanted? Or even horns?"

Lin nearly collapsed into the upholstered chair, trying to grasp the new possibilities that she hadn't even considered. She wondered what might come next. It intrigued her and terrified her at the same time.

"Okay, I'll need some time to absorb all that. This gets crazier all the time. So, back to that candy—why did you make it disappear? And my brush, and the salt? What's this all about, Gabby?"

Gabriel rummaged around in the backpack that had somehow arrived unnoticed, looking for something with apparent desperation. Lin couldn't help laughing at the bag of cookies that appeared.

As Gabriel took a huge bite out of the first one, Lin heard the answer.

"I'm sure it doesn't feel like it to you, but you're following a natural pattern. It starts with a long trauma, some impossible battle. And if it's met with strength and resolve, there's a chance that a power will develop. You call that power your mayhem. But that's just the beginning.

"From that space in between a person's spirit and their body, you're able to do all sorts of things, good or bad. But remember how you launch your mayhem: you focus on the person you're targeting. And that's very effective. It puts you right in there. But it also blinds you to something."

"I see infinity when I use my mayhem. I see limitless layers of magic, too, propping up this real world of ours. I'm seeing more than anyone else can see. I don't think I'm missing anything."

"Yes, you've seen how a person's spirit is connected to their body. But you haven't seen something else while you're busy using your mayhem."

"And what is that?"

"That everything in this world is connected to the magic. Each object that you see, every tiniest part of it, is connected to the magic. You knew that, I'm sure, because how could it be any different?"

"Of course, Gabby. You're right, I've never thought about it. Everything has magic below it, holding it up."

"Okay, we've gone far enough with how we describe it, Lin. It's been useful, but it's time to understand it more clearly. You do know there's no such thing as 'beneath,' don't you? There's no flat surface of the world with endless magic below it?"

Lin felt more pieces of her loosening and breaking away inside. She felt a panic to find solid ground, anything that was real, anything that she could depend on.

"But that's how I see it. Every time I've used my mayhem, I see the world as a flat, calm surface, and there's crazy magic beneath it. What are you saying?"

"I'm saying your mind has to interpret it somehow. Remember, your mind has limits. It works great in the world, but the world is only a small part of all the wonder that surrounds us."

"Well, if it's not like that, what is it like?"

"Once again, words will fail us, but I'll try. Instead of 'beneath,' think about the endless magic being 'inside and outside.' Your mind can't handle that, right? Every grain of sand, if you look at the magic that supports it, it goes on forever. It's infinite. For every tiniest thing that exists, there's infinity feeding it from every direction, both inside and outside. So, your mind organizes it in a way that makes sense. And that's fine—that's what our minds do. Your mind can almost understand infinity going forever in one direction beneath a surface. But from every direction, leading to every part of every single thing, all at the same time, overlapping in countless ways? It's madness!"

Gabriel laughed and took a big bite. "And this is delicious!"

Lin crumpled into the chair and held onto both of its arms. She felt she was trying to walk on quicksand. The world kept changing, too quickly for her to adapt. No, she had to admit to herself, the world wasn't changing at all. She was only learning the truth of it.

"I think I really am losing my mind. And I don't mean in a good way. Just a normal human way."

"That's no longer possible for you, Lin. What you're feeling is only weakness, and it will be chased away as your strength grows."

"But what am I supposed to do with what you're telling me? You want me to learn how to make candy disappear? I've been doing that for years!"

Lin laughed out loud herself, a bit hysterically, and she felt even crazier.

"Yes, Lin. Candy. That's a good start. But not by eating it."

They laughed together, best friends for over thirty years, discussing the boundless magic of the world.

"Gabby, I'm laughing, but really, I think I'm losing my mind."
"Let it go, Lin. But keep your intent."

*   *   *

Lin and Gabriel had pulled into the restaurant parking lot to wait for Jack and Lee and sat waiting in her Temt8tion. After Lin's own laughter had scared her, not another word had been spoken. She was content to sit in silence until Jack and Lee arrived, hopefully with Nomad. She needed to know that Nomad was safe.

Gabriel broke the silence.

"Lin, you've already learned something today, an improvement to your mayhem. But I don't think you noticed."

"You're right, I haven't noticed anything. What are you talking about?"

"At lunch, you invaded those two men, and you were kind."

"Yes, I was. There was no reason to hurt either of them."

"And did you see any converts?"

Her mouth hung open, and she stared out over the steering wheel. Of course, she thought—there had been other customers in the restaurant, and some were rather close. But none of them had been converted like John and Tommy.

"You're right about that. But why? Am I getting weaker?"

"No, Lin, just the opposite. You focused on those two men, and I mean, you really focused. You didn't send out a wave blindly, washing it through anyone close enough. You targeted them alone."

"But I didn't even know it. I didn't think about it. How did I do that?"

"Well, not by thinking. It's all intent, Lin. Yours is getting stronger."

"But, Gabby, I—"

Before she could finish, she saw Jack's truck approaching from the east. She and Gabriel got out of the car, and her heart rejoiced at seeing Nomad's massive red head sticking out of the passenger side window, catching wind in his mane like a sail.

She could barely see Lee on the seat beneath him. His two-hundred pounds dominated that half of Jack's truck, but Lin caught a glimpse of her black hair and mirrored sunglasses. She gained more respect for Lee, seeing how she would risk being crushed for Nomad's happiness.

The passenger door cracked open and Lin imagined she could feel the Earth shake as Nomad hit the ground running. In seconds he was on her, his massive paws pressing down on her shoulders and his huge tongue washing her smiling face.

"Nomad, my wonderful Nomad!" Lin could barely get the words out.

Her relief knew no bounds. Nomad had forgiven her completely, she could sense it. Only days before, she'd tried to use her mayhem on him, and it didn't go well. She found that she couldn't squeeze in—there was no narrow space with him. The more she tried, the more it aggravated him. It had taken a while to regain any of his trust. And even then, he remained more cautious with her.

But not anymore. He was her sweet fluffy boy again. She felt ready to face whatever future awaited her.

As Nomad dropped with a heavy thud, Lin turned to look toward the truck. Both Jack and Lee were walking toward them, and Lin watched with a smile.

Until she felt a pinch in the side of her neck. She had a quick glimpse of the parking lot rushing toward her, then everything went black.

Chapter 16 – Dreaming & Dying

Gabriel saw Lin falling and eased her to the pavement. The dart hung from her bare neck, drooping down onto her shoulder, and Gabriel quickly pulled it out. But it was too late—she'd lost consciousness.

And four strangers approached from the west, walking through the tall grass.

Jack and Lee began running to help Lin when they saw her drop. Nomad stood guard, staring at the four figures approaching them. He began a savage growl and would have charged, but Jack held him back. Lee stood and watched the events unfolding with no change of expression.

"Stop right there," said Jack. "Who are you? What do you want?"

They all stopped, and one spoke up.

"Step aside. We only want Lin. We have no intention of harming her, but we desperately need her help."

"They're with a group known as The Shield, Jack," said Gabriel. "They do need her help but not like this."

"I said stop. Don't take another step."

Jack suddenly wished Ben were there.

"I'm afraid we can't stop. Jack, isn't it? She'll be safe with us, Jack. But if you don't move aside, things are going to get pretty damn shitty for you."

Jack watched as two of the men continued walking toward them, while the man speaking and a woman stayed back. The two coming nearer didn't look like much of a threat, and he prepared himself for a fight. Until he saw that they each had a pistol. The older man's gun could be seen shaking, but the younger man looked focused and determined. Obsessed, even.

Jack had no idea what to do. He only knew that Gabriel and Lee were no help at all. As the two men got closer to the edge of the asphalt, Jack's panic rose, and he felt on the verge of a last-chance, desperate attempt to save Lin.

* * *

Lin had watched the hard pavement getting closer and closer, but everything slowed down, and she never noticed an impact. All she felt was a velvet darkness that wrapped her up and kept her safe. She had no idea why she'd fallen asleep, but it was okay. Sleep was a good thing.

The night stretched forever in every direction as if she were floating in space. Before long, she could make out the faintest bits of light, which she figured must be distant stars. The universe was beautiful, she thought, and its magic had no limits. She reveled in watching the stars trace their paths across the empty blackness.

* * *

When Father Steve saw Lin, he wailed and turned back to Benson and Daria.

"No, no, I can't. I can't get near her. Don't make me, please. Please . . ."

Joel had stopped and stood staring at Lin. His back straightened, and he flexed his arms, swinging the gun up and down. He let out a low laugh as he nodded repeatedly.

Benson pulled his own pistol and pressed the barrel into Steve's forehead.

"You should be more afraid of this, padre. This will end you immediately. At least you have a chance with her. Turn around and march."

Father Steve only stared at Benson and trembled.

"Don't get any bright ideas, priest. Did I forget to mention? Your gun ain't loaded."

Steve looked more scared than before as his eyes turned down toward the useless weapon in his hand.

"Daria, put that stupid phone away. This is no time for that shit."

"Just one, okay? This would be a fantastic shot. No one has ever seen—"

"You think this is a goddamn game? Your mother won't be happy when she hears about your bullshit."

He looked back at Steve.

"Get moving, padre."

Steve turned and walked up beside Joel, and he stayed mostly behind him as they both faced Lin.

"Joel, you've really gotten us into some shit, haven't you? What the hell are we doing? And I'm terrified of her, Joel. Why? I know her. Why am I so scared?"

"Shut up, Steve, and do what you're told. I'm not afraid of her at all. I'm not afraid of anyone. Go back there and get your head blown off, I don't care. I got this."

Steve turned to look at Benson and his gun, then at Lin lying on the parking lot. He stumbled his way to fall in behind Joel, who was walking briskly toward Lin, raising and lowering his pistol in time with his steps, his eyes clamped down to thin slits.

*　*　*

The longer Lin watched, the more stars she could see. There were endless patterns of them strewn across every direction she looked. Some were brighter than others, but all were beautiful.

One star in particular seemed to be moving toward her. Its motion was so slow she could barely detect it. But she was sure that that star would eventually fly past her in all its radiant glory.

When it got closer, she saw that it was actually a twin star system. How amazing, she thought. Two stars traveling through the universe together. That alone was a special kind of magic.

As Lin watched the two stars, she began to notice that they didn't shine with a simple, unidentifiable light like all the rest. Each had a coloring, a hue that carried a beauty of its own—their own personalities. She realized they were planets, or comets, or something else but not stars. Soon, they'd be close enough, and she'd get a fantastic view of them. What a great fortune to be at the right place, at the right time, to witness such a celestial miracle.

* * *

Jack struggled to guess when the best time would be to attack. Too soon, and they'd have plenty of time to gun him down. Too late, and they'd be upon him and by then, too close to Lin. They'd made it to the parking lot. Maybe a few more steps. Patience, he told himself. Take the young one out first. He's clearly the more aggressive. Take him out quickly, then deal with the older man. Maybe even use the younger man's pistol on the old man. Then, turn the weapon on the other two.

No one would take his Lin. Just a few more steps . . .

* * *

Something was wrong, and Lin could feel it. The comets, or planets, or whatever they were, no longer appeared to be aimed off to one side or another. They were coming directly at her. Two large shapes, two huge planets, barreling through space on a collision course with her.

She'd never survive that! There must be a way to deflect them, send them off in a slightly different direction. But she didn't have time to figure out how. She could only think about how massive they were and how quickly they were moving.

And of course, she saw, they were connected to the endless depths of magic. She'd almost forgotten! Everything was connected to the magic, and the two planets were no different. Lin focused, and she found her intent, even out there in the nearly empty wasteland of space.

The dangerous planets were supported by the magic. She needed to focus on the magic. She'd learned to control magic. Her mayhem. She sensed each of the planets. How solid they seemed. Magic held them in place. Allowing them to exist. Creating them. She needed to go to the magic of each. Instantly, her intent brought her there. It was so clear how each one existed. She got a strong grip on the magic of each. As if she had giant hands. She felt the magic flowing. Creating the two planets. New in every moment.

And she squeezed. She squeezed the magic tight.

* * *

Just as Jack was about to lunge for the younger man's gun, he heard and saw something that knocked him to his knees. It was the sound of a large eggshell cracking open, quickly followed by another one. He watched as each approaching man's head exploded gently, one after the other, with all the contents spilling down the fronts and backs of their headless bodies. The corpses stood in a ghastly display before silently slumping into their own puddles on the cold asphalt.

Jack's eyes popped open wide as his heart raced and his breaths rushed in and out. What had just happened? How was that even possible?

He turned to look at his companions. Gabriel only nodded, not disturbed in any way. Lee's eyes were like saucers above her sunglasses, the most change in expression Jack had ever seen from her about anything. So, that's what it took to get a reaction, he thought. Nomad had stopped growling and prodded Lin with his snout. The man and woman had fled.

Lin still lay there unconscious, but Jack couldn't deny that he saw a trace of a smile.

* * *

Ben had dozed off shortly after Taylor had talked herself into oblivion. She'd exhausted herself with stories of her childhood, all the good times with Lin, how she fell ill, and how she regretted that things had become difficult with her mother. Taylor knew she'd pushed Lin too far by prying into her past. They never should have had any kind of argument like that. And now, Taylor was ill, and it seemed insurmountable to rebuild their relationship.

He'd listened attentively, genuinely caring and wishing he could help. He knew that the only way he could make a difference, at least since things had gotten dangerous for Lin, was to protect Taylor. And maybe even be her friend. He found that he'd like that. But maybe without so much talking.

An unfamiliar footstep rhythm awoke him. Like an animal, he adapted to his environment, quickly remembering sounds that were safe and expected. The new sound was neither. Ben opened his eyes a crack to view the scene before committing himself to any type of action. The sound came from just outside Taylor's door. Nothing could be seen.

The door swung in slowly, and Ben prepared himself for violence if it were needed. A man stepped into the room, treading lightly, proving that he was up to no good. Ben began to rise from his seat just as the man raised a pistol and fired. The dart missed his thick flannel shirt and easily pierced his t-shirt only inches from the knife hole. It had sunk in deep and stuck straight out from his chest.

The dose was strong, but not strong enough to take Ben down. He charged forward, closing the distance in no time, and got a solid grip on the man's throat. Two other men tried to pull Ben's hands loose to the point where they were both hanging from Ben's arms. But Ben never let up. He felt something in his hands snap, and the man went limp.

But so did Ben. His last thoughts were that he'd failed. He vowed that if he ever awoke from their drugs, he'd make every last one of them pay. His last sight was of a man injecting Taylor and another removing her from her equipment.

Then, it all went black as night. A night that, for Ben, permitted no dreams.

Chapter 17 – Shovels & Hoses

Jack ran after the two remaining attackers, jumping one bloody heap and dodging the other. The parking lot ended in a wide expanse of wet grass, which gave way to a dense evergreen forest. He got as far as the edge of the trees when he heard a car start and speed away on the nearby road, spraying gravel and snapping twigs.

A quick sprint brought him back to Lin's side. With his lungs still pumping, he stood looking down on her as she slept, and a thick tear crept down his cheek.

"She's going to be fine, Jack," said Gabriel.

"Thank God," said Jack. "What did they hit her with? Do you know? Either of you?"

They didn't.

"And how long . . . how long will she be out?"

"Not long," said Gabriel.

As if on cue, Lin began to stir, stretching her limbs like she was waking up in the comfort of her own bed. Her eyes opened, and she smiled at Jack, then at Gabriel and Lee. Nomad continued his nudging of her, his big wet nose rooting around her throat.

"Oh, Nomad, thanks for waking me up," she said as she tried to get her arms around his thick mane.

"Lin, are you okay? How do you feel?" said Jack.

"A little groggy but not bad. What happened to me?"

"Some people shot you with something. They knocked you out," said Gabriel, holding the dart for Lin to see.

"Well, thanks for not letting them take me. Whatever you all did, it worked."

"We didn't do anything," said Lee.

"We really didn't, Lin, but some . . . something happened. You probably shouldn't look," said Jack.

"You mean, whoever came for me didn't just give up and leave?"

"Hardly. Two did run away but only after the other two, they, um . . . they—"

"They're dead, Lin," Lee said.

"How? I need to know."

Gabriel helped Lin up. She straightened her skirt and tried to pull it down some, but like usual, there wasn't enough material. Lee handed Lin her beret, which she placed above her flowing hair like a crown. And the four began the short walk to the dead bodies, Nomad trailing beside Lin and nosing her hand.

Lin stood over the gruesome scene without any change of expression.

"The priest and the organist, right? I recognize their clothes."

Why on Earth were they involved? she wondered. Could her short visit to the church have led to them losing their heads in that cold parking lot?

"Yes, Lin. The ones from the diner."

"Did any of you see this happen?" said Lin.

"I was looking right at them," said Jack. "Their heads, they just exploded, but not like bombs. They popped like bubbles. On a sheet of bubble wrap. Just one little pop. Then another. Both heads."

Jack laughed and rubbed his face with both hands.

"I was watching. Just a pop. Then another pop. I saw it . . . I—"

"Jack, Lee, can you both take Nomad back to the truck and give me a minute with Gabby?"

Jack turned quickly and began walking, but he had to tug on Lee's leather jacket to get her started. Nomad didn't want to leave Lin's side, but he let out a deep whine and followed Jack.

"Broken hearts or broken bones," Lin said under her breath.

"Yes, Lin. But only bones here this time."

"Gabby, I'm not confused at all. I had a dream while I was out, but it didn't involve people. Not real people. But I'm sure my dream killed them."

"Yes, Lin, your mayhem protected you even while you slept."

"It wasn't my mayhem. It was something else."

"Oh? What did you experience?"

"It seemed like a normal dream for a while. I saw the two men as planets out in space, and they were coming at me. Somehow, I knew to go to the magic of each. My intent took me right there, wherever 'there' was. I grabbed ahold of the magic for each one, and I felt it flowing through my hands. I saw what you meant—that things are continually being created. I didn't believe it, Gabby. And then, I squeezed. I squeezed the magic real tight."

"And that's the result," said Gabriel, pointing at the two corpses.

"Yes, that's what I did. And it was something new. It wasn't my mayhem. Not like I've understood it. I didn't mean it."

"I know. I'm sorry, Lin."

She looked down to see the organ player's puddle had formed a thin stream trickling into a rusty storm drain. She brushed at one eye, thinking how an unfortunate series of events had led to his life flowing into a sewer, unnoticed, as the Earth continued to spin.

Before she could put it behind her, one final thought flashed and was gone—that their last human contact might be just a guy with a shovel and a garden hose. Making minimum wage.

"Gabby, they really want me bad. It's all because of that scroll?"

"Yes, they've been trying for many lifetimes to find another person capable of reading the Scroll. It was read twenty centuries ago, but he wouldn't tell The Shield what it said. Instead he went about trying to help people, trying to teach them in a way that they could understand."

"There's more to his story, that's for sure."

"Yes, I think you know that it didn't end well. Even without him revealing the Words, he changed the course of civilization. You can see just how important the Words are. What happened to him was a shame and a waste."

"So, he wasn't who he said he was? Just a random guy that learned to use the magic?"

"Oh, no, Lin. He was exactly who he said he was. And of course, he could use the magic too. We'll never know how things would have gone if he'd never read the Scroll."

Gabriel took several more bites, finishing the cookie, and reached into the bag for the next.

"I won't always be here to protect you, but you won't need me much longer anyway. It's important that you stay safe, but it's also important that you read the Words.

"I suspect the Words were meant to be known by everyone. I don't understand why the reading of the Scroll was made to be so difficult. The description of the Words left by that powerful woman who heard them, I've heard that it all sounds rather disheartening. But even so, people have the right to know."

They stood in silence over the two dead men in the cold Pennsylvania air.

"Gabby, I've never been just an abused child, just a bounty hunter, just a woman playing with magic, have I?"

"No, definitely not, Lin. You came into the world with at least the beginnings of something extraordinary. But you added to it and became stronger. You're living a life, and seeing the world, like few ever could. Or ever have before."

"And it's okay to still wear short skirts and crave chocolate?" Lin said with a smile.

"Yes, of course. You just be you, Lin. Magic will sort it all out."

And Gabriel smiled, too, before digging back into the cookie bag.

*　*　*

"Ms. Kelgina, you don't understand. You don't know just how crazy things were. We tried—"

"Slow down, Benson. Just take me through it step by step, okay?"

117

Anna had known it would be difficult if The Shield ever did encounter someone with the kind of power that they sought. But how bad could it have been? So the two extras had died. In her mind, that was an acceptable price to pay.

"Ms. Kelgina, I don't know how else to say it. Their goddamn heads exploded. Really, their heads just exploded. And then, they just dropped to the ground. And Lin, she—"

"There is no need to curse, Benson. Then, you ran away? That is not like you."

"I, uh . . . Daria was scared. I wanted to keep her safe."

"Lin must not have been fully sedated. Did you increase the dose to twice normal like you were instructed?"

"Yes, of course, and she was on the ground, she was out, I should have shot—"

"Benson! You have not been authorized to shoot anyone. Right now, I need you to keep your head clear. Do you understand?"

"Yes. Yes, of course. I won't fail again. I *will* bring her in, whatever it takes."

"What you will do is follow instructions. Report back to headquarters. We can go over this in great detail when you are back. I need to know everything so that our next attempt will succeed. We will figure this out. Just bring Daria back. Hey, is Daria okay?"

"Yes, she's fine. We only sent those two stooges in."

"You did the right thing by bringing them back from Georgia. You and Daria, report back here."

Anna ended the call, wondering if the whole operation had begun to fall apart. For centuries, The Shield had waited and watched, and finally, the person they needed had arrived. She knew she couldn't let a couple of deaths and some minor problems stop the mission. They'd get Lin to read the Scroll, no matter what it took.

"Oh, Mr. Wolfe, I did not hear you come in."

"No one ever does, Anna. I'm clever like that," Wolfe said with a smile.

"I overheard part of your conversation just now. It pleases me that you take this work so seriously. And I'm thrilled that we're coming so close to our goal. I believe we will soon know what's recorded on the Scroll. That excites me, Anna."

She sat looking up at Wolfe, still stunned by his youthful good looks and physical intensity. She wondered how he could maintain that after the twenty-plus years since they'd first met.

"You please me, Anna. You're doing God's work. And you're very important to me."

He stepped closer, and she looked up at him through her large glasses as her hands fought to smooth her skirt down across her thighs. The door had closed behind him, and they were alone.

He reached out and removed her glasses, setting them on the conference table. With one hand, he scooped up Ozzy and placed him on the table. A soft caress to smooth out Anna's hair was followed by both hands resting on her shoulders. Anna's heart raced as he pulled her face toward him until she felt her cheek pressed up against his hard body hot like a furnace. He stroked her hair like she was his pet.

Anna dared not resist, hoping that she was safe, but in some perverse way, hoping she wasn't.

Wolfe's hands slid down the outside of her arms as he leaned in to kiss the top of her head. His hands found her elbows, and he gently coaxed her out of her seat. He kicked the chair aside and turned her to sit against the edge of the table, where he stared into her eyes as he reached for her skirt.

Anna leaned back and rested her elbows on the table, and her lips parted as she welcomed whatever would come next. She smiled at the freedom of being unable, and unwilling, to say "no."

*   *   *

Anna woke to find herself flat on her back on the table with Ozzy whining and licking her ear. She slid off of the table and pulled down her skirt. A quick look around showed that Wolfe had left, and the door was closed. She shook her head, thinking it must have been a dream. But she could feel that it had been all too real.

She couldn't imagine what had gotten into her. Why had she allowed that? She'd been with The Shield for over twenty years, doing God's work. It was no place for an encounter like that.

She couldn't stop the feelings of guilt.

But she did manage to stop her smile.

She held Ozzy close as she exited the conference room. She felt an overpowering need for a cool shower, something that would clean her, help her look beyond what had just happened. Perhaps a glass of vodka would help, she thought.

But first, she needed to make a call.

Chapter 18 – Scaring & Sharing

"Something's wrong, Gabby."

They both watched Jack and Lee walking back to join them at the edge of the parking lot, where the remains of her two assailants lay silent, their red puddles thickening in the cold air. And Jack had his cell phone out.

"Lin, I just got a call from someone, some woman. She didn't identify herself, but she said she was with the same group. I don't know how to tell you this—"

"Just get it out, Jack. You know you can tell me anything."

"They have Taylor."

Lin froze on the spot. She stared at Jack with her mouth open but without saying a word. Ben was there and protecting her, she remembered. What had happened?

"The Shield took Taylor? Is she okay? What did she say? Jack, what did she say?"

"She said Taylor's fine, that they have someone monitoring her. She's stable and will be taken care of. And they have Ben too."

"Give me your phone."

Jack handed his phone to her, and she searched until she found the number. She called it back. No one spoke.

"Talk. I know you're there."

"You are Lin?"

"Where is my daughter?"

"She is safe. We will take care of her. You will do as we instruct."

"You have *no* idea what I'm going to do when I find you."

"We will call tomorrow with an address. You will come."

"You better—"

Lin pulled the phone away and stared at it a second. She handed it back to Jack.

"Did she tell you what they wanted, Jack?"

"She said they need you to read the Scroll. Lin, she sounded very determined. Desperate. What are we going to do?"

She looked from Jack to Gabriel to Lee. She fought to push her panic and anger down.

"First of all, we need to get out of here. There are two headless corpses that will bring down a lot of scrutiny. We can't be around. We need to get back to the suite right now.

"Then, we can plan to get Taylor. And Ben, of course. And the Shield needs to be dealt with."

Lin swept her long blond hair back over her shoulders, and a look of dangerous determination set in her green eyes.

*　*　*

Lin and Gabriel led their hasty departure with Jack, Lee, and Nomad following in Jack's truck. Back at the suite, Jack and Lee moved their things inside, and Nomad was the first to find a comfortable spot to claim as his own.

Lin suspected Jack was still kind of shaken, and she wanted badly to have some time alone with him. She knew her stress needed to be pushed aside, at least for a while. She needed to clear her mind. And Jack's.

"Gabby, I noticed driving in that there are lots of restaurants close by. That should help, don't you think?"

Gabriel nodded with an understanding smile.

"Exactly right, Lin. And since I'm hungry again, I think I'll wander around and see what's cooking."

Lin smiled at the thought of Gabriel's cheeks again being packed with whatever delightful meals could be found.

Even Lee seemed to know to give them some space.

"I have some things I need to pick up, things I didn't have time to pack. And I need to call Alessa too."

"Alessa?" said Jack.

"Alessa's my daughter. She's back in Jacksonville with her grandma. I need to tell her I'll be gone for a few days. It'll be fine."

The door closed, and Lin let out a deep breath as she looked to Jack.

"Jack, I'm sorry life is so complicated. I've become quite a complicated woman."

"I don't understand much of anything that's happened. My head is spinning. On the drive up here, I tried to put together a poem for you to tell you how I feel. I can't find the words, though."

"Aw, Jack. You'd still write poetry for me?"

"Of course. Even with all this . . . whatever it is . . . going on, you're still the only Cowgirl for me." He gave her a hopeful smile.

She let out another deep breath and returned his smile.

"I'll always need a Cowboy, Jack. Still interested in the job?"

She smoothed her hair back and smiled again. A smile that told him exactly what she wanted.

"Lin, I . . ." Jack said but fell silent. After several seconds, he took three strong steps toward her and placed his hands on either side of her face. He took a long look into her eyes.

Then, he kissed her. A deep kiss. A kiss that swept away all the clutter in their lives. It was only the heartfelt kiss of a Cowboy for his Cowgirl.

Lin slipped her arms around his waist and returned his kiss with a warm, wet intensity that Jack welcomed with a deep groan.

Still holding him tight, and with her lips open against his, she backed up until she bumped into the bed. She felt her mayhem rising along with her passion.

He stopped when he noticed the very slight green glow in her eyes, but he quickly closed his eyes and continued to kiss her and hold her tight.

That's right, Lin thought. Just let it happen, Jack. Like that night in St. Simons, when you nearly went insane loving me.

She had a brief thought of suppressing her mayhem and making simple love with Jack. But the lure of that power, the ecstasy of infinity, had already begun, and she wanted to abandon herself to it. Still, somewhere in her thoughts remained a desire to not take complete control of him, to not terrify him out of his mind.

Holding her intent tightly, she focused on her breath, all the while thrilled with Jack's ravenous hunger for her. She knew her eyes had begun to glow more brightly as she saw infinity spread out from her in every direction. Such a magical world, she thought, as she drew in a deep breath and held it.

Lin found herself happy to believe what she sensed—that the world of reality was a calm surface, and endless depths of magic twisted and churned below it, supporting it, creating it in every moment.

From the breath she held inside, she felt the magic flowing up into her, swelling her to the point of bursting. The pleasure from that breath was a slice of heaven, and she held it as long as she could.

And then, she had a feeling of falling from the stars, racing toward the surface of the world, as she sharply set the breath free. Instantly, a mountain crashed onto the calm surface of the world, and a powerful wave of magic rose up. Lin's life broke free of her body and traveled straight to Jack, the focus of her intent.

As the wave carried her to him, she saw the narrow gap between Jack's body and his spirit, between the reality and the magic. Instead of rushing into that region and taking control, she slowed herself down, and she eased herself into the tight space. She felt she was gently sliding her fingers into a snug glove. She sensed no terror in Jack, only his anticipation and acceptance. And his noticeable excitement.

Jack didn't shriek silently, and no terror settled in.

She'd taken control of him, but she'd left him in control too. There were now two spirits sharing control of Jack's body. Lin sensed him acquiesce and let her call the shots, and her eyes glowed more brightly. She wondered if he'd accepted that her spirit was much stronger, overpowering even. Or perhaps it was his eagerness to experience whatever she would have him do. He remained silent, letting her intent carry them both

Lin viewed herself through Jack's eyes and felt the touch of her own lips on his, as she broke free of her own embrace and had him take a step back. She watched as she methodically undressed herself, pausing only to smile at him. And herself.

She left on the stockings and heels and crawled onto the bed. She and Jack watched her crawl up and roll onto her back, with her legs crossed and off to one side, smiling and waiting after flicking her hair back.

Lin saw the glow in her own eyes.

She moved Jack's hands down to his belt buckle, unclasping it and sliding it out of the loops of his jeans. She pulled his t-shirt up over his head, smelling the leather of the belt as it hung there, feeling his long hair resist at first, then allow the shirt to come off. She smoothed his hair back, and she let him smile on his own.

With the belt still in his hand, she coaxed him, whispering to him in a silent way that he was the Cowboy, and she was the calf, ready to be taken. It was rodeo time, she told him.

She had him approach her, and he knelt beside her on the bed. She watched through his eyes as she let him reach down and wrap his belt around her ankles. She felt his rush of excitement at having subdued her, and she felt her own flirtatious fear at being captured.

She stepped him onto the floor, where the rest of his clothes were soon cast aside. And she watched through her own eyes as he stood before her naked, smiling down at her. Eager for her. She saw her own hands sliding up and down her thighs, with her eyes big and glowing, welcoming Jack to do as he wished.

And as she wished.

She moved his hands to grab the belt and lift her legs straight up. She felt his rough hands caressing the backs of her thighs gently, followed by a sharp smack to her bottom. She saw her eyes only become brighter.

Lin quickly lost herself in touching Jack and touching herself through Jack. It all blended together into an unimaginable feast of sensations, where they both scaled impossible heights of pleasure, their wills mingling and becoming indistinguishable.

The belt had long ago been removed, having served its playful purpose. She looked deep into his eyes, seeing a pleasure there that could drive him insane if she'd let it go much further. And she also looked into her own glowing green eyes, seeing the same pleasure but also a level of control that took her aback. She barely recognized herself for a moment, but the pleasure quickly replaced any doubts.

Unlike their other encounter with her mayhem back on the Island, this time she didn't force Jack to wait so that she could take her own satisfaction first. She worked her magic on Jack and herself together, raising their ecstasy to a crazy level. And she held both of them there, seeing the sweet agony in each other's eyes.

Then, she tore the wall open, and the immense surge took them both into uncharted worlds of pleasure.

When at last they'd both returned from wherever the wave had taken them, Lin lingered in Jack a while longer, feeling his deep satisfaction and near exhaustion.

Before returning to herself she looked into her own green eyes, still glowing and staring intently into Jack's, with an intensity softened only by the pleasure that had washed through them.

Her eyes startled her. They were the eyes of a predator. She held her own gaze until they'd returned to their normal shade of green.

* * *

Back in her own body, Lin breathed deeply and delighted in having Jack pressed up against her. He was largely unconscious, his breathing strong and slow. But he was alert enough to hold her, to touch her, to show how much he adored her.

They lay there in peace for longer than either could know until finally, Jack began to wake up completely.

"Lin, I don't even know what to say. I—"

"It's okay, Jack. There's no need to say anything."

"Just when I think I know you, that you have some power that can terrify me and paralyze me, then you do something like this, something that—"

"Jack, this was new to me too. I only knew that I didn't want to scare you. I only wanted us both to feel good with each other. I had no idea something like that was even possible."

He rolled onto his back and looked up at the ceiling, but he still held her hand.

"I wasn't scared, Lin, but I wasn't in control either. Were you controlling me? Is that what I felt?"

"Yeah, I guess you could say that. But I wouldn't use the word 'control.' I'd say it was more like suggestions for you. Does that make sense?"

"Uh . . . yeah, I think so. I mean, I probably could have resisted, but I didn't want to. I didn't want to stop you from whatever you wanted me to do. I loved it, Cowgirl."

Lin smiled, remembering how Jack didn't call her "Cowgirl" for a long time after she'd first used her power on him. She rolled over, draped her long leg over his, and snuggled close.

"Oh, Jack, what a crazy world, huh?"

But a worrisome foreboding crept up on Lin's thoughts as they drifted off to sleep. What side effect might the new mayhem have on Jack? He'd given up his will to her completely. That's not something people normally do. People are meant to act through their own will, not someone else's.

She wanted to think about how to rescue Taylor and also what she might have done to Jack. But the fatigue she felt from using the magic to defend herself and to play with Jack overpowered her, and they both slept.

Chapter 19 – Reports & Portents

Anna returned to the meeting room and glanced down at the tabletop. Before looking up, she cleared her throat and said, "Tayo, you are early."

Tayo quickly closed the file he'd been reading and placed it in its proper place on top of the others.

"Good morning, Anna. Yes, I never feel I've studied enough. But I'm prepared to brief you on several reports."

"Yes, please do—I need to know everything you have found out. I understand Benson also gave you his findings from the site near Pittsburgh. He has been in the field but without much success, I am afraid. I am eager to learn of what you found in South Georgia."

Anna squirmed in her seat and picked several dog hairs off of one sleeve. She pushed her glasses up and nodded for Tayo to begin.

"Perhaps we should go chronologically, if you'd find that acceptable?"

"Yes, of course, Tayo." She picked Ozzy up from the floor and cradled him like a baby. She scratched his belly and said, "Please proceed."

"Very good. The first report, for which we have very little information, details an incident that happened in Erie nine days ago. A bail jumper was delivered by a bounty hunter to the local authorities. Nothing out of the ordinary about that. I'm sure you've read Daria's report. The odd condition of the man is what caught our attention. By all accounts from several interviews Daria conducted, the man had been an outgoing, talkative sort. But when he was brought to the police, he was barely responsive. Yet there were no signs of injury. A medical examination showed that there was no physical reason for him not speaking, but he wouldn't. Not a word. And he wouldn't make eye contact with anyone either. We have no information on how he came to that condition. As of now, that's a dead end."

"Yes, I recall Daria's reporting on that. We will keep a file open on him, and perhaps more can be uncovered later."

"Good. Very good, Anna. Now, the next two reports stand on their own, but they also have a deeper connotation, if one were to look. Which, of course, I tend to do. I take my work here quite seriously."

"I know you do, Tayo. You are of immense value to The Shield. I was fortunate to meet you in Makurdi. And despite your obvious anger,"—she paused to look at his shirt—"you are the most calm and rational man I have ever met."

"Thank you, Anna. Your kindness is surpassed only by your wit. I will discuss the reports individually first, then offer my observations on a more profound, perhaps startling, interpretation.

"There's a location between Erie and Pittsburgh, on a less-traveled road and near a pond, where we're fairly certain Lin Finity used her power. I understand that you've already gone over Benson's report, so I won't cover the same information. You know that there was another victim there, who is now also unresponsive. But this man had clearly been injured and in a peculiar way. Also, there were two probable witnesses to the incident named John and Tommy. We still haven't been able to identify them.

"So, you know the basics of what happened. Here's one thing not in Benson's report, though: I was able to locate precisely where Lin used her power. The exact spot. That might not seem possible, sitting here at this table."

Anna looked down at the table and felt a smile struggling to the surface.

"But if you were to visit the site, you'd see immediately. Well, forgive me, but the casual observer might not. However, I strive to gather details. Next to the gravel parking area where the victim was found by the medical specialists, there's a circular segment where—"

"A what, Tayo?"

"A circular segment. If you were to lay a circle on the gravel area, with just a slice of it extending beyond the gravel, that part that's not on the gravel would form a circular segment."

"Okay, please continue."

"The segment extended into an area thick with dried cattail stalks, many of which had been bent over, likely by local wildlife seeking the pond's water. Anna, the stalks within the boundaries of that segment are green and appear unaffected by the changing seasons. Some of the stalks showed a clean transition between withered and rejuvenated. And there is also an unexpectedly high concentration of insect life."

"And what does this tell us?"

"I'm not proud to admit that I needed to review basic geometry to determine the radius of the circle represented by the segment. That radius was very nearly nine feet ten inches. We can say ten feet without compromising the conclusion."

"And what is that conclusion?"

"Lin stood at the center of that circle when she used her power."

Anna sat back in her chair, the one from which she'd been seduced and lifted up by Wolfe, and she looked at the ceiling before holding Tayo's stare.

"Photographs of the site are included in the file."

"Tayo, how is that possible? Do you have even a theory about that?"

"Sorry, Anna. No, I don't. Shall I continue?"

"Yes, please continue."

"I also visited South Georgia, a seldom-used road northwest of Brunswick, which was the site of another unexplainable occurrence. Two convicts, also jumping bail, were found by authorities in most perplexing conditions. As a side note, this led to my conclusion that Lin Finity is working as a bounty hunter in addition to her employment at the veterinarian's office.

"One of the victims was found dead, and at first, it was considered a heart attack. His autopsy, though, revealed that something odd had happened to his heart. It appeared compressed. Slightly crushed. The medical examiner had no explanation for what might have caused that.

"The second victim was found nearly blind. But in this instance, the man was able to speak."

Tayo paused to look through the folder before continuing.

"His name is Ivan, and he'd never had eye problems before. He was able to speak, but he remained mostly incoherent. A transcript is included in the file for you to review if you wish.

"Ivan mostly ranted about what he called a 'witch.' He said she was a beautiful witch, but even when pressed, he couldn't give a description. It was clear to the interviewer, though, that he'd become quite obsessed with her—but only in a negative way. When prompted to discuss her, he was near tears. He blamed her for his eyesight being mostly destroyed."

"He used that word? He called her a witch?"

"Yes, Anna. More than once."

"Damn."

"Anna?"

"Nothing. Please continue."

"So again, we have two victims in South Georgia with unexplainable injuries plus two more in Pennsylvania. We suspect it was Lin responsible for all of them.

"And here's the other interesting aspect of the South Georgia incident. The same unlikely changes in growth of all plant life were found at the site in Georgia. Again, it was easy to identify the precise location where I believe Lin stood. For a radius of approximately twenty feet in every direction, all plant life was thriving. On the ground, grass and weeds were thick, like a tall carpet, in contrast to regions outside the circle, which were more sparse. Even the trees up above showed leaves of larger size than the rest. And there were absolutely no dead leaves to be found within that radius of twenty feet. I know because I spent time up in the branches. And again, insect life was thriving, much more than in adjacent regions."

Anna pushed her glasses back up her nose and looked into Tayo's eyes. "And to what do you attribute these phenomena?"

"I do not have a theory on that, Anna. I've performed some literature searches, but as you might guess, this topic is not referenced in any respected scientific journals. May I continue to my report on Allentown?"

Tayo pushed his own thick glasses farther up.

"By all means. Please continue. Your phone call earlier was difficult for me to accept. I need to hear all of this from you in person."

"Yes, I understand. I'll go through these events chronologically too. I staked out Lin Finity's house, and I hid behind the shrubbery in front. Before long, she came home, put the car in the garage, and then there were many minutes of silence. Finally, a large, single bark told me that she'd gone into the house. Many more minutes of silence passed, and I heard the dog shriek. I don't know what happened in there, but I didn't risk my surveillance by trying to look inside. Perhaps I should have—"

"No, you did fine, Tayo. Please, go on."

"There were no more sounds, and I remained there until early the next morning."

"You sat there in the cold all night?"

"Yes, Anna, that's what was required. In the morning, she left for work at Dr. Grayson's Sweet Pets in Allentown. After she'd gone into the building, I tried to plant the tracking device on her car, but there were too many witnesses.

"The exact times and durations are contained in the report, but I will approximate for this discussion. Several hours later, she left work and traveled back home. After a couple hours at home, she again drove to Allentown, to a restaurant. It was there that I was able to plant the device on her car as I entered the building. I understand that led Benson's team to her?"

"Yes, it did. But the mission failed."

"I'm sorry to hear that. But this is where it gets much more interesting.

"I followed her in and took a seat up in a second-floor balcony, where I had a perfect view of Lin sitting at the bar. I must say, Anna, Lin is quite striking. In full disclosure, I could have forgotten my mission. But I was able to refocus, and that will never happen again."

"That is not like you, Tayo. But I do believe you will be able to maintain your focus in the future. Perhaps that affected your interpretation of the events you witnessed?"

"I don't believe so, Anna. My momentary attraction to Lin's appearance was an aberration and had no effect on my perception and recording of all that occurred.

"Many more people showed up and gathered around Lin. Finally, a large, rough-looking man pushed his way through the crowd and stood facing Lin, who had stood up to face him as well. The tension in the air was obvious.

"And then, this is where I must repeat what I relayed to you in our phone call. Lin partially closed her eyes, and I kid you not—you know I don't joke—her eyes began to glow. Really, Anna, her eyes were glowing green."

"You cannot be serious, Tayo. You must be mistaken."

"Perhaps I've lost my mind, but that's what I recall. Truly. But that's not the strangest part. I also saw some kind of a wave emanate from Lin. It rushed out from her in all directions, and it appeared to pass through everyone within a twenty-five-foot radius. And Anna, I feel I must be wrong, but I saw everyone go slightly out of focus as the wave passed through them."

Anna sat and stared through her broad lenses.

"A wave? You are certain Lin can send out a wave of some kind?"

"As you recall, Anna, I saw renewed plant growth near that pond to a distance of ten feet. In South Georgia, the radius was twenty feet. And then in Allentown, I estimate it at twenty-five feet."

"It is increasing. Every day, every time she does it, she is getting stronger," said Anna.

"My thoughts exactly."

"Do you have a theory on what that wave might be? Why it would affect plant life too?"

"Sorry, no. I can only report on what I find."

"Very well, Tayo. And your investigation and reporting are top-notch, as always. The Shield is fortunate to have you."

"Thank you, Anna. I know I'm doing God's work. I will continue to do my best."

Anna found herself admiring Tayo's dedication. And she also found herself wondering what it would be like if he were to take her, right then, right there on that table, while she ran her fingers through his long, tight curls, his smooth skin hot against hers as she—

She shook her head and pushed her glasses up.

"And what happened after the wave?"

"The large man in front of her dropped to the floor immediately. Lin gathered her things and headed for the door. And a man who'd been two tables over on the same balcony as me, whom we've since identified as Jack Madison, he joined her, and they left the bar. The crowd that had experienced the wave clogged the entrance, all trying to get out at the same time. By the time I was able to get outside, it was only to see Lin driving away. I attempted to follow her, but with her head start and her tendency to drive at high speeds, I never caught up with her. I should have anticipated that possibility and brought the proper electronics with me."

"Planting the device was enough, and your reporting is first-rate, Tayo. Now, you wanted to point out some other interesting aspect to all of this?"

"Yes, if you'll indulge me. I'm no scholar, and I can't draw any conclusions from this. But I do have several observations that might interest you and likely the Director too.

"The incident in Pennsylvania, near the pond. No one has pointed this out yet, but that occurred just north of New Galilee. Nothing odd about that—it could have happened anywhere. But I've listened to the recording of John and Tommy. It's obvious that John had become totally enamored with Lin. Why? Did something happen? Did she do something that won them over? Did they become disciples of some kind?"

"What do you mean by 'disciples?'"

"There are Biblical stories about disciples at the Sea of Galilee. I realize this was just a pond, and it's near *New* Galilee, but still . . ."

Anna felt a cold fear in the pit of her stomach. Could that be just a coincidence, or was there some deep significance to it? She leaned in and urged him to continue.

"That alone is just one data point, and by itself, it can be dismissed. Now, let's consider again the events in South Georgia. I don't believe the death of Doc, as he was called, the convict that suffered some sort of heart trauma, is of any significance. But the other man, Ivan, remember that he was mostly blinded."

"Yes, I remember. But so what?"

"Anna, that happened on Jericho Road."

"And?"

"And there's a biblical story of a blind man being healed in Jericho. I'll find the exact passage for you. I apologize that I haven't already."

"Wait. You mean, back then, a blind man was healed in Jericho. But this time, on Jericho *Road*, a man was nearly blinded? Are you sure of all this, Tayo?"

"Yes, I am, but I don't know what it all means."

"Neither do I. But it is troubling. I will need to brief the Director as soon as possible."

Alone, thought Anna. I need to brief him alone with the conference room door closed. And locked. She trembled from the foreboding of what Tayo had revealed and from anticipation of what might again be coming her way.

Chapter 20 – Planning & Taking

After Tayo had left the conference room, Anna sat and collected her thoughts. Before she could arrange a meeting with the Director to discuss Tayo's cryptic observations, she received a text message that the team she'd sent to Philadelphia had returned. And they'd been successful. Finally, she thought, something was going their way.

Without leaving the room, she summoned the team's leader. He arrived promptly and gave Anna a summary of their excursion. They'd accomplished their objective. Their presence hadn't been observed, and only one of them had been injured. Killed, actually. His throat crushed. Lin's daughter and a man visiting her had both been brought to headquarters. They were contained in their own rooms, and the man had been restrained. The girl was under medical care for an as-yet unknown condition. The team had neglected to collect her medical charts.

* * *

Anna gathered up Ozzy and walked the silent hallways to the detention cells. Without further thought, she walked in on Ben, who had been strapped to a chair at the far corner of the room. He was awake and almost completely alert.

"Tell me your name," said Anna.

"Go to Hell," Ben said as he flexed against the zip ties holding his wrists.

"We mean you no harm. We only wanted the girl. Who are you, and what is your connection to the girl?"

He eyed her coldly, imagining his hands gripping her throat, squeezing so hard that even if he were pried away from her, the damage would be too great, and she'd continue to choke.

"That's nice. But I do mean *you* harm. Whoever you are, you have no right to take Taylor. And who the hell are you anyway?"

Anna held Ozzy close and smoothed out her skirt, picking off a few dog hairs.

"We should back up. I do not mean to be confrontational. And I assure you, you and the girl will be free soon. Now, would you please tell me your name?"

He stared at her and shook off the last of his drowsiness. Sure, I'll play along, he thought.

"Ben. My name's Ben. Who are you?"

"I am Anna. I run this group. We are called The Shield. We have a single purpose, and we need Lin's help. We only brought the girl here to convince Lin to help us."

"Is Taylor okay? You do know that she's not well, don't you? She belongs back in the hospital."

"I assure you that Taylor is fine. Now, Ben, what is your connection to Lin and Taylor?"

"I'm just a friend that was visiting Taylor. I really have no involvement. I can't help you, so maybe you should let me go."

"I am afraid I cannot do that. Not yet. We need to bring Lin here to help with something. If you can think of any way to convince her, it would be in your and Taylor's best interest. After she helps, you will all be free to go."

"Lady, I have no idea what you're talking about. I barely know Lin, and I barely know Taylor, so don't expect much help from me."

"Well, Ben, this will all be resolved soon, I am sure. But in the meantime, we will need you to stay put. And Ben, just cooperate, okay? Let us all pitch in to make sure things work out best for everyone."

What a bunch of crap, thought Ben. He knew that as soon as Taylor was safe, he'd beat down Anna and anyone else that got in his way.

"Sure, Anna. Whatever you say."

* * *

Lin awoke with a start, and reality crashed in. It was time to save Taylor.

"Jack. Jack, wake up."

"Alright, I'm awake. I had the strangest dreams, Lin. I was just floating somewhere, not really going anywhere. It sure was peaceful, though."

"Jack, we need to focus." She shook him and his head flopped from side to side. "Taylor's in trouble, and so is Ben. We need to get dressed. We need to wake up Gabby and Lee, and we can put together a plan. That call should be coming any minute."

"I'm in for sure, just tell me what you need. I'll do anything. Anything you want."

"I believe you, Jack. You don't need to convince me."

* * *

"Lee, did you make your call? Will your daughter be okay?" said Lin.

"Yep, she'll be fine. I still want to talk to you, though, when we have time."

"Sure thing. We'll get a chance. Right now, all I can think about is getting my own daughter back. And where's Gabriel?"

"I understand. I'll help too—whatever you need. Gabriel left a few minutes ago."

"Thanks, Lee. I don't know what we can do, but we can all put our heads together and come up with something."

Just then, Gabriel walked in with bags of take-out breakfast for everyone.

"Gabby, you're the best. I'm starving, and I bet Jack is too. How about you, Lee?"

"I'm always ready for breakfast."

The four sat around the dining room table and mostly ate and looked at each other. Nomad crunched noisily from his bowl before his big eyes started to focus on everyone else's.

Jack's phone rang, and after looking at it, he handed it to Lin. She listened and wrote down the address.

Since they had all finished eating, except for Gabriel, Lin spoke up.

"They have my daughter. Some group called The Shield. Gabby, who are these people?"

Gabriel swallowed a large bite of egg and cheese on an English muffin and looked up at Lin.

"They've been around forever, or at least, it seems that way. They are in possession of the Scroll, an ancient artifact said to contain the Words of God. I believe they *are* the Words of God. How they got the Scroll, I do not know.

"The problem they face is that no ordinary person can read it. Everyone that's tried has gone completely mad. Well, except for one man. Lin, they think you can read it. I believe they're right."

"Why don't they just bring the Scroll to me, maybe in the parking lot somewhere. I'll read it, and then they can leave us alone and let Taylor go."

"It's not that easy. An ordinary person can't even stay close to it for any length of time. It eats away at you. Drives you mad. I'm sure they have it stashed somewhere safe. They're probably reluctant to even try moving it."

"So, if I read this thing, that's it? They'll go on their way?"

"That's what they say. But I don't trust them, Lin. I remember, I mean, I've heard, that the last person who read it wouldn't tell anyone what it said. And it didn't end well for him. You might be in trouble whether you read it or not."

Jack and Lee looked at each other before focusing again on the conversation. Lin looked only at Gabriel.

"Why wouldn't he say what was on the Scroll?"

"There's also a narrative recorded by the woman who heard the Words and committed them to the Scroll. I've never read that, but I've heard that it's not very encouraging. I believe the Words don't give a comfortable answer like many would wish. The last person who read them likely felt the same way and kept them to himself."

"What on Earth are you two talking about?" Jack said. "Some ancient scroll, the Words of God, and they want Lin to read it? This all sounds crazy."

"It is a little crazy, Jack," said Lin. "But you know that there's something different about me, don't you?"

"God, yes. Of course, there is."

"I've seen it too," said Lee.

"So, even though it's crazy, it makes sense that they'd believe I could read it. You can both see that, can't you?"

Jack and Lee nodded.

"Gabby, what do you recommend? I trust your judgment. You've been an amazing friend of mine for so long, and I trust you more than you probably know."

Gabriel pulled another sandwich out of a bag and looked back up at Lin.

Gabriel said, "You should surrender yourself to The Shield," before biting into the sandwich.

The silence in the room was broken only by Gabriel crunching on the burnt muffin.

"You can't be serious. These people seem to be murderers. They're certainly kidnappers. And you want me to turn myself over to them? Do you believe that would keep Taylor safe? Do you believe I can actually read the Scroll?"

"Yes to all of that. I'm sure you'll be fine, Lin," Gabriel said with a smile.

* * *

"I know you can handle our hostages, Anna. You have a more urgent reason for seeing me here in the alley. Don't you?"

"Yes, Mr. Wolfe, it is about Tayo and what he found. He said—"

"No. No, I don't believe it's about Tayo. Is it?"

Anna held onto the dog hair she'd been picking off her skirt, and when Wolfe powered down her window, she rubbed her fingers together for the wind to take it. Before she could answer, he grabbed her left wrist and pulled it up close to his lips. With his eyes fixed on hers, he slid his hot tongue across the back of her hand before giving her a bite.

"Oh . . . Mr. Wolfe, that is—"

"A good idea? Come closer, Anna." He powered her window back up.

"But, Mr. Wolfe, about Tayo, I—"

"Shh. Tayo's not here. I am."

"But we are out here, in the light, where—"

"Shh, shh." He removed her glasses, placed them on the dash, and pulled her closer.

With his left hand hot against her neck, his right hand smoothed back her hair, stroking her like a kitten, until she relaxed and closed her eyes. He drew her in until her parted lips were but an inch from his, and then he squeezed her throat, and her eyes popped open.

"Shh. It's okay, Anna. Don't expect to feel safe when you are in my hands. Do you understand?"

With his firm hold of her neck, he nodded her head several times.

"Yes, it's hard for you to understand, but you will. And you will never fight me. I always know exactly what needs to be done. And you will always perform as I instruct you. Do you understand?"

She appeared to understand.

He relaxed his hold of her throat and pulled her in until his steamy kiss filled her with a frightening vision of scorched lands, burning forests, and boiling seas. And it felt like home.

"I need more than just a kiss from you, Anna. Do you understand?"

With the help of his tightening grip, she appeared eager to comply.

*　*　*

A short while later, Anna grabbed her glasses and put them back on. She powered down her window and inhaled deeply, and she cleared her throat before speaking.

"Mr. Wolfe, that . . . I only wanted to tell you what Tayo reported."

"You're a liar, but I admire that." He smiled. "We can talk about Tayo now. Go ahead."

Anna put the window up and rubbed her hands down her skirt.

"Tayo has uncovered some disturbing details in his investigations. Maybe they do not mean anything. They might all be coincidences. Because it is just too—"

"Get to the point, Anna."

"Okay. There are correlations between things Lin Finity has done and stories from long ago. Stories of that man who read the Scroll. You told me about his involvement with the Scroll. I had never heard that before, and—"

"I'm waiting."

"Yes. You have seen the reports about what we think Lin did in Pennsylvania near that pond. There were two witnesses—John and Tommy. Mr. Wolfe, that pond is near New Galilee. And John and Tommy—"

"Are you sure it's near New Galilee? Are you sure their names are John and Tommy?" Wolfe held the steering wheel tight and glared at Anna.

"Yes, we are sure, and there is more. In Georgia, we believe Lin almost blinded a man named Ivan. Mr. Wolfe, that happened on Jericho Road, and—"

"You don't need to explain. I know all those stupid stories in that blasted book. Hell, I feel like I'm the star in many of them."

"Mr. Wolfe?"

"My sense of humor, Anna."

"And don't forget where Lin lives, Mr. Wolfe."

"I remember. Of course, that's where she lives," he said with a laugh before snarling at her. "This isn't funny, Anna. He's mocking me."

"Tayo would never—"

“Not Tayo. Don’t be a fool.”

“Sir?”

“God couldn’t have sent him back. Not like this. Not as a hot blond in a short skirt. Now *that* would be evil, wouldn’t you agree?”

“You . . . you do not think—”

“Forget it, Anna. I’ll handle it. Thanks for the report. And everything else. Now, you’d better get back down there and keep an eye on things.”

“You are not going down too?”

“Hell no. I need a drink. Call if you need me.”

He clicked to unlock her door, and after a short, awkward stare, Anna stepped out into the cold air.

Within seconds, Wolfe’s car had sped down the alley and turned a corner.

Chapter 21 – Shafts & Tunnels

She'd parked her Temt8tion near the entrance to the empty warehouse in Baltimore, dodged trash in the alley, and entered the dark room. If the intercom button hadn't been lit, she'd never have seen it. She pressed it and waited patiently.

"Yes?"

"Lin Finity. Let's get this over with."

After several minutes, the elevator doors opened, lighting the room, and two large men, thick muscles stretching black t-shirts, stood looking at Lin. Their eyes immediately dropped to her long legs beneath her short skirt and ending in her favorite black heels. They looked at each other, then back at her. She took a quick look around the room and didn't see any security cameras monitoring their activities.

Before they could complete a single step, Lin focused on her intent and felt infinity spreading out in every direction as time slammed to a stop. She found herself at the center of a beautiful, calm surface—the world of reality. And beneath that, she saw the bottomless depths of magic, swirling and dancing in unimaginable complex patterns.

She drew in the deepest breath she could, though there was no need. But still, it felt so good to take in the magic and hold it there inside. To feel the limitless volumes of magic flowing into her, expanding outward to every cell of her body. Lingering on the edge of magic filled her with an ecstasy that she could never become accustomed to and take for granted.

She watched all of that happening without planning it or even thinking about it. Her mayhem had risen up to protect her. And she let it.

With a focus still on the breath inside her, she exhaled sharply. Instantly, a massive wave of magic rushed out and washed through the two men. In the blink of an eye, the wave had passed, and Lin allowed time to resume.

Smiles took over their stern faces as they continued their walk toward her.

"Stop," Lin said, and they stopped.

"You're unbelievable. You're Lin, right? We were told to go meet you, to take you—"

"Quiet, the both of you. Here's what I need from you. I want you both to remember how much you adore me and how you'd do anything for me. But you must hide that. Keep it our little secret, okay?"

"Yes, of course, Lin," said the other man.

"Good. I want you to act as if nothing has changed. Behave as you ordinarily would, even if that means being rough with me. When the time comes, I'll have other work for you both to do. Do you understand?"

"Anything you want, Lin," said the first man in his normal, gruff voice.

"Good. Take me wherever you were instructed. Do as you were told by your boss. Let's go."

* * *

Lin rode the freight elevator down with her newest converts. None of them spoke a word, and the men watched her, like guards would do and just as Lin had instructed them. The camera up in the corner would reveal nothing out of the ordinary to whomever watched.

The elevator doors slid open, and the guards led her into a bright hallway that smelled clean and fresh. She looked in both directions and saw that there were turns at each end. I'd better not get lost down here, she thought.

Her guards pulled her to the right, and she counted thirty steps, then right for another twenty, before opening a door on the left. Twenty steps from the elevator, they'd passed a monolithic concrete block on the right side of the hall, and Lin could sense some significance. But the men never slowed or even looked at it.

She shook her arm free and walked into the room, followed by her guards, to see a tastefully dressed woman sitting on the far side of a small table. Her brown hair hung in an orderly clump, and she held a small black dog in her arms. They both looked at her with a controlled curiosity.

"Lin Finity, is it? Please, take a seat. Thank you so much for coming to help us."

One guard closed the door behind him, and they stood on either side, both watching Lin and rarely blinking.

"Yes, my name's Lin. And you are?"

"Anna Kelgina. I am the Assistant Director of The Shield. Please, have a seat." She studied Lin's short skirt and heels and smoothed out her own drab skirt.

Lin brushed her long blond hair back over her shoulders and made a conscious effort to keep her eyes from glowing, even though her mayhem lurked the tiniest distance beneath her surface. She sat and stared at Anna.

"Lin, I do not know what you have heard about our work here, but I would like us to start fresh. I will explain everything I can and answer any questions you have. Does that sound reasonable?"

"You took my daughter. There's nothing reasonable about that or about you. I'd advise you to get to the point while you still can." Lin stared calmly.

Anna leaned back, and her mouth opened silently. She quickly closed it and pushed her glasses up.

"Yes, well, we mean your daughter no harm. I can explain the importance of our work, and I think you will be able to appreciate what we are trying to do. Please forgive us for doing our best to—"

"There will be no forgiving. You want something read? You think I can do it? Fine. Bring it in here."

Lin knew that was likely impossible. She'd reasoned that the Scroll was probably behind that concrete barrier they'd passed. They were terrified of it.

"Um, we cannot bring it in here, but we can certainly bring you to it. And when you read it, Lin, it is very important that you tell us word for word what it says."

"I have no interest in your scroll or whatever is written on it. You can keep it. I'm here only for my daughter. I thought this would be the least bloody way of getting her back."

Again, Anna shrank back and stared at Lin for several seconds with her eyes wide and unblinking.

"Yes, of course. I think we agree completely. I will walk with you and the guards and arrange for the tunnel to be opened. I cannot thank you enough. We are really talking about the Words of God here, Lin."

Lin sneered and shook her head. She figured they were probably deluding themselves and maybe there was nothing even written on the Scroll. But she'd take a look to free her daughter.

"And Ben. Ben better be okay too."

Lin stared directly into Anna's eyes, and Anna flinched, seeing the ferocity that waited only for the slightest provocation to rip it loose.

* * *

Lin, Anna, and the two guards stood to one side of the concrete door. Anna reached inside her jacket, retrieved a key, and handed it to one of the guards.

"Here. Move the block enough for her to go in."

Lin sized up the block and saw that it was taller than her, as wide as its height, and as thick as the length of her forearm. It had no features other than a thick metal hoop embedded in each side just above the floor. Cables led from the hoops to large motors on each side, which were attached to the floor with huge bolts. Lin noticed that the floor had been kept clean all around it, and there were no scratch marks to be seen. It hadn't been moved in many years.

The guard didn't speak, but he turned the key to power on the device. When he pushed a button, the motor whined, and the block scraped across the floor.

Anna and the other guard moved to not remain in front of the opening. She extended toward Lin a pad and a pencil while giving her instructions.

"Please, Lin, copy down the Words onto this paper, will you? Every little detail is important, so please try to capture everything that you read."

Lin never moved to receive the offering, continuing instead to stare into Anna's eyes.

"You can't be serious. If that scroll is so important, take one of the walkie-talkies from these guards, and I'll read the thing to you."

"We cannot. We really cannot. I am not sure I can even explain this properly, but that thing in there drives people mad. Not you, we think, but everyone else."

"So, don't come with me. You stay here, and I'll read it to you."

"No, you do not understand. If any part of our senses is in contact with the Scroll, it has a horrible effect. Looking at it is the worst. It destroys a mind in no time. If you were to speak the Words to me while standing next to the Scroll, I am afraid that is still too direct of a link. I cannot take that chance. Write down the words, and I should be safe reading them."

"Well, that just sounds crazy. You know that, don't you?"

Lin reached out quickly, causing Anna to wince, and took the tablet and pencil.

"Fine, I'll go take a look."

"Thank you, Lin. You might not know it, but you are doing God's work."

"We'll see about that. And lady, if you don't honor our agreement, you'll suffer like you can't even imagine."

Lin allowed her eyes to glow for just a second, causing Anna to take a step back and almost drop her phone.

She began the walk into the dimly lit tunnel, observing that there were no footprints on the dusty floor. The tunnel's rough stone walls curved gradually to the right, making a line of sight from the entrance to the Scroll impossible. As she neared the tunnel's end, she saw a small table with an odd box resting upon it. She'd counted thirty steps to the table, where she stopped and looked down on it just as she heard the concrete scraping back into place.

Just wonderful, she thought as she placed the note pad and pencil on the table. But she knew those people truly wanted to learn what the Scroll contained, and she felt confident that their goal wasn't to trap her in there. Fear forced them to keep the tunnel sealed.

She looked down on a box about the size of a large microwave oven but only half as tall. It had been built of a material that she didn't recognize, but its glossy surface reminded her of a metal. She imagined it must be quite heavy.

She reached out and ran her hands along the top and then down the sides. It was smooth to the touch and felt warmer than the tunnel air.

Lin tested the weight by squeezing the box from both ends and lifting, having prepared herself for a strenuous effort. The box almost floated up on its own—it had no weight that she could notice.

She put it down gently and stepped back, doing nothing more than staring at it for a few minutes. The enormity of what was about to happen finally hit her. She'd already seen the unusual nature of the box, and she was beginning to believe that its contents might indeed be something she couldn't anticipate.

Lin recalled the stories Gabriel had told her, about staying too close to it and about opening the box. How madness would result to anyone without enough strength. She looked inward, studying her feelings and thoughts and saw that, so far at least, no harm had come her way.

She brushed her hair back over her shoulders, and a look of determination set in her green eyes. With both hands, she lifted the lid off and set it to one side.

Her heart sped up as she gazed upon something more beautiful than she could imagine, something so impossible that it shouldn't exist. Yet there it sat, in the plain interior of the box.

She saw the rollers nearly filling the box's length, and wrapped around them a material, somewhat like paper. But it couldn't be a complete scroll, not the way the material was wound. She knew that if the rollers were continuous, and if there were only two of them as it appeared, then the Scroll couldn't possibly be unwound.

Covering the middle area of the Scroll sat a plain clasp. It was flat and smooth and appeared to be of the same material as the rollers. She reached out and touched the top of it with one manicured finger. It, too, felt warmer than the tunnel air. The secret of the Scroll clearly lay waiting beneath that clasp.

Lin paused again to take inventory of her thoughts and senses. She felt nothing out of the ordinary other than a growing excitement.

It was time to read the Scroll.

Chapter 22 – Madhouses & Messengers

Lin thought back once again to what Gabriel had said. The warning was clear: removing the clasp was potentially the single most destructive act one could take, short of outright death. Losing her mind would be almost immediate. But Gabriel had also warned of opening the box, she remembered, and she still felt fine.

She looked at the clasp from several different angles and noticed that along the back edge, there was a hinge. Apparently, it didn't require that it be removed, only opened.

With both hands, she reached out, grabbing the top section with her left and the bottom with her right, and she carefully pulled them apart. The two parts of the clasp separated with barely any resistance.

Lin stared directly at the mystery of the Scroll, the place where an impossible construction existed.

And she saw that it was completely possible. Of course, she thought, it's just a scroll. It was made to be unrolled and read.

She turned her head to look around the tunnel again, but her eyes felt glued to the Scroll. Up, down, left, right—her vision remained tethered to the perfectly reasonable scroll before her.

And from the corner of her eye, at the extremes of what she could see, there was a commotion. An upheaval. A circus of insanity devouring the rational. A cold fear coiled around Lin's spine as the madness around the edges began to expand, to grow wider, until it filled her view, and she was again able to look around.

The tunnel had become a madhouse. Her footprints in the dust stomped about on their own, and they appeared to be dancing. The stone walls fell toward her like crashing waves but never reached her.

The tablet on the table fluttered open and closed, and each sheet of paper had at least three sides. The lights on the ceiling shined darkness. She could feel her own hair growing—on the inside—and squirming like snakes. Her pounding heartbeats felt like shattering glass. And when she raised her hands, she saw—

Lin shuddered and locked her vision on the Scroll, which sat in perfect calm, plausible in every way. While all around, an unimaginable nightmare welcomed her, just waiting for her to join it.

She felt a swarm of screams boiling up, straining to break loose. But she clamped them down, refusing to ride them into delirium. She fought to focus inside herself and not succumb to the horror clawing at her from every side.

Lin searched for and found the stillness deep within her, and there, she found her intent.

She focused on the unbreakable hold she had on her intent.

With every tiniest part of her life, she held her intent.

Feeling only stillness, she quietly held her intent.

For how long, she could not know . . . she held her intent . . .

. . . and the tumult began to recede. Walls became still and the tablet ordinary paper. Lights shined on footprints in the dust, and her hair draped down over her shoulders. She felt a normal heartbeat. And her hands were . . . only hands.

Lin saw at the same time that the Scroll couldn't possibly be unrolled, and still, it would open like any other scroll. She accepted the contradiction. And her world remained.

She took a step back, looked around the tunnel again, and took note of her thoughts. They still seemed sensible. With the tight hold on her intent, she focused on her mayhem, and she felt it begin to rise. Everything felt normal, even the green glow that had ignited in her eyes.

With her mayhem rising, everything before her became a calm surface, the world in which she lived. And below that, even though she knew that she saw things only how her mind dictated, she saw endless mountains and valleys of churning, chaotic magic.

Again, she focused on the Scroll.

And she gasped at the sight.

There was no Messenger Scroll.

Lin saw the Scroll. *And* the Messenger.

"Who are you?" said Lin.

"I am Renato. I have been trusted with the Words by my Queen. I have not forgotten them. Who are you?"

"I'm Lin. How is this even possible?" she said, her green eyes glowing down on the Messenger.

"My Queen is very powerful. I have been transformed to carry the Words."

"But how do you exist? How can you survive this way?"

"I do not know. But I do survive. I am happy, Lin."

"How long have you been like this?"

"I cannot know. It seems only yesterday that I last saw my Queen. I have spoken the Words only once before."

Lin found herself unable to speak. The Scroll's true nature must not have been known by anyone, she concluded. Even Gabriel didn't know. She swept her hair back, and her eyes glowed even more brightly. The more her mayhem rose up, the more she saw Renato in his human form.

"Renato, how can you be happy like this?"

"I am happy to honor my vow to my Queen. There is no other path for me."

"Your queen has been gone a long time. Must you remain this way forever?"

"No. I have only one lifetime. I am living a small part of it with you."

Despite her mayhem revealing infinity in every direction and the fearlessness that it brought, Lin shook inside at the unimaginable power over the magic she witnessed. She didn't quake from fear. Only respect. And awe. Her heart wanted to race at seeing how much power was possible. But she stayed focused on Renato.

"Renato, I didn't mean to ask if you'd live forever. I want to know if you'd like to be human again? If there were a way that—"

"My Queen said there would be no way to return to what I was. I accepted that. I will happily continue to do as my Queen has asked."

"But if you tell me the Words, I can be the source of the Words for whoever wants to know them. You wouldn't need to be a scroll."

"I was told that can never happen."

Several seconds passed in silence.

"The last person to read your words . . . did he meet you, like I'm doing now?"

"No. When I spoke the Words, he believed that he read them. He saw only a scroll."

Lin shook her head and said, "Renato, that can't be. We know that he could do unbelievable things."

"And you cannot?"

Lin paused and stared into the box.

"I can do *some* things. But not like that."

"Yet *you* see me."

Lin closed her eyes and held the table with both hands. When her trembling began to lessen, she looked again at Renato. And the Scroll. She straightened up and took a step back.

"Tell me the Words, Renato, please. You can trust them with me."

Renato began reciting the Words slowly and deliberately as Lin committed them to memory. They weren't at all what she'd expected. She'd anticipated a message of hope, despite what Gabriel had told her. How could the Words of God not inspire hope?

When Renato had finished, Lin stepped toward the box and asked again.

"Renato, if there were a way, would you choose to be a man again? Only a man?"

He didn't answer quickly. Lin sensed his struggle.

"If it were possible, Lin, I would like to be just a man again. I cannot describe to you the comfort I feel here as a scroll. I could easily remain this way for all my seasons. There is endless magic here.

"But feeling sunshine on my skin is a powerful magic too."

* * *

Lin replaced the lid, grabbed up the blank tablet and pencil, and hiked down the hall to face the concrete barrier. She could plainly see that there could be no conversation through the door, so she pressed the intercom button.

"Remove the barrier."

"Lin, how do you feel?"

"I feel fine. Now, move the block."

"Do you have the Words?"

"I do."

Lin heard the faint whine of the motor through the concrete, and within seconds, the block had slid to her right, leaving an opening only wide enough to reach through.

"Very good, Lin. Just pass the tablet through so we can verify it."

"No. Move the block."

"We need to see the written Words, Lin. Surely you must understand."

Lin shook her hair back over her shoulders, and her eyes continued to glow.

"*You* must understand that you're in danger if you don't move the concrete."

Anna backed away from the opening and looked to the guards on either side of her, then back through the opening. They had only looked back at her blankly.

"Do you think the guards can protect you if I get angry?"

"I do not know, but I feel better with you behind that block for now. Please, Lin, just let me see the Words."

Lin stood still, feeling her breathing slow and steady and magic billowing up into her from the bottomless depths. Her eyes glowed with an intense green, and she threw the tablet to the floor.

"Guards," she said, "it's time. I want to get out of this tunnel."

Instantly, one guard grabbed Anna from behind with one hand over her mouth; her muffled screams would be heard by no one. Ozzy was tossed to the floor, and he cringed silently against the wall. The other guard pressed the button and began dragging the barrier aside.

Just as the slack in the cable tightened, and the concrete had begun to grind across the floor, and Lin knew she'd soon be out of the tunnel, she heard both guards groan, and their bodies hit the floor. Seconds later, Anna's face appeared in the narrow opening. She looked in on Lin's glowing eyes, and her voice shook.

"Lin, we have taken precautions. The guards, *your* guards, are unconscious. We do not understand what you do, but we learned from the events in the diner that you can control people. Everyone here is wearing a shock collar, and it is turned up high enough to knock us out."

"You know that I can kill you as easily as taking my next breath, don't you?"

"Yes, I know that. But that will not get you out of the tunnel."

Lin took a step back and allowed her mayhem to recede. She felt trapped, and the rage that went with it, but she knew that Anna spoke the truth. Killing her wouldn't help.

"Then, I'll make you move the block."

"I am being watched. I will get shocked and knocked out too."

She let her mayhem disappear altogether, and her eyes returned to their usual shade of green. Her rage could wait, she thought.

"Who's watching you?"

"I am, Lin," said a voice over the intercom. "My name's Lancaster Wolfe. I'm Director of The Shield. Nice disguise. You're a lot different than before."

"Before what?"

"Last time I had to deal with you."

"What the hell are you talking about?"

"Go ahead and play dumb. I'm onto your tricks—that's all you need to know."

"You sound like a fool. Do you really want me as an enemy?"

"No, not at all," said Wolfe. "We can be allies, if you can find it in yourself to see it that way. Let's do it right this time, okay? We both want your daughter released safely. And the gentleman that was with her, too, of course."

Lin's silent thoughts were interrupted by Wolfe.

"In case you're wondering, no, you can't take control of me. I've studied the reports, and I believe I know how far your power reaches. I don't understand it, and maybe you don't either, but I doubt it can reach me. I know what you've done in Erie, near New Galilee, and on Jericho Road. Even in Allentown. Your reach is increasing, but it won't make it this far. I'm at ground level. You're seventeen stories underground."

Lin's heart sank. She knew she was trapped. Physically trapped, unlike the emotional trap in which her uncle Ray had ensnared her. And her mayhem wouldn't get her out of it.

"Fine. What do you want, Wolfe? The Words?"

"Yes, that's all I want. Just like last time."

"Last time?"

"Just the Words. Then, you can go do whatever it is you hope to do this time."

"Sure, you'll let me go. Or maybe once you have them, you'll find a way to kill me. Or leave me here until I die."

"I only want the Words, Lin."

"And you'll get them after you let me out. The Words are obviously important to you. It might be a long time before anyone else comes along that can survive them."

"I can be very patient."

"Two-thousand more years?"

Lin noticed the pause. That got to him, she thought. She let the silence drag on.

"Your daughter needs more medical care than we can provide here. I suggest you make a decision soon. I won't claim that I can wait two-thousand years, but neither can your daughter."

"This won't end well for you, Wolfe." Lin switched off the intercom.

"Anna, do you want to die for this? I'm considering killing you whether it gets me out of here or not."

"I believe in what we are trying to do, Lin, but I might have chosen other methods. Please do not kill me. I want you and your daughter safe, but I also want the Words. They are the Words of God, Lin. Damn it, you have to know how important that is . . . to all of us."

"That Wolfe character probably doesn't care if you live or die."

"Yes, I know. I wish there were another way."

"You better figure it out. Soon. Neither one of us knows what you're awakening in me now . . ."

*   *   *

Lin walked back to stand in front of the table at the end of the tunnel. She looked at it a moment, not knowing what exactly she sought. She focused her intent and raised her mayhem. She saw infinity spreading around her in every direction, and she rejoiced in seeing massive, thick fields of magic below, twisting and turning in eternal chaos. With eyes glowing, she removed the lid with both hands.

"Lin, I am happy to see you again. How long has it been?"

Lin struggled to grasp Renato's predicament. Time had no meaning for him.

"I've only been gone a short time, Renato. You really can't tell the passage of time, can you?"

"No. It could have been many more seasons. Magic is timeless. Magic can be madness too. Are we still in the desert lands?"

"There are no deserts here, Renato. Did you live in the desert with your queen?"

"We lived on islands, but the islands were dying. They were sinking into the ocean. Before I spoke the Words to the man, I heard him speak to his father about a desert. That seems like only moments ago, Lin."

"I think that was a lot longer ago than you can imagine, Renato. And you're not in the desert anymore."

"Is he with you? Can I see him again?"

"No, I'm sorry. He died long ago. You must have seen so much of the magic. Do you understand how everyone else can see you only as a scroll?"

"I did not at first, but now I do. I can see the real world, where you live, and I can see the magic. I see both at the same time."

"But how do you stay there, able to see both?"

"It became clear to me. My spirit has been reshaped. My magic has been reshaped by my Queen. My spirit is part man, part scroll now. In the world, I am seen as a scroll. In the magic, I am a human. I can no longer be just one or the other. My Queen was very strong."

Lin remembered her experience in the parking lot, when she'd unconsciously killed the two men by grabbing hold of their magic. It had been more of a reflex, and she didn't have a clue how to focus her intent on such an act.

"Renato, do you believe your magic can be reshaped once more so that you would be completely a man again?"

"I do not know, Lin. But I feel different since I met you. I believe you are changing me in some small way."

"But I'm not doing anything. I'm only talking to you."

"Yes, but you are with me as a scroll in the world, and you are also with me as a man in the magic. I believe to anyone else, I can be only one or the other. You are reminding me of being a man. Less like a scroll."

"My mayhem must be affecting you . . ." Lin thought out loud.

"Tell me, Renato, how did your queen reshape your magic? Could you feel it happening?"

"I do not understand anything about magic. But yes, I felt it happening. All that I knew of the world around me ran together and nothing made sense. There was no firm ground for me. I remember howling like a madman, but the sounds were far away. I was very scared."

"Your senses ran together? That's what you felt?"

"Yes, and I felt like some part of me was being squeezed, some part that I never noticed before. It happened quickly, and then I became a scroll."

Lin felt more shifting inside herself. Other parts breaking loose. A new arrangement forming. She allowed her mayhem to recede and began the short walk back to the concrete barrier.

Chapter 23 – Hot Shadows & Homes

Jack pulled back his wavy brown hair and tucked it under a ball cap before looking over at Gabriel, who was lost in a nap.

"Gabriel, wake up. It's been hours since Lin left. And I still can't believe you told her to turn herself in to those maniacs."

Gabriel woke slowly and turned to look at Jack.

"Jack, it's really the only way. You probably won't believe this, but I assure you that Lin will be fine."

"How can you possibly know that? Those people are crazy."

"She's special, Jack, and even she doesn't know how much power she has. Believe me, she'll be fine."

"Just how do you know her anyway?"

"We met many years ago back in St. Simons Island. We've been friends ever since, but I like to stay mostly private. She's respected that and not talked about me."

"It's just a little difficult, you know? I never heard of you or her daughter. I feel like I don't really know her sometimes."

"You know her, Jack. You know her in the best way. Taylor and I don't make her who she is."

Lee had been sitting against the wall, only half asleep, and she stood and stretched. She'd removed her leather jacket long before, and her straight black hair fell almost to her waist. Jack couldn't help but notice her lean, muscular figure as she walked over to dig into another breakfast bag.

"You don't say much, Lee. What is it you want from Lin?"

Lee only looked at Jack calmly as she continued to chew.

"I just need to talk to her. I know she's special, and I want to ask her about some things, that's all."

"How do you stay in such great shape?" said Jack.

"I just do. This is how I want to be."

"But don't you have to work hard at that? I can't believe you're eating all this fast food."

"I used to have to be careful but not anymore. Let's just say that I've figured some things out."

Gabriel sat quietly, listening closely to Lee.

"But you look like a bodybuilder or something. And you don't do anything special to stay that way."

"Oh no, I do something special. Something I learned along the way."

"Lee," said Gabriel, "what exactly do you want with Lin?"

"Right now, I want to make sure she's safe. We should figure out a way to help her."

"She can handle herself," said Gabriel.

"I'm with Lee. I think we should go help her any way we can. I know those people are kind of vicious, but I don't care. We need to get Lin back. And Taylor and Ben too. Gabriel, she told you where she was going, didn't she?"

"Yes, Jack, but—"

"Just tell us, Gabriel. If you're really her friend, you'll help us help her."

Gabriel wrote down the address and handed it to him.

"Good luck. You might need it, but Lin won't."

Jack could barely hide his disappointment with Gabriel. He expected some level of help, but none was offered.

"I guess it's you and me, Lee. I need to make a run for some supplies. I'll be back soon. Just hold tight."

* * *

"Take the elevator and come up here, Anna. We need to talk strategy."

"Okay, I will be right up."

Anna rode the long distance in silence, not knowing what to expect from Wolfe. But she felt an odd sensation, an anticipation of what might happen. What might be expected of her. Just as the door began to open to the filthy room, she realized that her hands were on herself, and the surprise caused her to jerk her arms straight down.

"Good, I see you left that dog down below. I need your complete attention for myself."

"Of course, Mr. Wolfe. We have a problem down there with Lin. She is not handing over the Words. And she terrifies me."

"Yes, she's really something. But so are you. Don't be afraid."

Wolfe had moved in close, and with his right hand, he brushed her hair aside as he leaned in and kissed her. She didn't resist.

"Mr. Wolfe, I do not know if—"

"You did good by calling me right away. I'm always close for you, my Anna."

"But, Mr. Wolfe, did we not just—"

"And I still have need of you."

She heard her own feeble protest and felt she'd met her obligation. His presence seemed dark, even within the mostly dark room. He seemed more hot shadow than human, and she felt herself falling into his darkness. He grabbed her wrists and held them near her hips, pressing them against the cold brick wall. Her breaths were slow and measured, and she only awaited his instructions.

His directions were quite clear, spoken with a calm, authoritative voice that she suspected never failed to get his desired result. He freed her wrists, and she turned as she'd been told, placing one hand against the rough bricks while the other pulled at her skirt.

His darkness seemed to fill her, and she knew she could never resist him.

* * *

Jack had left, and Lee found herself alone with Gabriel.

"You eat almost as much as me, Lee. How do you manage that?"

"It's a private thing. I don't think you'd understand."

"I understand Lin. I'd probably understand you too."

"What exactly do you understand about Lin?"

"I'd like to know about you first. You've stopped aging, haven't you?"

Lee felt like she'd been punched in the gut. They'd only met a short while ago. How could Gabriel know that?

"What? That's nonsense. What the heck are you talking about?"

"I've watched you. Every time you eat, you stop for a few seconds and close your eyes. What are you doing?"

She stared into Gabriel's eyes, not knowing what to say or how much to trust.

"Before you deny your nature again, let me tell you that I understand what Lin does. I'm her best friend. You might find that I can be a good friend to you as well."

Lee had longed for a friend that truly understood her ever since she'd learned how things work. But there had been no one she could trust. She'd hoped Lin could be that person. Could Gabriel be trusted? She decided it might be worth a try. She figured Gabriel couldn't hurt her anyway.

"Alright, Gabriel, here it is. I've learned how to keep myself healthy. I've even healed myself. I struggled for a long time until I learned how. You can't imagine how difficult it's been."

"Maybe I can. I understand how hard life can be. What were you struggling with?"

"I was born with serious medical problems, things that the doctors couldn't fix."

"So, you fixed the problems yourself?"

"Not right away. I only knew I couldn't let them beat me. And they didn't. I won that battle."

"How?"

Lee felt she'd already said too much, but she had to admit to herself that it felt good to tell someone. She'd fought a war inside and won, but it had also brought isolation from a story she could tell no one.

"Beginning when I was really little, I looked inside, and I tried to imagine I could see what needed to be fixed. I didn't understand what all was wrong with me. And even if I understood what people told me, I could never have figured out how to fix any of it. I knew enough to know that I'd never know enough."

She looked into Gabriel's eyes and saw a calmness, an acceptance, and she continued.

"There was a big turning point when I was seven. I decided to not try to figure out all of my anatomy. Instead, I started to view my body like it was part of a dream. I'd close my eyes and try to find a place where I felt better. I eventually did. It's a peaceful clearing in a quiet valley. The grass is thick and very green, and there's a clear sky and bright sun above me. After I found that place, whenever I look inside, that's where I go. It didn't take long before it felt like home. I think of it as home.

"But just going there didn't help. I felt that I needed to do something while I was there. I needed to fix myself somehow. But how? It still felt like it was just a dream.

"At first, I tried to smooth down all the grass to point it all in one direction. It looked beautiful except for the footprints I was leaving in it. And when I came out of the dream, I felt more hopeful, but nothing had really changed.

"That went on for a long time, and I knew I had to try something else. I saw a smooth white rock off to one side of the clearing. It's about as big as a softball. I put it at the center of the grassy area, and I just looked at it for a long time. I sensed it had some importance, and I spent years just looking at it. But again, nothing really changed in my life.

"Eventually, I saw several more rocks in different areas of the grass, and I was surprised I'd never noticed them before. I gathered them up, and I counted forty of them altogether. I piled them all up. And I even smoothed the grass to point away from the rocks, then toward the rocks, then all in one direction, but nothing seemed to work. More years went past.

"Then, I don't know why, but I felt something change in me. I knew that piling the rocks would never work. So, I arranged them all in a circle. It looked beautiful there in the grass under a perfect blue sky. I must have looked at that circle for a year, and still, it never helped me.

"So, I tried different arrangements. I put the stones in a square, then a triangle, even one circle inside another. Nothing worked, and I was getting desperate. My illnesses were getting worse.

"I knew I was dying, Gabriel. But I wouldn't let death take me. Not then. I wasn't done trying.

"I went back to my home, too ill to even think straight. I felt I was in a trance. My mind had stopped. There were no more thoughts. I felt something shifting inside me, and I watched my own hands arrange the stones in a figure eight.

"I expected nothing, but I got everything I ever wanted. I felt it immediately. If you can imagine a million million puzzle pieces all coming together at once. I felt all the pieces moving, and then, after they'd all lined up, they all snapped together at the same time.

"I left my home, and I could feel that I'd been healed. I'd healed myself. It took many years to learn it, but the figure eight is the key."

Gabriel showed no surprise and no emotion. Lee marveled at that, knowing that what she'd just said must sound like nonsense.

"And after you eat, Lee, you go back to that place? To your home?"

"Yeah, I go back to my home. And I see that some of the stones are moved from where they should be. Not much, but I can tell. It doesn't take me long. I set them in the proper arrangement. A figure eight."

"Lee, that's not an eight. That's infinity."

"What do you mean, 'infinity?'"

"That shape that you're making—it's the symbol for infinity."

"So? Who cares what it's called? I'm only arranging those stones."

"Those aren't stones, Lee. That's your physical body. That's how you've learned to see it."

Lee stared without saying a word.

"And your sun, Lee. In your home. It's not the same as our sun, is it?"

"I've said too much already. I—"

"What color is it?"

Lee's eyes opened wide, and she moved her mouth, but she didn't speak.

The rattle of a key in the door told them that Jack had returned.

*   *   *

"Mr. Wolfe, I have never—"

"We need to focus back on our work, Anna. You've spoken with Lin. What are her weak points? How can we coerce her into handing over the Words?"

"She scares me, Mr. Wolfe. She—"

"Just call me Wolfe."

"Wolfe." Anna repeated it and felt something warm her inside. She felt as if she'd growled the name.

"Wolfe, she is impossible to push around. I saw her eyes glowing, and the only reason she did not kill me was because that would not free her from the goddamn tunnel. Otherwise, she would not have hesitated one second."

Wolfe paused and rubbed his chin, looking around the dim room. He focused his gaze back on Anna.

"What about her daughter? How concerned is Lin with the girl's safety?"

"She is very concerned. But she is not convinced that you will ever let her daughter go anyway. And Wolfe, I get the impression that even if you let them both go, Lin will come back for us."

"We don't want that, Anna. So, let's just treat her nice. Go talk to her. Move the stone, and let her out. I'll bring the elevator back up and lock it, and I'll be watching too. Maybe that way she'll feel more like she can trust us."

Anna shook her head back and forth slowly, and her eyes were open wide.

"She scares me, Wolfe. And maybe whatever is on the Scroll is not that important. Maybe they are not the Words of God."

"No, that's exactly what they are. And I need to know every word of it," he said with his voice rising. "Don't ever say again that they're not the Words of God. Those *are* the Words of God. On that goddamn Scroll!"

Wolfe paused and rubbed his hands over his face.

Shaking and staring into her eyes, he continued. "The Words *must* have a message of hope. For everyone, Anna. Not just the sheep, doing as they're told. Following those ridiculous rules. Our choices change us, Anna. Even me. *My* choices. So long ago . . ."

He broke his gaze into Anna's eyes and stared at the cracked brick wall above her head.

In a voice that could barely be heard, he said, "I need to know . . . if there's still hope . . ."

"I . . . I do not understand, Mr. Wolfe. You make it sound like life or death, and—"

His eyes burned into hers.

"What do you know of death, Anna?"

He locked a set of hot fingers around her throat.

"Or even life?"

He leaned in until their eyes were inches apart. Anna couldn't breathe.

"Go. Do as I command. And do not fail me."

He released her.

Chapter 24 – Fantasies & Summaries

Jack swung the door open and walked in, carrying two plastic bags from a sporting goods store. And two bags from a bakery. He handed one of them to Gabriel and the other to Lee. They both got started on chocolate cupcakes.

"I don't get you two. I really don't."

Gabriel and Lee looked at each other while continuing to chew. Gabriel shrugged.

"Okay, I picked up some basic stuff. Flashlights, pocket knives, stun guns, and some pepper spray. And some walkie-talkies too. I don't know what we're going to need. I hope this stuff helps."

"It'll be fine, Jack," said Lee. "For all we know, by the time we get there, Lin might have been released. Why don't we just pack up and head out?"

"Yeah, I'm sure you're right. Let's do what you said. I put some gas in the truck, too, so we're good to go."

"Gabriel," said Lee, "we need to continue that conversation, alright?"

"Yes, Lee. Be safe, the both of you."

Jack stared at Gabriel for several seconds before shaking his head and walking out with Lee.

* * *

"I can open the door myself, Jack."

"I know. Just being polite."

Jack slammed Lee's door, climbed in, and got his truck headed for Baltimore.

"Lee, I don't mean to be nosy, but why exactly are you here? What do you want with Lin?"

Jack waited for a response, but he saw from the corner of his eye that Lee had reached into the bag for the last of the cupcakes.

"Alright, even more importantly, how is that you can eat all that junk? My God, you're in fantastic shape. I don't get it."

Lee rested the hand holding what remained of a cupcake on her lap and turned to Jack.

"Jack, about the food. That's hard to explain. It's just something I learned along the way. I think I just know how to make it work. I know how I want to look, how I want to feel, and I make it happen.

"And about your first question. About why I'm here. I saw Lin do something back in Jacksonville. I need to understand what she does and how she does it. Somehow, she seemed familiar to me. Like we both know something. A secret.

"We need to get her out of there."

"You think you two have something in common? Do you think you can do the same things as she can? The same things?"

Visions of the night with Lin in St. Simons Island invaded Jack's mind, followed quickly by memories of what she'd done with him more recently. He shook himself out of his daydream and knew he loved Lin. Only Lin.

"I don't know, Jack. Maybe."

He stared straight ahead and fought to focus only on the road.

*　*　*

"Yes, I know you're back. I heard the elevator."

Anna peered through the narrow opening into the tunnel with her eyes wide and unblinking. She was greeted by a direct stare from Lin, whose eyes were a normal shade of green.

170

"As a show of good faith, I am letting you out of the tunnel. I know you could kill me from in there, so I hope this does not cause you to do anything rash. Please, we can just talk. I do not want to die for this."

"Fine. Move the concrete."

Anna had brought another guard with her.

"Let me keep this guard, okay, Lin? I need him to get these bodies out of here."

"Bodies?"

"Yes. It seems these collars can kill too."

After several minutes of hearing the guards dragged off to some other room, Lin heard the motor start and begin to move the block. A second later, she heard the new guard groan, and the block froze in place. It had moved only an inch.

"Lin, I've changed my mind," Wolfe said over the intercom. "I pride myself on my negotiating abilities, and since you're a captive audience, I'd like you to hear this offer."

Lin felt her mayhem rise a small amount, and Anna took a step back at the sight of her eyes glowing.

"I'm listening," said Lin.

"It's simple. Give Anna a summary, in your own words, of what's written on the Scroll. Tell her enough that we understand the basic message. You must understand that right now, we have no idea what's written there. After that, when you're on ground level and free to leave, I'd like you to tell us all of the Words."

"There's nothing written there, but the Messenger told me the Words."

The intercom remained silent for a full ten seconds.

"Lin, I don't understand."

"No, you really don't."

Lin switched off the intercom and walked back to the opening.

"Okay, write this down."

Anna scrambled to get out a pad and pencil and waited for Lin to continue.

"Just remember that we are being watched. I hope this is not a trick, because now I know Wolfe can kill me with this damn thing around my neck. And Lin, I want you to know that the elevator is locked at ground level."

Lin glared at her through the crack but accepted the situation.

"Lin, I said Wolfe is watching, and he is. But he is not listening. We can speak freely."

"I have little interest in what you have to say. I'm here for Taylor and Ben. You and your boss can go to hell."

"I understand," said Anna. "But we really do need to know what is written on the Scroll. And I will be honest with you. I do not know if Wolfe will set you free even if you tell him the Words. I do not want to die, and I do not want you to die either. Please just do as he says—tell us what is on the Scroll."

"You really don't understand, neither of you. He's a Messenger, and his name is Renato. He told me the Words."

"What are you talking about? Who is Renato? You are not making any sense."

Lin laughed. "Yes, now you get it. There's no 'sense' involved."

"I . . . I do not—"

"Just get ready to write, okay?"

Anna looked up from her paper and met Lin's stare. She nodded her head meekly.

Lin continued staring into Anna's eyes as she said, "Your lives are meant to be hard. You are all here to suffer and find joy too . . . if you can. Don't waste your time praying. No help is coming. No one is even listening."

Anna shook as she wrote Lin's words on the tablet. When she'd finished, she looked up, and her eyes showed a desperation that caused Lin to feel some sympathy. Until she remembered that she was still a prisoner.

"There, that's my summary. Take it to your cowardly boss. You'd be wise to release me now. This tunnel won't hold me forever."

Anna backed away from the opening with her mouth open, shaking her head slowly.

"But, Lin, that cannot be right. That is what you read? That is what is on the Scroll?"

"You're not listening. There's nothing 'on' the Scroll. The Messenger told me God's Words."

Lin watched as tears welled up in her captor's eyes before she moved out of her sight. Anna slowed only to take the key back from the guard's hand. Seconds later, Lin heard the elevator doors open and close, then no more sounds.

Many minutes passed before Wolfe spoke through the intercom.

"Lin, listen up. I like your summary. From what you've told me, there's no hope. Not for anyone, no matter what. That's a relief! But your summary is not enough. I need all of the Words, exactly as they're written. I need every stinking little detail of what God had to say."

"You're a liar and a coward. I expect you to honor our deal. You have the summary. And you seem to like it. Why, God only knows."

"Yes, he damn well does."

"What the hell are you talking about?"

"I need the exact Words. All of them. Until you wise up, you'll stay in the tunnel. I urge you to do exactly as I tell you. You might find that you like it. Remember that we both want what's best for your daughter."

Lin heard Wolfe switch off the intercom. With their conversation over, and Anna gone as well, Lin walked back to the tunnel's end. Back to the Scroll.

She found her intent, and instantly, she saw the calm surface of reality spreading to infinity in every direction. Below that, massive mountains of magic writhed and twisted in endless chaos. With glowing eyes, Lin opened the clasp.

"I'm back, Renato. It's been only a few minutes."

* * *

They'd driven in silence for several hours and had just reached the outskirts of Baltimore. Jack's old pickup didn't have a GPS unit, so he relied on Lee serving as a copilot with a map on her lap.

Jack welcomed having the excuse of looking over at the map, when in reality, he couldn't help himself from looking at Lee's thighs straining against the thin denim. Her talk of having powers like Lin's had captivated him. He felt powerless to whatever powers she had. But he loved Lin. He knew that to be true. But—

"We're almost there, Jack. Just take a right over here and park along the road. We can walk the last quarter mile."

"Yes, you're right. That sounds good."

He parked, and they made sure they had their modest equipment secure in their pockets. They climbed out into the chilly air and began their walk toward the address Gabriel had given them.

Jack invited Lee to take the lead. Not because she was the leader, but because he wanted to enjoy the view. He barely noticed the decrepit buildings adorned with broken windows behind metal grating as he stumbled along, watching only Lee.

Her short leather jacket left a lot for him to see, and he couldn't stop imagining Lee taking control of him in whatever way she could. He knew he'd never be able to stop her. He didn't even know if he'd want to be able to stop her. It wouldn't be his choice, not his fault—

"Jack, there's the place we're looking for across the alley. I see one . . . no, two guards standing outside the door. Let's hold back and observe a while. We need some kind of plan. We can't just charge in there."

He returned from his daydream, saying, "Yeah, you're right. That's what we should do. Let's sit tight and see if an opportunity presents itself. Like you said."

They found a small area out of sight behind a large trash container.

"That's Lin's car right there behind the red one," Jack said, pointing at Lin's Temt8tion.

The two guards stood motionless outside the door. Jack and Lee settled in and waited.

Chapter 25 – Rage & Focus

Ben shook off the last of the drugs they'd pumped into him and looked around his room. Zip ties held his wrists to the arms of a solid wooden chair. They were tight, and even without him struggling, they'd begun to dig into his skin. He looked from one side to the other and saw that his ankles were also restrained the same way.

The room held nothing of any obvious use. A small conference table sat in the middle beneath a dim, recessed ceiling light. Anna had left her coffee mug on the table, and Ben could see traces of her lipstick on the plain white. His own chair sat in the corner farthest from the door. He looked for any signs of surveillance cameras and found none.

He'd lost track of time, but he knew that no more could be wasted. They had Taylor, the one he'd sworn to protect. And they wanted to somehow take Lin too. The two most important people in his life. He needed to free Taylor and find a way to protect Lin. And then, he'd deal with anyone involved in Taylor's capture. He vowed he'd make them pay dearly.

He looked down at his right wrist, where the zip tie had already worn a groove in his skin. He pulled against it, testing it, and he found that even his strength probably wouldn't be enough to snap it. He quickly concluded that sliding his hand through the loop was the only option.

Even a gentle pull caused skin on his wrist to bunch up behind the thick plastic strip.

Ben paused and thought of Lin. Their time together in their youth. His feelings for her then and still. And how she'd saved his very soul in Allentown.

He thought of Taylor. The few precious moments they'd shared. How he wished he'd had a daughter of his own. How Taylor deserved a better life even if he couldn't be a part of it.

And then he began to pull in a serious way.

He didn't need to look and only stared straight ahead. He felt the skin bunch up, and the strip began to cut in. He didn't hesitate, and the strip dug in deep. He laughed out loud at the realization that the blood actually helped the raw meat of his wrist slide under the plastic as his skin was peeled back.

But he stopped laughing when he'd gotten as far as the joint of his thumb. Without looking down, he knew that the worst was yet to come. He thought of Lin. He thought of Taylor. And he pulled with all his strength, feeling the zip tie sharp against the bone. And he felt his pants soaking up blood beneath it.

With images of Lin and Taylor in his mind, so real that he felt they were there watching him, encouraging him, he found more strength and pulled. His bone met the unyielding plastic strip and refused to go farther. But he continued to pull. He searched for and found yet more strength as the blood continued to splatter onto his lap and across the floor.

With the desperation of a wild animal in the jaws of a trap, and with his heart racing, Ben pulled even harder. And he finally felt the strip weaken and then break.

He still didn't look down. What had happened to his wrist and hand were of no consequence. He'd worry about it later.

But Ben knew he might not be able to do that with his other wrist. He accepted that even he had limits. There had to be another way. And he saw what he needed there on the table. He sat, listening to the steady drip, and let his heart slow down.

It didn't take long, rocking the chair side to side, before it fell over to his left. The impact was harder than he'd expected, but he'd landed close enough to the table that he could reach its nearest leg with his free hand. He grabbed it tight, and a pool of blood formed below as he lay there and focused for what would come next.

Although his hand throbbed and screamed for him to leave it alone, he gripped the table leg as hard as he could. He imagined his hand around Anna's throat, seeing Anna silenced while her eyes bugged out, and he rotated the table up so its surface leaned toward him. Despite his valiant effort, the coffee mug wouldn't move.

Ben dug down deep inside again, still imagining a death grip on Anna's neck, and he pulled the table up even higher. He heard the mug begin to slide, and he waited as it inched its way to the edge, where it dropped and shattered on the concrete floor. He let the table down softly.

With his bloody hand, he grasped the handle, which had a sharp point still attached, and cut the tie holding his other wrist. After freeing his ankles, he stood and looked down on the mess he'd made. Pools and streaks of blood glistened in the dim light, and more continued to drip from his wounds. He worked his way out of his flannel shirt, leaving only the t-shirt beneath it, and he wrapped it around his hand and wrist.

He held the sharp piece of porcelain in his left hand and tested the door, finding that it was locked. So, he took a deep breath and stood ready. He had only one objective, and that was to cut to death anyone that walked through that door. Anyone except Lin or Taylor. Through the pain and weakness, he fought to remember their images as his quiet, murderous rage settled in.

* * *

"Renato, please tell me more about what happened to you. Tell me as much as you can remember."

"Yes, Lin, I am happy to tell you. You remind me of my Queen. She was beautiful too.

"There was a ceremony high in the tower. Many important people were there, and I felt I was not worthy of so much attention. But my Queen had selected me. I felt honored.

"After the ceremony ended and everyone left, I was alone with my Queen. She had given me permission to look directly at her. That alone was a great honor. I looked into her eyes, and I saw that she was tired. And sad.

"Her eyes began to close, and they glowed with a light of their own. I felt something rush through me, and it tingled. I have never felt such happiness, Lin. I adored my Queen. Everything about my life and about the world seemed right. I looked around and saw that even the walls surrounding us had been touched by whatever had touched me. The walls seemed to be like water, shimmering and swirling.

"I looked back into my Queen's eyes and became startled. They glowed brightly, and they were fierce. I became afraid. But the tingling was so comfortable. And the feeling got stronger as her eyes glowed more brightly.

"Then, I saw that the walls had begun to settle. It felt like when I had seen the sea wash over a low part of the island, and it had been forced to rush through a narrow channel. I was that channel. What had been touching the walls all around was now touching only me. All that my Queen had caused became focused on me. I could not even scream any longer."

Lin quaked inside imagining the magical event that had transpired so many centuries before, transforming Renato into something that shouldn't exist. She sensed a lesson in what he'd recounted, almost as if the queen were speaking to her across time. It sounded like she'd sent out a wave, much like Lin's mayhem wave. But she'd focused the wave, narrowing it down, and pouring it all into Renato.

A realization hit Lin with a force and certainty that she couldn't question. Of course, it was so simple. Back in the diner with Gabriel, she'd used her mayhem on the two men, but she hadn't affected anyone else. She'd focused her wave, much like what the queen had done so long ago.

And Wolfe, seventeen stories up, felt confident that her wave couldn't reach him. No, a complete wave could not. But a focused wave? How far might that reach?

"Renato, what happened next? After you felt all the magic focused on you?"

"Oh, Lin, it was something I cannot describe. I could not find the words."

"Please, try. I'm in danger, Renato. Whatever you tell me might help."

"Yes, I will try."

There was a pause, and Lin imagined it would be a good time for Renato to clear his throat. But Renato was no longer flesh and bone.

"As the tingling grew so high that I could barely see the world anymore, I felt as if I had been grabbed. But not my body. Some other part of me. It felt like a hand squeezing me. It did not hurt, but nothing in my life ever felt like that. I felt that whatever made me a man was being changed. I continued to see the world and my Queen, and I also saw unbelievable oceans of magic. A final hard squeeze left me how I have been ever since. I see the world, and I see endless tides of magic. I am a scroll, and I am a man."

Lin's eyes had been glowing so brightly that she saw green reflected off of parts of the Scroll and its box. The tunnel had become barely noticeable, and the fields of magic below flowed in every direction, colliding and mingling and spinning in mad patterns.

She visualized where she stood at the end of a curving tunnel. She knew the length of the tunnel from counting steps. She added to the tunnel the length of the hallway beyond the concrete barrier all the way to the elevator. From there, Lin imagined a distance of seventeen floors above and the room at the top, where she'd converted the two guards. Wolfe was likely right there in that room and near the intercom.

With eyes glowing bright green, Lin took the deepest breath she could, and she held it. All the magic from the chaotic fields below began to flow into her, expanding her and filling her every cell. She felt the sweet pressure of it, the pleasure of swelling full of magic ready to burst and send her life out. How she longed to be part of all that magic, all that wonder.

But it would have to wait. She felt the distance and direction to the room at ground level. She lingered one more moment on the edge of insanity, magic rippling through her, her eyes glowing brightly, and she exhaled sharply while holding the image of that room and Wolfe.

A tight, focused wave rushed out from her through concrete, steel, soil, and anything else the real world could contain. The wave rushed upward, sent to convert Wolfe and bend him to her will.

* * *

But the wave had missed its mark. Wolfe remained safe near the intercom as the wave rushed through one of the guards in the alley outside the door. The guard immediately smiled and relaxed his posture.

"We need to get Lin out of there. She doesn't deserve to be a prisoner down there. C'mon, let's go get her."

"What are you talking about? She's evil, remember? Just do what you were told to do."

"No. No, man, I'd do anything for Lin. If you won't help, then get out of my way before I move you myself."

He reached for the doorknob. A fight ensued, with both guards wrestling first against the door, then down to the ground. Wolfe heard the brawl and looked outside.

"Goddamn it, Lin . . ." he said and bolted the door.

* * *

Lee kept watch of the two guards, and Jack watched Lee. She broke his reverie when she swung her hand back and hit him in the shoulder.

"Jack, something's happening. Look."

They watched as one guard slouched against the brick wall for a second before standing up and talking to his companion. He seemed to be asking him for something as he reached for the doorknob. The other man pushed his hand away from the door, then pushed him away altogether.

"Should we rush them now?"
"No, Jack. Let's see what happens."

Chapter 26 – Scrolls & Men

Lin's eyes continued to glow as she walked to the intercom.

"Wolfe, get in the elevator and come down here."

"No, that's not going to happen, Lin. You see, you missed your mark. You don't own me. You never will."

The light of Lin's eyes flared.

"I'm truly sorry that you, and your daughter, and that other fellow, will remain down there forever. Or at least until it's safe for us to return and drag out your dead bodies."

Lin's eyes glowed more brightly, and she didn't take the time to enjoy the magic in a breath. She focused a narrow distance away from her last target and sent out another tight, sharp wave.

* * *

"Wait," said the second guard. "Wait! I'm on your side. Stop hitting me, alright? I want Lin safe too. I adore Lin even more than you."

"Well, that's not possible, but we can fight about it some other time. Let's go get her."

"Right, we'll have plenty of time for that later."

He turned the knob and pushed, but the door wouldn't open, so he pounded on it. The other guard joined him.

"Goddamn traitors . . . no use to me," Wolfe said as he drew his semi-automatic pistol. He looked through the grimy window at the two men, Lin's two men, knowing he couldn't be seen in the darkness. He watched patiently, noting each man's motion. He observed that they barely moved, and their heads remained mostly in the same locations.

He took a deep breath and let it out slowly. With the pistol raised and pointed at the head on the right, he quietly slipped the bolt free. The guard had quit turning the knob, but they both continued to pound on the door. Wolfe gently rotated the knob, moving the gun to the door's edge and still pointed at the head on the right.

"Time to lose your heads, boys," he said with a smile.

He pulled the door in quickly and fired one shot into the head on the right, then another shot to the head on the left. He stood over both bodies and put another round in each head.

*　*　*

Lee reached back and grabbed Jack's jacket when she saw the door open and both guards were shot. Jack froze alongside her as they watched another man exit the building, shoot both bodies again, then climb into the other car. It started quickly and sped out of the alley, past them in their hiding place, dragging newspapers and plastic bags in its wake.

They rushed over to the door and stood over the dead guards. Jack started to check for pulses, but Lee stopped him.

"Don't waste your time. Get their guns."

He handed one pistol to her, and they entered the dark room. In the faint light, they found Anna huddled down in a corner. She stared at the floor and didn't move, but Lee pointed her pistol anyway.

"Get up."

She didn't look at Lee, but she did rise to her feet.

"Where's Lin?" said Jack.

"Down there," she said and pointed to the elevator doors.

Jack rushed over and hit the button while Lee used her pistol to persuade Anna to accompany them.

After a quiet ride to the bottom, how far down neither Jack nor Lee knew, the doors opened, and all three stepped out into the hallway.

"Where? Tell me where!"

Anna pointed to the right, toward the tunnel. On the way, they found Ozzy still crouching against a wall and whimpering.

"May I?" said Anna.

Lee only gestured with the barrel of her gun, and Anna scooped up her dog.

When they'd gotten as far as the tunnel entrance, Jack saw the huge concrete slab blocking it and the winches connected to it at each side. Anna pointed at one, nodding her head. The cable was still attached, and Jack pressed the button.

"Damn it. Where's the key? Tell me!" said Jack.

"Wolfe has it. The man who just left. The one who just shot those two guards."

"So, how do we move it? It's got to weigh a ton," said Lee.

"Much more than that," said Anna.

"Are there more of you people down here?" said Jack.

"No. Not alive anyway. I was the last. And even if there were, it would not be enough of us to drag that aside."

"Jack?"

He heard Lin's voice through the intercom, and a smile spread across his face.

"Lin! Are you okay? We'll get you out, don't worry."

"Jack, listen to me. I'm fine. I want you to find Taylor and Ben. I believe they're down here somewhere too."

Anna spoke up. "Yes, they are. Lin, this is Anna. Things have not turned out so well. I am so sorry. Wolfe . . . he is a madman. He is possessed. I will take your friends to your daughter."

"That's the most important thing. Make sure Taylor is okay."

Jack smiled and said, "What's a nice Cowgirl like you doing in a place like this?"

"Oh, my Cowboy. You came to my rescue. Find Taylor, Jack. And Ben too."

Anna led Jack and Lee to the end of a hallway, where two doors remained closed, one locked from the outside.

"Taylor is in this room," she said as she turned the knob and led them inside. Jack and Lee followed, with Jack gasping at the sight of Taylor connected to monitors and receiving an IV. She was conscious, but she appeared weary and confused. Jack approached her cautiously.

"Taylor, my name is Jack. I'm a good friend of your mom's. We've come to get you out of here. Do you think you can walk?"

"I don't think so, Jack. I haven't stood on my own in a long time."

"Okay, that's fine. Just don't worry—we'll figure this out. You'll be safely out of here soon.

"Lee, can you wait here with Taylor while I get Ben?"

"Sure, Jack, just take her with you," Lee said, gesturing toward Anna. "And don't trust her."

Jack leveled his pistol at Anna and motioned for her to lead the way. Outside Ben's cell, Jack saw that a large padlock secured the door. He glanced at Anna, who only shrugged her shoulders.

"Alright, let's go back to Taylor's room."

"Taylor, we need to get you out of here. Lee and I will help you, and I promise, you won't have to go far. We'll have you safe in no time."

With Taylor's arms limp over Jack on one side and Lee on the other, and Anna in front with a gun pointed at her, they walked back to the end of the hallway. The three of them sat, and Jack continued walking to the concrete barrier.

* * *

"Jack, are you still out there?"

"Yeah, Lin, I'm right here. Lee is with Taylor. We need to get you out, but I don't know how yet."

"What happened upstairs, Jack? Is Wolfe still there with his guards?"

"It's a mess up there. Wolfe killed them both and took off."

"I think I left him no choice. Jack, give me a few minutes."

Lin felt she was being pulled down a road that she never knew existed. With an unexpected calmness, she walked back to the tunnel's end, feeling her mayhem rising to new levels. She removed the box's lid and opened the clasp. Her bright green eyes greeted Renato.

"I've been away only a few minutes, Renato. I need you to consider your life now. You have done all that your queen has asked of you. The Words are safe in my memory. Do you want to be a man again?"

Renato didn't hesitate.

"Yes, Lin. But I do not know if it is possible. I was told there would be no path home for me."

"What was required of you when you were changed?"

"I was told I needed to offer my unconditional submission to the transformation."

"And how were you able to do that?"

"My Queen made me repeat something many times. The more I said it, the more at ease I felt. I became ready to be changed."

Some part of Lin understood what he meant. Somehow, the chanting had focused Renato. Something inside him had become aligned. Lin knew what to do without knowing how she knew.

"Renato, repeat after me: 'I have done all my Queen has asked. I will be a man for all my remaining days.'"

Renato began repeating Lin's words, tentatively at first, then with more confidence. He continued as her green eyes glowed down on him, and she felt the changes taking place deep inside him, in his magic.

With her mayhem already raging, Lin took in a breath and felt even more magic swelling up into her. She felt the ecstasy of infinity, the longing to break out of her limits and join the magic. Such sweet pleasure, she thought, as she felt herself falling through the sky. And she sharply exhaled.

She focused on Renato's magic with her intent, and the wave carried her there. She felt that she'd wrapped her arms around it. She felt it flowing—timeless streams of magic creating him in every moment. She felt the magic's shape. She sensed a man, and she sensed a scroll. She learned the shape of each.

Lin didn't notice, but the tunnel walls around her had begun to swirl and glimmer.

Without letting go of any of Renato's magic, Lin focused on the shape that made him a man. It was a distinct pattern, a collection of dreams and feelings and hopes no words could ever describe. But she understood it. She held that shape, in whatever gaze she used, and she began funneling all of his magic into the man shape. Renato began to scream. Like a madman.

As Lin pulled the magic tighter, drawing it all down to fit into Renato's human shape, the swirling all around her began to fade. Renato's screaming stopped. In an instant, the walls became completely solid, and she forced all of his magic into Renato's human self.

She staggered and grabbed the table with both hands to support herself, and when her glowing eyes looked down, she saw a young, naked man lying across the table. The box had been cast aside, and no scroll would ever be found. It no longer existed.

Renato opened his eyes, sat up, and looked first at his surroundings, then down at his outstretched hand. A smile spread across his face as he touched his own body and felt that it was real. *He* was real. He laughed out loud, almost hysterically. But not like a madman.

To Lin his laughter was the sweetest thing ever. Despite her weakness she laughed with him, and they shared an embrace.

With her mayhem still blazing, she said, "Let's go, Renato. We're not done yet."

Chapter 27 – Beaches & Alleys

"Are you okay, Renato? I can help you."

"Thank you, Lin, but I do not need help. Only yesterday, I was running along the ocean. But I can help you if you want."

"No . . . let me try."

A slow walk on the dusty floor brought them to the tunnel entrance.

"Jack," Lin said over the intercom. "I need you to back away from the concrete. All of you."

She said no more, and Jack didn't ask. He took a spot at the far end of the hallway, joining Taylor, Anna, and Lee, and choosing to not get between Anna and Lee's pistol.

Behind the concrete barrier, Lin stood with Renato. She looked at the massive slab and wondered how much effort it would demand. She reminded herself that the concrete block, like everything else, was connected to the magic. It didn't matter what size or how much magic. She would have to find the strength.

She let go of Renato's hand and nudged him to the side of the tunnel. She approached the cold concrete and placed her hands against it, and when she closed her eyes, she almost collapsed. With her head hanging forward, she held a hand out to calm Renato's concerns and did nothing but breathe for several minutes. She searched deep inside and found the strength she needed, and she stepped back from the block.

Once again, Lin drew in a deep breath and felt endless currents of magic flowing into her. Though weary, the ecstasy of infinity still captivated her, and a faint smile formed beneath her glowing eyes. She let the breath out gently, confidently. She focused her intent, and like riding a wave, it brought her to the magic of the heavy block—the magic that made it real.

She found that the block possessed a quiet magic, darker than that of a living thing. Even the magic of the Scroll had had some brightness to it. The stone's magic felt still, like deep water that hadn't stirred in ages. Lin felt like her arms were wrapping around the magic, struggling to hold all of it. She felt as though she were stretching, her arms getting thinner, until they finally reached completely around.

Holding the concrete's magic, she discovered that it, too, was creating the block anew in every moment. What a miracle, she thought—even concrete doesn't exist on its own. She celebrated the truth Gabriel had shared: that only magic cannot be created or destroyed. Magic continuously creates even concrete.

Jack and the others sat dumbfounded, staring at concrete that had begun to swirl about within its rigid shape. It appeared to be a liquid, threatening to break through a thin glass sheet.

Ozzy wiggled loose from Anna's careless hold and trotted to the shimmering wall. Jack held Anna back, and they watched as the dog approached the baffling sight. He whimpered as he extended a paw toward the swirling surface.

Lin had the sudden realization that magic was magic, and only the patterns changed. And the patterns determined what form the magic would take in the world of reality.

An image of Renato on his island appeared before her. The sunshine fell on him as he walked along the ocean's edge. Salty water splashing up with every step. Water flowing into his footprints behind him. Water reflecting the hot sunlight. Water sparkling and sloshing, wave after wave after—

She squeezed the concrete's magic with the last of her strength.

Just as Ozzy was about to touch the molten concrete, it became a wall of water. It rested there impossibly for an instant before it collapsed, washing the dog to the far wall and nearly tripping up Lin and Renato. Some of it splashed up, a stray drop landing on Lin's lips, and she tasted salt.

Jack, Lee, Taylor, and Anna stared and said nothing, even as a few streams of water reached them and soaked their clothes.

Lin allowed her mayhem to recede but not disappear, and she stumbled, feeling a weakness like she'd never known before. Renato quickly held her and kept her from falling. Together, they walked out into the wet hallway.

Jack began to speak but stopped at seeing Lin walk out of the tunnel with a naked man. He finally managed to get up and rush over to help her.

"Lin, are you alright?"

"Yes, I think I'm okay, Jack. Just tired. How's Taylor?"

"She's safe. Come on, she's right over there."

He helped her travel down the hall, and she faced her daughter for the first time in years. Lin saw the shock on Taylor's face, and she saw the ravages of her illness too.

"Taylor, I'm so sorry for everything . . ."

"Mom," was all Taylor could say before sobbing took over.

Anna and Lee held Taylor up so she could accept Lin's embrace. Everyone there offered their tears except for Renato and Lee. Renato still grinned, thrilled to be alive again. Lee held her pistol tight, still pointed at Anna, and studied Lin.

"I have a million questions," said Jack, "but they'll have to wait. We need to get Ben out. He's locked in a room. And we need to get out of here. You two can catch up later."

"Take me to Ben," Lin said as she struggled to hold her eyes open.

Jack and Lin walked the short distance and stood outside Ben's cell. He pointed to the padlock, and she nodded.

Despite her extreme fatigue, she raised her mayhem higher. And even in her much-weakened condition, she felt the pleasure of seeing infinity sprawling out in every direction. She didn't bother with a captive breath. After all, she thought with a smile, it was only a lock. She focused her intent, and it took her to the magic of its metal.

Jack stood back and watched her work, her eyes glowing. But they were much more than half-closed, something he'd never seen before. There were only two thin lines of bright green.

She found it took barely any effort to get a grasp on the lock's magic. She felt as if only one hand was enough.

Again, she had an image of Renato walking along his shore so many centuries before. She looked at the sky above him, a dome of bold blue dotted with puffy white clouds. The clouds had a beauty that called to Lin across time. Soft, peaceful, and floating. Just floating. Weightless. She squeezed the lock's magic, and she felt the last of her strength drain out.

Jack looked down to see the metal of the lock swirling and shimmering before it changed to a puff of white smoke. He looked back at Lin just as she began to collapse. He hugged her tight, but her weight pulled him to the floor, where he sat cradling her.

"Lin, Lin, are you alright?"

She didn't answer. Jack sat with her several minutes, praying out loud that she'd recover.

After many minutes of silence, without opening her eyes, she said, "Jack, I'll be okay. Just get Ben. We need to go."

He left her sitting against the wall and turned to face Ben's cell. He pulled the door open and looked across the dark room, expecting to see Ben sitting in a chair like Anna had described.

Just as he stepped into the room, a bloody arm wrapped around his neck, pulling him in. While struggling to breathe, Jack saw a hand coming toward his chest with something sharp and dripping. With both hands, he grabbed that wrist and fought to hold it away.

He could taste the warm blood on the cloth of the arm that held him tight, threatening to suffocate him or break his neck. And it took everything he had to hold the other arm away. His attacker's breaths were deep and full, and his strength was overpowering. Jack knew he couldn't hold on much longer . . .

"Ben! Ben!" Lin said as loudly as she could.

The struggle continued.

"Binge!" Lin screamed.

Ben's grip loosened.

"Binge! That's Jack! Let him go!"

A second later, Jack felt the arm pull away, and he crumbled to the floor, gasping for breath. Ben's name for the last thirty years finally got through to him. Jack looked up to see Lin at the door, leaning heavily against the wall, her eyes completely shut.

"Lin, my God, you're here! And Taylor, is she okay?" said Ben.

"Yes, we're all fine. But Ben, you really need to stop attacking Jack," she said with a smile.

Ben looked down and offered Jack a hand up. Jack hesitated, looking from Ben to Lin and back to Ben.

"Yeah, Ben. You need to stop."

He accepted Ben's help.

"Sorry, Jack." He laughed. "Next time, knock."

"Funny."

*   *   *

Lin slumped back down against the wall, and Jack sat beside her, wishing he could help. But he had no idea what to do. Ben stood guard, even though they saw no immediate danger. Even though blood still dripped from the tips of every finger on his right hand.

"What can I do?" said Anna after walking silently up to them.

Ben turned and looked about to leap at her. His left hand still held the shard from her coffee mug.

"Ben, easy. It's okay. She won't cause any trouble," said Jack.

Ben relaxed but continued to stare at her.

"Will Lin be okay?" said Anna. "I have never even imagined anything like I have just seen."

"You don't know her very well," said Jack. "Maybe now you people will leave her alone."

"I will, Jack. Please believe me. I do not agree with anything that has happened. I joined The Shield only to learn the Words of God. Lin knows them now. I hope she tells me. But I will never do anything that might harm her again."

"You're right," said Ben. "You won't."

Anna took a step back as the big man glared at her.

"We need to get out of here. Anna, if you're serious about not helping them anymore, tell us what other dangers we're up against."

"None, Jack. Wolfe fled like a coward. I feel like he had me under some kind of spell, but when he shot those two guys, he lost me. He will not come back to this place for a long time. But he will not give up. I want to know the Words, I truly do. But not like him. He is obsessed. He is a goddamn madman."

Anna looked down at Lin, who appeared to be resting comfortably in Jack's arms.

"You know, Jack, I think I can actually help you. The Shield has few members, but it is a wealthy corporation. I think after all this, the company will disband. Wolfe will probably set up something new. But there is cash here. Lots of it. I want you to have it. You will all need it."

Jack looked at Ben, and Ben nodded his agreement. Jack looked back at Anna.

"Yeah, you're right we can use it. Go get it."

Jack couldn't help himself—he stared intently at Anna as she walked away, wondering if she had any powers too. The way her hips swayed while her hair remained in place. The sight of her legs beneath the long skirt. After she rounded a corner, he spoke.

"Lin, are you awake? Can you hear me?"

"My Cowboy, you came for us."

"Yes, I always will. Can you stand?"

"I think so."

He helped her to her feet, where she wobbled a few times before straightening up.

"I can stand, Jack, but walking won't be easy."

"I'll help you," he said as he wrapped her arm around his neck.

"What about Taylor, Jack? She can't even stand on her own."

"I'll carry her," said Ben.

Only then did Lin notice Ben's injuries and the pool of blood at his feet.

"Ben, you're unbelievable. I can't thank you enough."

"I'm just happy to help. Let's get out of here."

Anna had returned with a backpack stuffed with crisp new bills. Jack helped Lin walk to the elevator, Ben carried Taylor, who had both arms around his neck, and Lee kept her pistol and a wary eye on Anna. Renato stood off by himself, watching only Lin.

"Come on, let's all get in. You, we'll get you some clothes up top, alright?"

"My name is Renato. Lin saved me."

"Alright, Renato. We have to go."

Jack hit the button, and the door opened, allowing them all to enter. He held the door open as Anna hesitated in the hallway.

"Wait, there is one more thing I must keep."

She hurried off and returned with a plain, letter-size envelope, which she tucked into her jacket pocket.

No one spoke on the ride up, and the doors opened to a dim, quiet room. The exit door stood partly open where the dead guards' feet blocked its closing. Daylight waned, and a cold draft blew in.

"Everyone wait here a minute," said Jack. He allowed Lin to sit in the corner and instructed Lee to hold open the door. He reached out and dragged both of the dead guards back into the room, where he removed all of one's clothing.

"No, Renato. Hold it with both hands. That's right, now step into it, one at a time. Good."

Minutes later, Renato had helped dress himself, and Jack could again focus on their escape.

"Alright, we're just about out. Ben, I don't know what happened to you, but I think you belong in the hospital with Taylor. You can take my pickup. I'll pull it up here in a minute. The rest of us will cram into Lin's Temt8tion and head back to our place. Does that sound okay?"

Ben and Lee nodded but not Renato, whose exuberance at being alive seemed to be getting pushed aside by shock. He shivered and stood in the corner, his eyes silently pleading for Lin to help him.

"Lee, can you come with me to get the truck? I might need an extra set of eyes out there."

"Sure thing, Jack."

He handed his gun to Ben, who easily held Taylor with one arm as he took it and stuffed it into his pocket.

Jack and Lee walked through the doorway, into the cold Baltimore air.

"Lee, I think we're going to be fine. We just—"

Jack's heart thundered when he saw a fountain of red explode from Lee's chest and heard the gunshot hammer the brick walls all down the alley.

Chapter 28 – Wine & Cookies

"Oh no . . . goddamn it!"

Jack embraced Lee, heard a bullet ricochet off the wall above them, and dragged her back into the building. He pressed his shoulder into the door, pushed it closed, and bolted it. The sounds of three more shots striking near the doorway rang out. He dragged Lee to the far wall and sat her down. She'd been conscious since the bullet had found her, but she hadn't made a sound.

"Stay quiet, everyone. We're safe in here, but it's better if they can't hear us—they'll think we went back underground."

Jack removed Lee's jacket and pulled her loose sweater down over her shoulder. The bullet had entered from the back and left a ragged hole out the front just above her heart. Blood streamed down from both holes, and Lee gazed at him as her eyes glazed over and closed.

* * *

Lee went home. She found her green meadow with a cheerful blue sky above. The sun shined brightly from directly overhead, and she laughed to herself, remembering that her sun never moved, no matter how long she remained. No matter how much work needed to be done.

She looked down at her collection of rocks, all scattered to the point of showing no pattern at all. She knew she needed to work quickly. She hadn't seen the stones in such disarray since the time when she was dying, when she was forced to find the correct pattern or give up her life.

She started with her original stone, the first one she'd found so long ago. She placed it at just the right location. It would serve as the anchor for all the rest. But the others had rolled in every direction, and when she counted them, she found that several were missing.

She gathered up as many as she could and dropped them all around the anchor stone. It didn't take long before the correct arrangement could be seen growing from the chaos. She felt a renewed strength as the figure eight, infinity as Gabriel had called it, took form.

A methodical sweep of the fields around her meadow revealed the remaining stones. They'd rolled farther away than Lee had seen before, but she'd found them all. She couldn't be sure, but she thought one of them had moved to dodge her grasp.

She proceeded to fill in the pattern, and finally, the figure eight, infinity, looked perfect.

But Lee still didn't feel at her best. She studied the stones closely and found a few that needed adjustments. She moved some closer to the middle, some farther away.

At last, the arrangement was complete, and Lee felt whole again. She knew it was time to rejoin the world, so she opened her eyes.

* * *

Jack stared at the severe damage Lee had taken from the bullet, and he fought to keep his breaths under control. He knew he couldn't help her. No one there could. And from the looks of the bleeding, he didn't feel optimistic about getting her to a hospital in time.

As he stared at the oozing hole in Lee's chest, the leaking blood slowed to a dribble, then stopped altogether. The ragged edges smoothed out and began drawing together. Within seconds, the hole had closed, and only a small red dot marked the location. Another second, and the dot had disappeared. He stared at her chest where the hole had been, and he could see only perfect skin, with blood all around the area and soaking into her sweater.

Lee's breathing had been slow and steady, and she took one large, deep breath, exhaled, and opened her eyes.

Jack flinched at the sound of a single gunshot in the alley outside the door. But he continued to stare at Lee, unable to speak.

Several seconds later Lee's eyes had regained their shine and focused on Jack's.

"It's like the junk food, Jack. It's what I do, although I've never done *that* before."

She gave him a smile, the first one he'd ever seen on her face, and then she closed her eyes, still smiling, and breathed comfortably.

Jack continued to stare at her until a pounding on the door interrupted their unlikely conversation. He walked over to see a young woman with thick black hair looking back at him. It was the woman from the parking lot when they'd tried to take Lin. No one else could be seen.

"You again. Get the hell out of here!"

"Help me! I just shot Derek!"

Jack could see she was near tears. He retrieved his pistol from Ben and approached the door. He pointed the barrel at the woman, unbolted the door, and cracked it open.

"Please, I had to do it. I'm not like them. I just started working for The Shield. This can't be happening!"

Anna spoke up. "Please let her in, Jack. That is Daria. She is my daughter."

Jack never moved his gun, but he turned to look at Anna with a frown.

"Who the heck are you people?"

"Really, she is. She did not belong with this group even before it all went to hell."

Jack sighed and opened the door. Daria ran in and sat close against Anna.

"He was crazy, Mom. We got the call from Wolfe, and we got back as fast as we could. As soon as Derek saw people coming out into the alley, he started shooting. He seemed crazy. We got close to the door, then he turned his gun on me . . . he shot but missed . . . and I shot right back—"

"Why would he want to shoot you?"

"Hell if I know. He was nuts."

"Goddamn Benson . . ."

"Since when do you swear, Mom?"

Anna wrapped her arm around Daria and shushed her, and Daria trembled in her embrace. But her eyes continued to scan the room and everyone in it.

Jack bolted the door and stood looking at the two women, shaking his head in disgust.

Without dropping Taylor, Ben leaned over and snapped up Daria's gun, which he stuffed into his own pocket. His blood continued to drip.

"What a crazy mess," said Jack. "Okay, the plan's the same. Ben and Taylor to the hospital, in my truck. Lin, Lee, and you, Renato, you're all with me, back to our room. Anna, you and your daughter— you're on your own. Just stay the hell out of our way."

"You cannot be serious. He is bleeding all over the place. Ben, where do you and Taylor need to go?" said Anna.

"Back to Philadelphia."

"I will drive you there. Daria and I will drop you wherever you want."

"Why would you do that?" said Ben.

"Because we need to get out of here anyway. And then, we are going to disappear for a while. It is the least I can do for you."

Ben nodded his agreement. Jack too.

"Anna, here's the key. I'll get them into Lin's car, and then I'll guard your group to the pickup."

"Good, Jack. And Jack, don't forget the cash," Ben said with a smile, despite his own exhaustion nearly dragging him to the ground.

Jack walked over and pulled the backpack roughly from Anna, and he helped Lin to her feet. He kicked Lee lightly to wake her. Renato still shivered in the corner, staring intently at Lin with a lost look in his eyes.

Jack poked his head out and looked both ways. A body slumped against the brick wall near Lin's car. He took a cautious step out. No gunshots.

"Come on, let's get to Lin's car."

After Lee and Renato got in the back seat, Jack eased Lin into the passenger side before closing and locking the doors.

After helping Ben place Taylor in the backseat of his truck, Jack watched as they disappeared around the corner, with Anna driving.

Back at Lin's Temt8tion, Jack sat behind the wheel and looked over at Lin. Her eyes were barely open, showing only a normal shade of green. She smiled.

"Jack, sure you can handle the power of this thing?"

"This car? Oh, well, if I can handle you . . ."

They shared a quiet smile, and he started the big engine.

*　*　*

Ben sat in the truck's back seat with Taylor, and before many miles, they'd slumped to opposite sides, both still awake. He saw that she was scared and weak, so he didn't expect her to speak. Anna and Daria remained silent.

"Taylor, it's going to be okay. You're going to be fine. I'll stay with you as long as you want. No one will ever take you again, not while I'm watching you."

Taylor managed a smile.

"Your mom's fine, too, and I bet she's going to figure out some way to help you get better. I know your mom. There's no stopping her. You saw what she did down there."

Taylor nodded, and Ben could see the fear and distress in her eyes.

"Just don't worry, okay?"

It was a much longer drive than Ben had anticipated, and he was grateful to not be driving. Anna pulled Jack's truck near the main entrance, and Ben took Taylor back into his arms. He felt the pain in his torn-up hand and wrist, but he pushed it aside.

"It's fine now, Taylor. We're back."

Taylor couldn't keep her arms around Ben's neck, and she rested like a baby in his arms as he walked solidly into the hospital.

At the sight of them entering the lobby, security called for help, and soon, they were both in wheelchairs being rushed to the emergency room. At one point, they'd wanted to separate them, but Ben got up from his chair and convinced them that he intended to stay with Taylor. No one cared to argue.

The head nurse spoke to Ben, saying, "Mr. Barlow, is it? What happened? Who took Taylor?"

"I don't know. I was visiting, and some masked guys came in and knocked us out. I managed to escape with Taylor, but I got this in the process." He held up his bloody hand.

"Well, that certainly is a bad one. I'm going to give you something for the pain, and then—"

"No, you're not. I plan to stay ready. I will take a cup of coffee, though."

"Okay, suit yourself, but patching you up won't be pleasant."

"Doesn't matter. Just don't take Taylor out of my sight."

* * *

Lin fell back asleep for the return drive to their suite. No one spoke again until they were all safe inside, where they found Gabriel watching a movie on the couch with Nomad, both eating cookies. Jack shook his head at the sight.

"We're fine, Gabriel. I hope you weren't worried about us."

He helped Lin into one of the bedrooms and laid her down. Her eyes opened for only a moment, and she was out again. Lee walked in under her own power but still struggling. Renato came in and sat in a corner, still shivering despite the room's warmth.

Gabriel switched off the TV, set a tray of cookies in front of Nomad, and walked into the bedroom to see Lin.

"Lin, I knew you'd be alright."

Jack continued to shake his head as he left the room.

"Gabby, you were right," she said without opening her eyes. "I *was* alright. And the magic, oh, Gabby, I'm exhausted from it."

"You'll shake that off in a while, but you need to rest. I see that you didn't lose your mind from the Scroll," Gabriel said with a smile.

"Oh, I came close. I felt it—the insanity fighting to take over. When the Scroll made sense, nothing else did."

"But you were able to survive. Your intent saved you?"

"How did you know?"

"That's the only way. You must never lose your hold on it."

"I won't. I promise."

Her cheek leaned into the pillow, and she said no more.

* * *

Gabriel had remained by Lin's side, and half an hour later, she opened her eyes, sat up, and stretched. She looked around the room before focusing on Gabriel.

"I know the Words. Renato told me in the tunnel."

"Who's Renato?"

"The guy we brought back with us. Gabby, he's the Messenger. He used to be a scroll. I restored him."

Gabriel's eyes grew wide before a big smile appeared.

"The Scroll is a man, Lin?"

"He was both, actually. That powerful woman you spoke of, she used his magic to change him. Gabby, at first I saw only a scroll, then my mayhem started up on its own. Somehow, it knew. When I saw infinity, and all the crazy magic below the world, I saw Renato too. I saw them both."

"How did you know how to change him back to a man?"

"I didn't know—I just did it. I grabbed the magic, the magic that was creating Renato and the Scroll, and I sensed the difference between them. Somehow, I brought all his magic back to him and away from the Scroll."

"You're learning many things quickly, Lin. But your strength hasn't caught up yet. It will, though. You might not need me here much longer."

Lin bit her lip and looked down at the blanket covering her.

"No, Gabby, I'll always need you around. I can't imagine life without you." She looked back up at Gabriel.

Gabriel held her gaze, and once again, she saw the profound love in Gabriel's eyes, a love so deep and peaceful that she felt near tears. But she couldn't focus on Gabriel leaving. Not yet. She brushed the tears aside and continued.

"I did more than restore Renato. I was trapped in the tunnel behind a huge block of concrete. There was no way to move it. I would have died down there."

"How did you get out?"

"I turned the concrete to water. To seawater."

Gabriel laughed out loud before grabbing hold of Lin's hand.

"You turned concrete to water. What's next—water into wine?"

"Do you want some wine with your cookies, Gabby?" she said with a laugh.

Gabriel released her hand and took a step back.

"You've truly learned a great deal, Lin. Like I always ask you, did you hurt anyone?"

"No, I didn't. And I saved Renato from a near eternity of being part scroll."

Gabriel's understanding eyes looked deep into Lin's.

"And now what?"

She only stared back at Gabriel, and no answer came to her. She didn't regret saving him the way she had, but she realized that life must be overwhelming for him. And how could she help him? She didn't even know where he used to live. Or when.

"One thing I don't understand is how he speaks English. Wherever and whenever he came from, he probably had a different language, don't you think? He even spoke English as a scroll."

"I don't know for sure, Lin, but you said you shaped his magic back entirely into that of a man. When you did that, it was in a shape you understood—a shape that speaks English. That's all I can think. And while he was still a scroll, I guess the magic just made that work. There probably wasn't any real speaking going on anyway."

"I'll figure out what to do with him. I'll help him. Somehow, I think my mayhem will know what to do when the time is right."

"I don't doubt you will. In the meantime, while we have a few minutes, why don't you tell me the Words?"

"Sure, it's as good a time as any.

"Every garden—" Lin fell silent and closed her eyes.

"Lin, are you okay?"

"Yeah, but I must be weaker than I thought from all that."

"You probably are. Would you rather rest a while?"

"No, I'll get through it, then I'll rest some more.

"Every garden needs water—" Lin stopped again.

"I felt something inside. I don't know what."

"Perhaps you should rest more before telling me?"

"No, I should be able to say a few sentences. I don't feel *that* tired."

Lin continued to recite all the Words to Gabriel, getting weaker with each sentence, sometimes with each Word.

When she'd finished, Gabriel said, "Lin, you don't look so good. Are you alright?"

"Gabby . . . I don't know. I felt something, something with every Word. Something inside. Things shifting around. I feel . . . different."

"I'm glad you told me the Words, Lin, but you should stay in bed awhile. You're more tired than you know."

"I expected something a lot different in the Words."

"So did I, but the truth is the truth. We don't bend it to our needs. *We* must bend."

Chapter 29 – Gods & Terror

The sun had set, and Jack had pulled the curtains closed before lying down for a nap. After her shower, Lin wrapped herself in a thick white robe and nudged Nomad to the floor to take a seat next to Gabriel on the couch. Gabriel still wore the same jeans, sweater, and hiking boots and continued to poke around in a bag of popcorn.

"How did you know I'd be alright? I didn't think I would be. I was trapped in that tunnel and left to die. I never would have guessed that I could find a way to do what I did."

"It's the same for you now as it was over thirty years ago. Every day of abuse that you experienced from your uncle Ray led to you getting stronger. Because you took your problems head on. Last week, I encouraged you to put yourself in danger, and you gained control of your mayhem. I knew The Shield could be dangerous, and I believed you'd end up in some kind of trouble. But that's what works. Because of who you are. You don't back down and look . . . you learned so much."

"I don't know. I feel complete confidence in my mayhem, but so many new things are coming at me. I can't keep up. There are too many things I don't understand."

"Like what? We have time. Maybe I can explain some of it to you."

"I'd love that. How about converts? How does my mayhem turn people into such adoring fans, people that would do anything for me?"

"I guess that would seem pretty mysterious to you, but it's really quite simple. You'd eventually figure it out for yourself anyway."

"Really? I'm not so sure. Why don't you just tell me? I love it when you can explain things to me. Sometimes, this is all kind of frightening but not when I'm with you."

Lin swept her hair back and settled into the plush cushions.

Nomad approached Gabriel and sat perfectly still. Only his big eyes moved to take turns looking into Gabriel's and Lin's as Gabriel scratched his ears and the top of his head.

"What's today . . . Wednesday? Only three days ago, you tried to use your mayhem on Nomad. You found that he had no space in between his spirit and his body. Or at least, not enough for anyone to get in there. We talked about that the other day. I told you that space, that narrow gap that people have, that's free will. And no other living thing has that.

"Your first reaction was to feel sorry for them, but I stopped you. I told you they have something else, something you can't even imagine. I can tell you what that is, but you won't truly understand it until you experience it.

"Lin, what they have instead of free will is the absolute knowledge of God's presence. They have no doubts. They know exactly what they're supposed to be. What God *wants* them to be. And they know exactly where they'll go when their life is done. It's a comfort that no human can imagine."

Lin brushed her hair back again and said, "Well, if it's so comfortable, and they're so happy, why are they so afraid to die? Why do they fight so hard to stay alive?"

"That's not fear, Lin. That's gratitude. They never forget what a precious gift they've been given. They're aware of that gift in every moment of their lives."

Lin stopped and stared at Gabriel, trying to process what had been revealed. Of course—it made perfect sense. It was the opposite of free will. They're content being what they were created to be. And they have no doubts.

"Okay, so what does that have to do with my mayhem making converts?"

"Simple. When you use your mayhem, when you send your magic into a person's narrow space, you're closing their gap. You're taking away their free will. And they, like every other living creature, have no doubts. You've taken away all the anguish and confusion. It's more contentment than they've ever known before or ever will again. You have become like God to them."

Lin shook deep inside, feeling the enormity of what her mayhem could do. What an incredible power. She thought back to John and Tommy, her first two converts, and how annoying they'd been to her. But it all made perfect sense. They'd adored her. She'd taken away all of their doubts. At least for a while.

"I don't even know what to say. I had no idea."

"Very few do, Lin. And it works on you too. You must have noticed—when you're using your mayhem, you have no doubts."

"Yeah, I did notice. I feel unstoppable, and I have no doubts at all. But when I invade someone, why does that terrify them, then?"

"That's different. You're not filling that gap with your wave of magic. You're getting in between their spirit and their body. They feel their soul being separated from their body. They're experiencing a more profound death than any natural death. They're remaining completely aware *after* you've taken their lives."

Again, Lin did nothing but stare, remembering the terror all of her victims had felt. No wonder they would never get over that fear, she realized.

"You said every living thing except humans knows where they'll go when their lives are done. Where?"

"My words won't convince you, but I'll try. They live every moment with the knowledge that God is with them. They've never known anything else. They know they've always been part of God, and God has been part of them. They know death won't change that."

"But they still suffer while they're alive, don't they?"

"Yes, of course, they do. There's no escape from that. But it's different for them. They know their ultimate future."

"So, they don't suffer as much as we do?"

"No, I didn't say that. This is part of what you can't understand. Your mind is not made to comprehend it. They suffer like we do, oftentimes more. But it's different. They know God. We don't. I'll give you a good example, although it's not exact. But it will give you some idea of it.

"Ben is injured badly. You told me you saw the blood. And yet, he ignored it completely to carry your daughter and to do whatever she needed. Without Taylor, it's just pain and suffering. With Taylor, he didn't care. Same pain either way. See the difference?

"And that was only from a distraction of his mind, helping him to ignore the pain. It wasn't from something fundamental to his existence, something built-in."

"Yeah, I sure do see. You told me you could show me that someday, but I needed to be much stronger. You said I wouldn't come back. Did you mean I wouldn't be able to come back?"

"I meant you wouldn't *want* to come back. You would trade your magical life as Lin Finity in a heartbeat, if you felt what the lowest, most disgusting thing you could think of, felt. Being human is the hardest thing . . ."

Lin could barely focus on the room or on Gabriel. When she'd journeyed into the magic, it had rocked her deep inside, learning that so much more existed beyond her reality. She hadn't even come to terms with that yet. And she just learned the true cost of free will.

It was a good thing to be able to shape the slow magic of the real world. But it came with a high price. It left everyone stranded, not knowing what their lives were about or what they're supposed to be. Or where they'll ultimately go.

"If every other living thing knows they're going back to God, doesn't that mean we will too?"

"As long as I've been around, I don't know the answer to that. I believe we will, yes. But do I *know* it? No, I don't. I think our free will makes it impossible for us to *know* it. I'd hoped the Words of the Scroll would tell us something positive."

"Yeah, well, that hasn't worked out, has it?"

*　*　*

Jack awoke from his nap with a start, curled up on the floor not far from Renato. Nomad, also close by, continued to snore, with an occasional twitch of his huge paws. Lee had been pretending to sleep, but she'd been listening to Lin and Gabriel. Gabriel had seen her look their way several times but acted as if no one overheard.

Jack spoke first. "Lin, did you get some rest? Are you feeling better?"

"Yeah, I feel mostly fine. Just a little tired but more like an ordinary tired. We've all had quite the afternoon."

"Yeah, we sure did. Do you need anything? Can I get you anything?"

"Jack, I'm not injured. Really, I'm fine. You don't need to wait on me."

"I know. Just happy to help."

Lin couldn't ignore that something seemed to have changed in him. Her mayhem always changed things.

"Thanks. I'm fine, Jack. It's just good that we're all back here safe. And I got a text from Anna. She dropped Ben and Taylor at the hospital, and they're both getting the care they need."

"Great. What's next? Whatever it is, count me in."

"I don't know. I just want to get back to my life."

As if on cue, Nomad shifted and jumped on her lap.

"Ugh . . . thanks, Nomad!"

She hugged him tight, and he nuzzled her neck and licked her face.

"How long, Gabby, before everyone from the restaurant turns back?"

"Hard to tell, Lin. But I'd guess you have about a week yet."

"Okay, why don't we eat and get a good night's sleep, and tomorrow morning, over breakfast,"—Lin paused to smile at Gabriel—"we'll make plans."

Everyone agreed, and long after, a room service feast had been devoured. While Gabriel still picked at the unfinished dessert plates, Lee went off to the other bedroom for the night. A short while later, Gabriel took the couch. Renato had eaten, and he seemed to have enjoyed it, but he looked most comfortable remaining in his corner. Jack stretched out on the floor after kissing Lin goodnight.

Lin went back into her bedroom and lay staring at the ceiling, wondering where her life would take her next. It still seemed to be too much. The mayhem, the magic, things not being real, things not making sense. And Jack . . . how had she changed Jack?

She knew it wasn't fear that Jack felt like when she'd taken him with her mayhem. She'd fixed that, sort of, by sending a wave to convert him, using just enough.

No, it was something else. Something related to her having pushed his will aside. He'd given it up, and he'd only been along for the ride. What might that have done to him? How could it be fixed?

She heard a light knocking on the door before it pushed inward. She saw her smiling Cowboy waiting to be invited in. Her heart sank—permission was usually the last thing on Jack's mind.

Still, she smiled and invited him in.

Chapter 30 – Teased & Crazed

Lin's robe lay in a bunch next to the bed, and she snuggled deep under the thick blankets. Her fatigue left her at the sight of Jack about to join her.

He walked up to the bedside and smiled down at her. With one hand, he smoothed back her hair, and she pushed aside her doubts and smiled back. No matter what she'd done to him, she thought, he was still her Cowboy.

"I'd like to get undressed and get in there with you, if that's alright. You're not too tired for some company, are you?"

Lin's heart sank again, but a voice inside whispered a plan to her. She liked the plan.

"Do you want to, Jack?"

"Yeah, I sure do. But if you're tired . . ."

Lin held his gaze and rolled the blankets down just far enough to expose her bare breasts. He couldn't help but look with a smile, and it grew as he stared. She thought of using her mayhem, but she knew that wasn't the time. It was time for ordinary magic, and she had plenty of that.

Jack didn't ask again. He stripped off his clothes and slipped under the covers. Together, they pulled the blankets tight up to their chins. Jack lay close to her, but their bodies barely touched.

"Do you want to kiss me, Jack?"

"I sure do. It's all I can think of. Is that what you want too?"

She didn't answer. She only parted her lips just enough for her tongue to be seen. He watched as it traced a pattern across her top lip, then back across the bottom. She never stopped looking into his eyes, but he only stared at her wet tongue sliding slowly along her wet lips.

He leaned in to kiss her, and just as his lips brushed against hers, she pulled back. He looked into her smiling eyes, then down at her tongue sliding across her lips. He leaned in again, and again she pulled back, still smiling.

He reached for her and held her head with both of his rough hands, his callouses snagging her hair. He pulled her toward him until their lips met. She felt his powerful grip on her, and his lips hot against hers. She yielded, opening her mouth, her tongue playfully toying with his.

He kissed her so long that she needed to break free to breathe. And still, her tongue teased its way across her lips, lips now wetter from Jack's kisses. Again, he pulled her in for more, his mouth hungry against hers.

Lin slowly rolled the blankets down to her waist. She took one of Jack's wrists and positioned his hand right above her breasts, and she held it there. She pulled away from his kiss, smiling, tongue dancing along her top lip. And she watched as Jack's eyes moved to his own hand, so close to touching her.

She felt him pushing against her hold, gently at first, then with more determination, reaching for what his imagination must have already felt. Lin pushed back but only enough to keep his hand mere inches away. Slowly, she allowed his strength to overtake her, and they both watched as his hand moved nearer, nearer, and finally, she felt his roughness against her softness.

Lin let go of his wrist and moved her hand to his shoulder as Jack's hand squeezed and caressed her, cautiously at first, then with more abandon. He looked back into her eyes, and they resumed the deep kiss with more urgency.

His hand moved from side to side, enjoying all that Lin had offered. She smiled through their kiss, seeing traces of the old Jack, the Cowboy she knew and loved and had changed with her mayhem. But she needed more from him. She needed his will to be once again strong enough to take her. Without questions or doubts.

As she continued to kiss him, she reached across and grasped his other wrist, the one still holding her head in close so that he could press her lips into his. She placed his hand against her wrist, and his instincts didn't disappoint her. She felt his iron grip wrap around her wrist, and he forced her arm into the sheets.

Within seconds, Jack ended his playful fondling and grabbed her other wrist. Lin let out a sharp gasp as he stretched both of her arms straight above her head until both of her hands were trapped tightly against the headboard.

Now, she thought, now I see my Cowboy again . . .

With his Cowgirl subdued, Jack's natural inclinations continued to rise to the occasion. He hesitated only a second before Lin heard a low growl from deep within him, sounding as if it were fighting to break free. She felt his hold on her wrists tighten as he rolled her onto her back.

Every exhale from Jack was a muffled roar, and he'd stopped kissing her. He looked down on her, her eyes only a normal shade of green, she only his Cowgirl. And Lin felt his strong motions rocking her, bumping her hands into the headboard. Quickly, his desires became more powerful, unstoppable, as his grip tightened even more.

Lin's normal green eyes continued to gaze into Jack's, and she puckered her lips. Fueling the fire. Provoking the animal. Jack stared into the eyes of his captive Cowgirl, and Lin saw the change there even as she felt it with every rough, unapologetic push.

She resumed sliding her tongue over her lips as her eyes smiled at seeing the fire of his will burning bright once more.

Jack appeared to have no consideration of whether Lin would join him in the final act or not. He was ready . . . a crazed, selfish beast. Whatever walls her mayhem had built into him came crashing down all at once. And Lin felt his spirit set free as his body offered her that spirit, his very soul, in the only way his animal nature could.

Lin fought to not laugh out loud with relief and joy in a celebration of Jack's return. But her smile said it all, and when he returned that smile with his own, she saw without any doubt that her Cowboy was back.

* * *

They'd made barely a sound, and after resting several minutes, they awoke in each other's arms. Lin beamed with a satisfied smile. She'd gotten everything she'd wanted from him.

Jack brushed back her long hair, working to get it over her shoulder, playing with it much more than was necessary. There was no hurry. Everyone was safe, and the precious moments they shared in that quiet bedroom felt like an eternity.

"Lin, I have no words to express what I feel for you."

"Yet somehow, you find a way to tell me anyway, don't you, Jack?"

"You just drove me nearly insane, and I know that you didn't use any of your powers. That was all you."

"That was all us, Jack."

He gave her a smile, and Lin felt sure that after all he'd been through, with fearing her, with mindlessly adoring her, with giving up his will . . . all he felt now was love. Like he had before she'd ever used her mayhem on him.

"Yeah, you're right. We have our own kind of magic, don't we?"

"Yes," Lin said with a smile. "Yes, we do."

* * *

After Anna had dropped Ben and Taylor back at the hospital, she decided to keep Jack's truck. Easier than a cab, she figured. She made a call to Wolfe, who'd been waiting impatiently to hear from her.

"Things went okay, Anna?"

"Yes, Wolfe, no one suspected a goddamn thing. I dropped the two at the hospital, just as you instructed. We are ready to join you to finish this operation."

"Excellent. The less people in the way, the better. And I'd rather those two join me someday anyway. I'm still in Baltimore, but I'll get up to Allentown. I want you and Daria to meet me there."

"Where in Allentown?"

"The restaurant where Tayo witnessed Lin using her power."

"Is there some reason for meeting there?"

"No, none at all. But Tayo will join us, too, and he said the steaks there are to die for."

* * *

"Mom, I don't want to go. He's creepy. He scares me."

"He is different, I will admit that. He is just very intense, Daria. That is not always a bad thing. Besides, he requested you."

They walked in and saw Wolfe and Tayo seated in the balcony.

As they approached the table, Wolfe set down his martini and stood to greet them. He hugged Anna tightly, and as his hands slid down below her waistline, he stared into Daria's eyes with a grin.

"I've enlisted Tayo to help us out. Our ranks are meager these days, especially after Lin's antics at the HQ. I had to put down two guards after she'd taken control of them. And maybe I should have read the instructions for those collars," Wolfe said with a laugh. "I must have had them set to incinerate! So, basically, they're all dead."

Anna said, "We cannot just leave bodies all over like that, can we?"

"No, it'll be handled. I sent a text to Benson, instructing him to clean it all up."

Anna and Daria exchanged a quick look.

"That leaves us with Tayo. Right this minute, he is our only army!"

Wolfe smiled and held his glass up in a toast.

"Yes, but Mr. Wolfe, I'm mostly a scientist and an investigator. I'm not sure if—"

"You'll be fine," said Wolfe. "Time to step up, Tayo."

Wolfe looked Tayo in the eye, and Tayo quickly looked down at his menu.

"That Lin is something else, wouldn't you say, Daria? Beautiful, but oh, so deadly. What was your impression of her?"

"I . . . don't know what you mean. She was blond, she dressed well, she—"

"No, no, who cares about that. How did she act? Like she was better than everyone else? Preachy?"

Daria looked quickly at Anna and said, "No, she just seemed tired."

"Tired. That's it? Okay then, we'll all get another look at her soon enough.

"Now, Anna, Daria, I want to congratulate you on doing so well back there. Offering the cash to Lin and her gang was brilliant!"

He raised his drink to salute them, downed it, and ordered another.

"We know exactly where they are. I have our last Northeastern U.S. agents en route even as we speak. And drink," he said as the server placed his next one in front of him.

"We have every reason to believe they haven't found the device. It hasn't moved from a location we've determined is a suite in a building just west of here. They're probably all resting peacefully, believing they're safe."

"Mr. Wolfe," said Daria, "I'm not sure I'm cut out for this. Can I please just head back home?"

Wolfe looked at her closely, so closely that Daria shrank back into her seat. He only smiled after his examination of her was complete.

"No, you cannot leave. I'm good at reading people, Daria, and I think you're exactly the kind of person we need. I believe you're capable of taking drastic actions when required. I believe you wouldn't hesitate to kill if you needed to. The Words of God, remember? How thrilling is that?" he said before taking another large swallow.

Daria looked down at her menu and said no more.

"Here's what we're going to do. We'll have a good meal because Tayo, you said the food here is excellent. Excellent, right?"

Tayo cringed.

"We'll eat and head out to intercept our targets. I'll get those damn Words, and then we'll destroy them."

Chapter 31 – Friends & Things

Weak morning light streamed past the crisp curtains, waking Lin as she still lay in Jack's arms. She felt only a moment of peace before a difficult possibility hit her hard, something she hadn't even considered. The cash. Anna had been eager to give them the cash. Too eager. And there was a lot of it.

She tiptoed past Gabriel sleeping on the couch, and she rummaged through the backpack. She quickly found what she feared might be there: a tracker. Anna had fooled them all. A sharp wave of terror ran through her.

Fearing the worst, she called Taylor's hospital.

"Yes, Taylor is here, and she's doing well. She's a little more tired than when she left, but she's doing okay. Yes, Ben is fine too. He's sustained quite a wound, and he wouldn't say how he got it. But we've treated him, and he'll be fine too. If he lets it heal. A police detective was here earlier and talked with them, but now, they're both resting quietly."

Lin ended the call, satisfied that Anna had honored that agreement at least. But she'd also betrayed them.

Jack walked out of the bedroom, rubbing his eyes, the beginning of a smile intruding onto his still sleepy face.

Lin only held up the device, chasing away Jack's smile.

He said, "Oh, Lin . . . I had no idea. Let me drive that thing the heck away from here and leave it. Far away. They'll never—"

"It's too late, Jack. While we've been sleeping and laying around, they probably have this place surrounded. Or at least, they're getting close. I don't know how many people Wolfe has, but he's probably rounding them up. We need to get our things together and go."

Gabriel had awakened, and while rummaging through bags for any food that might be left, said, "Lin, tell me about Wolfe."

She set down the bag she'd begun to pack, but she didn't let go of it.

"Sure, Gabby, what do you want to know?"

"Have you met him?"

"No, I only heard his voice on the intercom."

"How did he speak? Was he confident?"

"Yes. Very. And I'd guess pretty persuasive too. Anna even spoke about him having her under a spell of some kind. She said that spell had been broken, though, when Wolfe shot the two guards."

"It looks like maybe the spell is still holding, don't you think?"

Gabriel held up the tracker before setting it down and taking a few moments to consider the situation as everyone waited impatiently.

"We should wait for them to come to us."

"Oh, come on, Gabriel," said Jack. "We need to get out of here."

"Yes, and we will, but for now, we're safer here, Jack. Let's not throw away the value of being in a solid building among many other guests. If they come to us, they will be exposed, not us."

Jack shook his head as Gabriel took Lin aside for a private conversation.

"Lin, if what I suspect is true, Wolfe himself has no chance against you. They have available to them only the tools of common criminals. They're not able to use the magic."

Lin's eyes opened wide.

"Gabby, who ever said they might know anything about the magic?"

"No one. But Lin, I need to meet Wolfe."

Lin couldn't comprehend Gabriel's interest in Wolfe, or even whether staying there was the best option. But Gabriel had been her best friend for over three decades. She'd take the advice.

"Okay, everyone," Lin said, "let's just lay low for a while. I'm convinced this is the best strategy. If nothing happens, if no one comes after us, we can venture out. But for now, let's stay put."

Gabriel quickly began taking everyone's order for room service as Lin smiled and shook her head.

Her smiled evaporated at the urgent knocking on the door.

Lin looked at Gabriel a few more seconds, then looked to Jack.

"Well, that settles that," said Jack. "Looks like they *did* come to us."

Jack took the lead and walked toward the door, leaving everyone else standing and staring. He first looked through the peep hole and reported to the group that it was Anna outside the door, and he could see no one else.

"Jack, chain the door first, and see what she wants," said Gabriel.

With the door secured, Jack cracked it open, and Anna's and Ozzy's faces appeared in the opening.

"Jack, first, I hope all of you are okay. And I want to assure you that Taylor and Ben are fine. No one will bother them again. But Jack, we still need to know the Words. All of them. Not just Lin's summary."

"You fooled us with a tracker in the bag of cash. That's obvious since here you are. Why should we trust you at all about anything?"

"I am sorry, Jack, but this is just too important. My boss is here, and he would like to ask Lin himself. Let us in, please. Just to talk."

Jack closed the door, locked it, and turned to face the group.

"Alright, well, it looks like this Wolfe guy is out there too. They both want to come in. She says they only want to ask Lin about the Words. I don't like it, not a bit. I'm not letting anyone get close to—"

"Jack," said Gabriel. "It'll be okay. I can't explain right now, but they can't hurt Lin. Her power will keep her safe. And it'll keep us safe too. I say let them in."

Gabriel looked to Lin for her decision.

"Let them in, Jack, but just the two of them."

She felt her mayhem begin to rise.

Without any formalities, Anna and Wolfe soon stood inside the closed, locked door. Lin was surprised at Wolfe's appearance. He seemed so young—too young to be on such a quest. And she could sense his intensity, a singular focus and obsession for his mission. The martini in his hand seemed out of place. And the sight of Ozzy in Anna's arms struck her as comical too.

Anna spoke first. "Jack, here is the key to your truck. It is parked out front. Sorry, but I had to borrow it."

"Lin, we've never really met, not in this time anyway," said Wolfe. "I'm Lancaster Wolfe, Director of The Shield. I think you know by now that our only purpose is to learn the Words written on the Scroll. You've read them. No doubt you remember them, even though you wouldn't write them down. Please. Tell me all the Words. Your summary isn't enough."

Gabriel stood close behind Lin, watching Wolfe intently. The others had backed away, giving them room to talk.

"You ordered the kidnapping of my daughter, and you took my dear friend Ben too. That's not something I'm about to forget, Wolfe. You must know by now that I'm not someone you'd want as an enemy."

Lin flicked her long blond hair back over her shoulders, and the glowing green of her eyes was impossible to ignore. Anna stepped back, but Wolfe only gazed into the light as if he were hypnotized by it.

"You're not seventeen floors away from me now. You're right here. I could take you in less than a heartbeat. I could take you, or I could kill you, or—"

Gabriel stepped between the two, facing Lin.

"Lin, there's no need for broken bones. You're not in any danger."

She looked into Gabriel's eyes, and she knew what Gabriel must see—the eyes of a predator. She felt her mayhem flare up, and she let it back down. But it remained just beneath her surface, ready to rise up and stop time if needed.

Gabriel turned to face Wolfe.

"So, your name is Gabriel," said Wolfe.

"It is."

"How original."

"And your name is?"

"Wolfe. Lancaster Wolfe."

He held out his hand to shake Gabriel's. Gabriel ignored it.

"No. Your real name."

Wolfe laughed and looked at the ceiling before focusing again on Gabriel's eyes.

"Only Wolfe," he said with a laugh. "That's been my name for a long time."

"And before that?"

Lin met Jack's gaze, and she shrugged, and they both looked back at Gabriel.

Wolfe's smile disappeared, replaced by an impatient sneer.

"I know what you are, Gabriel. I know your kind. You can't interfere with me. Step aside."

"I don't need to do anything, Wolfe, or whoever you are. Lin doesn't need my help with you or anyone like you."

"Wonderful! So, move aside, and let her tell me the—"

"But if you bring any of your *friends* into this drama, know that I *will* act."

Wolfe's cocky attitude deflated, and he looked to the floor briefly before regrouping himself.

"There will be no need for that, Gabriel. I just want the Words. Then, Lin can live her life in peace."

Gabriel took a strong step toward Wolfe, and they stood close, both staring.

"I could recommend to Lin that she destroy you right now. And maybe I will."

They continued to glare at each other.

"Take your minion and go. Lin will consider your request."

Wolfe's unblinking gaze bored into Gabriel's eyes, and the silence blanketing them threatened to drag on forever. Jack stared at the confrontation, and his shock at seeing Gabriel's courage was obvious on his face.

"Very well. We will go. For now."

With that, Wolfe and Anna left the room, and Gabriel latched the door.

When Gabriel turned around, it was to everyone's surprised faces. Even Lin's.

"Gabby, what was that all about?"

"That thing doesn't belong here, Lin."

"Thing?"

"Lancaster Wolfe has been gone for years."

* * *

The silence in the room lingered long after Gabriel's declaration. The group looked around at each other, staring and not speaking. Only Renato seemed as he'd been before Wolfe had entered the room. He sat quietly, his eyes imploring Lin to reassure him in some way. But Lin had more pressing issues.

"Alright, so they did come to us. Now, what? Shouldn't we just get out of here already?" said Jack.

"Yes, now we should go. Now we know who we're dealing with."

"Maybe you do," said Lin. "Gabby, what do you mean, Wolfe is gone? Who was that, then?"

Gabriel looked around at the questioning eyes of Jack and Lee and even Renato. A nod prompted Lin to follow Gabriel to the far corner of the room.

"This isn't the best time to discuss it, Lin. All I can say is, remember how I was a, um, close friend of yours for a long time? That's what happened to Wolfe. The real Wolfe. But Wolfe's friend never had good intentions. Wolfe's spirit couldn't survive long that way."

Lin nodded her head, understanding exactly what Gabriel meant. Wolfe had picked up something. A spirit, like Gabriel, but not a good one. She felt ill imagining how that must have been for Wolfe.

"But Wolfe . . . he's not still in there, is he?"

"There's only enough of him left to suffer. He's only along for the ride. Did you feel the heat?"

"Yeah, and I wasn't even that close. What's going on?"

"Whatever that is, it's burning up Wolfe's, the real Wolfe's, body."

"Can we help him? Wolfe, I mean?"

"We can only end his suffering. We can't restore him. Those things are very good at what they do."

"I know my powers are incredible, and I'm not scared of that Wolfe thing. But this whole situation—all the magic, the Words that leave us nowhere, all of it, it's just—"

"This will all work out, Lin. Remember that you're getting stronger every day. As your strength increases, your doubts will peel away. You'll see."

"But what's this all about? Why is there magic at all? Why am I able to use it?"

"I don't know, Lin. I seek an answer as well. I truly thought the Words would explain it all."

"Look," Lee said from across the room, "I hate to interrupt, but maybe we should get the hell out of here?"

"I agree," said Jack. "I don't want to wait for Wolfe to come back with more of his people."

"People will never be a problem, Jack," said Gabriel. "It's what else he might bring that I'm concerned with."

Jack's mouth hung open, and even Lee's eyes grew wide. Neither said a word.

Lin spoke up. "Let's all get our things and get out of here. I need to see with my own eyes that Taylor and Ben are okay. After that, I don't know. We'll figure it out."

As everyone packed their belongings, Jack watched Gabriel pick through what was left on the dinner plates that were scattered on the counter. He didn't shake his head. He only watched curiously for a while, then continued to gather his things.

* * *

Lin had hoped that Renato would ride with Jack and Lee, but he'd seemed desperate to remain with her. So, he climbed into her Temt8tion's back seat, and Gabriel took the passenger seat. She pulled out for the drive to Philadelphia, with Jack's truck trailing her with Lee up front, and Nomad had the back seat to himself.

The drive on I476 and I76 remained quiet and uneventful. No one spoke much, only enough to acknowledge that they were being followed. By three cars.

Chapter 32 – Doves & Oaks

"Mom, I can't believe you're here," Taylor said after seeing Lin, Jack, and Lee walk into her room.

Lin walked up to the bed, and the other two stayed near the doorway. Gabriel had chosen to remain in the hallway. Nomad had protested, but he had no choice but to remain in the car.

Ben sat up straight in his chair, rubbed his face, and gave Lin a smile that almost matched those of John and Tommy.

"My dear Taylor, I had to see you. I'm so sorry for how things have been. I understand now why I couldn't talk to you about my childhood and how that caused a huge problem between us. I'm ready to tell you anything you want to know. We'll have time for that, I promise."

Lin leaned over the bed and embraced her daughter, who was connected to several monitors and IVs. Taylor still appeared quite sick, and her voice betrayed the weakness that had become part of her.

Ben watched the long hug, still smiling, but Jack turned to Lee to whisper an idea.

"I don't know, Jack. I have no clue how to do that."

"Can you at least try? I saw what you did after you were shot. Maybe you really can help her?"

Lee held Jack's gaze a few seconds, shaking her head, then with a sigh, she turned and walked to stand near Lin.

"Lin," said Lee, "you know what I've been able to do for myself, with those problems I had. And you know what I did after that gunshot. Maybe . . ."

Lin knew exactly what Lee had in mind. But she wondered if such an attempt could be dangerous. A quick study of the situation told her that Taylor was miserable, and she looked as though she were ready to give up. She knew that it was worth a try. The last round of treatments had been disappointing. And besides, she felt she'd be able to invade Taylor's narrow space, that gap between her magic and her body, if necessary. From there, she might be able to help in some way. They had to try.

She felt her mayhem rising on its own, and her eyes lit up.

At the sight of Lin's glowing eyes and faint smile, Lee nodded her head.

The three of them watched Lee approach Taylor and look her up and down. Only Taylor's eyes moved to look up at her, and it seemed that turning her head required too much effort. Lee got a firm grip on each of Taylor's hands, and she closed her eyes.

Taylor looked at Lin and gasped at her shining green eyes. She glanced at Jack, who only nodded. Her eyes turned to look at Ben, seated on her other side, and he smiled. She could manage only another quick look at Lin before her eyes rolled up high and closed.

* * *

Lee quickly found her home, that bright green patch of grass in a peaceful valley, with a vivid blue sky above. She smiled at her old friend, the sun, as its brilliant green light shined down from directly above her. A quick look at her stones, her figure eight, told her she had some minor repairs to do. Must be from the lousy food, she thought with a laugh. She quickly set them in the proper arrangement, and she felt her health and power increase.

With a mild shock, she saw footprints in the grass on the far side of her stones. She knew she hadn't gone there, having made all her adjustments from her side. And she'd never before seen evidence of anyone else's presence in her home. The footprints looked fresh and disappeared at the edge of her clearing, where she could see the taller plants trampled down.

Lee walked around her stones and carefully placed each of her steps in the footprints in the grass. With every step she took, she sensed her awareness changing as if she were turning into someone else. There was a darkening sky above, and the sun, her sun, struggled.

She followed the footprints to the edge of the grass, feeling weaker with every step she took. The taller weeds and plants were smashed down, and she knew she had to keep going. She had to follow that path. And she continued to get weaker as she walked.

Lee barely made it to another clearing, one that had no grass, only dry, cracked earth, with jagged stones protruding up and pointing at the sky. At the center of the clearing sat a pure white dove, inside a tangled cage built of countless branches and twigs.

She froze as she heard the dove singing a sad song, and she couldn't help but weep. With tears streaming down her cheeks, she kept walking until she'd reached the imprisoned bird. She'd become too weak to take another step.

The bird's melody haunted her. The lonely bird repeated it many times as if she'd been singing it for all time. Lee shuddered when she remembered the song—she'd sung it herself, so many years before! She hadn't heard it in so long, not since she'd found the proper pattern. Not since she'd healed herself.

Lee looked into the bird's eyes, and she knew that the bird had no illness and no injury of any kind. She'd been trapped long ago, and she'd gotten more despondent with each passing day. The bird had been all alone, helpless for so long. No one had come to help her. No one even knew.

She wanted nothing more than to free the sad dove. But how? The cage had been constructed in a complex pattern, and no obvious solution presented itself. Lee looked at every branch, each woven among many others, twisting from side to side and joined in impossible patterns. She moved one branch, and another shifted to take its spot. She pulled two out, and three appeared in their place. She tried to lift the entire cage, but it seemed anchored into the Earth, and Leé grew even more tired.

She looked up at the sun, her sun, and smiled when she felt that it had whispered to her an idea.

Lee stopped her thoughts and focused on her desire to set the bird free. She felt something move deep inside herself—a force, a purpose, a part of her she could never describe. Something she'd never noticed before began to take shape. She smiled more as she felt it expand and work its way toward the surface.

As her tears began to dry, a new confidence flowed through her, and she saw how easy it would be. It took only a simple lifting of one branch, then a rotating of another, a sliding of a third and fourth at the same time, and finally, pulling a fifth one out completely. She removed the cage's top and cast it aside.

She looked up and smiled again at her sun before looking into the cage.

The bird still sat, free but not knowing it. Not knowing what to do.

Lee reached into the cage, and the dove crawled up and perched on her wrist. She lifted the scared bird out of her prison and placed her on her shoulder. Her sad song had ended.

The dove cooed and rubbed her head against Lee's cheek as she began to retrace her steps, walking backward the entire way. She felt that the dove was offering advice to her, helping her place her steps correctly. Returning Lee to herself.

Back in the grass of her home, Lee saw her stones had scattered but not badly. With the bird's constant encouragement, she arranged all of her stones until they were perfect again. Until she felt perfect. She reached up, and the dove climbed back onto her wrist.

Both of them basked in the sparkling, nourishing sunshine of Lee's home. She held the now radiant bird in front of her, and they looked into each other's eyes. They held the gaze a long time under the bright sun they shared.

Lee felt immense gratitude, knowing she never would have made it back on her own. The dove seemed to understand, and she thanked Lee in the only way she could—by bobbing her head and cooing.

And then, she flew.

She fluttered, weakly at first, in a tight circle around Lee's home. Then, she began to rise higher into the blue sky with each turn, feeling her wings, turning them loose at last, and leaving her prison far below her.

And then, she was gone.

* * *

Lin watched closely, and only a few seconds had passed before she saw Lee take a deep breath. She let it out slowly, and her eyes opened, looking first down at Taylor, then at Lin. Lee looked back at Taylor and continued to hold her hands but without saying a word. Several minutes passed.

Taylor opened her eyes. They were focused on Lee from the moment they'd opened. She smiled and looked to Lin, who silently rejoiced that no harm had come to her daughter. But had it worked? Had Lee's power accomplished anything?

"Mom, Lee . . . I've never felt this way. Never in my life. I feel good. I don't feel weak at all. Is this what it's like to be healthy? Am I really okay?"

She began sobbing, with Lin joining her after letting her mayhem recede. Lee only smiled down at her and released her hands.

Lin rushed forward and leaned in to hug Taylor, who continued to cry softly through her smile.

"Oh, Taylor, my sweet girl, are you really better? How do you feel?"

"I feel good, Mom. No, I feel perfect. Can we get out of here? I don't belong here anymore. I know I don't."

"Oh my God, Taylor, this is amazing. Yes, let's all get out of here. I just need to have a nurse or a doctor check you out, just to make sure."

"Sure. Okay, Mom, let's do what we need to do. Call them right now, okay?"

"They'll think it was a miracle, Taylor."

"Mom, it was."

* * *

Taylor's doctor had insisted that she remain there several more days just to be safe. Lin couldn't agree, and she made it quite clear that they were leaving. Jack sat patiently next to Lee, who had again closed her eyes. Everything had been packed, and they were ready to go.

"Lee, are you okay?" Jack said.

"Yeah, sure. I'm fine. Just tired. That took something out of me."

"Alright, you did good. I hope you know that. Just rest. We'll be on the road soon."

Lee nodded but didn't answer.

Ben had stayed off to the side, smiling at Taylor's recovery and at Lin's obvious happiness. He rose from his seat, the chair from which he'd guarded Taylor, and he approached her. She sat on the high bed, looking full of energy and ready to find her life. She looked up at him with a big smile.

"Taylor, I'm so happy for you. I don't understand Lee or your mom either. But somehow, they're able to do unbelievable things."

"Thanks, Ben. I've only known you a short while, but you've become my best friend. After my mom, of course."

"You know I'd still carry you if you'd like."

"I don't think I need that, but I'd like it a lot. For old times' sake," she said with a laugh.

Until she glanced down at his heavily bandaged hand and wrist. A look of surprise and sadness clouded her cheerful features.

"I didn't know that you were hurt, Ben. You carried me . . . like that? You still carried me?"

A single tear rolled down her cheek.

"Of course. It was nothing. Whatever you need."

Taylor looked over at Lee, still resting with closed eyes, then at Jack. Jack nodded.

"Lee." Jack shook her gently. "Lee, we need to ask something of you. Just one more thing, alright?"

"What, Jack?" Lee said with her eyes shut.

"It's Ben. Do you remember his injury? Is there any way . . ."

Lee shook off the last of her sleep and sat straight up. She brushed her long black hair back and blinked several times.

"Sure, Jack, just . . . um,"—she fell back into her seat—"bring him over here, okay?"

"I'm fine, Lee. You've done enough. You just get yourself back to normal."

"Ben, stop," Taylor said in a stronger voice. "You think of everyone before yourself. I can see that already. I want you to be better. Do it for me, then, okay?"

Ben just shook his head and smiled before walking over to stand in front of Lee. She remained seated, but she took both of his hands in hers. She closed her eyes, and almost immediately, they popped back open.

"Somebody, drag a chair over here for Ben. Something he can't fall out of. Just a precaution."

Once Ben had seated himself in the upholstered chair, his guard chair, Lee again took his hands, and her eyes closed. Several seconds later, Ben's eyes closed, and he slumped into the soft cushions.

* * *

Lee returned to her home, a field of lush green grass in a quiet valley, where time stood still beneath a dazzling blue sky. She looked up at her familiar sun and smiled. She felt her sun might have smiled back at her. She looked down and remembered why she'd returned.

A look at her stones showed that all were in order. No footprints were to be found anywhere in her meadow. The grass looked perfect. A moment of hesitation ensued, with Lee wondering what to do.

She realized quickly that there might not be an easy trail to lead her to Ben. She looked all around for anything out of order, but she saw nothing unusual. Except that her stones didn't shine as brightly as they had every other time. It shocked her to see shadows covering most of her stones, leaving very few alone in the intense sunlight. She'd never seen shadows in her home before.

She looked up again and saw a collection of branches, crowded with leaves, fanning across the sky and hampering her sun's efforts. She looked along the largest branch and saw that it extended out past her meadow and faded from her view.

She began a cautious walk in the branch's direction, feeling a growing pain with each step. Her right arm throbbed and curled itself in close against her body. But she continued her march, putting herself farther into the shade with each step.

She'd reached the edge of the grass, and still, she couldn't see where the branch would lead her. Into the tall weeds she stepped, taking her time and feeling the pain increase, wondering how far she'd be able to go. Her entire arm ached, and it had wound itself tight against her ribs and around her waist. She felt it weakening and withering, and she could no longer move it.

Struggling to think clearly through the pain, Lee passed into a clearing of low ground cover. The complete shade must keep grass from growing there, she thought.

Then, she saw it. A thick tree trunk, a mighty oak, planted firmly in the center of the clearing. She saw that near the trunk was total shade, and she knew she'd never make it that far—the pain would kill her. There had to be another way. A look to the left showed nothing unusual, but to the right, she saw that one of the branches had been bent to the Earth. And to Lee's welcome surprise, there were random patches of sunlight still reaching the ground.

She walked closer, into more darkness, feeling the pain spread to her shoulder and down her back. And when she was close enough, she could see that large stones had pinned to the ground many of the outer branches. She could feel the tree's frustration, its inability to lift up its trapped branches. It cried softly inside, and it sounded like only the wind.

Lee struggled to roll the closest stone away, using only her left arm, and she freed one of the branches. It took most of the strength she had left. The branch sprung up as far as it could, but its neighbors were all trapped, too, and they held it close to the ground. She moved the next closest stone, and the two branches together rose slightly farther.

She continued working in the shade, pushing herself to finish, all the while feeling her agony increasing. The pain had spread to her lungs, and she struggled to take in air. But the tree needed help. It might somehow free itself to once again raise all its branches to form an unbroken canopy, but when? How long might that take?

Nearing the limits of her abilities, her entire body racked with pain, Lee rolled aside the last stone, and in a rush, the entire branch sprang up to its natural height. The wind sound, the tree's soft crying, had ceased.

She stood in the shade, feeling near collapse in the darkness beneath the giant tree's leaves. She took joy in the oak's restored freedom, but she felt her left arm beginning to sag to the Earth too. And her head began to tip forward, too heavy to hold up. Her right arm had become a slender twig cramped to her side. Soon, she knew, she'd waste away and be reclaimed by the Earth.

Then, a thin strip of sunlight lit up her cheek. She looked up and saw that the branches had moved aside, from bottom to top, allowing a sliver of light to land on her.

She felt her pain decrease, and she took only one step before the agony returned. She was again in shade, and her misery was overwhelming.

Once again, the branches parted, and Lee's entire face basked in the light of her old friend, the sun that never moved. She took another step, and the branches moved again. So it continued, branches parting and Lee feeling her pain recede just enough to allow her to take another step, until she'd reached her home. The thick green grass in the quiet valley, beneath a sun that warmed her head to toe.

The pain that had nearly consumed her faded and her power began to return. She basked in the sunlight, lingering there in the silence and feeling her health return until she felt whole again.

She looked up at the branch which had begun to recede, allowing her stones to again shine brightly. She listened for the tree's cries, the sound of wind. But there was only silence. The branch had vanished. It was once again only her home.

* * *

Jack watched Lee again take a deep breath and let it out slowly. Her eyes opened, and they showed a fatigue worse than before. But she smiled at him. Several seconds later, Ben awoke.

He looked first at Lee, then Lin, then back at Lee.

"Who are you people? How can . . . how do you—"

He stopped himself and peeled away his bandages under the watchful eyes of everyone there. The unwrapping took half a minute, and no one spoke a word. Finally, his hand and wrist could be seen, and aside from the stains of antibiotics and traces of adhesive from the bandages, it was perfect. He'd been healed completely.

He looked at Lee with a big smile until he saw her eyes roll up, and she slumped into her chair.

"Taylor," said Ben, "if you don't mind, I'll carry Lee instead."

Chapter 33 – Infinity & Eternity

Heads turned in the hallways and out through the lobby. A blond woman in a short skirt and heels, with her hair flowing flawlessly from under a blue beret, walking and chatting with a younger blond woman that looked frail but moved with a surprising energy and strength. A large, rough-looking man with a bald head, carrying in his arms a black-haired woman in tight jeans and snakeskin boots, her hair covering his shoulder and her own black leather jacket. And a rugged man with wavy brown hair, his t-shirt stretched over tight muscles, walking silently next to another of their group who looked only forward.

*　*　*

Lin brushed her hair back, crossed her arms, and leaned against her Temt8tion. She looked at the questioning faces all around her and smiled.

"Taylor, Ben . . . you're healed, but we're not out of this yet. All of us, we need to get going. I'm sure The Shield will tail us once we leave just like coming here."

"We can't go back to the suite, can we, Lin?" said Jack.

"No, I have someplace much better in mind. The family cabin near St. Mary's. It's a drive, but it has what we need most right now."

"We'll be safe there, Mom?"

"No, there's no place safe from them. What it has is privacy. And we'll need that for what's coming."

Lin looked at Gabriel, who only nodded.

"Let's go."

They split up and formed a short caravan near the parking lot exit. Lin rode with Lee in the Temt8tion, and Renato still huddled in the backseat. Behind them followed Ben, driving his truck after he'd cleared the passenger side for Taylor. Jack's truck brought up the rear, with Gabriel in the front and Nomad in the back.

Before they'd made it to I76, the same three cars fell in behind them. Lin led the convoy at a comfortable pace, and she was well aware of the pursuers, who made no effort to conceal themselves. She shifted in her seat and tried to pull her skirt down some before she looked over at Lee. Lee had fallen asleep with the seat tilted back, one hand reaching into a cookie bag. Lin just shook her head and smiled.

*   *   *

The Temt8tion's big motor purred a deep tone, leading them all north on I76, then I476. At the transition to I80, instead of taking it west, Lin chose Route 940 and headed east. The entire procession joined her.

When they rolled through a secluded area, Lin quickly applied the brakes without any warning. All the vehicles behind her had bunched up before they came to a stop. She switched off the Temt8tion's engine and stepped onto the pavement. The breeze carried her mane up and back, but she flicked it on each side to be sure. A look of dangerous determination set in her green eyes.

Lin began a steady walk, her hips swaying and her heels clicking smartly on the cold pavement. Lee had just barely awakened after hearing the car door slam, and her sleepy eyes watched Lin walking away before she fell back asleep.

By the time she reached Ben's truck, he'd rolled down his window, but she never paused. Never even looked over. Ben and Taylor could only watch her pass their vehicle. Jack didn't even roll down his window. He and Gabriel watched her walk past, a woman with a purpose. And even Gabriel couldn't have known what to expect.

Lin's mayhem began to rise on its own, and her intent stopped time. She reveled in the world being so still—such a quiet, slow magic while she gazed at the endless, swirling sea of magic beneath it. She looked at the infinity all around, smiling at her own name of Lin Finity, and she drew in a deep breath of the fresh forest air.

She felt lost in the rapture of magic billowing up into her, swelling her spirit to the point of bursting. She continued her walk through a world frozen in time until she stood outside the driver's window of The Shield's lead vehicle. The green glow of her eyes bounced off of the glass, and she paused to view her reflection. But only for a moment.

Lin cracked open the door and looked inside. She noticed that Wolfe wasn't there and that the driver's open shirt revealed he wore no collar. She slammed the door shut just as she felt she was falling from the sky, and she exhaled sharply. Her sharp wave invaded the two men inside the car, and she traveled with it into their narrow spaces. She felt their silent screams, and then their terror settled in, and their silent shrieking began. She turned their heads to look at her, to see her eyes burning into them, as she took complete control. She smiled even more. No one would ever hurt her daughter. Or her friends.

It took only a moment for her to cause the driver to turn the steering wheel to the right. She removed his foot from the brake and pressed it down hard on the gas. The tires screamed against the road, spraying gravel on the car behind, as Lin drove it off the road and down the embankment. She'd chosen the place carefully, and the descent was gradual and long. The car came to rest hundreds of feet away in the tall grass, where it bogged down in cold mud with its headlights burning.

She released the two men but continued to hold time still as she walked to stand at the passenger window of the second car. Wolfe sat in the passenger seat, locked in place like the rest of the world. Behind him, Lin saw Daria and Anna, with Ozzy like a stuffed toy on her lap.

She allowed her mayhem to recede. With her mayhem fading, time continued, and Wolfe turned his head to see Lin outside his window.

Then, Lin immediately raged her mayhem to its highest level as she stared in on them. But she didn't stop time.

* * *

Wolfe sat in the passenger seat of the second car in line, and he shook his head slowly without making a sound. He'd seen Lin approaching their lead vehicle, and it shocked him, even though he'd stared into those glowing green eyes before, to again see them shining bright against the dark pine forest behind her. But no previous experience with Lin could have prepared him for what he witnessed next.

Instantly, he saw an empty space where the car in front of his had been, and Lin standing outside his own window. In less than a heartbeat, he saw her eyes flare bright green, so bright that they might melt the glass. It had all happened in less than the blink of an eye.

"Drive. Drive!"

"I can't, boss, he's right behind me!"

"Ram him. I don't care. Get me the hell out of here!"

His driver obeyed, throwing the car into reverse, gunning the engine, and spilling Wolfe's drink. The crash into the car behind them was loud, but Wolfe didn't hear it. He could only see her eyes calmly watching him, and he knew he was still inside her range.

"Go! Go! Go!"

Wolfe's car sped back the way they'd come, followed closely by their third vehicle.

* * *

Confident that they wouldn't be back, Lin let her mayhem drop to nothing, and she began a quicker walk back. She saw that Jack had rolled down his window, so she stopped to look in.

"Lin . . . that car . . . how—"

"Jack, we're safe from them now, at least for a while. That's all that matters."

She reached in and rubbed and scratched the big red head that eclipsed Gabriel.

"Gabby, I know you're back there somewhere. I bet you're hungry, aren't you?"

"Very much, like always, Lin. But I still have some cookies in my backpack. I'll be okay for a while. And Lin, it's good that you were kind."

"I want to be kind, Gabby. I really do."

Nomad retreated to the back seat, and she and Gabriel shared a smile, two travelers in a magical world, before Lin continued her walk.

*   *   *

"Ben, is everyone okay in here? Taylor, how do you feel?"

"Mom, I feel fantastic. I have no clue what's going on, though, so, maybe soon, if we get a chance, we—"

"Yes, Hon, I'll tell you everything I know. But really, I don't know how much I can explain. Ben, you taking good care of my girl?"

"Nothing could stop me, Lin."

He smiled at her like a proud father.

"I know, Ben. I can't thank you enough. We need to drive awhile. Will that be okay?"

"Of course. Lead the way."

*   *   *

Lin slammed the Temt8tion's door and sank into the contoured black leather. What a machine, she thought. It must have its own kind of magic.

Lee stared at her without speaking a word, so Lin fired up the motor and led her parade west, back to I80.

*   *   *

"How does she do that?"

"Do what?"

"Make things disappear."

Jack questioned Gabriel, even though he suspected Gabriel didn't have a clue either. He looked over, but Gabriel continued to look straight forward.

"The car? It didn't disappear. The man drove it down the hill."

"Alright, sure, but when? I saw her walk past us, and then the car was gone. It might as well have disappeared."

"She's special, Jack. She's a very special person."

"You've known her a long time, you've said. Has she always been like this? How much have you seen over the years?"

"Oh, there were times. But she's getting more impressive every day. The best thing you can do, Jack, is remember that you love her."

Jack looked out at the approaching roadway, his headlights reflecting off the dented chrome of Ben's rear bumper. Of course, he'd remember. He knew that he'd always love Lin. That part was easy. But understanding her—that was the challenge.

"I will, no matter what happens."

"And Nomad too," said Gabriel without looking over.

"Yeah, of course. Nomad too. But Gabriel, you know this group, The Shield. Will this ever end? Will she ever be free of them?"

"Yes, she will. The time is coming. Soon, I might even join in to help."

Jack let out a short laugh and shook his head.

"That's great, Gabriel. I'll be looking forward to seeing that."

"You might not believe your eyes, Jack."

Jack felt a chill run up his spine, and he turned to look at Gabriel, who only continued to stare out through the windshield.

* * *

"She healed us both, didn't she?"

"Yeah, she sure did."

"How did she do that? And why were my mom's eyes glowing like that? How could anyone's eyes do that, Ben?"

Ben wished he had an answer to more than just Taylor's first question. But he didn't. He knew only that Lin had some strange power when they were fifteen, back in St. Simons Island. And again, in the hotel room, over thirty years later, when she'd knocked him out without so much as a touch. She'd healed him in Allentown, too, restoring something that he'd lost, some damage he'd carried with him. And just now, he'd witnessed the car disappearing. And whatever she did, she'd terrified the rest of them so badly that they'd burned their tires to get away from her. He had no other answers.

"I don't understand Lee or your mom. But Lee healed us. We know that. I felt it, even though I was out cold. Did you feel anything?"

"Yeah, I sure did. But I don't think I can describe it. It felt like something opened up, like Lee opened up something inside me. And then I felt free. Inside. I don't know what that was, but when I woke up, I was all the way better, like I've never felt before. Ben, I feel so good!"

"It's the same with my hand. It throbbed real bad, and I know it would have taken forever to heal. I felt the pain getting less and less, and I woke up. That's all I remember."

Ben held his right hand up for Taylor to see.

"It's perfect. Like it never got hurt."

"Do you know this place where we're going?"

"No, I don't. But I do know that I'd follow your mom anywhere. I owe her my life. But I also owe Lee my hand."

Ben laughed, and Taylor joined him.

* * *

Lin felt something unsettled deep inside like more parts of her, parts without names, were finding a new arrangement. But she still smiled at the road approaching quickly and disappearing beneath the leading edge of her car. A quick glance in the mirror confirmed that her eyes weren't glowing, but she saw again a ferocity. And unyielding, unexplainable power. It made her smile and scared her at the same time.

"Lin, I think I must have slept through something. Weren't we being followed before?"

"Welcome back, Lee. Are you feeling better? You looked exhausted after your work at the hospital."

"Yeah, I'm mostly back to normal. That was difficult. But I did it, didn't I? Your daughter's better now?"

Lin forgot the sight of her own eyes at the mention of Taylor. She smiled a normal smile, happy to finally have time for a chat with Lee.

"I know that feeling. After what I did in their lair, I was more tired than ever before. Now, I feel much better, though. Yes, Taylor is perfect. So is Ben. How did you do that, Lee? I've mostly been able to hurt people. The only one I've helped has been Ben, but that was his spirit, I think. I don't understand what you're able to do."

Lee realized her hand was still in the cookie bag, and she retrieved one, holding it up, ready to take a bite. She reconsidered and turned to look at Renato, and she handed it to him instead. He accepted it and ate silently

"I don't understand it either. Somehow, I've taught myself to look inside, and when I do, I go to this place. The same place every time. I fix myself there, even from a gunshot."

"Do you fix everything? Every little thing that might be wrong with you?"

"Yeah, I think I do. I feel great. All the time."

"I have two questions. First, does that mean you'll never age?"

Lee's jaw dropped as she turned to look at Lin. "That's the same thing Gabriel asked me. Who is Gabriel anyway?"

"Oh, a very good friend. But really, you don't age, do you?"

"No, I haven't since I figured out what needed to be done."

Lin appeared ready to ask her next question, but she stopped and smiled instead.

"My name used to be Lin Finnerty. I've changed it to Lin Finity. Get it? Like 'infinity?'"

"Wow, that's really cool. It fits you too."

"What's your last name again? Turner?"

"Yeah, Turner."

Lin thought a moment and said, "From now on, to me at least, you'll be Lee Ternity."

Once again Lee's mouth hung open, and it quickly turned into a big smile. They laughed together as Lin Finity and Lee Ternity.

"I like it. I really like it!"

"You've earned it, that's for sure. But okay, my other question: how do you eat whatever you want? How is that possible? I'd love to be able to eat lots of chocolate every day. I'd probably be okay but maybe not. If I could fix it like you do . . . wow. How about some tips?"

"I'll explain it in more detail sometime, maybe when we're not on the run. But the simple version is that I go to a place inside, a place I call 'home,' and I arrange some stones. I put them in the exact arrangement that works. And it does work. Every time. It even fixed the bullet wound."

"That's incredible, Lee. And how did you help Taylor and Ben?"

"In some weird way, they were there too. In my home. I sensed what needed to be done. With Ben, he was a giant oak tree that had a branch pinned to the ground. I freed the branch, and the tree helped me get back, to return to myself somehow."

"Wow. Well, that makes sense—Ben as a big oak tree. How about Taylor?"

"That was different. Taylor was a bird. A dove. But the dove wasn't hurt. Not at all. She was trapped. All I did was set her free. And she helped me get back too."

"Taylor was a trapped bird? Are you sure?"

"No doubt about it. A beautiful bird. Trapped, but not hurt. Not even sick. I knew it."

Once again, Lin felt a mild breaking up inside. The nameless parts continued to shift, to find new patterns until they settled, and she knew.

"I trapped her," Lin said with a weariness in her voice. "I never knew. She must have been trapped since before she was born, and it took years before it showed itself in an illness that no one could cure."

"What do you mean? How could you have trapped her?"

"When I was fifteen, I locked away my power. It scared me, and I was afraid of what it could do. I only knew I couldn't control it. So, I buried it in a box inside. It's been locked away until last week.

"That's where Taylor began her life."

Lee remained quiet as Lin felt waves of guilt wash through her, carrying away the exhilaration of the magic, of her mayhem, of all the wonder in the world. A reflexive look in the mirror showed Renato still huddled in the back, his eyes wide and unfocused. The guilt of Renato's impossible life hit her hard too.

Lee noticed a single tear rolling down Lin's cheek.

"Lin, Taylor's fine now. Whatever happened, and however it happened, it wasn't your fault."

Lin couldn't answer. She only watched the road race up and vanish beneath her car as she led her friends west. And then, a harsh possibility hit her.

"Lee, how long have you had your power?"

"I started working on it when I was really little, but I only got it figured out nine years ago."

"And how old is Alessa?"

Lin didn't expect an answer and focused again on the road. From the corner of her eye, she saw that Lee's cookie bag had dropped to the floor.

"She's eight," Lee said, and the only sound that followed came from the car's big engine.

Chapter 34 – Time & Tents

The overgrown two-track road led them through a rapidly darkening forest. Lin's Temt8tion rode low above the ground, bending all but the shortest weeds and sometimes scraping against the earth. She led the procession through several twists, up and back down a few hills, and they spilled out into a large clearing. The fading light showed a solitary cabin set in the middle, with the nearest trees several hundred feet away. A cold moon looked down silently.

When all the engines had been shut down, Lin sat quietly and listened to the night sounds of the deserted Alleghany Mountains. She knew feelings of guilt had to be pushed aside, and she stepped out into the chilly air. Lee and Renato joined her.

When Jack opened his truck's door, Nomad leapt to the ground and charged straight to Lin. She welcomed him with open arms, and his kisses pushed her guilt further away.

"Okay, we should probably get our stuff inside before it's completely dark," she said.

"All this dog food too?" Jack said with a smile. "The sun will be up by then."

Tears collected in her eyes as she walked toward him.

"Oh, Jack . . ." she whispered to him as she wrapped her arms around his waist and pressed her face into his chest, unable to say any more.

Jack's face showed his surprise, and he laid his arms around her.

"My Cowgirl, we're fine. Everyone's fine." He rocked her gently.

The others had collected their things and filed into the cabin, while Lin and Jack continued to hug in the near darkness.

"I want to still be your Cowgirl, Jack. I . . . I just—"

"You'll always be my Cowgirl, Lin. We'll get through all of this. You and me." He rotated her to face the cabin. "And all of them too."

"I feel so strange, Jack. I'm exhausted and agitated. I'm scared of what my mayhem does, how it changes everything. But I'm thrilled with it too—it's amazing. But I wish I never had any of it. And still, I want more, just like that powerful woman Gabby told me about, the one that made Renato a scroll, and—"

"What woman? How could Renato be a scroll?"

"Oh, I don't even know anymore, Jack. I'm just tired. I'm not making sense. I just know I don't want to hurt anyone else. Especially not you or Taylor. And not Nomad. Ever. I'll never hurt that sweet fluffy boy again." She wiped at the last of her tears.

Jack hugged her, and they began a walk toward the house. Gabriel came out onto the porch and studied Lin closely.

"Lin, you're exhausted. You've done too much. You'll be fine, but you need to rest."

They led her inside, where Ben had started a fire that crackled and added a dancing light to the rustic room. Lee sat with him, gazing into the flames. Lin collapsed onto a couch, and Taylor brought over a blanket to cover her up.

"She's going to be alright, isn't she?"

"Yes," said Gabriel, "but she's very tired. I think we all are. Why don't we all find a spot and get some rest?"

* * *

Lin awoke to the logs on the fire hissing and snapping. A look around the wood-paneled room showed that everyone was asleep except Renato. He sat near the fire, gazing into it and looking lost.

She recalled her emotional display outside the cabin. How she'd felt broken as if too many pieces didn't fit. That feeling had begun to pass. She felt stronger and more confident, ready for what she knew had to come next.

"Gabby." Lin shook Gabriel gently. "Gabby, wake up."

"Uh . . . Lin . . . okay, I'm up. What's wrong?"

"Nothing. Well, no, not nothing. It's Renato—he's not going to make it. He wanted to be a man again, but I think he believed he'd be back in his world, the only one he's ever known. He'll never understand this world. What can we do?"

"There's no way for him to go back in time, Lin. It never stops. It just—"

"Wait. Hold it. When I use my mayhem, time stops. Everything in the world comes to a stop. Things freeze in midair. So, what do you mean that it never stops? I've seen it many times, and I—"

"Lin, think about it. How could time stop around you and nowhere else? You don't believe you're stopping time for all of creation, do you?"

"So . . . what, then? How does it make sense?"

"Do you remember that color, in the magic? Okay, trick question. Of course, you don't remember it. You can't remember it. But you remember seeing it. In the magic, things are different. And just as that color doesn't exist in our world, time doesn't exist in the magic. The world's not stopping around you, Lin. You're in the magic. You're outside of time."

Lin sat and stared at Gabriel, struggling to answer as she felt more subtle shifts inside. A new arrangement. A new understanding.

She still couldn't speak, so Gabriel continued.

"That's how Renato could exist for so long. He was mostly in the magic. He only has one lifetime. But in the magic . . . well, that could take forever."

Gabriel had found part of a sandwich and took a bite.

"How do you think I've been around for so long?"

Gabriel took another bite and looked at Lin, this time waiting for a reply. It took a while.

"Gabby, that fits. It doesn't make 'sense,' but I know it's right. The world just looks like it stopped. And to anyone in the world, no time has passed. Wow, I don't think I'm ever going to accept all this. It's too much."

"It's the easiest thing in the world, Lin. Just don't fight it. You're still trying to have things make sense, to fit into your mind in this world. There's so much more."

"Okay. Okay, I'll deal with all that in a while. Right now, we need to figure out what to do about Renato. Yes, we can't go back in time. He'll never go home. But he can't live like this. Not here and now."

"I think you're right. He needs help. And there is a way. We can't know how it will turn out, though. Perhaps we need to take that chance anyway."

"What are you thinking?"

"I was with you for over thirty years. My spirit shared your world with you. There were countless times where I, in a way of speaking, closed my eyes. During those times, I had no idea what you were doing. You always had your privacy. But I'm getting off track. I just wanted you to know that.

"The same can be done with Renato. His spirit can join someone else's. Someone from here and now. He'd have all the feelings and memories of this time and place, and that anguish he's feeling now will be gone."

"But what about the other person, Gabby? What will that do to them? It doesn't seem fair."

"I've never done this before, but I think there's a way. Renato's spirit will not have an active role in the person's life, but Renato will have all the benefits of fitting into the world again. The host will never know. He might notice a slight change in the beginning, but he'll never even know Renato is there."

"So, how would Renato be happy that way? That sounds like another type of prison for him."

"No, not at all. A large part of his spirit will be focused on the magic, and he'll feel mostly what every other creature on Earth feels. He'll feel content. And here's the best part: he'll gradually become a part of the other person. They'll merge after many years, and Renato will be a new, complete person. They, together, will be one person."

Lin brushed her hair back over her shoulders and leaned into the couch cushion. She stared straight ahead, considering the options. She knew that Gabriel's plan was the best and maybe the only good option. They had to give it a try.

"How do we pick this person that's going to adopt Renato?"

"We're in the mountainous area of Pennsylvania, and there are many campsites around. Let's take a walk to one nearby and see what we find. I'll look for a solitary type, maybe someone who's disenchanted with the world anyway and ready for some kind of change. There are more people like that than you can imagine. The actual transfer of Renato will take hardly any time.

"In fact, it will all happen in the magic, so it won't take any time at all."

* * *

The nearest campsite wasn't hard to find on a map. Lin's Temt8tion rumbled into the parking lot, and she killed the engine. The flashlights Jack had purchased for her rescue were finally put to good use as the three of them hiked down a path to within a five-minute walk to the camp. From there, they went off-trail and circled around to come in from the cover of the forest.

The moon lit up the area enough to make two tents visible. One was large, and lights could be seen inside it, and a nearby fire was tended by three people. The other tent was small, dark, and silent. It sat off near the perimeter, close to the tree line.

"Lin," Gabriel whispered, "use your mayhem. Stop time long enough to go peek in that small tent. My guess is there's a man in there by himself, but we need to know for sure. Take note of anything you see in there, and tell me your impression of him."

Lin didn't hesitate. She focused her intent and found the switch, the switch to begin her mayhem. She knew it was nothing more than being what she needed to be, but she liked the idea of there being a switch. She flipped that switch, and she became what her mayhem demanded her to be. And her mayhem rose. Her eyes began to glow, and she let them, knowing that she preferred bright green eyes to a halo. Or horns.

Infinity spread out from her in every direction. The world again appeared as a calm, flat surface, and she observed sparks from the fire locked in place above it. Thin trails of smoke hung like twisted icicles. Not a sound could be heard in the forest all around them.

She rejoiced in seeing the immense masses of magic rolling into and over each other, creating shapes and patterns that would never be repeated and that could never be remembered. She felt her spirit longing to break free, to join all that magic and be part of it, even before she drew in a deep breath. When she did, it filled her with unknowable scents and tastes and textures and feelings of magic until she thought she'd burst. The pressure continued to grow, forcing its way to every part of her body, until she felt she could take no more. She felt she was falling as she let the breath out sharply. A massive boulder crashed onto the still surface of reality, and she focused her wave straight up at the stars.

Lin made her way to the small tent, where she unzipped the flap and peered in. A lone man lay there in a sleeping bag, lit up by her glowing eyes. She saw that he'd fallen asleep with a pen and tablet in his hands. She read the note, which was only a beginning of a message, and she knew that Gabriel had led them to Renato's new life.

Halfway back to Gabriel and Renato, Lin paused to look up at the sky. She heard the silence all around her, and she saw things that should be moving but that were waiting. Waiting for her to return from the magic. Looking from star to star, her gaze finally rested on the moon. It looked down on her, and she tried to discern if it had a life, a spirit of its own. Her mayhem allowed her to see the limitless, unimaginable amounts of magic that created it new in every moment. The beauty, the miracle of it, made her want to weep, and she wondered if the moon would feel the same about her. But she sensed nothing from it. Only indifference. So be it, she thought.

Back at Gabriel's side, she let her mayhem fade. She saw the swirling fields of magic below become hidden once more. Infinity could no longer be seen. Sparks rose from the fire along with trails of smoke, and the forest sounds came alive. The world's time had never stopped.

"Gabby, we found the right guy."

"That's great, Lin, but why all the breathing and glowing eyes and sending a wave up into the sky?"

"Oh, that. I like it. Anyway, he's our guy."

She told him what the man had written on his tablet, the first sentence of a note to a woman. But he'd never finished before he'd given up, and sleep had taken him.

"I agree. This is good. Is there anything you want to say to Renato before he's gone?"

Lin turned toward Renato, who only looked at the ground. Although he must have heard their discussion, he'd had no reaction. He'd stopped speaking shortly after they'd left Baltimore.

"Renato, I wish there was a way to send you back home. But you know that your islands don't exist anymore. And I don't know how you could ever be happy in this world. Heck, it's nearly impossible for us too. You trusted me once, Renato, and now, please trust me again. Allow us to help you. You'll be happy. I promise."

He looked up and said, "I trust you, Lin. But I am afraid. Will I have to forget my life? Can I never tell anyone about the islands that were my home?"

"Renato, it will take a while before you could do that anyway. You'll be comfortable and content, and you'll watch the world and enjoy it. But when you're able, go ahead and shout it from the rooftops. Hell, write a book. No one will believe you anyway."

He smiled at her, and he seemed to be more at ease. He appeared ready.

With Renato standing between them, Lin and Gabriel both focused their intent and the world seemed to stop. Lin never felt anything but awe when seeing infinity extending from her in every direction and endless depths of magic churning below. The three walked to the small tent.

She released Renato's hand, and he stepped forward to stand next to Gabriel. Lin saw Gabriel's eyes light up brighter than ever before, and she felt a powerful wave wash over her, lifting her impossibly high and snapping her back down. Her senses overlapped in a familiar madness until they all broke a boundary and came to rest in the magic.

Without Gabriel's hand to guide her, she felt a moment of uncertainty. But she found her intent deep inside, and she held it tight as she witnessed the chaos storming all around. She knew she wouldn't be lost there, at least not right away. But she stayed close to Gabriel anyway as they traveled toward the lone camper.

From there, Lin could only watch in amazement. She witnessed Gabriel guiding Renato's magic, his spirit, and interweaving it among the stranger's. The man's magic still shone brightly, but if Lin looked closely, she could see traces of Renato's mixed in. In an instant, it was done.

Lin felt another immense wave, and after breaking the barrier and sailing high in the sky and quickly back down, she stood next to Gabriel in the real, but still silent, world. Their eyes continued to glow brightly.

As Gabriel's eyes returned to their normal color, she felt her mayhem dwindle and finally disappear. She gazed up at the silent moon looking down, offering no opinion on what had just happened in that lonely tent.

Lin stood listening to the forest's night sounds next to her best friend, a being she hoped she was beginning to comprehend.

Chapter 35 – Life & More Life

Back in her Temt8tion, Lin and Gabriel sat and looked out at the darkness before heading back to the cabin. Although the mountain air carried a chill and a hint of campfire smoke, they kept the windows down. Pale moonlight bathed the car's hood, and she could make out individual points of it reflecting off of the line of lights down the hood's center.

"Gabby, I feel strong and healthy, but I'm weary too. These last ten days have blown my world apart. I wonder if I'll ever feel comfortable again."

Gabriel's arm continued to wave out the window as if sculpting the moonlight into some creation more likely to be found in the magic.

"Yes, you are strong and healthy. You've learned a lot, and you've done a lot. You've earned every bit of your weariness."

"But where do I go from here? What is this all about?"

"What exactly are you asking, Lin?"

Lin paused to collect her thoughts. After Gabriel's direct question, she realized she'd had only vague concerns darting through her mind, coming at her from every angle. She respected Gabriel's wisdom. She knew she needed to at least focus her questions.

"I'm still in my old life, with everyone I know. Everyone in the world is still going about their business. None of that has changed. But I see now that it's an illusion, or rather, a clever disguise. There's so much more. I feel like I cracked that disguise into pieces when my mayhem first rose up and destroyed Ray. I tried to hold the pieces together by hiding that part of me away—by putting my mayhem in a box inside.

"But it wouldn't stay in there forever. And I wouldn't have survived without you. Or I might have destroyed everyone around me. I just don't know. But here I am, with my mayhem and so much more. I can summon my mayhem anytime, and I see infinity. And such unimaginable magic. I even changed my name, Gabby."

"And what is your question, Lin? What do you need to know?"

"Why? Why is the world like this? Why does everyone struggle through their lives, unaware of the magic that creates them, the magic that I can see and use? Why me?

"Why is it possible for me to know the magic?"

"There it is, Lin. That's the question. Why indeed . . ."

Lin waited, holding her breath, expecting an answer from the wisest being she could imagine—the friend who had guided her and kept her safe for more than three decades.

"I don't know."

Lin's heart sank a bit, but she wasn't surprised. She'd learned earlier that Gabriel had no answer to that question. But she'd hoped that somehow, at that time, under the moonlight, alone in the woods, an answer would be revealed.

"The Words," said Lin. "The answer must be in the Words. But I've gone through them so many times, and I haven't found an answer. It's all about suffering, that that's the point of it all. How could that be, Gabby? Is this some kind of Hell?"

Gabriel turned to look at Lin, unblinking eyes locked on hers.

"No. Of that I'm sure. I've seen great evil. I've fought it. It wants you to believe that this world is pointless, that none of what we do matters. But it does matter, Lin. And the magic is part of it. I just don't know what it all leads to. What the purpose might be."

"So, we just keep trudging along, fighting to choose good and not knowing why?"

"Yes. That's all we can do. No expectations. No hope for rewards. You asked once why I can't involve myself in normal human conflicts, and you wondered if it was a rule. I reminded you that you didn't need to read an exact rule telling you to be kind to small animals. And when you're kind, when you don't act in a cruel way, are you expecting a reward?"

"No, of course not. I guess I see your point. We choose good because it's the right thing to do. And I will. With your help, I've learned to choose good. I'm just wondering why. Why all the magic.

"Why me."

* * *

Lin lost herself in her thoughts, looking back on her life from the moment her mayhem had first erupted. She recalled the anguish and struggle that had led to her mayhem. How she'd bottled it up out of fear. How it came back so many years later. And all she'd learned since then. She felt dizzy trying to wrap it all up into something cohesive, a life that made sense. She laughed out loud at that, remembering all the proof of the magic not making sense.

Gabriel had kept quiet, but at Lin's laughter, began a new conversation.

"Lin, you know that I can't stay with you forever. I'm not leaving yet, but that time might be approaching. There's something I want to show you. In the magic. Like when we saw that color that exists only there, not here. We can leave now."

Lin laughed again, saying, "Gabby, let's go. Show me something else in the magic that makes no sense. I'll leave my mind here."

Gabriel didn't take her hand, but she saw green light reflected off the dashboard in front of her. She felt her own eyes glowing brightly, followed by a wave that both washed over her and emanated from her at the same time. Together, they rode their wave to an impossible height, where they lingered briefly, Lin anticipating the fall. Then, they crashed down through a barrier, where her senses mingled and overlapped. They came to rest amid a swirling storm of magic that writhed all around them.

Only then did Gabriel take her hand, and to Lin it was a feeling, an idea, a memory. It was madness. It was the magic, and it existed outside the realm of her mind.

Gabriel led her to a quieter region, and though Lin knew it didn't make sense, because it couldn't, she had the feeling that they were rising to a surface. She wasn't prepared for the sight. She and Gabriel were below the calm surface of the world, treading in the chaotic magic. Above them, she saw the campsite, the large tent with three people huddled around a fire. Farther away, she could see the lone stranger, who was now also Renato, lying quietly in the darkness. But Gabriel had brought her to the other campers, for what she didn't know.

They rested there, two beings of calm among the storming magic all around, until they'd slowed even more. Lin felt her intent focusing like it never had before, and she could make out the separate magic of each individual. A shock wave raced through her when she saw that each person's magic was shaped like their physical body. Their bodies were mere reflections of their magic!

Several minutes passed, or it might have been centuries, and Lin calmed further, and her intent focused more sharply. She saw that each person's magic glowed softly—a light, green glow that infused every part of their magic with uncountable thin strands passing through the barrier, connecting them to their bodies.

But each of them was also connected to the limitless magic below, which Lin could see flowing into them, creating them anew in every moment. Lin quaked inside at witnessing the miracle of life, the miracle of creation. Creation didn't happen once long ago. It was happening in every moment, sustaining everything.

Gabriel nudged her to one side or somehow focused her perception on the fire. She saw that it, too, was connected to the magic, but the magic had no light. No green coloring. No life. It was also being created in every instant.

She knew that Gabriel had shown her those things for a reason—it was a lesson. Unbidden by Gabriel, she shifted her focus to the magic of a stone, just one of the small rocks ringing the campfire. She saw no green light, just endless magic creating it, allowing it to exist in the real world. She felt Gabriel's hand begin to pull her, to take her back to reality. To end the lesson.

But she lingered, holding the view of the rock's magic. She calmed herself even further until not the slightest thought could be found.

And a subtle, barely noticeable sight rocked her to her core.

She shivered inside, even while in the magic. But Gabriel's grip allowed her no more time. After tugging her away from the campsite, Gabriel released her again, and together, they broke the barrier. Lin felt that she raced to the clouds with Gabriel, where they paused before they dove through the sky and opened their still-glowing eyes in her car.

* * *

Their eyes slowly returned to normal, and Gabriel turned to her.

"Lin, did you see life in the magic? How living things have a light but no other things do?"

She opened her mouth but closed it without speaking. She continued to stare into the darkness beyond the glass, studying the tiny points of moonlight trailing along the curved hood.

"Lin, are you okay?"

She turned to look at Gabriel.

"Gabby, it's all alive."

Gabriel's mouth hung open, eyes big and staring directly into Lin's.

"What are you talking about?"

"Not just people. Not just animals and bugs and plants. It's all alive."

Lin felt tears trickling down both cheeks, but she knew she wasn't crying. Her breathing was calm and steady, and her voice betrayed no strong emotions.

"Lin, only living things have the green light. It's a magic thing. It's why our eyes naturally glow that color. No other thing has that green light."

"You're right. You're absolutely right," she said. "Nothing else has that green glow. But it all glows. It's hard to see, but I saw it. I saw the magic of a stone glowing."

She waited for a response from Gabriel, but she was met with only silence. Many long seconds passed.

She turned to look back out into the night, the night of a world much more mysterious and majestic than she ever could have imagined.

Gabriel only sat looking at her, completely silenced.

She turned back to face Gabriel.

"Lin, that can't be life. Whatever you saw, it's not life as we know it."

"No, you're right . . . not as we know it. Not as we *have* known it."

She closed her eyes, squeezing the last tears onto her cheeks, and leaned back against the headrest. But a small smile showed, even in the weak moonlight.

"Lin, I think maybe you're still tired. I probably shouldn't have taken you there. Why don't we get back to the others?"

Many quiet seconds passed before she answered.

"Okay, Gabby. I am tired. I'm not sure of anything right now. Let's get back."

Lin opened her eyes and brought life to her Temt8tion.

Chapter 36 – Hope & Evil

The warmth and comfort of the cabin greeted Lin and Gabriel as did questioning eyes.

"What happened to Renato?" said Jack. "Is he okay?"

"Yes," said Lin, "he's going to be fine. But he won't be with us any longer."

Jack and Lee looked at each other, then back to Lin, but they didn't question her further.

"I won't be with you much longer either," said Lee. "I need to head back home in the morning. I need to get back to Alessa."

Lin understood Lee's need to get back more than anyone else could have. She knew that Lee must be wondering how her own powers had affected Alessa. It must be tearing her up inside, and she needed to be back with her daughter.

From near the fire, Ben spoke up. "Me too, Lin. I called Luanne and left a message. At least, she knows I'm still alive. But I gotta get back there. I don't think you need me anymore anyway."

"Ben, I hate to see you leave. You've helped me so much."

"Don't go, Ben!" said Taylor. "We need you here. I need you here. You can't go."

Ben looked over at Taylor, who had tears in her eyes, and said, "Don't worry, I'm not leaving yet. But soon. I have thirty years of crap that I handed to Luanne, and I gotta make up for that. I'll see you again—I promise."

Taylor wiped at her tears and sat back down, and Nomad let out a low whine and nuzzled her hand.

"Lin, you and I still need to talk," said Lee. "Maybe we can spend some time, um, comparing notes?"

"Yes, of course. I really want to. We will."

"What are we going to do, Lin?" said Jack. "Those people aren't done with you, are they?"

"Those people can't hurt her, Jack," said Gabriel. "Even if they come back, which they might not."

Gabriel turned toward Lin.

"Lin, I'm already thinking about breakfast. Is there a diner close by?"

"Mom, can I come back home with you?" said Taylor. "I don't even have my apartment anymore."

Lin scanned the room, looking at all the questioning faces just as her cell phone rang. She recognized Anna's number and switched on the speaker. The room fell silent.

"This is Lin."

"Lin Finity! This is Wolfe. Got a minute?"

Gabriel whispered, "Lin, Wolfe is gone, remember? That's something else."

"Yes, I have a minute. What do you want? Haven't you had enough?"

"We've lost some people, that's true enough. And you've scared a lot of us—me included!" Wolfe said with a laugh. "But we're back to the same, simple, nagging question, Lin. What was written on the Scroll?"

Lin glanced at Gabriel, who only shrugged at her smile.

"God, you just don't get it, do you? That wasn't just a scroll. Oh, you know what? Never mind. It doesn't matter. You want the Words? Fine. I'll tell them to you. You can write them down, you can record them, whatever the hell you want. If you're looking for comfort or reassurance, you'll have to keep looking. Tell me when you're ready."

The room remained completely silent, with every pair of eyes focused on Lin.

"Go ahead," said Wolfe. "Let's have them."

Gabriel whispered again to Lin, who covered the phone with her hand. "Lin, are you sure you want Wolfe to know the Words? You'll become expendable to him."

"Gabby, I'm done putting everyone in danger. If Wolfe still wants me after this, I'll destroy him. This has to end."

In a calm, clear voice, Lin began reciting the Words that Renato had spoken to her:

"Every garden needs water, every plant needs rain . . ."

She stopped and held her abdomen with both hands. Gabriel stood next to her with a hand on her back.

"Lin, are you okay?"

"I think so. Just tired. I need to get through this. And I will."

"Every garden needs water, every plant needs rain,
For my children mankind, not water, mostly pain.
To see what I see, you must continue to grow,
And if you have time, I might be one you will know."

"Set sail toward pleasure, if you waste your days,
If you think not of me, your soul will stray.
If your life were too easy, you might let down your guard,
And the end of your days will be cold and hard."

"Let friends desert you, still try to find the light,
It is there holding you up, but use not your sight.
Recognize me there, learn what I am,
To know me better than any woman or man."

"Your strength will fail, you will feel death beside you,
You will have to stop running, there will be no place to hide you.
If it is trying you have forsaken, asking for help instead,
Know that no help is coming, only more that you dread."

"Death will take you, and chill you to the bone,
And even with friends, you will be all alone.
If you have not found me, can you be sure where you will go?
No, you chose free will, and with it you cannot know."

Lin's legs began to buckle, and she would have fallen, but Jack and Gabriel held her from each side.

"Lin, what's wrong?" said Jack.

She covered her phone.

"Nothing, Jack. I think I'm still exhausted, though."

"Lin," said Gabriel, "you felt fine before you spoke the Words."

"I know, Gabby. When I finished, I felt something like last time. Something inside."

She held her phone up again.

"There. Now you know the Words. Are you happy?"

Everyone in the cabin waited to hear a response through Lin's phone, but only long seconds of silence followed.

"Actually, yes," Wolfe said and laughed. "I'm very happy." He continued to laugh.

"And what exactly is so amusing to you?"

"It's hopeless. We're all in a world without hope. It's like you summarized before, Lin. Don't even waste your time praying. No one's coming. No one's even listening. You're here to suffer."

"And why on Earth would you be happy about that?"

"Because it doesn't make a goddamn bit of difference what we do. When people hear these Words, and they know the truth, they'll turn to *me*. Not God. Me."

Gabriel cut in. "You're still going to lose, Wolfe, or whatever you call yourself. We will find hope, even in those Words."

"No. No, you really won't. You heard her, Gabriel. We're all here for pain, and our ending will be cold and hard. 'No help is coming,' Gabriel. Lin, tell the whole world what God has said. If you don't, I will."

He continued to laugh until the call ended.

Lin put the phone down on the coffee table and sat on the couch. Gabriel sat next to her and Jack on her other side.

"It can't end like this, Gabby. It can't be hopeless. And why is Wolfe so happy about that?"

"Wolfe isn't really a man, Lin. Think of all the evil you've known in your life. Think of Ray. Think of Doc, whom you put down on that road in Georgia. They were evil. That evil was encouraged by Wolfe. Think of the young man in the diner, ready to inject you and take you. He didn't want to. That was encouraged by Wolfe."

"It all comes from Wolfe? How can that be?"

"No, not exactly from Wolfe. But he rejoices in it. He's given his existence to it. He believes those Words will bring even more to his side. He feels stronger just from hearing those Words. But Lin, this won't stop him. He won't want you going around performing miracles, telling people to choose good. He'll be back."

"Then, I will face him, whatever he is. But all of you," she said, looking around the room, "I want you all safe. You should go."

"I'm not going anywhere, Lin," said Jack. "I will never desert you."

"Thanks, Jack," she said with a big smile, looking into his adoring brown eyes.

"But the rest of you—Ben, Lee, even you, Taylor—I need you to be safe, at least until this is over. Wolfe wants me. Only me. Like Gabby said, he needs to stop me."

Ben and Lee looked down, not happy but agreeing. They both had lives they needed to continue. Taylor had a look of anguish on her face.

"Mom, I just now found you again. And I'm cured—Lee cured me! I want to stay with you. Maybe I can help somehow?"

"Okay, Taylor, but let Jack keep an eye on you if anything happens, okay?"

Taylor nodded.

"Ben, you should get back home. I'll be fine. I really will. And you too, Lee. Your daughter needs you. In the morning? Both of you?"

They nodded.

"Gabby, you're not leaving yet, are you? I'm sure Wolfe will be back, and I know you can't intervene with people, but it will still help to have you here."

Jack watched Gabriel silently, the look of disgust replaced with curiosity.

"Yes, Lin, of course, I'll stay. And don't worry about Wolfe. I'm sure *we'll* be fine," Gabriel said with a smile.

Chapter 37 – Secrets & Laughter

After everyone had consumed a hearty late meal, and while Gabriel still picked at the crumbs left in the pie tin and a donut box, Lin and Lee made their way to a quiet corner to talk. Lin had changed into jeans, hiking boots, and a thick sweater. Lee still wore her tight faded jeans and black snakeskin boots. But her leather jacket had been tossed aside, and a fresh t-shirt had replaced her blood-soaked sweater.

Lin brushed back her hair and leaned into the chair cushions. Lee did the same. Each chair faced the fire, and they settled in with a bottle of Merlot. Lin uncorked it, poured two glasses, and handed one to Lee.

"Lin, I traveled here to find you because of what I saw in Jacksonville. Well, I didn't really see anything, but you know what I mean."

"Yes, I do know. I took over Alex because of things he said and the things I thought he might do. I didn't mean to hurt him. Just scare him."

"Yeah, you scared him alright," said Lee. "He was a crybaby after that. I put him on his plane, and I haven't heard from him since. He'll be back, though. I hope that changed him some."

"Good, that's all I wanted. He reminded me of someone from my past, someone abusive. I had to do something."

"What exactly did you do, Lin? I felt something funny, but I didn't see anything. And in no time at all, Alex was on the floor."

Lin smiled and took a big sip, thinking back to using her mayhem, how effortless it had become by then.

"I can try to explain it, but even to me, it doesn't make sense. Well, I'm learning that 'sense' has nothing to do with it. Anyway, let me try. God, I need to go all the way back, don't I? Back to when it first started?

"Okay, here goes. I was sexually abused by an uncle from the age of twelve to fifteen. To keep my family together, I didn't tell anyone. So, there was no help for me. But I faced it with all the strength I could muster as just a child. And somehow, Lee, I got stronger until one day, something erupted out of me. I blacked out, but Ray, he was finished. Since then, I've remembered what happened. I invaded him, and I destroyed him."

Lee stared with eyes stretched open, but she still managed a swallow of wine.

"Right after that, the power I had, it wrecked Ben too. It didn't kill him, but he was ruined. On the inside. But that ended well. I repaired his damage Monday evening when I thought he was attacking me. I could see what was wrong, and somehow, I knew how to fix it. The Ben you see here isn't the same Ben the world has known for the last thirty years.

"After I hurt young Ben, I buried it. I buried it deep, too afraid to face it, too afraid of what it might do. Until Monday of last week. It erupted again a couple of times, and it hurt some people. But I eventually got control of it. I was dying on a road in Georgia. I was being strangled, and I looked inside, and after all that time, all that confusion, it was as plain as can be. I just had to be what my mayhem demanded of me."

"Your mayhem?"

"Yeah," said Lin, "that's what I call it. All I had to do was calm myself and focus something inside, something that Gabriel calls 'intent.' When I do that, time stops. Or at least, it seems that way. But I see infinity, Lee, in every direction, and so much magic . . ."

Lin looked up at the ceiling, smiling like a child seeing something so amazing, so incomprehensible, that all they can do is forget themselves and gaze at the wonder of it.

"And I can send out a wave. At first, it seemed like it had something to do with my breath, but Lee, it's all intent. I can ride that wave and invade someone, like I did with Alex. And from there, God, the things I can do."

Lee's face betrayed some fear, and she shrank farther back into her seat.

"And I can do other things too. Like that concrete wall. You saw what I did. What my intent did. It's all magic, Lee, and intent is the key. My intent is getting stronger every day. I don't know where it's taking me, though."

"But how do you . . . how can you—"

"Lee, I don't think I can explain it and certainly not teach it. It started with the abuse and my facing it. Looking back, I think that every time I withstood the abuse, my intent was getting stronger. I was learning how to focus it. And now, it's so easy. Like flipping a switch."

Lin flipped that switch, and Lee recoiled as Lin's eyes blazed a bright green before fading back to their normal color.

"But I have to tell you, Lee, that nothing is free. Many times, I think I'm doing something simple, something that's only good, and there are unexpected results. Probably the biggest one, though, is Taylor. Her entire existence began inside me, where I'd hidden a huge part of myself in a box. Locked it up tight. That's where Taylor began her life. And you saw the result. A bird, you said? A bird in a cage? You saved her, Lee. You did that, and I can't thank you enough. But I have no idea how you did it."

Lin finished her glass and poured another.

Lee stayed silent and held her glass out for a refill.

"Lin, none of that even sounds possible. If I hadn't had such strange experiences myself, I'd think you were just crazy or evil. Or both. But I get it. There's magic. And you've learned to use it, affecting people around you. Oh yeah, and concrete too."

They shared a laugh and clinked their glasses.

"I've always focused on myself because of my health. Yeah, focus is the right word. Just like you did, but with me, it was all inside. I know this will sound weird, but I go to this place where there's bright green grass in a peaceful valley. And up above, there's a clear blue sky, with a sun right over me, and it never moves.

"It took a long time to figure this out, but now I know. There's a proper arrangement, a pattern I make with stones that I found there. I call it a figure eight. Gabriel called it infinity. When I arrange the stones exactly in the right places, I'm back in perfect health."

"Wait," said Lin. "You do this all the time? That's how you eat so much crap and still look good?"

"Yeah, that's all it takes for me. I can eat anything. And like I said, I've stopped aging from it."

"You've earned the name Lee Ternity, that's for sure. I need to learn what you do. I want to eat junk too."

They laughed again, each taking a sip.

"So, Lin, how do we learn from each other?"

"I don't think we can. No one taught us any of this. We each faced something and took it head on. With me, it was outside. With you, it was inside."

"You're right. We fought alone. Because we are alone," said Lee. "That's how it works."

"For me to ever learn what you've learned, I'd have to battle something on the inside. I think that's the only way. But how could I do that? What would I fight?"

"It would have to be the same for me. I'd need an outside battle."

Lin ran her fingers through her hair and smoothed it to the back. A smile lit up her face.

"Okay, these are probably terrible ideas, but hear me out. And they'd probably never work because for each of us, it took a long time to learn. But for me, what if I intentionally contracted some fatal disease? I'd feel it starting to kill me, and that would be my challenge. I'd have to figure it out or die. And you, you could put yourself in a dangerous situation, one that you knew you wouldn't survive. Where someone was about to kill you. You'd have to figure it out."

"Lin, I don't think we should try any of that. There's no way either of us could learn that quickly. No. I'm not doing anything like that."

"Of course, you're right. Just thinking out loud, I guess. Instead of doing any of that, why don't we find a way to team up? We won't need each other's powers if we have each other."

"Team up and do what? What's the point?"

"To keep learning. I don't understand it, Lee, but I think that's what's important—to keep learning. Why don't you go back to your daughter tomorrow morning. Think about all this. Maybe get things in order and come back, at least to visit. Give it some thought, okay?"

Lee looked skeptical, and she paused a long moment before nodding her head.

"Okay, Lin, I'll think about it. Because I really want to learn what you do."

"And I want to eat junk."

They interrupted their own laughter only to finish the bottle.

Chapter 38 – Cowgirls & Cowboys

Lin and Lee rose from their chairs and embraced, feeling a bond that went beyond anything the world had likely seen before. With big smiles, they rejoined the group.

"What was that all about?" said Taylor. "We heard you laughing a lot, but Mom, what's funny about any of this?"

"There's nothing funny. You're right. We just shared some experiences from our lives, and you know, why not laugh once in a while?"

"It's late, everyone," said Lee, "and I'm tired. I'm going to use one of the bedrooms, if no one minds."

No one cared, so Lee retired and closed the door.

"I'll take the couch," said Jack.

"Sitting by the fire is good enough for me," said Ben.

"Me too. I want to sit there too. I want to sit up and watch the fire awhile. It feels so good just doing anything. Or nothing. I've never felt this good before."

"That sounds good, Taylor," said Lin. "But I'm exhausted too. If no one cares, I'll take the other bedroom. Gabriel, how about you?"

"Oh, I'm not quite done here yet. And there's a box of crackers in that cabinet I want to get into. After all that, I'll just curl up somewhere. Like a dog. I'll be fine."

The rummaging through the pantry continued, a serious Nomad standing near and watching every move.

Soon, everyone had found a place for the night, with the only sounds coming from the kitchen. Finally, those noises stopped as well. The cabin and its inhabitants enjoyed the quiet of night.

* * *

Lin felt weak sunlight hitting her in patches, and she looked up to see a quilt of tree branches blocking the sky. The sun struggled to send its warmth through the narrow openings. She followed the covering with her eyes and saw that it enclosed a carved-out cell, cut into the Earth, with barely enough room for her to lie down. Very much like a grave.

One by one, twigs and smaller branches began falling into her prison, laying across her in odd patterns, new ones covering older ones, fresh ones falling every second, until the sunlight dwindled, and no more reached her. She felt the weight of the branches, knowing they were stacked high, and she attempted to raise her arms, hoping to push the branches aside. But she couldn't move. The weight was too great.

Lin knew she had only minutes before the mass above would crush her or she'd be unable to continue breathing, and she pondered her predicament. She couldn't remember how she'd come to be in the cage. She couldn't remember, and she knew it didn't matter anyway.

This was her life, and no one was coming to save her. She couldn't even call for help. She knew she was meant to suffer. To suffer there and die. Without ever knowing why.

* * *

Jack awoke on the couch, stretched, and rubbed his face. He sat up and listened, hearing only Gabriel snoring. A ravenous hunger deep inside caused him to rise up, where he stood a moment before beginning a slow, careful walk to Lin's bedroom door.

A gentle turn of the doorknob led him to a dark room, and he could hear short, difficult breaths from the bed. A quiet walk to the bedside gave him a view of Lin in the weak moonlight. She was covered with blankets up to her chin but still shivering even though the room was quite warm. He could see the blankets shaking, and without thinking, he peeled them down from her. The light of the moon revealed her thin t-shirt stretched over a chest that struggled to rise and fall as if a heavy weight were upon her.

* * *

As she was about to give up, knowing that death was the only purpose of her life, she felt the weight above her decrease. And before long, stray bits of light landed on her skin, warming her and giving her hope. Soon, she knew, she'd be able to take a deep breath, a breath of the sweet air of the world, a breath that would give her life. The last several twigs and branches fell to the side, and Lin opened her eyes.

* * *

She saw Jack standing beside the bed, looking down at her. And even in the faint light, she could see the warmth and love in his eyes. She reached for him as he leaned in close.

"My Cowboy, you saved me. Again."

"Always, Cowgirl." He said no more.

He leaned in to kiss her, his lips hot against hers, and she pushed the blankets farther down as she sat up. Jack ended the kiss and sat next to her, facing her. He wrapped his strong arms around her waist, and she reached around his neck, where she ran her fingers through his long, wavy hair. They kissed again, and Lin pulled him into her, needing him as much as the air she breathed.

She felt his hands searching for the bottom of her shirt, and when he found it, he rolled it up above her, where she pulled her arms free. And it held there a second, finally allowing her long hair to cascade down onto her bare shoulders.

Their lips joined again, and she felt his hard muscles pressing against her. She felt his deep breaths becoming more urgent the longer he touched her. She released him and lay back against the pillows, and from there, she kicked the blankets down the bed, where they dropped to the floor.

She knew that she didn't need to tease him—she'd cured him of any trace of her mayhem. She didn't need her eyes to glow, and no mayhem tricks would join them this time. She looked into his eyes as she held his face with both hands.

Jack smiled and said, "My Cowgirl," and he turned to lay next to her. As he reached for her face, Lin moved her hands to hold him around his trim waist. He moved in close and kissed her while he twirled her hair and caressed her ears, touching her in the gentlest ways.

Until he began raising her head off the bed as he rolled onto his back. His hands had moved to her waist, and he pulled her over on top of himself, where Lin rose to her knees and looked down on him.

Jack extended his arms back and got a firm hold on the headboard, and his smile showed his lustful, teasing hopes. Lin knew exactly what he wanted. Her hands got busy, holding his enthusiasm, teasing him like she knew he deserved. With closed eyes, he smiled and reached for her hips, which she slowly lowered, guiding herself and finding the perfect place.

Jack gasped, but he said nothing. There was no motion in the room for several seconds. Lin felt her mayhem wanting to rise up, but she resisted.

Until Jack whispered to her.

"Light me up, Cowgirl . . ."

Lin let out a low moan as she released her mayhem, controlling it, allowing it to rise only a small amount, and her eyes glowed brightly down on her Cowboy.

Jack held her hips tightly as she began to move, two glowing green eyes in the darkness, bobbing up and down, a wanton smile just below them. When she took in a deep breath and held it, so did he. She felt time stop as infinity opened up in every direction.

The mesmerizing expanse of magic beneath them began a slow slide into her, and the magic filled her—every part of her. She held the magic in, feeling like she'd burst from the pressure and from the pleasure. And she slowly let out a trickle of her captive breath.

She aimed her mayhem at only a part of Jack—the part that had become her own.

The magic rushed into him there, and his eyes grew wide, but his smile never stopped. He smiled like a madman. Lin continued to rise and fall, her green light raining down on him.

Warming him. Teasing him.

Leading him into insanity.

She hadn't invaded him. She hadn't taken control. Jack was still Jack, only she knew that he now felt the endless depths of magic where they had become one. And he felt no fear.

His calloused hands slid up her sides and reached her breasts, where they lingered, playfully exploring and caressing. Then, he continued until he held her face in his hands, where they lingered again, touching, feeling. Adoring. He looked straight into her glowing eyes, smiling like a man in heaven.

Lin gradually increased her mayhem, focusing it where it counted most, as she continued to rise and fall. It seemed an eternity must have passed for the two lovers as they played with magic under the moon's dim light. But through her endless, impossible pleasure, she knew that he could take only so much.

Without changing the motion of her hips, which bounced effortlessly above tireless legs that flexed like coiled springs, she leaned close and looked into his eyes. He'd moved his rough hands to hold her from behind, and his eyes remained open when her lips met his. Both of their mouths hot and wet, tongues toying with each other's.

They'd waited long enough. Lin felt Jack's soul in his kiss, and she felt his love, a love so deep that it seemed to match the bottomless magic swirling beneath them. She knew that only a thin wall separated them from the oblivion of pleasure that would soon take them. She pried at that wall ever so slowly, so that both of them remained there, staring into indescribable ecstasy, hungering for it with every fiber of their existence until . . .

. . . she tore the wall down.

Together, they felt an immense wave wash over them, picking them up, tangling them and blending them until they had no sense of themselves as individuals but only of them as a pair, journeying into unknown realms of pleasure.

Just a Cowgirl and her Cowboy, alone together in a world afloat on infinite magic.

Chapter 39 – Tellings & Verses

The dim moonlight had retreated under the cautious advances of daylight. Lin pulled the blankets up tighter and felt a profound peace inside, welcoming the bed as a safe refuge from the realities she still faced.

The Shield would never quit. Wolfe likely wanted her dead, and he wouldn't stop. She worried about Renato, hoping that his new life would bring him joy. And Gabriel. She couldn't forget that Gabriel would have to leave someday.

Still, she reminded herself of all the good in her life. Taylor had been healed and so had Ben. Lee had become a trusted friend, and maybe they could learn from each other. Jack was just Jack, and he loved her more than ever. And she him. And Nomad had forgiven her. She had her sweet fluffy boy back.

And she remembered that Taylor shared the cabin with them.

"Jack. Jack, wake up. You need to get out of here."

Lin shook him lightly at first, then more urgently. He'd spent the night in a sleep so deep she feared he might be dead. But the dead don't wear such satisfied smiles, and she knew he was in there somewhere.

"Huh . . . alright, I think I'm awake. What's wrong?"

"Nothing's wrong, Jack," she said before kissing him. "You just need to get back out to the couch or wherever you were sleeping. Taylor's here, remember?"

"Oh, yeah. Alright. It's just hard to walk away from Heaven, Cowgirl."

Lin's heart leapt inside her, and she pressed her smile into his lips. It was Jack. Just Jack. Her careful mayhem hadn't changed him.

He got up slowly and stood stretching, smiling down at her. It took only a few seconds for him to get dressed, but before he finished his belt, he searched for something in his pocket. He found it and couldn't hide his smile.

"Lin, I—"

Through the closed bedroom door, they heard a rapid knocking on the cabin's door.

"Jack, that can't be anything good. Get going and check it out, okay?"

His empty hand appeared, and he cinched his belt tight. He held her gaze several long, silent seconds before he shook his head, smiled, and exited the room.

By the time Lin peeked out, Jack had already cracked the door, and she could see Anna standing on the cold porch. Her face showed a controlled desperation, and she held an envelope close to her chest. Along with her dog.

"Jack, can I please come in? I am alone."

He looked her up and down, then poked his head out to look in all directions. When he looked back inside, Lin was standing near, and she nodded. He opened the door, and Anna walked in, treading softly, seeing that most of the group lay sleeping.

"How the hell did you find us?"

"It is Wolfe, Jack. He is more resourceful than you can imagine."

"And what do *you* want?"

"I want to help. I am really not a bad person. Wolfe, he keeps me under some kind of spell. I am trying to resist it. But I came here alone. I think I can help you with—"

"And why the hell would we trust you? Some kind of spell?"

"It's okay, Jack," Lin said as she put a hand on his shoulder. "I believe her. Wolfe isn't a good guy."

He frowned and stepped aside, and Lin stood in front of Anna.

"How can you help?"

"I was devastated hearing the Words of God, Lin. All these years trying to learn them too. I had a rough life, and I have always wondered why life is so hard. There has to be an answer, right? And when you told me the Words that you read—"

"I didn't *read* anything. I told you that."

"I know, but the Words, they have to mean more than what you said. I have something that might help."

She shifted Ozzy to her left arm and held out the envelope. Lin took it.

"What's this?"

"This has been handed down through time. We call it the Telling. It is the story from whoever wrote down God's Words to begin with. I have read the Telling so many times I have lost count. I do not know what it means or even if it can help. But you know the Words better than anyone. And you do not seem evil to me."

"Why would I?"

"All I mean is that you seem good. Maybe this will help you. Please, just take a look."

Anna looked at the door.

"I do not want to go back to him."

"So, don't," said Lin. "Just leave. Go somewhere else."

"I cannot. I must go back."

Anna turned and walked toward the door, which Jack opened for her. She stepped into the cold air and turned back to Lin.

"Please, Lin."

Lin looked up from the envelope and said, "Just don't be with Wolfe if he's stupid enough to come here. Do you understand me?"

She allowed her eyes to glow in the ferocious way they do when she knows she must kill. The eyes of a predator stared at Anna, who shrank back and scurried to her car.

* * *

"Gabby, read this story, and tell me what you think."

Lin handed Gabriel the letter she'd removed from the envelope. A cold slice of pizza had to be set down, and Gabriel unfolded the sheet and read it.

"I don't know what to make of this, Lin. Do you?"

"I suspect something. I think there are more Words. Maybe Renato didn't tell me all of them."

"What makes you think that?"

"This story came from that powerful queen long ago. And here,"— Lin pointed at one part of the story—"she talked about how she heard the Words. They weren't spoken. They came to her in different ways. *Six* different ways. I think Renato only told us the last five.

"The first verse from Renato says, 'Every garden needs water.' I think that matches how some of the Words came with the 'morning's light rain.' Same thing with the second verse. It starts with, 'Set sail toward pleasure.' That matches the Words that 'came on a warm mid-day wind.' You see, Gabby? The verses go with all the ways she heard the Words."

"That's pretty astounding, Lin. But how does that help us?"

"The first Words she heard—they 'shone with the rising sun.' Nothing Renato told me matches that. She heard the Words in six different ways. Renato told me only five. Renato must have left the first verse unspoken."

"We need Renato," said Gabriel.

"Yes, but he's gone."

"There's still a way, Lin."

"How? You buried him so deep in that stranger. It'll take years before he can rise to the surface."

"I can hurry that process, but it won't be without some danger for the man who carries Renato."

"I think it's worth it."

"So do I."

Lin paused and looked at Gabriel a moment before sweeping her hair back over both shoulders.

"Gabby, does God really speak in poems?"

"I doubt that, Lin. But that's how the queen heard it. She must have had a love of drama."

* * *

The sun had risen, but the air hadn't yet warmed when Lin parked, and she and Gabriel hiked through the wooded hills to the campsite. A stillness hung heavy all around them as they stepped quietly over twigs and leaves, planning to not use any more powers than was necessary. Lin's weakness hadn't completely left her.

Before venturing into the clearing, they stopped, and Lin turned to Gabriel.

"Gabby, I need to know all the Words more than Anna. Sometimes, I feel completely lost. I mean, I know how to use my mayhem, and I've learned so much more. But it eats at me that I have no idea why any of this exists. Why I'm able to learn about the magic. Why any of us suffers so much too. What is this world all about?"

"When you first remembered who I really am, I told you that you were important. And you are. This world is about good against evil. I believe they both naturally occur like two sides to a sheet of paper. But which of them will triumph? I've devoted my life to that battle. I'm betting on good.

"You're important because with all the power you're gathering into yourself, you can help immensely in that battle. For good *or* evil. It has to be your choice. I want you to choose good. I think you know that by now."

"Yes, of course, I know that by now!"

They laughed softly together as they looked into each other's eyes.

"And I will choose good. But I can't understand what all the magic is about. Why does it exist? Why am I, or anyone else, able to learn about it and how to use it?"

Gabriel shrugged. "I don't know, Lin. How about we go ask Renato?"

Lin only laughed again as Gabriel led the way to Renato's tent. The camper was awake inside, and she and Gabriel stood nearby, out of the sight of the other, larger tent.

"Before I do this, Lin, I want you to remember to keep as lighthearted as you can about the world. Make your actions serious, deadly serious if they must be. But let your heart be at peace."

"That seems mostly impossible, Gabby. It's all so serious. It's life or death so often."

"Maybe I should point out something humorous to you, then?"

"What could possibly be funny about any of this?"

Gabriel stopped and looked at the clouds above them. Several long seconds passed before Gabriel looked again at Lin and spoke.

"I've told you that the key to using your mayhem, and all the magic, is in your intent, not your mind. Do you remember that?"

"Of course, I remember. I can feel my intent. It's a part of me. I can't explain what it is, but I always find it inside me."

"Yes, you find your intent inside you. And now . . . let's see what we can find 'in tent' beside you."

Lin couldn't help it.

A loud, "Oh, Gabby!" caused a noisy clamor inside the tent, and Lin saw Gabriel's eyes instantly glow bright green, and time stopped.

Gabriel took Lin's hand, and she felt a powerful wave hit her, lift her impossibly high, and snap her back down. They'd broken the barrier, and they stood among towering waves of magic, flowing and crashing in every direction, mixing mad designs for few to ever see.

They found their way to the magic of the camper and Renato, his hidden companion. Lin knew that she couldn't help, so she tried to learn what Gabriel would do. She was able to discern Renato's magic, his spirit, mingled with that of the camper. It didn't glow as brightly, and she understood that Renato remained in the background, focused mostly on the magic. Just as a flower opens to sunlight, she thought, so would Renato's spirit open to the world. But it would take a while. Unless Gabriel hurried it along.

She could sense Renato's magic being pushed, being channeled toward the camper's physical form. It seemed to take forever, but she reminded herself that in the magic, time didn't exist.

The last thing Lin saw before they exited the magic was that Renato's spirit had become the brighter one. The camper, the man who had penned the beginnings of such a remorseful note, was now in the background, finding his peace in the magic.

The journey back to the world never ceased to surprise her. They broke the barrier, and she felt herself soaring into the clouds and instantly dropping to the world's surface. She opened her eyes and felt her hand still in Gabriel's.

Lin tugged her hand free and unzipped the tent door. They both looked in on Renato, for it really was mostly Renato.

"Hello, Lin. It is so good to see you again. I know how long it has been. It has not been long!"

"Oh, Renato, have you been well?"

"Yes, very well. I have been at peace viewing the magic, and I have been living a life too. But something has changed. What has happened?"

"We had to bring you back to ask you something. Then, we'll leave you be, I promise, and you can go live a good life."

"What is it, Lin?"

"The Words. Did you tell me all of them?"

"I did. My Queen told me the Words to tell whoever I spoke with."

"Did she tell you anything else?"

Renato paused and took off the camper's hat, scratched his head a few times, and smiled.

"Yes. She wished me well. And I think she believed I would see her again. That everyone on our islands would somehow see her again. I did not believe her, Lin. Our islands were sinking. Almost everyone had fled."

"How did she wish you well? Can you remember the exact words?"

"Yes, I remember them as if it were yesterday. And for me, it was. And I was already part scroll, so I could not help but remember them:

"You will begin each day with the life I give,
All I ask is you find me, but if you fail, I'll forgive.
When your time is done, fear not the opening door,
For all who have tried will be with me once more."

Lin fumbled blindly and grabbed Gabriel's sleeve to keep herself from falling.

"Renato, I'm so glad you remember that. That makes all the difference in the world. You've done very well. Your queen would be so proud."

"I do not understand. Why is what she said to me so important?"

"That wasn't just for you, Renato. Those were also the Words of God."

Chapter 40 – Faith & Death

They'd left Renato to continue his camping vacation after removing the note the camper had started. Renato needed a fresh beginning, Lin knew, and the message might have clouded his life.

Lin and Gabriel hadn't spoken a word on the drive back to the cabin. She was lost in thought, and Gabriel must have known to let her be. The entire excursion had taken little time, and they returned to a cabin full of peaceful sleeping. Even Jack had curled up under a thick blanket and snored lightly.

Seated on the couch, Lin and Gabriel spoke in hushed whispers.

"Do you see what I see in those other Words?"

"What do you see, Lin?"

"The best possible thing. The first Words, the ones Renato told me in the tunnel, they're dark and depressing. We're here to suffer, and there's no mention of why or if there's anything good waiting for us."

"That's true. They weren't encouraging."

"But what Renato just told us . . . God said we should try to find Him. And later, the Words said, 'try to find the light, it's there holding you up, but use not your sight.' He said, 'recognize me there.' Gabby, is God talking about the magic? About that vast expanse where everything is possible?"

"It would seem so, Lin."

"And we'll find God there? Is that why it's even possible for someone like me to find the magic and to see infinity?"

"I believe you might have figured it out. God wants to be found there, in the magic."

"And is that why our lives are so hard? Why we must struggle so much?"

"Your struggles led to your mayhem, Lin. It led to you knowing the magic. It was the same with me."

"Our lives are meant to be hard. It's the only way, isn't it?"

"The only way to know the magic, yes."

"Have you seen God there?"

"I've seen endless possibilities and endless beginnings. Wonders that can't be explained, can't even be remembered. That's what I've seen. You've seen that too."

Lin slumped back into the cushions with a huge smile.

"Faith, Gabby. I know why. I know why the message he preached was that we should have faith."

"What about it?"

"The magic is something our minds can't understand. You showed me that many times. But that's where we'll find God. Don't you see? We have to leave our minds behind to know the magic . . . to find God. That's faith—we must let go.

"He never heard the first verse from Renato. All he had was the last five verses, telling us that humans have nothing but misery and challenges. All he could tell anyone was to have faith!

"And Gabby, those Words that Renato just told us, they say that as long as we try, we'll all be with God once more. Like every other living thing, Gabby. Us too. We just can't feel it. We can't know it. Because of our free will? That's why?"

A loud, steady knocking resounded about the quiet room. Gabriel rose and walked to the door, which shook and rattled from the frantic pounding. Everyone inside had been jarred from their sleep. Gabriel opened the door to see Wolfe standing outside, leaning his head to each side to peek into the room. Although the air had a chill, he held a martini in his hand.

"Gabriel, my dear friend, please let me in. I'm not too dangerous. You know that."

"Let him in, Gabby," said Lin. "I need something from him anyway."

Wolfe strutted into the room as if he owned it or thought he soon would.

Lin focused on her intent and became what she needed to be for her mayhem. It rose up in an instant, and she felt her eyes glowing a piercing green as the limitless rivers of magic began flowing into her. She focused her eyes directly on Wolfe, and despite his cockiness, he stepped back and hesitated before he spoke.

"Lin, there's no need."

"I'll decide that. Remember, Wolfe, I can kill you instantly. Or I can torture you for an eternity first."

"I know. I get it. What do *you* want?" He sipped his drink with a trembling hand.

"Two friends need to leave this cabin. They're packed and ready to go. You won't interfere with them in any way. Do you understand?"

"Lin," he said with a smirk, "I have this place surrounded, and they're outside your range, even with your new targeting tricks. I'll decide if they leave or not."

Her eyes flared up even brighter as she took a step toward him, and she said with a smile, "You're willing to die for that, right now? Sounds good to me . . ."

Wolfe looked down and quickly backed up, his drink shaking in his hand.

"I will let them go. Even the dog."

"Nomad stays."

"Fine."

Ben and Lee were ready to depart and they said their goodbyes, grabbed their things, and headed toward the door. Taylor held back her tears. Ben stopped to stare down on Wolfe, glaring at him with eyes ready to kill until he turned to look at Lin.

"It's fine, Ben. We'll be fine. And I'll be in touch. I just want you and Lee safe, okay?"

"I'll do as you wish, Lin."

Then, he faked a lunge at Wolfe, who flinched and spilled his drink. Lee took one last look at Lin from the doorway, much like how Lin had looked at her in Jacksonville. And then, Ben and Lee were gone, Ben's truck rattling off through the quiet of the Pennsylvania woods.

"Well, that was more uncomfortable than it needed to be," said Wolfe. "The truth is, all of you can go. Except you, Lin. And you, Gabriel."

"Nobody else is leaving. Just you," Lin said with her eyes blazing.

"Sure. But only for a minute or two. You see, I can't have you out performing miracles or anything. I know the Words of God now. And they prove that this world is hopeless. Most people already believe that, and I won't let you try to spread a pointless message of hope."

"Oh, but it's not hopeless. There are more Words, some that the Messenger didn't tell me at first."

"That you didn't read?"

"Oh . . . you'll never understand. The new Words tell of endless hope. Hope for everyone, no matter whether they succeed here or not. Everyone that tries to find God, in whatever way they can, will return to God when their time is up.

"That's the message that I'll spread. People will believe me. I'll work a few miracles if I have to."

Wolfe's jaw clenched, and a sneer took over his face. Through that, he managed to relax enough to tip his head back and finish his drink anyway.

"No. It can't be just for the fools that follow the rules. It has to be for all of us. All of us!"

"It's pretty clear, Wolfe. Our choices change us, you know. There are consequences."

"No, no, no. You'll never leave this cabin alive. None of you. Not even your dog. The rest of the Words will die here with you."

He turned and stormed out, and Lin allowed her mayhem to recede until her eyes were again a normal shade of green.

"Gabby, I will *not* be kind."

"No, Lin, you won't. Wolfe and his minions have chosen their fate."

"Jack, I'm glad you're here with me. But if anything happens, please protect Taylor. I know Nomad will help you."

She rubbed the big dog's ears and scratched under his chin. He let out a low whimper as he looked into her eyes.

"I will, Lin. If they come at us, you know I'm happy to help in any way I can. I'm not as big as Ben, but I'm sure I could still take that weasel."

"I know you can, Jack. Please, though, the three of you should just stay back. Let Gabby and me handle it, okay?"

"Gabriel? Really? Alright, I'll gather up our stuff so we can leave quick if we need to."

"Thanks, Cowboy." She kissed him then hugged him like there would be no tomorrow.

* * *

"Lin," Gabriel said from near the front door. "Come here and take a look."

She released Jack and walked to stand near Gabriel, and they both craned their necks and looked out in every direction they could.

"I see Wolfe's people scattered all around. They're hiding behind rocks and tree trunks, and they're moving. It won't be easy for you to focus a wave at them."

"It's never easy, is it? How many do you count?"

"I think maybe three. And that's just this side of the cabin. There are probably more around back."

"You heard Wolfe. He doesn't want any of us left alive. Not even Nomad. What a sick man."

"Lin, you know he's not really just a man anymore."

"I know. But he'll die like one if I have any say in it."

"You do have a say. Free will, remember?"

"Yes, of course, I remember. But I'd like him to hear death whisper in *his* ear too."

"Death whispers?"

"Did to me. When I was being strangled by Ivan in Georgia."

"You never mentioned that before."

"I'm trying not to dwell on it. I was right there, Gabby—almost dead. And then, I found my intent. I got an unbreakable hold on it. Death knew it right away. He whispered in my ear, and I could hear him laughing after he had to let me go."

"Death is a 'he,' Lin? What did he say to you?"

"It was only one word. He said, 'soon.' And that one word seemed to take forever. It was like ice water that he poured right into my head. That's what Wolfe deserves."

"Oh, Lin . . ." Gabriel said and laughed.

"What, Gabby?"

"You probably don't want to know."

Gabriel continued to laugh softly.

"What's so funny about me dying?"

"Nothing. You dying isn't funny at all. But Lin—death isn't a 'he' or anything else. And death doesn't whisper. It can't."

"You weren't there, Gabby. How would you know?"

"Where was I, Lin?"

Lin looked down at the floor and smiled. Without looking up, she said, "Okay, you *were* there. But I didn't completely know it. So, you saw the whole thing?"

"I saw you almost dying, yes."

"But you didn't know he had a hold of me, and then he whispered and laughed?"

"I knew that you almost died. The rest . . ."

Gabriel continued to smile.

"Gabby, what's going on?"

"The human mind, Lin. It's made to understand things. That's how this world works. And when it can't understand something, it turns it into something that it *can* understand."

"So, you're saying death isn't like a person? Not in any way?"

"It's not. Your mind turned it into something familiar, something less frightening."

"No, Gabby. It was terrifying."

"But the truth that your mind hid from you—it's even more frightening."

"And what exactly is the truth?"

"Death is something that has no interest in you at all. Nothing you are, or have done, means anything to it."

"Why is that more frightening?"

"Because it takes you as if you never were anything. No anger or passion. No feeling about us at all. We want our lives to mean something. It's very profound to be wiped out as if we're nothing."

"But our lives do mean something, don't they?"

"Yes, of course. But not to death."

"Why did I imagine death whispering and then laughing too?"

"I guess you have a strong appreciation for drama too, Lin."

They laughed together, looking into each other's eyes before looking back out at their adversaries.

"They're not attacking. I don't know, but I think they're scared. Maybe Wolfe has all of them in some kind of spell."

"They're just humans, and yes, he's very persuasive."

Lin froze with her eyes wide.

"What else could they be?"

"Let's not worry about that yet. For now, you just have a bunch of people determined to kill you. You have every right to defend yourself. And I think, to protect the rest of us, you don't have to be kind. Not anymore."

She turned to look into Gabriel's eyes.

"Gabby, you've been around a long, long time. Where were you before I needed you?"

Gabriel didn't answer right away.

"I was in the magic, Lin. Fighting."

"Fighting what?"

"Evil."

"How? How does that work? You punch each other around until one gives up?"

"In a way of speaking, yes. But there are no fists. There are no chins to strike."

"Well, what, then? How can you fight evil in the magic?"

Gabriel paused, and Lin continued to stare, waiting for an answer.

"When you were confronted by Ben in the restaurant, you believed you would injure him greatly. That was the direction you'd chosen. But when you saw his condition, that he was damaged, injured by your mayhem and so many other incidents in his life, you chose a new path. You chose to heal him.

"It happened so quickly for you that you probably didn't notice. When you changed directions, you discarded your plans for violence and retribution. You fought those feelings and embarked on a new path. A path of good.

"During that brief moment, you fought evil. And good prevailed. That was a turning point for you. I knew it was time for you to remember me."

"I don't remember fighting anything. I only made a choice."

"Yes, it was very quick. But look at it as changing directions. There's a point where the old tendency has to be resisted, and it takes a force of your intent to launch yourself down a new road. A better road."

"What does any of that have to do with you fighting in the magic?"

"That brief moment you had, where your free will would let you travel down either path, was a tiny battle. When I'm in the magic, all of the time, I'm in that moment. I don't see anything. I'm not touching anything. Certainly not punching anything."

They both laughed.

"I exist in that feeling of choosing good over evil. That's how the battle is fought. You waged a tiny version of that war. I spend every moment at that change of directions choosing good. It's not easy—free will always gives us a choice. I can't do it indefinitely. I welcomed the break to spend time with you.

"But the war continues, and I will rejoin it."

Lin shook inside, unable to imagine the strength, the power, the constant choosing of good that Gabriel's existence had become.

Gabriel, and others, fought that war every moment of every day, in a place without time, keeping evil at bay. Fighting a war that would never end. Trying to tip the balance.

"Why am I so important? I need the clearest answer you can give."

"You're needed in that war, Lin."

"Oh, Gabby, I don't think I could ever do what you do. I'm not that strong."

"Not yet, no. Soon, though, I will ask you to join me. You're not obligated, of course."

Lin couldn't respond. Her head spun with the realization that she wasn't just dabbling in magic. The stakes were high. And she would be needed. But not yet, she comforted herself.

Gabriel took another look outside.

"They're starting to move in. But mostly, they're just moving around. I'm sure they have this place surrounded."

"What can I do? I can't send out a huge wave in every direction—it'll never go far enough. And the way they're moving, I don't know where to focus a wave either. There's got to be another way . . ."

"Yes, there is. The final chapter for these individuals. No broken hearts this time. Magic, Lin. You killed two men in a parking lot using their magic. Concrete became water. You even turned a scroll back into a man. It's in the magic, Lin."

And then, Lin knew what had to be done.

She flicked her long blond hair back over her shoulders, and a look of unyielding power filled her green eyes as her mayhem began to rise.

Chapter 41 – Miracles & Waste

"Tayo, do you have eyes on the cabin?"

Lancaster Wolfe took another swallow of his drink before he repeated his query.

"Tayo, come in. Are you in position?"

"Yes, Mr. Wolfe. I don't think anyone saw me either. I'm on a branch that's twenty-seven feet up in a pine, and I have a perfect view of the whole scene. I can see the cabin and four of our six agents positioned around it. No, one just moved behind a rock. I see three. Awaiting further instructions."

"For now, just sit tight. When our people start moving in, report on what you see. And Tayo, do you have line of sight?"

"I do, sir."

"Wolfe out."

"Anna, Daria, I want you two to stay put. You don't need to get involved in this little skirmish. Best if you don't even see it. But oh, you'll hear it. And keep that little dog quiet."

Wolfe sneered confidently and emptied his glass.

Anna stroked Ozzy's back and held him close. Daria pressed up against her where they sat behind a large rock, far from the cabin.

* * *

"I wish you could help, Gabby, but I understand. Not with people."

"Yes, but you don't need me."

They walked out onto the porch, causing more movement from Wolfe's agents. They were in constant motion behind rocks and trees. Lin guessed she could never focus a wave on them.

She stepped to the edge of the stairway leading down from the porch, and she let her mayhem rise up until she was sure all of the hiding Shield agents could see her. For a moment, their activity stopped. Then, they began moving again with more urgency.

"I'm not sure I have enough strength. What I did before weakened me."

"You will find the strength you need. Trust yourself."

* * *

"Okay, Tayo, send the first man to the cabin. Don't be shocked by anything you see. Remember, this is only a test. And hey, he volunteered," Wolfe said while laughing and pouring another drink from a large thermos.

"Jim, it's your time," Tayo said into his radio. "Walk to the cabin. Don't pull your gun until you're within the distance at which you qualified at the range."

* * *

Lin and Gabriel watched a solitary man step out from behind a fallen tree and begin a slow walk toward the cabin. Her mayhem was blazing, and she could stop time in an instant, so she let the man approach. He got within twenty feet and stopped. His long coat hung down to the tops of his brown cowboy boots, and he stared at her from under a wide-brimmed hat.

"This isn't the Wild West, you loser. If you're going to draw, draw."

"I will. And look," he said as he pulled his shirt open. "No shock collar. I volunteered for this. I'm here to send you back to Hell where you belong. Yeah, I'm that fast."

Lin felt a brief twinge of sadness as she watched the man reach inside his coat. Her intent stopped time, and his weapon never saw the light of day. She saw infinity in every direction and towering mountains of magic below, crumbling down and thrusting up, constantly in motion, with mad patterns that would never be seen again.

She took in a slow, deep breath, and she felt expansive rivers of magic flowing into her, seeping into her every cell, swelling her to the point of bursting. Such ecstasy, she thought, as she gazed at the man who would bring death to her.

Lin needed to find the man's magic, and in no time, her intent took her there. She studied his magic and saw that no dark spirit had fused into it. He was simply a man who had chosen an evil path.

She felt as if her hands wrapped around his magic, and she became aware of the magic flowing into him, creating him, allowing him to exist. Such a miracle and such a waste, she thought as she began to squeeze. She took her time and heard his silent shrieking but no confession. There was no repentance. And there would be no mercy.

One final, hard squeeze, and his life ended.

Lin allowed infinity to recede, and time resumed.

*   *   *

"Mr. Wolfe, I . . . I just saw—"

"Out with it, Tayo. What did you see?"

"He . . . he exploded . . . his body . . . it's just a puddle . . . and his legs and his arms . . . they're still moving . . . they're—"

"Forget about him, Tayo. He knew the risks. And we learned how powerful she is. Now, we know she's not interested in taking control. Just killing. He died a good death."

"But—"

"Stay focused. You will not lose it up there, do you hear me?"

"Yes. Yes, sir."

"What's going on at the cabin?"

"Nothing. She's still standing on the porch. And Mr. Wolfe, her eyes are so bright, I can see them without the binoculars."

Wolfe cringed then managed a weak laugh.

"Never mind about that. It won't help her against what you have. Wait for my signal. Don't fire until I give the order. You got that?"

"Mr. Wolfe, she's special. I know that now. Those eyes, they're . . . we shouldn't kill her. She—"

"I told you what she is: evil."

"No, she can't be, Mr. Wolfe. Her eyes, she—"

"Complete your mission when I tell you to. If you don't, don't think that Nigeria is that far away. I have friends that would just love to visit your family. Do you understand?"

"Yes, I do, sir. I do. Awaiting your order."

* * *

"Gabby, I didn't want to do that. He left me no choice."

"Yes, you're right, Lin. You have a right to survive and to protect those you care about. And he would have killed you and anyone else here."

"So will the rest of them. Broken hearts or broken bones," she said with sadness in her voice.

"Yes. I'm sorry."

Her mayhem already raged, and she looked back out from the porch as her intent stopped time. She once again found herself at the center of a calm world, with infinity rolled out to every horizon. Beneath the calm world, timeless magic swirled and churned and danced, tempting her to join it, to return to it. Not now, she thought. Someday, though . . .

Her blazing eyes scanned the horizon, seeing the magic of each attacker, and she plotted the order of their demise. She took a deep breath and rejoiced in the sweet pressure of magic filling her to every corner. She knew that they didn't have a chance.

Her intent brought her to the first man, who hid behind a thick fallen tree. She saw that his magic and the tree's magic were so close that they almost touched. She got a grip on his magic, but she didn't squeeze. She nudged his magic toward the tree's until they bumped together. With a final push, using her intent, she merged the man's magic with that of the tree. His life as a human stopped instantly.

The next assailant crouched behind a large rock, and Lin again saw the magic of each. Days earlier, she might have been intimidated by the rock's magic. It was deep and dark and much more still than the magic of a life as she'd known it. She paused when she again noticed something unexpected, a quality that could be easily missed. Something about the rock's magic . . .

But there was no time. She remembered the danger she and the rest of them faced. She wrapped her arms around the rock's magic, and she didn't squeeze, she only moved it like an armful of laundry, feeling the magic flowing, a constant stream, creating the rock anew in every moment.

She set the magic onto the man's magic, and he never had a chance for silent shrieking. She knew that there was some humor in the man having literally turned to stone, but laughter eluded her.

The third attacker lay in the tall grass, barely noticeable from the cabin. To Lin, his magic seemed to be swimming on the surface of an endless ocean of magic. The Earth's magic. It took scant effort for her to dunk part of his magic, the portion connected to his head, into that vast sea of magic. She realized how horrifying the sight would be to whoever found him, and the waste saddened her.

She continued that way all around the cabin, eliminating every nearby threat.

At last, she let her mayhem recede, and she fully opened her eyes to see Gabriel next to her.

"You did good, Lin. You fought evil, and you won. You protected all of us."

"But, Gabby . . . I'm so . . ."

Gabriel caught her as she fell to the floor, where they sat in a warm embrace in the cold Pennsylvania air.

* * *

"Now, Tayo. Now!"

"But, Mr. Wolfe, she's already down. I can't—"

"Do as you're told, Tayo!" Wolfe said and cackled hysterically.

Tayo raised the large weapon to his shoulder and uncapped the sight. It took several seconds to focus on the porch, to get wind readings, and to make the calculations necessary for a successful launch.

* * *

"I've never felt this weak. Am I dying?"

Gabriel laughed. "No, Lin. What you did will never kill you. You're beyond that. But you sure have weakened yourself. They were all far away—that alone made it more difficult for you."

"And how long will it take for—"

Lin's intent caught the single flash of the rocket launcher high in the trees, far past all of the agents that she'd just killed. Without a conscious thought, her eyes instantly blazed like the sun. Time stopped. The world stopped. And she saw the point of a rocket no more than twenty paces from the cabin and trailing frozen fire.

Although still very weak, her intent knew what had to be done. It took her there, to the magic of a rocket which would have reached their cabin in no time at all. Except for Lin's intent.

The rocket's magic was dark, in contrast to the bright flames motionless behind it. Lin had just barely begun to squeeze its magic when she sensed that it was only the tiniest distance from exploding. She remembered that the calm surface of the world didn't stop completely—it was just dreadfully slow. She could sense the power of the imminent explosion, and her intent took her back to the porch. In the briefest of instants, she opened her eyes completely, and she and

Gabriel watched the rocket self-destruct, sending streams of burning material in every direction. The shock wave gently lifted her and Gabriel's hair.

Lin thought she was done, and her weakness made it almost impossible to focus. She relished the warmth and safety of Gabriel's embrace. But without another thought, her intent brought her to the source of the rocket—a man in a tree far from the cabin.

She studied his magic and found that he was a reluctant participant, a man with a good heart. She would not kill him. She simply nudged his magic, toppling him to the ground, where he lay broken and unable to hurt anyone.

"Gabby, I hope we're done. I'm . . ."

She slumped into Gabriel's arms and said no more.

While holding her as they sat on the wooden porch, Gabriel stood and carried her into the cabin, laying her on the couch. Jack rushed over and sat with her, holding her hands in his. The explosion had startled all of them inside the cabin, but they'd stayed away from the war as Lin had wanted.

Taylor had come over, too, and so had Nomad. He whined softly and nudged Lin with his big wet nose, but he got no response.

"Is she going to be okay?" Taylor said to no one in particular.

"She will," said Gabriel. "But she really pushed herself. She did good. She saved us."

Taylor smiled and looked at Jack, who returned her smile. Nomad's attention finally filtered into Lin's deepest of sleeps, and she opened her eyes and sat up. Immediately, her eyes closed again, and she started to tilt to one side. Jack sat close and kept her from toppling, and Taylor squeezed in close against her other side. Nomad seemed content with his massive head on her lap, watching her with rarely blinking eyes.

The sound of slow, steady, sarcastic clapping could be heard in front of the cabin. Gabriel swung the door open, and through the doorway and windows, they all could see Wolfe, flanked by a dozen ragged figures, faces hidden by hoods pulled forward. He stopped clapping his hands, and one of his horde handed him his drink.

"Time to get serious," was all he said.

Chapter 42 – Demons & Destroyers

Lin's eyes opened, and her heart sank at seeing Wolfe with a fresh army.

"Ladies and gentlemen," said Wolfe, "time for the final act. That was very impressive, Lin. Your tricks have been fun to watch. But they won't work anymore. Like I said, none of you are leaving this cabin. Not even your mangy dog."

Lin groaned and tried to get up from the couch. But her eyes drooped shut, and she collapsed back into the cushions, where Jack and Taylor and Nomad gently held her down.

"Gabby," Lin said with closed eyes before pausing to take another breath. "I can't. I have nothing left."

"I got this, Lin," said Jack. "I'm not afraid of any of them. I still have a couple of pistols, and I'll—"

"No, Jack. Your bullets won't work."

"What do you mean? They have body armor or something?"

"Something. I will handle this."

"You? I've never seen you do anything risky. No offense, Gabriel, but I don't think you have it in you. Sit with Lin. I'll deal with them."

Jack started to rise.

"Sit," bellowed a voice that rattled the cabin's timbers.

Jack sat, with eyes wide and mouth open and speechless.

"Gabby, you can't. You said so," said Lin.

"Not with people, Lin. But those are not people."

Even Nomad seemed to freeze up at Gabriel's last comment. No one moved from the couch. They only watched, silent and staring in disbelief. Despite Lin's great weakness, she managed a slight smile, and a faint glow lit up her eyes. She knew that her mayhem sensed a change coming.

A voice came from Gabriel, deeper than any of them had ever heard. It echoed about the room lined with stained wood and warmed by a quiet fire.

"I can be a babysitter, Lin. It was good to rest. But I was born in battle, and I am made for war."

All eyes were fixed on Gabriel.

"I am a destroyer."

They all watched in surprise and fear as Gabriel's features began to change. Sharper angles developed. Ancient scars became visible. The face became hard, like granite barely softened by the centuries. It was a face that had forgotten how to smile.

Gabriel's eyes burned with a cold light, like two green suns through ice. And when Lin gazed into them, fear gripped her heart. They were the eyes of a predator, a beast that might not recognize her or remember their friendship.

Still, Lin smiled, witnessing an unknown side to her best friend, a being that had saved her from darkness so many years before. She'd seen only peace and love in Gabriel's eyes up until then. She celebrated this other side, this dangerous side. And she felt the certainty of Gabriel's protection like she had when she was fifteen.

Gabriel had become several feet taller, and the wavy brown hair that had hung down now danced on a wind that no one else felt. With head lowered to clear the rough wooden beams, Gabriel turned and stepped solidly toward the door.

After leaning to get through the open doorway, Gabriel strode across the porch to stand facing the legion Wolfe commanded. Wolfe stumbled backward, still sneering, and his evil forces closed ranks in front of him. Gabriel descended the few stairs onto the dry ground, each footfall echoing in the quiet Pennsylvania air.

"We can talk about this," said Wolfe. "Or better yet, we'll just leave. I didn't know you were *that* Gabriel . . ."

"It's too late," boomed Gabriel, whose raised right arm swept from one end of the line of attackers to the other. "All I see, I claim as my own. And what I have claimed . . . I destroy."

"Attack, you fools!" screamed Wolfe as he feebly held his arms before him for protection.

Wolfe's minions became unnaturally still, with a pair of sharp red lights focused on Gabriel from within the hollow darkness of each hood. In unison, they took one step closer and again held their ground. A muffled roar seemed to creep up over the horizon from every direction as the outlines of shrieking, toothless mouths became visible below their red eyes.

The screaming from the attackers grew louder, then suddenly ended. But the eyes grew brighter, and the ravenous mouths gaped wider.

Gabriel stood as still as the adversaries, chest expanding and contracting with a sound like gathering storm winds. It was the only sound in the still air around the cabin.

With blinding speed, they all launched toward Gabriel as their screams instantly reached a fever pitch. Gabriel never moved, but raised a left forearm horizontal to the ground, and from the dry earth, a thousand roots sprang up and wound around their ankles, holding them in place.

The demons could advance no farther. Their bony hands stretched forward, desperate to get a grip on Gabriel, while they wailed and twisted like living smoke.

Gabriel's arms both extended level with the ground and pointed from one end of the horde to the other.

With Nomad's head still on her lap, mesmerized by her glowing green eyes, Lin watched Gabriel's hands turn to claws, each with talons longer than her fingers. She recalled what Gabriel had told her: that with magic, anything could be accomplished—not just glowing green eyes. Her smile grew. She was sure that the claws were for her.

Beneath each set of claws, a vortex in the dust sprang up. Each swirl grew larger and began to spin more quickly. Lin watched through her glowing eyes, seeing the magic in each dust storm. Gabriel had brought magic, pure magic, into the world. But to everyone else, she was sure, it appeared as only dust.

She felt like laughing at the realization that Gabriel had no need to stop time. She felt Jack and Taylor holding her more tightly, all of them watching the miracle unfold. Even Nomad had turned to see.

Gabriel pointed one set of claws at the closest of the attackers, and the vortex seemed to gallop over the ground as it had been commanded. It leapt up and enveloped the assailant, where it increased its spin, blocking it from sight. But not from hearing. Everyone heard its shrieking. Lin smiled and shook her head, so impressed with Gabriel for not bothering with silent shrieking.

Within seconds, only the red eyes could be seen, and then they vanished. The vortex grew tighter, spinning like mad until it had become a narrow strip, a single line of incalculable speed. It finally burst with a sound like a gunshot.

The wave from the explosion caught Lin by surprise. The sharp jolt left her smelling sounds, tasting colors, and hearing the texture of the dust. She fought to keep the room in sight, but she was carried into chaos with no way back.

But only until the wave passed. She shook off the confusion and looked to each side. Jack and Taylor were both unconscious, their heads flopped to the side.

She looked down and saw Nomad's bloodshot eyes staring at her. And past the top of his mane, halfway down his back, two red eyes also stared. Bony hands dug into Nomad's sides as the hooded darkness crept closer, eyes piercing, empty mouth snarling.

Nomad's eyes looked up as far as they could, but he didn't move. His eyes looked again at Lin, then back up, and he let out a low whimper.

Lin's heart echoed in her chest, and she saw beyond Nomad that Gabriel had launched another storm. Not now, she thought. No more waves!

And she heard the thing's voice. Soft. Slow. And warm. Asking a simple question: would she like more power? It was easy, it said. She could have immense power. All she wanted. If she'd just accept a partner. She'd never notice. It would stay quiet, it said. Just a harmless helper . . .

Again, Gabriel's attacker became wrapped in the dust spiral, shrieking hysterically, before it tightened and exploded, sending a wave into and over Lin. She held on and waited, praying that the wave would pass quickly.

The wave did pass, and she opened her eyes to see two red fires smoldering so close that she could see nothing else. Nomad wailed through his clenched jaw.

"Accept me, and I'll set the hound free." The voice was soothing, so convincing. "It would be good to release the animal, wouldn't it? Of course, it would. And you'll have power like you can't imagine . . ."

Power is good, Lin thought. Yes . . . more power . . .

But no, she thought—nothing is free. Nothing is given without a cost.

Still . . .

As Lin stared into the tempting promise of those red eyes, as she saw that its mouth wasn't all that horrible, that it *could* become a good friend . . . it became wrapped in a swirling storm of dust. In magic.

Its calm speech halted, and it shrieked like it was being ripped apart. Its howls were deafening, and Lin did what her heart told her to do: she covered Nomad's big ears.

The spiral above Nomad sped up, twisting and spinning like mad, until the eyes had been extinguished. And then, it blew up, and Lin felt a blast so strong she believed it must have peeled back her skin. She tumbled without coherent thoughts through mad landscapes.

But that wave passed too. She opened her eyes to see Nomad unconscious and breathing rapidly, his heavy head on her lap.

Lin looked up to see Gabriel holding her gaze without a smile before turning to send out more storms, more magic, over and over. Ending every last one of them.

Gabriel hadn't stopped time, but the attackers had been held back long enough for Gabriel to destroy all of them one by one. Including Lin's own personal tormentor.

Gabriel's claws remained in plain sight at the ends of arms stretched to each side, but no more storms swirled below them. One arm rotated and extended straight forward, claws pointing toward Wolfe.

"You," said Gabriel in a voice like thunder. "Stand before me."

Wolfe appeared unable to resist. No trace of his army existed any longer, and he reluctantly walked toward the cabin. He continually looked from side to side, nervously sipping his drink. He appeared to be hoping for reinforcements, but there were none. He had to face Gabriel alone.

"It doesn't have to be like this, Gabriel. That was very impressive—who knew you were *that* powerful. And who cares about them anyway. They were just a bunch of evil bastards.

"But you know you can't destroy me."

"No. I can't. But you will be gone from the Earth."

"I'll never be gone completely, Gabriel." He took another sip, defiantly sneering with his chest out.

"I will scatter you. You might someday be able to regroup. But you might not."

"Don't. Don't do it, Gabriel. Let me make you an offer. Just hear me out. You've learned a lot over the centuries, but there's more. So much more that I can show you. I can teach you things you've never imagined. Just let me go my way."

Gabriel stood motionless, chest heaving, green eyes flaming with wrath.

"Would you like to know how to go back in time?"

Gabriel's chest became still, and the claws that had been pointing at Wolfe began lowering. Lin felt a new fear race through her: a fear that Gabriel might not have the resolve to finish it.

Her fears were without merit.

The claws rose and again pointed directly at Wolfe. And a small storm began to brew in the dust. Gabriel's eyes blazed a blinding green.

"Don't, Gabriel. You know I'll be back anyway. More powerful. And I'll get you . . ."

The storm increased in size.

". . . and Lin and Jack . . ."

The storm began spinning like crazy.

". . . and that worthless dog too!"

Lin thought she could feel wind thrown off from the mad vortex, and Gabriel swept it toward Wolfe with the snap of a single claw.

The whirlwind wrapped itself tight around Wolfe and began to spin faster than Lin had seen any of them before. Wolfe could no longer be seen. But he could be heard. Laughing. Not shrieking. The laughter became insane, a howling like every dark force inside was being wrung out of him.

Finally, a single explosion shook the ground and rattled the cabin. Lin braced herself for the wave, but she never could have prepared for what hit her. The wave was immense, and she felt herself staggering through unknown territories, senses overlapping, no difference between laughter and tears, no up, no down, no good, no evil. She heard countless colors that didn't exist, saw sounds that flowed like rivers, tastes and scents piled high like mountains, planets and stars that spoke to her . . .

The madness engulfed her, threatening to dissolve her, to leave her without any memory of herself. But she looked for her intent, and even amid absolute chaos, she found it. And with it, she focused on her own heart beating.

It was a strong scent, and she could see it beating there inside of her.

The sound had a healthy flavor, and its shape seemed right.

She calmed herself further and found a place of stillness inside.

And it became only a sound. A simple heartbeat. She held onto that sound as if her life depended on it. And she fought to block out everything else, everything that would never make sense in the world.

Soon, she knew only that steady beat. She followed her heartbeat. She trusted it.

Lin opened her eyes to see Gabriel standing in front of her. The old Gabriel—the one she'd known for decades.

Not the scary one.

Not the destroyer.

* * *

"Lin, now I'm really hungry," Gabriel said with a laugh.

Lin laughed through her tears.

"Gabby, I don't know what to say. You saved me again. They're all gone? Even Wolfe?"

"The real Wolfe is finally released. But whatever that was, the thing that had taken over him, is gone."

"What were they?"

"Forces of evil from the magic. They rarely fight openly in the world. They're actually quite cowardly. It was an act of desperation for Wolfe to bring them here."

"What was Wolfe?"

"It was the same thing as the rest, but more powerful. That's how they operate—they prey on the darkest part of our nature, and they're very good at getting others to do their evil. The real Wolfe must have had a profound weakness, an opening for that thing. But it had no power over the magic like you do. It can have only as much power as the person it takes over. Which, in this case, was none."

"And the others? His minions? What could they have done?"

"They're cowards, Lin. They have no real power either. They rely on fear and trickery. But they're very persuasive. They can convince you to join their side if you're not strong enough to resist. I heard tempting offers from each of them, and to you it must have looked like a battle. That's what they do.

"But their dark magic is no match for the magic of good. When good stands up to evil, evil has no chance. You, though, might not have survived their attacks. Not weak like you are now."

"I believe you, Gabby. If you hadn't taken care of that one that came after me—"

"You would have been quite the prize for them. You fought that thing longer than you realize. Even when you're weakened, you're very strong."

She looked over Gabriel's shoulder to see Anna and Daria helping an injured and mostly unconscious Tayo onto the porch. Her mayhem quickly lit her eyes, weakening her further, and she was about to stop time when she heard Gabriel.

"Lin, be kind."

With her eyes still glowing softly, Lin called out to Anna.

"You have some nerve. Haven't you done enough?"

Anna spoke. "I am free. I am really free! We heard a bunch of explosions and then nothing but silence. And I feel the silence inside me too. I never realized that I had Wolfe's voice inside me ever since I met him. But he is gone. Somehow, he is gone!"

"And now, *you* need to be gone. All of you," said Lin.

Anna stared back at her but said nothing.

"Come on, Mom," said Daria. "Let's just go."

Anna looked to the floor and turned, keeping a hold on Tayo. Together, she and Daria began walking back toward the steps, helping Tayo as well as they could.

Before they'd reached the stairs, Tayo broke free of the two women and immediately collapsed. He struggled to turn himself around to face Lin on his hands and knees.

"Lin . . ."

"You. You fired the rocket."

"I did not want to. Lin, I saw your eyes. I know now. Please . . . please let me stay."

She stared at the crippled man, her eyes still glowing, focused like a beast ready to kill.

"You have all made your choices. Go now while you still can."

Tayo pressed his face to the floor and stayed silent. Quiet sobs shook him.

Anna and her daughter helped him to his feet. They walked away in silence, Tayo struggling to turn his head to see Lin. After Daria had pulled the door shut behind them, Lin's mayhem receded, and her eyes were again only their natural green.

"Gabby, The Shield is really done? I don't have to worry about them anymore?"

"Not for a long time." Nomad's eyes had opened and Gabriel rubbed his ears, prompting him to let out a long, low moan. "You can live your life. With Jack and Taylor. And Nomad too. And Lin, now that you're safe, and you've learned so much, I must return to the magic. To the war."

Lin felt a stab somewhere deep, and before she could begin to answer, Jack and Taylor awoke, their eyes wide.

"Lin," said Jack, "I only remember the sound of a gunshot and nothing else. What happened?"

"I don't even remember that, Mom."

Lin brushed at her moist eyes.

"Gabby and I convinced Wolfe to leave us alone. He and his entire group are gone. They won't be back."

Lin still felt the exhaustion from using the magic as much as she had, and she stayed sunk into the couch cushions with Jack and Taylor on either side. She also felt the somber weight of a future without Gabriel.

Nomad's big eyes stared only at Lin.

"Mom, why are Nomad's eyes bloodshot?"

"Maybe he's just tired, Hon. It's been a busy day."

Both Jack and Taylor reached over and played with Nomad's ears as his big head lay on Lin's lap.

"Gabby, maybe we can talk about that over breakfast—"

She stopped when she saw a green glow reflected in Gabriel's eyes.

"My mayhem isn't . . . are my eyes . . ."

Gabriel quickly glanced at Taylor before looking back at Lin.

Lin turned her head to look at Taylor, and she saw nothing out of the ordinary in Taylor's eyes.

But Taylor's hand was motionless just above Nomad, and she stared at the wall with an odd smile.

Lin turned to look again at Gabriel, who only gazed down at the floor.

"Lin, perhaps I'll stay a while longer . . ."

Chapter 43 – Long Ago Now

"I need a shower," said Jack. "God, this has been some crazy day. I'll feel better when I'm cleaned up."

"Sure, Jack, that's a great idea. Taylor, do you feel okay?"

"I do, Mom. Just tired still. But I feel incredible, like I've never felt before. I think I'll take a nap, though. I miss Ben."

"I know, Hon."

Both Jack and Taylor got up and left the living room area, Jack to his shower and Taylor to a bedroom. Lin and Gabriel were alone, and soon, Nomad lay down in front of the fire. Within seconds, his big, sleepy, bloodshot eyes closed.

"What did I just see?"

Gabriel sat next to Lin on the couch.

"What do you mean?"

"I saw green light reflected in your eyes. But I didn't feel my mayhem rising."

"Maybe you're still tired, Lin. You've pushed yourself much further than you should have."

"But, Taylor, she—"

"She's very tired too."

"Oh, that's for sure. I know I'm really exhausted. I'll rest a lot, I promise. And I'm relieved you'll stay a while longer. You will stay, won't you?"

"Yes. I will stay."

"Good."

Lin smiled and said, "Gabby, those claws. That was for me, wasn't it?"

"All of it was for you, Lin. There was no need for dust and storms spinning around those things or even the roots holding them back. The only thing that couldn't be avoided was the wave that hit you each time I scattered one of them. That was pure magic running into you."

"Scattered? You didn't kill them?"

"No, they can't be destroyed. That's why the war can never end."

"So, what actually happened? If there really weren't any dust storms or claws or any of that—what did you do?"

"It's only good against evil. My intent against theirs. They really aren't as powerful as people might think. They can be vanquished. Scattered. But those battles of good against evil will always continue."

Gabriel's brown eyes held Lin's without a smile.

"I can *never* stop my war."

Lin could only gaze into Gabriel's deep, kind eyes before again finding her voice.

"Gabby, you do all that, you've devoted your existence to it, and still,"—she dragged the back of her hand across her eyes—"you protect me. And guide me. And you make it fun too."

Gabriel's smile returned. "It's been a good three decades for me, Lin."

She wiped her eyes one more time as her own smile reappeared.

"You must have found your intent, even after the waves washed over you."

"Yes, I found my intent, and I used it to focus on my heartbeat. That's what got me back."

"Your heartbeat? It's good that that worked this time."

"What do you mean, 'this time?'"

"When you're in big trouble, Lin, always trust your intent. Nothing else."

"Okay, I'll remember that. But, God, I hope there won't be a 'next time.'"

"Me too."

"You really did all that for fun?"

"All except for letting you see the real me. The me that goes to war."

"You looked like you knew nothing but war."

"It feels that way sometimes, Lin. Like everyone else, my choices have changed me. You saw what my battles have made me. Can't blame me for savoring every bit of life while I'm here, can you?"

"No, I certainly can't. I understand now why you're enjoying everything so much."

Gabriel smiled for her, and for a moment, she lost herself in the peace and love that she saw. The fear she'd felt began to fade.

"But you seemed so scary. Even I was afraid of you."

"Well, I *am* scary, Lin. When I need to be."

"I'll say. You had me worried there for a while, though."

"Oh?"

"I heard what Wolfe offered you—to teach you how to go back in time if you'd let him live. You looked like you were thinking about it."

"I did think about it. Free will, Lin. Nothing is automatic. We must always choose."

"You were tempted?"

"Yes. And curious if it was even possible."

"You think it might be possible to travel back in time?"

"I don't know, but it might be. Remember that in the magic, there is no time. And maybe you can also say that in the magic, all of time can be found. You see? Every moment, past and future, might exist there."

"You don't know?"

Gabriel laughed. "No. I don't know everything. That's not *my* job."

Lin laughed, too, but the smile left her face as she leaned back into the cushions and held her waist with both hands. She felt something shifting, finding a new arrangement, as if Gabriel's observation of time were a key that had turned a lock. And something had opened.

Gabriel continued. "But witnessing the past isn't the same as traveling there. Like that color that you can see in the magic, maybe we can see other moments there too. But we'll never remember them. We can't."

Lin heard Gabriel's voice like an echo through a tunnel under water. She felt her mayhem flash but only for a second before it began to sink in a direction unknown to her.

It was no longer her mayhem. An invincible force had taken control.

Her eyes snapped open, and thin streams of tears began to flow.

"Lin, what's going on?"

"Gabby . . . I . . ."

She felt Gabriel take her hand, and though Gabriel's mouth continued to move, she could no longer hear a voice.

A tiny dot of darkness appeared straight ahead in her line of sight. Her eyes locked onto it, and they refused to look anywhere else. The single point began to grow, slowly at first, then speeding up, blocking out the world. It obliterated everything in its path until it engulfed her as if a giant black bowl had swallowed her.

When she saw only darkness, her breathing ceased. All feelings and thoughts left her. She was frozen, petrified in a timeless night. She knew only the sound of her heart.

Until it stopped.

* * *

A small point of light appeared before her, and her eyes could not turn away. The point grew larger, speeding toward her, and dragging a world with it. When it had covered her, and she could see no more darkness, her heart began a steady rhythm. Her thoughts returned, followed by feelings of relief and gratitude. She took a deep breath of ocean air.

Distant sounds of crashing waves and a fluttering from flying birds convinced her that she still lived. She found that she could move again.

When she looked down, she saw that she sat on a smooth white chair. She reached for it and held onto its edges, and she saw a stone floor below it. Large blocks had been fitted together in intricate patterns. And in front of her, a young man, dressed in a cloak and sandals, waited on his knees.

Lin stared at the teeth at the ends of his braids and then looked to her right. A line of people dressed in garments alien to her stood in silence, gazing at her. She looked to her left and saw that the line of onlookers encircled her completely. Beyond them, the floor ended at a wall made of the same stone. Her eyes followed the wall, seeing how it transitioned to a domed ceiling high above. Through an opening at the top, she could see a bright sky with swollen clouds drifting past.

She felt an urge to speak to the man, but before she could begin, her eyes locked on a black point straight ahead. It grew until it had buried her. Her breathing stopped, and her head emptied. Only one sound remained for her in the endless night.

Then it went silent.

* * *

A single point of light, growing, racing toward her with a world in its wake until it covered her. A strong, steady heartbeat, followed by a joy of surviving, thoughts full of questions, and a deep breath.

In seconds, Lin became filled with weakness and sadness and she sensed tears held back. She felt as though she were losing something, a strength or an achievement of some kind. A lifetime of effort would be stolen from her.

She looked down to see that she stood on the edge of the stone floor, a dizzying height above water that waved gently, barely lit by a sun about to rise from her left.

Lin looked to the sky, which was still mostly held by night, and she felt a deep, forlorn cry erupt from her. She voiced no words as her lungs emptied, and her anguished scream crashed into the dark.

All she felt was despair, and all she heard was silence.

As she hung her head, she felt the first rays of the sun land upon her. She understood. And she remained there, looking out over islands mostly covered by water.

Later, a gentle rain bathed her, and she knew its message. A warm wind dried her and helped birds flying above her. And soon, the sun set, warming her one last time. With the sun gone, a lonely moon looked down indifferently.

All had spoken to her.

And all had enraged her.

She vowed she would not leave. There would be no acceptance. Her existence would not end. Not ever. There would come a time—

Lin's eyes locked straight in front of her on a black point that grew as her captive eyes stared, and the blank night took her.

No breaths. No thoughts. No feelings.

Lin fought to find her intent, and she did find it, buried deep inside. Her grip slipped when her heart stopped. But her hold was unbreakable, and she clung to her intent in silence. In darkness.

In an emptiness like death.

*　*　*

After an immeasurable time, holding tightly onto her intent in the absence of everything else, the racing light brought her own world, and Lin's heart began again. Thoughts returned, and feelings. She took a deep breath of forest air and a warm breeze carrying scents of leather and coconut.

She felt the familiar comfort of a reclined seat and the warmth of a thick blanket bunched up to her chin. A look to her right revealed a dense pine forest nearby. She looked to her left and saw Gabriel, with one hand on the steering wheel and the other reaching for the stereo. Gabriel looked at her and smiled.

"Hello, Lin. How are you?"

"I'm good. How did I get here? I was on the couch."

"Yes, Lin, but now you're here. Do you feel okay?"

"Yeah, I'm okay. Just exhausted. But, Gabby, I was sitting on the couch, talking to you, when something . . . something happened. How did I get here? I *was* on the couch, wasn't I?"

"Yes, but . . ." Gabriel paused.

"Gabby?"

"That was three days ago."

Lin fell silent, and her eyes fixed on the air freshener hanging from the rearview mirror, being blown about by the Temt8tion's heater.

"I've been asleep for three days?"

"Not exactly."

A minute passed.

"We're in my car?"

"Yes. Some of us anyway." Gabriel smiled.

"Where's Jack?"

Gabriel pointed straight forward, and Lin sat up enough to see over the dash that Jack was seated at a picnic table, leaning forward with his face buried in his arms.

Another minute passed.

"Is Jack okay?"

"Jack will be fine now. He hasn't slept much, though."

"And Taylor? And Nomad?"

Gabriel pointed past Lin out through her passenger side window. "Taylor took the dog for a run on the trail. They should be back soon."

Lin reached down, powered her seat up, and looked to her right, then she looked back at Jack. Gabriel's classic rock was the only sound.

A long minute passed.

"Where are we? Gabby, what's going on?"

"We're traveling back to your home, Lin. Nomad got restless and convinced us to stop for a while. We're in Hickory Run State Park."

She leaned her head forward and looked past Gabriel to see Jack's truck parked in the next space.

She turned to look at Jack. Several minutes passed.

"How do you feel?"

"I'm okay, Gabby. Just . . . I don't know . . ."

Another minute passed as the music played.

"Lin?"

"I went somewhere, but it wasn't by choice. I was taken there."

"Into the magic?"

"No. It was different. Terrifying. It felt impossible."

"You weren't in the magic?"

"No."

Gabriel paused to examine Lin further.

"What happened?"

She remained silent, studying the blanket covering her, and a minute later, Gabriel said, "Lin, what happened?"

She looked up at Gabriel.

"I understand, Gabby. I saw it."

"What?"

"I saw what happened. When she heard the Words that she would tell to the Scroll. I lived it."

Gabriel's eyes grew wide, but only silence greeted Lin's revelation.

"She was angry. She didn't accept God's Words."

Gabriel hesitated but managed to speak.

"Who? Who *was* she, Lin?"

Lin closed her eyes and shook her head.

"She *is* Gloriana."

Gabriel continued to stare for many seconds before speaking.

"Lin, she lived long ago."

Lin opened her eyes but only stared through the windshield.

"Yes. And now."

Enjoy The Story?

Thank you for reading! Please consider leaving a review and/or a rating at your favorite bookseller or with your favorite book club. Help your fellow readers meet Lin Finity!

For more about Edward Allen Karr and his books, visit:

www.LakesideLetters.com

And follow him at:

Facebook: EdwardAllenKarr

Instagram: Edward_Allen_Karr

Appendix 1 – The Scroll

"The way that thing is made it cannot exist in our world. It simply can't. But anyone that looks at it will somehow see that it *can* exist. Why, now it makes perfect sense! And once *that* thing makes sense, the rest of the world–our world–will be a nightmare that does *not* make sense."

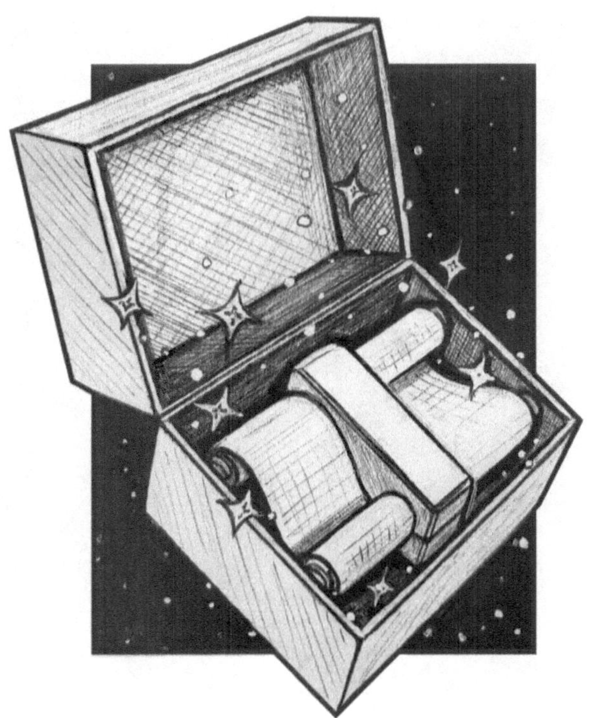

Appendix 2 – The Tower

"I looked to the Heavens and asked God, 'Why? For what reason are we subject to every imaginable nightmare, until the day when all our efforts are swept away, lost in oblivion? Why are we, for all our days, separate from your peace and truth?'

"God's Words came unspoken . . ."

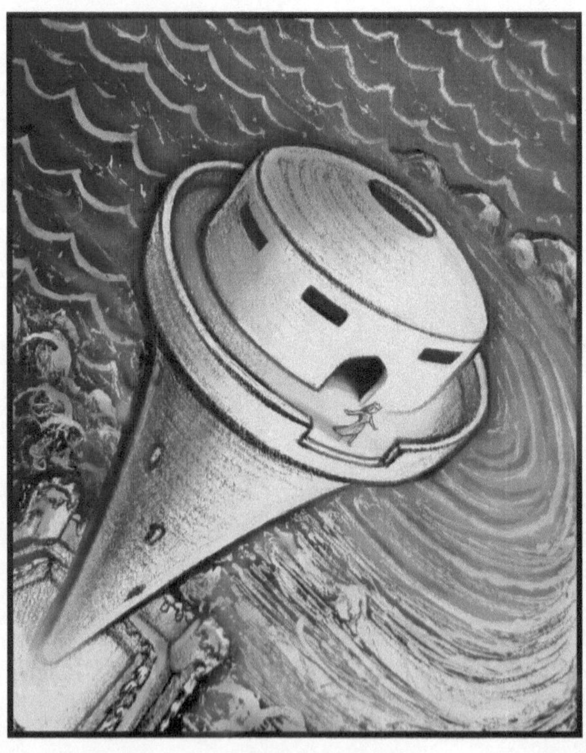

About The Author

Edward Allen Karr was born, raised, and continues to reside in Ohio, USA. His adult life has followed a meandering path, ranging from working an automotive assembly line to designing space flight hardware. And through all of it, he's seen that life is a captivating and ultimately unexplainable endeavor. His writing seeks to add a splash of wonder to a world already awash in it.

*   *   *

Lin Finity returns for more magic, adventure, and romance in:

Lin Finity And The Islands Of Time
Fringes Of Infinity Book Three

www.LakesideLetters.com

Next in time in the
Fringes Of Infinity
world:

Lin Finity And The
Islands Of Time
(Book Three)

AN ANCIENT QUEEN - No longer alive but too strong to die.
HER DIABOLICAL PLAN - A trap enduring across the centuries.
LIN FINITY - Sexy, magical, and the Queen's first hope in 2,000
years.

After Lin speaks the Words of God, the magic of powerful Queen
Gloriana snares her. She drags Lin to the Godless empty spaces
between the Islands Of Time where no life can exist. Gloriana has but
one chance to live again: only Lin's power can save her.

From Gloriana's attacks and from Gabriel's teachings, Lin learns that
there are endless possible lives for her—all too compelling to resist.
While fighting to hang on to the life she knows, Lin loves Jack more
than he can imagine, and she helps Taylor deal with an unbelievable,
long-lost power. But to save the Queen, Lin risks unleashing an
unstoppable death-bringer into the world of the living.

There are infinite ways to live on THE ISLANDS OF TIME.
In the end, Lin sees only one choice.